Ice-needle wind stung Shar's face.

Labored breaths fled from him, tattered gray veils of mist that vanished like dreams as he ran.

A phaser beam caromed off a stone wall above him, showering him with dust and sparks. He dodged left around a corner, shook off his overcoat, and sprinted for the dead drop.

Shar gave breathless thanks to Uzaveh the Infinite that the transom window facing the alley was open. He sprang upward as he passed by it and lobbed his tiny, precious cargo through the portal. As he landed, he crouched and turned over the empty feeding bowl that the uninitiated might assume was meant for the benefit of a stray *grayth*. That would be his contact's signal to retrieve the message he'd left safely behind the door.

All that was left then was to run.

Hoarse shouts and the crisp reports of booted feet resounded from the path ahead of Shar, and within moments they were echoed by similar harbingers from behind him. He took a chance and detoured down an unfamiliar passage, hoping it might lead him back to a major street where he could use a crowd for cover. Instead, he arrived at a dead end and a locked door. Then he turned back to see several Andorian Imperial Sentinels aiming phasers in his direction.

"Stop! Thirishar ch'Thane, you're under arrest!"

Shar heaved a tired sigh and raised his empty hands. "On what charge?"

"Espionage and treason."

Don't miss these other exciting novels in

THE FALL

STAR TREK®
THE FALL

A CEREMONY OF LOSSES

DAVID MACK

Based on *Star Trek* and
Star Trek: The Next Generation®
created by Gene Roddenberry
and
Star Trek: Deep Space Nine®
created by Rick Berman & Michael Piller

POCKET BOOKS
New York   London   Toronto   Sydney   New Delhi   Andor

Pocket Books
A Division of Simon & Schuster, Inc.
1230 Avenue of the Americas
New York, NY 10020

This book is a work of fiction. Any references to historical events, real people, or real places are used fictitiously. Other names, characters, places, and events are products of the author's imagination, and any resemblance to actual events or places or persons, living or dead, is entirely coincidental.

First Pocket Books paperback edition November 2013

POCKET and colophon are registered trademarks of Simon & Schuster, Inc.

For information about special discounts for bulk purchases, please contact Simon & Schuster Special Sales at 1-866-506-1949 or business@simonandschuster.com.

The Simon & Schuster Speakers Bureau can bring authors to your live event. For more information or to book an event, contact the Simon & Schuster Speakers Bureau at 1-866-248-3049 or visit our website at www.simonspeakers.com.

Cover design by Alan Dingman; cover art by Doug Drexler

Manufactured in the United States of America

10 9 8 7 6 5 4 3 2 1

ISBN 978-1-4767-2224-5
ISBN 978-1-4767-2226-9 (ebook)

For the dreamers

Historian's Note

This story begins nearly three years after the secession of Andor from the United Federation of Planets (*Star Trek: Typhon Pact—Paths of Disharmony*) and just three days after the dedication of the new Deep Space 9 starbase (*Star Trek: The Fall—Revelation and Dust*).

Concurrently, several Starfleet vessels have been deployed across the Alpha and Beta quadrants to bolster the Federation's security and ensure the safety of its allies (*Star Trek: The Fall—The Crimson Shadow*).

The main narrative of this tale transpires between August 31 and September 19, 2385, CE. Its prologue is set five months earlier, and its epilogue is set one year later.

All a man can betray is his conscience.

—Joseph Conrad,
Under Western Eyes (1911)

Dream me a better world and I'll find
a better way.

—John Fullbright,
From the Ground Up, "Daydreamer"

Prologue

There was so much blood. Viscous and cobalt blue, it sheeted down Selleshtala's thighs and traced erratic paths down her calves; it stuck to her hands and crusted her fingernails. Harsh light burned her eyes. Metal instruments colder than winter kissed her flesh as panicked whispers traveled the room. The world spun around her in a sapphire panic.

"Breathe, Tala." Shayl's voice was deep, but his angular face was cloaked in shadow and haloed by the surgical light behind him. The tall, slender *thaan* was the oldest of the four bondmates, and he struggled to project an air of soothing calm as he stood behind Selleshtala—Tala, to her bondmates—and cradled her head. "Breathe."

Anxious hands clasped hers; fingers entwined in desperate clenches meant to comfort. Huddled on either side of the bed, the bondgroup's delicately feminine *shen*, Mara, and its gracefully masculine *chan*, Thar, mirrored each other's grief. Thar's mask of courage betrayed only hints of his mounting fears, but the bitter tears on Mara's face belied her faltering smile.

The Bolian doctor's ridged, bald blue head poked up from behind a drape splattered with azure bloodstains. "You're doing great." His bland reassurance rang hollow. Like a nervous burrowing animal he ducked back out of Tala's sight and whispered a string of medical jargon at his Caitian nurse, who scurried away, treading like a breeze on tufted paws.

Uzaveh, help me, Tala prayed. *My children are dying and my fate lies in the hands of off-worlders.* She'd have preferred to have been attended to by an Andorian midwife. That had been the plan. The bondgroup's first *shelthreth* had ended in a miscarriage, a spontaneous termination of the two fertilized eggs inside Mara's womb before she could transfer them to Tala's pouch. That time the blood on her hands had been Mara's, but then, as now, the tears were everyone's. This time they had agreed to retreat to someplace quiet after the *shelthreth,* to get away from the stress of the cities and the pressures of their everyday lives, to give the new offspring a chance to grow and develop in peace. Shayl's family had kept a second home in the south, in a sparsely populated area of Andor that had escaped the ravages of the Borg attack years earlier. It had seemed an ideal location from which to escape the madding throngs of the new capital, Lor'Vela. Not until the group's second mating had taken a sudden turn for the disastrous did any of them realize how far they had traveled from qualified medical help.

Now, instead of a practiced Andorian obstetrician to guide them through this tragedy, they were at the mercy of off-worlders. The doctor and his nurse meant well, but they couldn't understand the true horror of this moment. No off-worlder could.

The physician gently grasped Tala's knee. "Hold still. This'll take a few minutes."

Tala reined in her wails of sorrow as tears kaleidoscoped her vision. She dreaded the inevitable reprise of old arguments the miscarriage would bring.

Thar would rail at the alien genetic sequences the fertility researchers had used to help him and Shayl fertilize Mara's ova, and he would curse the Yrythny, and Thirishar ch'Thane and Professor Marthrossi zh'Thiin, who had brought the Yrythny's biological legacy to Andor, and he would excoriate the Tholians for foisting the Shedai Meta-Genome upon them—while in the same breath denouncing Starfleet and the United Federation of Planets for concealing that same alien genetic data for more than a century while the Andorian population dwindled.

Shayl would blame himself, even though there was nothing he could have done to prevent the miscarriage. Mara would languish in guilt and self-recrimination and proclaim it all to be her fault for waiting too long—until she was nearly thirty years old—to conceive.

Tala knew no one would accuse her of failure, since *zhen* contributed no genetic material to offspring . . . but absolution brought her no comfort as the doctor began extracting the failed embryo from her weak and trembling body. She felt dull sensations of pressure through the dead zone of the local anesthetic.

Mara and Shayl whispered in her ears to distract her from the unpleasant scrapes at the end of the table and the steady drip of blood on the stone-tiled floor.

Shayl stroked sweaty locks of white hair from Tala's forehead. "Hang on, *zh'yi*."

"Try to relax." Mara squeezed Tala's hand a bit more tightly. "It's almost over."

It was a futile effort on their part. No matter how advanced, non-invasive, and antiseptic medical technology had become, there was no way to conceal the fact that the removal of dead embryos from a *zhen*'s pouch was a visceral horror. Tala closed her eyes and struggled not to hear the wet sounds of death that threatened to consume her.

Thar kissed her forehead. "We're all here for you, Tala. It'll be all right."

She knew he was lying, but she loved him for it all the same. She loved them all.

A soft click resonated in the claustrophobic room as the doctor shut the lid of a biological waste container. He handed it to the nurse, who took it in both white-furred paws and turned away before making a swift-footed exit. Medical instruments hummed and whirred for several moments, and then—just when Tala was certain she couldn't bear another moment of this ghastly but necessary procedure—the doctor leaned back and turned off the operating lights.

"All done." He pulled off his smock and surgical gloves, stuffed them into a matter reclamation bin, and sidled up to Tala. "There was no damage to your pouch, and I stopped your bleeding, but you need a transfusion to get your blood count back up." He looked at Shayl. "Can you three get her to a proper hospital in the next day?"

A small nod from Shayl placated the surgeon, who left the room with downcast eyes. By the time the door slid closed, the rest of the bondgroup had gathered around Tala, cocooning her in their sheltering embrace, shutting out the world so they could be alone with their sorrow and weep together, safe from the judgment of strangers' eyes.

They talked not of the past, nor of the future. Their pain was too raw, too deep for any of them to dare speak of trying again. There were no yesterdays, and there were no tomorrows. There was only that moment and its bitter truth.

One failed pregnancy at a time . . . the Andorian people were dying.

Five Months Later
September 2385

One

Though the metropolis of Lor'Vela had become the capital city of Andor after the Borg leveled Laikan, the city's poorer quarters were still no place for a *chan* alone after dark. Thirishar ch'Thane—Shar, to his friends—hurried from one shadow to the next, clutching shut the collar of his nondescript gray overcoat, eager to finish his errand and turn his steps homeward.

Once I would have been proud to be seen in my Starfleet uniform.

His idle musing stirred bittersweet memories. Part of him missed the freedom he'd enjoyed during his brief time away from home—first at Starfleet Academy, then aboard the *U.S.S. Tamberlaine,* and later as the senior science officer on Deep Space 9.

He'd surrendered that hard-won independence to return, at the urging of his *zhavey,* to fulfill his childhood vow to his bondmates . . . but not before his bondmate Thriss took her own life. Thriss had been special to him, beloved in a way that the other two members of their bondgroup were not. Her death had gutted him; her absence had left him hollow and incomplete.

Shar pushed the painful reminiscence down into the darkest corners of memory. Years had bled away since Thriss's tragic overdose. He had pledged himself to a new bondgroup and had helped sire a new child . . . who had perished, along with his bondmates, in the same Borg genocide that had reduced the planet's former capital to ionized dust and molten glass.

Why does nothing good ever last?

After the Borg attack on Andor, the galaxy had changed so quickly that Shar had all but lost track of it. Allegiances shifted, rivals turned into friends, allies became enemies. Andor, a founding member of the United Federation of Planets, seceded almost overnight, forcing Shar to choose between his oath to Starfleet or his kinship with the Andorian people. He had no ill will toward the Federation, but he knew where he was needed: here, at home, assisting Professor zh'Thiin in the ongoing search for a reliable, universal solution to the Andorian fertility crisis. To their shared dismay, that noble goal remained out of reach, though neither was sure why. They had tested every possible permutation of the Shedai Meta-Genome data they had received courtesy of the Tholians, only to find themselves burdened after each test with more questions than they'd had when they started.

A snap of footfall was met by sharp echoes, and Shar halted in mid-step to look back. He saw no one behind him, but he knew that meant nothing. Someone could be tracking him with a motion sensor or following the cues of someone observing his movements by means of a starship or a satellite in low orbit. It was also possible that he was just being paranoid, but recent experience had taught him to anticipate the worst. A host of reactionary elements in Andorian society resented the work he and Professor zh'Thiin had pioneered, and those foes had powerful friends in the civilian government. Making matters worse, Shar's current endeavor wasn't, in the strictest sense, entirely legal. Ethical? Yes. But that would carry little weight if he was caught.

He ducked down a narrow passage between two ancient buildings and scurried down a steep set of stairs hewn from the mountainside and weathered by millennia of foot traffic. The narrow lane afforded him a few moments of isolation from his pursuers.

Seconds mattered now. Clutching a fistful of secrets, Shar raced downhill and navigated hard angles as he fled. Wind and momentum tossed his dreadlocked white hair. He cleared a railing with a one-handed vault and then he was in free fall, dropping more than five meters into a sliver-thin alley's blank dead end. He crouched and rolled through the rough landing.

Above and behind him, frantic footsteps quickened. Sinister whispers spun into angry voices. The enemy was closer now. In the space of a breath, the hunt had become a race.

Ice-needle wind stung Shar's face. Labored breaths fled from him, tattered gray veils of mist that vanished like dreams as he ran.

A phaser beam caromed off a stone wall above him, showering him with dust and sparks. He dodged left around a corner, shook off his overcoat, and sprinted for the dead drop.

Shar gave breathless thanks to Uzaveh the Infinite that the transom window facing the alley was open. He sprang upward as he passed by it and lobbed his tiny, precious cargo through the portal. As he landed, he crouched and turned over the empty feeding bowl that the uninitiated might assume was meant for the benefit of a stray *grayth*. That would be his contact's signal to retrieve the message he'd left safely behind the door.

All that was left then was to run.

Hoarse shouts and the crisp reports of booted feet

resounded from the path ahead of Shar, and within moments they were echoed by similar harbingers from behind him. He took a chance and detoured down an unfamiliar passage, hoping it might lead him back to a major street where he could use a crowd for cover. Instead, he arrived at a dead end and a locked door. Then he turned back to see several Andorian Imperial Sentinels aiming phasers in his direction.

"Stop! Thirishar ch'Thane, you're under arrest!"

Shar heaved a tired sigh and raised his empty hands. "On what charge?"

"Espionage and treason." The sentinel in command stepped forward and clasped magnetic manacles onto Shar's wrists. The duranium restraints snapped closed with a cold finality—and then a sucker punch to Shar's solar plexus put him on his knees. He gasped for breaths he couldn't draw. The arresting sentinel loomed over him with a smug air. "That's for making us chase you."

Other sentinels stepped forward and lifted Shar by his arms. He kept his head down to hide his fear as they dragged him away. *If I've made a mistake, we're all going to die.*

"Who gave the order to have him arrested?" Ledanyi ch'Foruta, the Presider of the Parliament Andoria, stood behind the crescent-shaped desk in his office and raged at three of his senior advisers, all of whom hung their heads and avoided his accusatory gaze. Ferrathross zh'Rilah, his willowy but iron-willed chief counselor, scrutinized her subordinates: Seshivalas th'Larro, the senior counselor for intelligence, and Hennisar sh'Donnos, senior counselor for justice. The silence grew, stoking ch'Foruta's dudgeon. "I know it was one of you. Someone speak up."

Affecting a sullen cast, the gaunt and weathered th'Larro

cleared his throat. "Credible sources told us ch'Thane was about to share classified research with off-worlders. We had to move quickly." He shot an imploring look at sh'Donnos. "She signed off on it."

"I approved a *surveillance* order," the middle-aged *shen* protested, indignant.

"And then he ran!"

The chief counselor struck an incredulous note. "According to his statement, he had no idea he was being pursued by Imperial Sentinels." She added as an aside to the presider, "Judging from the sector in which he was arrested, that's a plausible defense."

Sh'Donnos scowled at th'Larro. "Not that he needs one. The law permits ch'Thane to move freely throughout the capital, just like any other citizen."

"And since the police found no data-storage media on him when he was arrested," zh'Rilah said, "we have no case against him for espionage or treason. Or anything else. At this point, we'll be lucky if ch'Thane doesn't sue the Imperial Sentinels."

Vexed by the evening's setbacks, ch'Foruta turned away from his guests, looked out his office's towering, curved transparasteel window at the capital city, and sighed. "I'm not worried about ch'Thane. His mentor zh'Thiin is the real problem. When she's not stirring up unrest by speaking out in support of the Progressives' push to overturn the secession vote, she's spreading false hope among the masses that she and her research team have almost found the *real* cure to the fertility crisis." He aimed a withering look over his shoulder at his counselors. "And the more attention she gets, the crazier the fringe elements become."

His observation seemed to amuse th'Larro. "Careful how you talk about our base."

"We need their votes, but that doesn't mean we let them run the party. They need to be kept in line. I won't have the *Treishya* name sullied. I guarantee you: One riot and we'll lose the moderates we need to keep this coalition intact."

It always disquieted ch'Foruta to think of how fragile his governing alliance was in the Andorian Parliament. His party, the *Treishya*, had seized power nearly three years earlier, during the uproar over the public revelation that the Federation had withheld scientific data acquired by Starfleet that might have helped reverse the downward spiral of the Andorian genetic crisis. But taking control was one thing; keeping it, ch'Foruta had learned, entailed very different challenges. Only a tenuous power-sharing agreement with the conservative True Heirs of Andor and several hard-liners from the centrist Visionist party had enabled the *Treishya* to wrest control of the parliament from the liberalist Progressives and their minor-party allies. But keeping his allies' political desires satisfied—and their rhetorical knives away from his back—had proved to be a constant struggle. Pleasing one friend often meant aggrieving another.

The counselor for justice sidled up to the presider and joined him in looking out the window at the throng gathering in the streets far below. "What do we do about ch'Thane?"

There was no perfect answer, so ch'Foruta chose the simplest one. "Drop the charges."

His order sparked outrage from th'Larro. "Sir! If we set ch'Thane free, we'll be turning him into a folk hero for the Progressives!"

"And if we keep holding him," zh'Rilah retorted, "we'll make him a martyr. And then he'll become a hero, when he humiliates us in court."

The justice counselor shook her head. "We can't just

drop the force field on his cell and let him walk out. Imperial charges were filed. Even with an executive order, it'll take at least a day to get the case dismissed and process ch'Thane's release." An anxious look transited her face. "I *will* have an executive order for this, won't I?"

Disdain creased the presider's brow. "Naturally."

Zh'Rilah rubbed her right thumb against her forefinger, a nervous habit she indulged when thinking on her feet. "Issue a statement saying the arrest was a case of mistaken identity. Be sure to apologize to ch'Thane, and to thank him for his co-operation. I want this story dead by tomorrow night. Let's not give the Progressives a ready-made issue for more than one news cycle." The *shen* and *thaan* wore blank expressions, as if waiting for the subject to change. She ushered them toward the door with a sharp tilt of her head. "We're done. Go."

The counselors slunk away like scolded children, and the chief counselor locked the door behind them. She trained her keen gray stare on the presider. "This is insane, sir. We can't hold off everyone forever. So . . . who do you least fear disappointing?"

It was another question with no good answer. "We've held the government for almost three years, and our control's as weak as ever. Our only saving grace is that almost no one outside this office knows how fragile the coalition really is. But if these protests continue . . . if the Progressives continue to win back the moderates and galvanize the backbenchers . . . then we'll have a public-perception disaster on our hands. We can't let that happen, Ferra."

"I understand, sir. Short of assassination, how should we deal with ch'Thane?"

"Why rule out our best option?"

"It would play badly in the press, sir."

"I suppose." She had a point. He and many of those upon whose support he depended were desperate for zh'Thiin's and ch'Thane's genetic research to prove successful. They wanted healthy children as much as anyone else did. It was strictly for political reasons that ch'Foruta and the rest of the *Treishya* needed that breakthrough to be postponed just a little longer, until their hold on political power on Andor became unassailable.

Ch'Foruta relaxed into his chair, smoothed the crisp fabric of his trademark white suit, and felt as if the power of his office were almost a tangible commodity rather than an abstraction. "Let ch'Thane go back to his work with Professor zh'Thiin—but rescind his travel credentials, and tell th'Larro to sign a secret order to have all of ch'Thane's communications monitored and recorded. He might have slipped one past us this time, but eventually, he'll make a mistake, or someone will send him a message that gives the lie to his immaculate reputation." The presider anticipated the future behind steepled fingers. "Then we'll have him."

Two

Green surf crashed upon a golden shore peppered with countless white shards—the remnants of millions of seashells, all of them broken like promises. B'hava'el, the star that Bajorans called their sun, held court high overhead, blanching the teal sky, and a sultry tropical breeze carried the scents of jungle flowers and salt water. Three gulls wheeled in tight, intersecting circles close to the water. Their shrill cries sounded faint behind the steady roar of breaking waves.

Walking on the beach, hand in hand with Julian Bashir, and knowing there wasn't another sentient being on the island, it felt to Sarina Douglas like paradise. It was so beautiful as to seem almost surreal, so idyllic that it felt like the creation of a clever holosuite programmer. But this was no simulation. She and Bashir had planned this vacation for months, and now that the new Deep Space 9 starbase was up and running—with its hospital and security systems both fully operational—the senior deputy chief of security and chief medical officer were treating themselves to some well-deserved and long-overdue R & R.

But though she felt the warmth of his hand in hers, she knew he wasn't fully there; his thoughts were distant, lending him an aspect of somber distraction that clashed with his beach attire: sandals, loose navy blue swim trunks, an off-white, tropical-weight linen shirt.

She gave his hand a firm but gentle squeeze. "Hey."

He hardly looked at her, despite the revealing quality of her violet bikini and the gauzy turquoise wrap tied unevenly around her waist.

They continued to stroll in silence. Douglas trod with care along the damp, wave-packed beach, mindful of sharp corners on the shells beneath her bare feet. "You okay?" She squinted against the beauty of a world almost too bright for her to see. "I almost feel like I'm alone here."

A sheepish smile brightened Bashir's face. "Forgive me." He looked away, toward a hazy white horizon. "It's just a bit hard for me to let go sometimes."

She pushed a windblown tangle of blond hair from her eyes. "Anything in particular?"

Drawing him out had grown difficult in recent weeks, forcing Douglas to become more patient. After he'd taken a long moment to find the right words, he replied, "The president."

The mere allusion to the assassination cast a pall over the moment. It was a tragedy whose effects the two of them felt most keenly. Douglas counted it as a personal failure that Nanietta Bacco, the President of the United Federation of Planets, the leader who had guided the Federation and its interstellar neighbors through the nightmare of the final Borg blitzkrieg, should die on her watch, the victim of a sniper attack aboard Deep Space 9. Five days earlier, despite all of Bashir's medical expertise and efforts, the mortally wounded commander in chief had expired on a transporter platform before she could be moved to the new starbase's state-of-the-art hospital.

Now the people of the Federation were in mourning; the entire quadrant was racked by political upheavals. No one had blamed them for the president's death, but Douglas knew that had it not been for the fierce loyalty and protection of

Captain Ro Laren, she and Bashir both could easily have been cast as scapegoats, drummed out of Starfleet, and condemned to take refuge in the fringe sectors, pariahs with a president's blood on their hands.

Instead, she was forced to seek comfort in platitudes. "It wasn't our fault."

"So I've told myself . . . again and again. Somehow, I never quite believe it." Dredging up the memory put an edge on his voice. "I keep going over those moments in my mind. Asking myself what else I might have done. What I might've done differently."

"There was nothing you could have done, Julian."

Bashir resisted her consolation. "So everyone says." He closed his eyes for a moment before breathing a dejected sigh. "I know it's true. But it's no comfort."

She halted him with a gentle tug on his hand. Turning, she pressed her pale palm against his brown, bearded cheek. "You and I are genetically enhanced, but that doesn't mean we can work miracles. We might be special, but in all the ways that really matter, we're only *human*."

"Maybe that's not good enough anymore."

Douglas recoiled, confused. "Meaning?"

He took a deep breath and looked away. "I don't know."

"I'm not sure I believe you."

He let go of her hand and waded ankle-deep into the rolling surf. The hunch of his back, the slump of his shoulders— they were the hallmarks of a man laboring under a terrible weight. "There are days when I feel like I've lost my way. Like I've forgotten who I am."

The timbre of his voice troubled her; he sounded as if he were making a confession. She hoped she was wrong. "This isn't just about the president, is it?"

"No." His eyes hinted at guilt and remorse. "I'm not saying it's anyone's fault but my own . . . but I think it started on Salavat."

It had been a few years since she and Bashir had returned from a covert mission to that frozen Breen planet on behalf of Starfleet Intelligence. The duo had infiltrated a top-secret Breen military shipyard to stop the Typhon Pact from developing a working slipstream drive based on designs it had stolen from Starfleet's shipyard in Mars orbit above Utopia Planitia. By all accounts the mission had ended in success, but Bashir had never spoken of it after his official Starfleet Intelligence debriefing—not until now.

Douglas waded into the balmy water, eased her way to Bashir's side, and rested a consoling hand on his shoulder. "Talk to me, Julian."

"What am I supposed to say? I knew what I was doing. For a while I even made myself believe that it was the right thing. I had a mission vital to Federation security. Presidential orders." Regret seemed to gnaw at him from some unreachable place deep inside. "A license to kill."

"You did what was necessary."

"Maybe. But I wish I hadn't been the one to do it." His sorrow was contagious. "All the times I'd played at being a spy in the holosuite, I never lost myself in the role the way I did on Salavat. . . . Something happened to me down there. I took lives I could've spared. I made choices I'd give anything now to take back. . . . I'm a doctor, Sarina. A healer. And I let myself turn into a killer because—" He cut himself off, and the incomplete thought alarmed Douglas.

"Why?" She sensed the truth in his averted eyes. "Because of me?"

"It wasn't your fault. I told myself all the lies I needed to hear. It was for the uniform. For Starfleet. For the Federation." He shot a bitter look skyward. "For my president."

"All good reasons."

"Not good enough to excuse murder. Not even when it's sanctioned by the state."

Douglas had no idea where to begin assuaging Bashir's conscience, or her own. Though she had told Bashir shortly after the Salavat mission about her long-term assignment within Starfleet Intelligence—attracting the attention of Section 31 so that she could infiltrate the shadowy agency and help orchestrate its downfall—she had never admitted that her reason for manipulating him toward such a bloody outcome on Salavat was to redeem him as a prospective agent for Section 31, which had tried and failed to recruit him on several previous occasions. Though her gambit had proved successful in deceiving her Section 31 handler L'Haan, she wasn't sure Bashir would ever be able to forgive her for coaxing him into lethal espionage.

Bashir's combadge chirped from inside the pocket of his swim trunks. He retrieved the tiny metallic device. It chirped again in his hand. "Don't they know I'm on vacation?"

"Could be an emergency." Douglas hoped Bashir was as eager for a change of subject at that moment as she was. "You should answer it."

He tapped it with his thumb, opening the channel. "This is Bashir."

A familiar nasal voice answered over the comm, *"Thank the Blessed Exchequer!"*

Bashir's brow creased with confusion and mild annoyance. "Quark?" After a moment he recovered his composure and pinched the bridge of his nose as he silently reminded himself of the Ferengi's elevated diplomatic status. "How can I be of service, Mister Ambassador?"

"I apologize for disturbing you on your vacation, Doctor, but I need you to come by the embassy as soon as possible."

Douglas and Bashir traded perplexed looks. "For what reason?"

"I'd rather not say over an open channel, Doctor. Let's just say . . . it's urgent."

Business was brisk and the profits were respectable at the new Quark's Public House, Café, Gaming Emporium, Holosuite Arcade, and Ferengi Embassy to Bajor—or, as most visitors to The Plaza aboard the new Deep Space 9 simply referred to it, Quark's.

Its proprietor and namesake hurried from his office, padd in hand, checking the latest inventory and sales reports from his second establishment, the one he'd left behind on the surface of Bajor when he'd opened his new flagship location on the Federation's impregnable new space station extraordinaire. He had left his planetside Bar, Grill, and Gaming House under the stewardship of Treir, a keen-witted young Orion woman who had climbed the ranks in Quark's organization, from *dabo* girl to general manager, in just under a decade. Some—including Treir herself—might have called her progress slow, but for a woman in an establishment owned and operated by a Ferengi, the upward trajectory of her career was nothing shy of spectacular.

Looking up from Treir's report, Quark saw diminishing profits at every turn. The portion sizes of the replicated desserts were at least three percent too large; his oaf of a bartender spilled another pitcher of Pacifican Sunrise cocktails; a faulty panel was frustrating a holosuite customer who no doubt would leave without renting a program unless his dilemma was fixed immediately; and he estimated that slow service by the waitstaff was reducing table turns by nine percent over the course of an average business day. *How am I supposed to stay in business when all my workers seem committed to driving me out of it?*

He grumbled under his breath and reminded himself to be thankful for the absurdly generous terms of his lease on the premium commercial space—an agreement made possible by the fact that Quark's bar was also the Ferengi Embassy to Bajor. Then he tried to forget he had become an ambassador only through an act of charity by his younger brother, Rom, who a decade earlier had somehow blundered his way into the exalted office of Grand Nagus of the Ferengi Alliance.

Ten years under the rule of Rom, and the Alliance is still solvent, Quark mused with well-earned cynicism. *Will the ironies of the Blessed Exchequer never cease?*

In one quick circuit of the main floor, Quark dispatched a repair technician to fix the broken holosuite menu, sent a terse order to his systems manager to fix the portion-control codes on the replicators, slung a few choice epithets at his butterfingered Bolian bartender, and told his hostess to send checks to the customers at tables 4, 8, 15, 16, 23, and 42, so that new patrons could be seated before the current ones put down roots and had to be phasered out.

Quark was about to ferret out another half-dozen crises in need of fast action when he noted the arrival of Doctor Bashir. Wasting no time on such niceties as apologies, he hurried through a cluster of customers who had spilled over from the gaming area, bladed through the crowd thronging the bar, and greeted the physician with a sharp-toothed grin. "Doctor!"

"You said it was urgent." He sounded upset, but still managed to add with grudging respect, "Mister Ambassador."

"Yes, I did. Follow me." He led Bashir through a dense knot of loudly chatting drinkers.

Bashir had to shout to be heard over the cheers of the crowd around the *dabo* table. "Where are we going?"

"My office." When they reached Quark's private sanctum, the doctor seemed just as relieved as the Ferengi to escape the sonic assault of the packed entertainment club, even though the human's puny ears couldn't possibly be as sensitive to noise as were a Ferengi's prodigious lobes. Quark stepped behind his desk. "Please, have a seat."

"I'll stand."

The doctor's manner struck Quark as oddly curt. "Are you sure?"

"I won't be staying long. Now tell me why I cut my vacation short to fly back here."

So much for courtesy. Quark unlocked his top desk drawer, took out a small isolinear chip, and pushed it across the desk to Bashir. "I was told to give you this message."

Suspicious but curious, Bashir picked up the chip. "Told by whom?"

"The Department of External Audits." He noted from Bashir's expression that he didn't recognize the agency's name. "Ferenginar's foreign-intelligence service. I'm speaking to you right now as a diplomatic agent of the Ferengi government."

The doctor turned the chip slowly between his thumb and forefinger. "Who's it from?"

"No clue. All I know is that it contains holographic data, and it's marked for your eyes only." He entered a few commands on his desktop's computer touch screen. "I've reserved Holosuite Five for you—and you have my word, its privacy controls are set to maximum."

Bashir clenched the chip in his fist. "Thank you, Quark."

"Thank me by paying your bar tab." He shooed the human out of his office. "Now, hurry up. I can't hold that holosuite all night, you know."

The doctor left, no doubt eager to see what was on the chip. Quark decided not to slow him down by telling him the holosuite time would be charged to his tab.

Sequestered inside the soundproofed privacy of a locked holosuite, Bashir felt almost as if he were up to something illicit. He studied the chip in his hand. *For your eyes only,* Quark had said. The expression echoed in Bashir's thoughts, kindling his curiosity. What could the Ferengi government's intelligence service want with him?

Only one way to find out.

He inserted the chip into a slot on the holosuite's control panel. The illumination inside the holosuite dimmed as the program on the chip self-activated with a low, sonorous hum.

A pale blue light suffused the room, enveloping Bashir. Alien symbols flowed from the deck to the overhead in long, translucent strings. Eyeing them more closely, Bashir recognized them as Andorian alphanumeric characters. A pentagonal icon flashed through a repeating sequence for a few seconds, then it vanished. A melodious, feminine disembodied voice declared, *"Counter-surveillance scan complete. Holosuite secure. Please identify yourself."*

"Doctor Julian Bashir."

"Voiceprint confirmed. Scanning." After a few seconds, the voice added, *"Genetic scan confirmed. Thank you. Program loading. Stand by."*

The upward cascade of alien digits and symbols faded and was replaced by the gleaming steel surfaces of a pristine, windowless laboratory equipped with state-of-the-art medical instruments. Standing at arm's length in front of Bashir, attired in gray scrubs and a white lab coat, was his Andorian former crewmate from the previous Deep Space 9 station, Thirishar ch'Thane. *"Hello, Julian. I hope you'll forgive the theatrics and intermediaries, but I had no other way to contact you. The first segment of this program is a prerecorded message. After it's finished playing, the interactive segment will engage, to try to help answer the many questions I'm sure you'll have."*

Holo-Shar half-turned and lifted his arm in a sweeping gesture. The program responded by making the laboratory vanish and summoning several overlapping screens of genetic code and helical scans, over all of which had been superimposed more data—this time in English, no doubt for Bashir's exclusive benefit. *"As you probably heard in the news,"* Holo-Shar continued, *"one of the key factors in Andor's secession from the Federation was that its people—or, to be more precise, reactionaries in its parliament—blamed the Federation for withholding intelligence about the Shedai Meta-Genome that had been gathered in the twenty-third century as part of Operation Vanguard. My people think that information might hold the key to solving our fertility crisis by filling in blanks that the Yrythny 'turnkey gene' couldn't."*

Several strings of alien genetic material enlarged as Holo-Shar went on. *"Over the past two and a half years, the Tholian*

*Assembly has shared a significant quantity of its own intel-
ligence about the Shedai Meta-Genome. But whether by chance
or by design, they never provide us with the sequences we need
to fix the flaws in our gene-therapy program. Of course, it
might be that the* Treishya—*the party that currently controls
our government—is embargoing critical data sequences from
the Shedai genome, in order to slow down our research until
they figure out how to take credit for it and solidify their own
hold on power.*

"*Either way, the program I run with Professor Marthrossi
zh'Thiin isn't getting the information we need. In the past, we'd
have requested data on the Shedai genome sequences from
Starfleet Medical or through the Federation Surgeon General,
but since the* Treishya *whipped up a bare majority to back
secession, we're cut off from those databases. And that's why we
need your help, Julian. Because we're dying . . . and we're running out of time.*"

A long list of file names appeared on Bashir's right. "*To
get you started, I've included on this chip all the research and
raw data my team has amassed on the Shedai genome and its
application to our fertility crisis. But I can already tell you there
isn't enough here to solve the problem. To finish what we've
started, you or someone else with access to Starfleet's secure
medical archives will have to retrieve the intel that we can't,
figure out how to put it to use, and then find a way to get that
data back to us.*

"*I know I'm asking a lot, Julian. But I don't know who else
to trust.*" The holographic Andorian gave a small half-shrug.
"*That's my plea, in a nutshell. The rest . . . is up to you.*" His ap-
peal complete, he stood calmly, hands folded in front of him,
waiting for Bashir to respond.

Bashir considered the scope of the mess he had been

invited to unleash. "Shar, unless I'm mistaken, the Shedai intelligence is still classified top secret by Starfleet, isn't it?"

"Yes, I believe it is."

"Has anyone else in Starfleet seen it?"

"To the best of my knowledge, until now only Doctor Beverly Crusher, chief medical officer of the Enterprise, *has been privy to the Shedai data contained in our research."*

That was something, at least. A place to start, a peer with whom Bashir might confer in confidence. But the urgency in Shar's tone during the prerecorded message troubled him. "You said the Andorian people are running out of time. Have you and Professor zh'Thiin estimated how long the Andorian people have left before their population decline becomes irreversible?"

"Factoring in the time necessary for a retroviral gene therapy to be disseminated to the entire population, the current mortality rates across all age groups, and the continuing decline in fertility rates, we estimate that unless a successful program is initiated within the next year, the Andorian people will be extinct by the end of the next century. We're at the tipping point."

Weighed against such stakes, Bashir suddenly considered the notion of a court-martial to be of little consequence or concern. "I understand. I'll get started as soon as I can. . . . Computer: End program." The simulation dissolved, revealing the interior of the holosuite. Bashir collected the isolinear chip from the control panel and unlocked the door.

He had awoken that day plagued with self-doubt and tormented by guilt. Now, all at once, he had a sudden clarity of purpose. Striding out of Quark's and heading for his office in the station's hospital complex, he felt imbued with a sense of mission. But he also knew this undertaking would present challenges greater than he could face alone. He would need help.

Fortunately, he knew exactly who to contact.

The tricky part would be not getting himself arrested in the process.

Three

Portered by a pair of sentinels as if he were a sack of refuse, Shar offered no resistance but also made no effort at compliance as he was hauled out of the capital city's Hall of Detention. Dim pools of light blurred past behind half-closed doors as he was carried down a long dark corridor. Then, as they crossed over the Andorian imperial emblem set into the floor of the main atrium, his eyes fixed upon a blinding light directly ahead, outside the main entrance.

Towering portals parted ahead of him, and then he was heaved without ceremony into the glare of the rising sun to face the day—and the media.

In the seconds it took Shar to halt his stumbling, find his balance, and face the rabid gaggle, his eyes adjusted enough for him to realize he was surrounded on three sides. Reporters from every media outlet on Andor—as well as dozens of foreign correspondents from off-world news services—harangued him with barked demands for information, for answers, for a statement, for some hint of how he was feeling at that moment. Hundreds of voices shouted at once, a sonic barrage of stunning force and volume.

Shar lifted his hands and descended into the media scrum. "Everyone, listen up! I've had a very long night, so if you don't mind, I'd just like to—" Wild shouts cut him off.

"Why were you arrested?"

"Is it true the charges were dropped? Do you know why?"

"Who secured your release? Did you call in political favors? Did Professor zh'Thiin?"

"Did your arrest have anything to do with your research at the Science Institute?"

"Is it true you were charged with espionage?"

A dozen variations on each question flew at him, each louder than the last, and for a moment Shar wondered if it might be possible to ask the sentinels to take him back into protective custody. Spending the day incarcerated seemed infinitely preferable to weathering a public inquisition by muckrakers. *If only I could punch a few of them,* he lamented, knowing that as satisfying as that might feel in the moment, it would only worsen his predicament when the recording made its way onto the global comm network.

Beyond the far edge of the press gauntlet he spied a personal transport whose markings he recognized. The tint on the rear side window faded for a few seconds, affording him a glimpse of his mentor and friend, Professor Marthrossi zh'Thiin. The middle-aged *zhen* reproved him from a distance with a shake of her head, then darkened the window to safeguard her privacy.

With effort, Shar tuned out the cacophony of the journalists pressing in upon him and with brusque determination shouldered his way toward the street.

Then the bystanders kicked into gear. Hoarse cries of "Traitor!" and "Butcher!" assailed Shar from his left, and when he looked for the source of the insults, he saw a mob of raging zealots, all wide-eyed and hungry for violence, held at bay by a handful of Imperial Sentinels in body armor. Opposite them, restrained by another line of stern-faced peace officers in battle dress, were equally fervid counter-protesters screaming at Shar's detractors, "Shut up, scum!

Lie down and die if that's what you want, but don't take us with you!"

Nothing like being a celebrity to make life interesting.

A rock flew past Shar's head and struck a journalist in the face. As the wounded *thaan* collapsed, pandemonium erupted on the steps of the Hall of Detention. Shar ducked under the melee and made a frantic dash to the transport. The rear door lifted open with a hydraulic gasp. He leaped inside the vehicle, and as he landed on the floor between the front and back seats, he heard Professor zh'Thiin command her driver, "Go!"

The hovercar ascended straight upward for a few seconds as the rear door closed, then the sleek craft lurched into motion and sped away from the fast-spreading free-for-all.

Scuffed and abashed but otherwise unhurt, Shar climbed onto the seat beside zh'Thiin and dusted himself off. "Thanks for coming to pick me up."

"What in the name of Uzaveh were you thinking?"

He feigned ignorance. "Excuse me?"

The professor was seething. "After all the discussions we had. After I expressly told you—no, *begged* you—not to do it . . . you went and did it, didn't you?"

It was impossible for him to look her in the eye and lie to her, so he faced straight ahead and expunged all emotion from his voice. "I don't know what you're talking about."

"Shar, we're long past the point of worrying about plausible deniability for me, you, or anyone else. The news said you got picked up for espionage and treason."

What was he supposed to say? "It was mistaken identity."

"I sincerely doubt that. Dammit, Shar, you knew they had you under surveillance. They've been watching us all for years, ever since the secession. It was a stupid risk to take." Her anger seemed on the verge of exploding, but then she looked away and drew a deep breath as she watched the capital's architecture blur past outside her window. "What did they find?"

After all the lies he had told, it was almost a relief to be able to answer a question with the truth. "Nothing. All I had was my ID, a credit chip, a comm, and the clothes on my back."

"Let's be grateful for small mercies."

A silence stretched between them, and he ventured another look in her direction. Her stark white hair was tousled, as if she'd been roused from her sleep in the middle of the night, and her normally fastidious attire was disheveled. The delicate features of her middle-aged face looked careworn that morning, with dark circles under her kind, sky-blue eyes. Perhaps sensing his unspoken concern, she muttered, "I'm fine. Just didn't sleep much last night, knowing you were in custody."

"I'm sorry to have put you through that."

She patted the back of his hand, apparently resigning herself to their current situation. Then she lifted a small insulated beverage cup from the caddy between the seats in front of them and offered it to Shar. "Tea?" Noting his skepticism, she added, "It's from my garden."

"I'll need more than herbal broth to jolt my brain into gear."

"I used the petals from the black flowers. Trust me, it has a kick."

He accepted the cup, rotated open the drink slot on the lid, and took a sip. Hot, sweet, and soothing, it also cleared the cobwebs from his thoughts in a matter of seconds. "Nice."

"I thought you'd like it."

Shar took a few more sips of the tea and let its recuperative effects suffuse his body. When he felt like himself again, he looked up and noted that the driver's route was carrying them not toward Shar's home but toward the Science Institute. He shot a questioning look at zh'Thiin. "Guess I'm not going home for a change of clothes before heading in to the lab."

"You're quick, Shar. That's why I keep you on my payroll."

"This is payback for you having to pick me up today, isn't it?"

"Like I said: You're quick."

The transport landed in front of the Science Institute as Shar finished the tea and put on his most optimistic demeanor. "So . . . what are we doing today, Professor?"

"The same thing we do every day, Shar." She opened her door and stepped outside, into the daylight. "Trying to save the world."

Four

"**W**eapons locked, Captain. Phasers and torpedoes standing by."

"Noted." Captain Ezri Dax acknowledged the report from security chief Lonnoc Kedair while maintaining eye contact with the civilian freighter commander on the *Aventine*'s main viewscreen. "Captain Valik, this is your final warning. Drop your shields or we *will* open fire."

The Rigellian's tattooed face contorted with righteous fury. *"You have no right—"*

"We both know that's not true," Dax cut in. "Your ship is off its registered flight plan and on a course for Andor, in violation of the embargo. Don't make me cite chapter and verse." Everything about the heavyset civilian's body language suggested he was spoiling for a fight, but Dax hoped it was empty posturing. "You have five seconds, Captain."

Valik's defiance bled away, supplanted by disgust. He gave a curt nod to someone offscreen, then turned his sour anger toward Dax. *"You can commence your plundering."*

The young Trill starship commander ignored the insult and made a tiny slashing gesture near her throat to signal her security chief to close the channel. The green-scaled Takaran woman cut the transmission, and then Dax issued a one-word directive to her first officer: "Go."

Commander Samaritan "Sam" Bowers snapped the crew into action with rapid-fire orders. "Mister Tharp, come about bearing seven five mark five, and put us ten kilometers off the *Okemah*'s bow. I don't want them to even think of making a run for it. Mirren, have Chief Jebreal beam boarding parties to the *Okemah*'s bridge, engineering deck, and main cargo hold. Lieutenant Kedair, tell your people to set all weapons for stun and to keep them holstered unless attacked. Mister Helkara, monitor the *Okemah*'s comms. If there's any suspicious chatter, or if they try to send any subspace signals, shut 'em down and alert me immediately."

Confirmations echoed back from all the senior officers, who set to work turning words into action. Satisfied the situation was well in hand, Dax pushed away her exhaustion by running one hand through her short-cropped black hair as she headed for her ready room. She cut off Bowers's half-formed but not yet spoken objection to her departure. "Keep me posted."

The door to the ready room hushed closed, and Dax followed a well-trod path in the carpet to the chair behind her desk. She sank into the chair, which had come to know her curves. As much as she usually preferred to be on the bridge, engaged in the business of the moment, the *Aventine*'s current mission had left her frustrated and ill at ease, qualities she preferred to conceal from her crew for the sake of morale. It had been nearly four years since she had been promoted from second officer to the ship's center seat after a battle with the Borg had killed her two direct superiors, and she had only just started to feel as if her crew was coming to accept that she belonged in command. She was determined not to jeopardize their hard-earned respect by letting them see her as anything less than fully committed to their current mission . . . no matter how pointless, spiteful, and misguided their orders from Starfleet Command might be.

Minutes passed without any new alerts being sounded,

giving Dax reason to hope the boarding operation was pro-
ceeding without incident. Then her door signal buzzed, and
she sighed, knowing who it would be, and what was in the
offing. "Come in."

She watched the portal slide open with a soft hiss, and
Bowers walked in clutching a padd in one hand. The lanky,
brown-skinned, shaved-headed human stopped in front of
her desk. "All boarding teams have reported in. The *Okemah*'s
cargo matched its manifest—medical supplies and pharma-
ceuticals, bound for Andor. We've started beaming over the
contraband cargo. Chief Jebreal estimates we'll be finished
with cargo transfer in ten minutes. The freighter's crew hasn't
offered any resistance."

He hadn't glanced at the padd, making Dax wonder why
he had brought it with him. She pointed at the data tablet. "Is
that for me?"

"Yes, sir." Bowers set it on her desk, then stepped back.
"It's an independent report by the Foundation for Interstellar
Medicine, documenting the spread of communicable diseases
on Andor. I'd recommend against it as bedtime reading."

Dax gave her first officer credit; he had become much
more subtle and oblique in his criticism of her command
decisions. "Any particular reason you're sharing this, Sam?"

"I know how much you like to remain aware of the big
picture, Captain."

"Knock it off, Sam. 'Coy' isn't a good color on you."

The by-the-book XO took the admonishment in stride.
"I'm sorry if it's inconvenient to be reminded that our actions
are hurting real people."

"I don't need to be reminded, Sam." She rolled her eyes
and drew a sharp breath, both as part of her fight to retain her composure. "You think I can't see these orders for

what they are?" She stood and paced to the narrow pane of transparasteel behind her desk. "I don't like being used as a political pawn any more than you do."

Bowers's frustration spilled out. "Then why don't we speak up? Everyone knows that Ishan's manipulating policy to score points for an election. Let's call him on it."

"It's not our place, Sam. You swore an oath—just as I did—to serve and obey the lawful civilian government. No matter what we think of his politics, Ishan is the one in charge. We don't have to agree with his rationales, but we're bound by law to obey his orders."

"But a full embargo against Andor? Food, medicine, commerce, even communications? This is *ridiculous*. They were a founding member of the Federation!"

"And last year an Andorian separatist colluded in a plot to steal the designs for slipstream drive and helped Typhon Pact agents destroy the original Deep Space Nine." Dax turned and held up one open hand. "Stop. We're not having this debate again. It's a waste of time."

Her peremptory stifling of the discussion darkened Bowers's already dour mood. "Opposing injustice is *never* a waste of time. . . . *Sir.*"

"Let me know when the cargo transfer is complete and our boarding teams are back aboard." She looked up as if she were surprised he was still there. "Dismissed."

"Aye, sir." He turned on his heel and left the ready room.

Dax sank back into the chair her body had spent years shaping to her contours . . . but now, no matter how she shifted her weight or posture, she could no longer get comfortable.

It was the faintest of sounds, barely a sigh above the white noise of the *Aventine*'s ventilation system, but it was enough to rouse Doctor Simon Tarses. He shuddered awake and cursed the sensitivity of his pointed ears, then he blinked and rolled onto his side to find his lover, Nerathyla sh'Pash, sitting up in bed beside him, staring off into space. Perhaps sensing the motion from his side of the bed, she turned her head and looked down at him. "Did I wake you?"

"No," he lied. "You all right?"

Her antennae twitched as her blue brow furrowed—telltale signals of simmering fury. "Kedair left me off the boarding detail." She clenched her jaw. "For no reason."

Tarses didn't know what to say to her. He was no stranger to the ostracizing effects of racism—his quarter-Romulan ancestry had ensured that, even within the proudly accepting polyglot culture of the Federation—but the latest rash of discriminatory behaviors toward Andorians, in the wake of their homeworld's secession from the Federation, was so thick with fresh bitterness and raw emotion that he had no idea how to address it without inflaming it.

It didn't help that sh'Pash had a talent for taking offense where none had been intended. In contrast to Tarses, who had smoothed his way through Starfleet basic training and, later, Starfleet Medical School by cultivating a persona of agreeable compromise, sh'Pash had earned a reputation for confrontation.

Which probably explains why I'm a doctor and she's a security officer.

He reached out and gently stroked his pale hand along her blue arm. "Thyla, are you really sure you'd *want* to help enforce an embargo against Andor?"

True to form, sh'Pash bristled. "What're you saying, Simon? You don't think I can do my job? That I'd let my racial identity trump my oath to Starfleet?"

Now I've done it. He sat up. "No, sweetheart. That's not what I'm saying."

"Then what *are* you saying?" If sh'Pash was guilty of embodying one species stereotype about Andorians, it was her propensity for seeking out fights. It might have been enough to scare Tarses off had the young *shen* not been so damned fetching, brilliant, courageous, and beguiling.

Only half awake and still bleary-eyed, the chief medical officer chose his words with care. "I'm saying that our current assignment is questionable on a number of levels. At the very least it seems unjust; at worst, I'd say it was designed to perpetuate the pain of innocent people on Andor so our president pro tem can polish up his security credentials for an election."

For a moment, he thought he'd gotten through to sh'Pash. Her anger shifted from a full blaze to a slow burn. Then she spoke, and he realized that in an Andorian, a long cold fire in the heart was a far more terrifying prospect than any moment of fury, no matter how intense. "Of course Ishan is hurting Andor to help himself. It seems like that's the new national sport of the Federation. But that doesn't mean I can't fulfill my oath. So if Kedair's bumping me from the duty roster, it's because she doesn't trust me. She might as well call me a traitor."

Tarses knew he had to tread carefully. "If there was something I could do to help, would you want me to try? Or would you prefer I stay out of it?"

The *shen* tucked her long bone-white hair behind her ear, so as to be able to fix Tarses with her pointed suspicion. "If you were going to help . . . how would you do it?"

"I'm senior staff, Thyla. I could *discreetly* suggest to Commander Bowers that he review Lieutenant Kedair's recent personnel choices for boarding parties. I might also hint that I've heard rumors of discrimination or favoritism in her assignments."

A crooked smile softened her mocking incredulity. "As if Bowers *doesn't* know you and I have been sleeping together for the last eight months? He'll know you're standing up for me."

"Maybe I want him to know." He kissed her shoulder. "Maybe I want everyone to know."

"Careful, Simon. Keep that up and you might start using the dreaded four-letter word. And then where would we be?"

A soft chuckle concealed his disappointment at once again being gently returned to arm's length from the object of his ardor. It had felt like this between them from the beginning: he in pursuit, she in resistance; he in declaration, she in denial; he in love, and she only deeply in like. At times such as this, he protected his naked feelings by changing the subject. "Let me ask you a hypothetical question. If we were sent into action against an Andorian ship, and Kedair ordered you to fire on other Andorians . . . would you do it?"

The question seemed to trouble sh'Pash, as Tarses had hoped it would. "It would depend upon the circumstances. I'd have to know what was at stake. What the consequences would be."

"What if it was life or death? Shoot to kill or be killed? Andor or the Federation?"

Grim resolve turned her hard and cold. She got out of bed and showed Tarses her back as she strode to the window. "Don't ask me those kinds of questions, Simon."

Sensing he had inflicted a deeper rhetorical cut than he'd intended, he filled with remorse. He got out of bed and moved with caution to stand behind sh'Pash. He knew she could see his dim reflection on the transparent aluminum window in front of them, and he was relieved when she did not tense at the touch of his hands on her shoulders. "I'm sorry." He kissed the tender spot along her right shoulder, where it met the nape of her long, elegant neck.

She reached back and covered his right hand with her own. "Not your fault." Then she bowed her head, as if maintaining eye contact had become too painful. "The reason I said don't ask is that I don't want you to think less of me if I admit that, sometimes, I feel like I *would* choose Andor. That I'd give up everything I've worked for"—she turned, pressed her bare flesh to his, and wrapped him in a fierce hug as her voice shrank to a breathy whisper tickling his ear—"and everyone I . . ."

Tarses almost had to laugh. Sh'Pash hated that "four-letter word" so much that even in an intimate moment such as this, she couldn't bring herself to say it out loud.

Maybe that's for the best, he decided. Because if she ever said it, he would have to admit the truth, too—that there was nothing he wouldn't do, and no oath he wouldn't break, for her.

And then where would they be?

Five

"The situation on Andor is becoming untenable." Thot Naaz, the head of the Breen Intelligence Directorate, knew this was an unpopular topic with his Romulan and Tholian peers, but it was one that could no longer be ignored. "It has been nearly three years since the truth of the Shedai Meta-Genome was revealed. Why have the Andorians not yet found a cure to their dilemma?"

Projected on one side of the vast holographic display in Naaz's office was Tozrene, the Tholian Assembly's current Facet for External Security—a job title he had been assured was analogous to his own; looming larger than life on the other side was Chairwoman Tesitera Levat of the Tal Shiar, the foreign-intelligence apparatus of the Romulan Star Empire. Levat's short temper was in clear evidence; gauging Tozrene's mood was a more challenging proposition.

"The Meta-Genome data is quite complex." Tozrene's reply, despite being filtered through a vocoder, came with a sharp edge of annoyance. *"Isolating the sequences applicable to the Andorians' genetic crisis has been exceedingly difficult."*

Levat's ire deepened. *"Had you allowed us to review the raw data, we might have been able to help you expedite the extraction of relevant sections of the genome."*

"Unfettered access to the secrets of the Shedai is forbidden," Tozrene snapped, his synthesized voice as metallic and shrill as an overheated drill bit boring into metal.

Naaz was thankful that his snout-shaped mask, a mandatory component of the uniform of the Breen Confederacy, concealed his reflexive contempt for the Tholians' xenophobia. "Now you sound like the Federation. Need I remind you that it was their reluctance to share this intelligence with their allies that led them into crisis? Would you have us repeat their errors?"

Tozrene's customary golden radiance took on ominous crimson tints. *"Forbidden."*

The Romulan woman looked tired; she was heavyset, her hair was graying, and the lines in her face betrayed her life's hardships. But as weary as she looked, her manner suggested that a core of iron will still dwelled within her. *"We all share an interest in Andor's future. Persuading them to turn their backs on the Federation was only the first step. If we wish to sway them to our side, we will have to give them a superlative reason to trust us."*

"She's right, Tozrene. We're on the verge of a break-through. We mustn't waste it."

Angry hues coruscated within the Tholian's crystalline torso and head. *"We have provided the Andorian government with more than enough information to complete this task. If those sequences have not been shared with their researchers, that is beyond our control."*

Naaz was baffled by the implications of Tozrene's reply. "Why would the Andorian government not share the Shedai genome data with its own scientists?"

"Political leverage," opined Professor zh'Thiin. "Why else would ch'Foruta and his cronies have set themselves up as gatekeepers for the genome data?"

Her guests at the Science Institute remained subdued. Gathered around a long table in the middle of the Institute's spacious research library, Ulloresh th'Forris of the Unity

Caucus and Narwanit ch'Szaan of the New Restoration Party volleyed anxious glances before both turned hopefully toward the third and senior member of the delegation from the Parliament Andoria.

It was Kellessar zh'Tarash, Leader of the Loyal Opposition and head of the Progressive Caucus, who first ventured an answer. The lithe *zhen*'s slight, delicate features belied the steely quality of her convictions. "I'm sure the presider and his advisers would argue they need to vet the Tholian data as a matter of planetary security, before clearing it for research purposes."

"A convenient excuse," zh'Thiin said. "Who would they trust to inspect the raw data? Who would understand it any better than I and my colleagues?"

Th'Forris sat forward and folded his hands atop the conference table and faced zh'Thiin with the apprehensive air of someone who dreaded speaking in public—a trait zh'Thiin found curious in a politician. "Forgive me, Professor, but isn't it possible the data is being scrubbed of—I don't know—malicious code?"

"Why would the Tholians want to sabotage our research when it was their contributions that made it possible in the first place?"

"If we're speaking hypothetically," ch'Szaan said, "why did they help us at all?"

That was the burning question behind the entire Shedai Meta-Genome controversy, and the one whose answer was both too obvious to deny and too damning to admit aloud.

Federation President Pro Tem Ishan Anjar interrupted his senior advisers' debate by slamming his palm onto his desk. "The only reason the Tholians got involved on Andor was to make us look bad!"

Admiral Marta Batanides, the director of Starfleet Intelligence, hid her distaste for Ishan's emotional outburst as she looked around the room to gauge the reactions of her peers. None of the other counselors gathered on the fifteenth floor of the Palais de la Concorde seemed eager to contradict Ishan's reading of the Typhon Pact's role in the Andorian fertility crisis. They preferred to admire the room's view of Paris by moonlight rather than confront Ishan. All of them except Rujat Suwadi, the irascible Zakdorn director of the Federation Security Agency.

"If the Typhon Pact was trying to embarrass us, they've done a poor job of it. Andor's scientists don't seem any closer to a cure for their genetic crisis than they did pre-secession."

"Not for lack of trying," shot back Galif jav Velk. The Tellarite was Ishan's chief of staff as well as his campaign manager for the upcoming special election, in which Ishan—a hawkish but relatively unknown councillor from Bajor, who was appointed temporarily to the presidency after the shocking assassination of his predecessor, Nanietta Bacco—was vying against a field of even less notable opponents to make permanent his installation as leader of the Federation. "The Andorians have been working on that cure non-stop. It's only a matter of time until they find it."

"And therein lies our dilemma." Lean, soft-spoken, and unassuming in his appearance, Councillor Cort Enaren of Betazed defied one's expectations when it came to Betazoid royalty. "If the Andorians find their cure using Tholian data derived from the Shedai genome, it'll give the Typhon Pact a significant edge in their efforts to induct Andor as a new, full member. If that happens, it won't just be our pride that takes a hit. We'll have to contend with our rivals having a permanent base of operations right in our backyard."

"That's not something we can allow," Ishan said.

"No, sir. It's not." In the wake of President Bacco's murder, Enaren had become a quiet but firm proponent of forceful diplomacy throughout local space.

The tenor of the meeting troubled Batanides. "How would you propose we prevent it?"

Velk counted the steps on a three-fingered hand. "One: Disrupt the Andorians' research with targeted acts of software-based sabotage. Two: Keep pressing the trade and travel embargo against Andor. And three: Make the Tholians halt the flow of Meta-Genome data by threatening to resurrect a technology we know scares them even more: the Genesis device."

Around the room, postures stiffened and eyes widened at the mere mention of Genesis.

It was an insane notion, mad enough to make Batanides abandon decorum. She confronted Velk at point-blank range, her patrician nose all but jabbing his broad porcine snout. "Are you out of your mind? If you even *hint* you might do something like that, we'll have every power in known space gunning for us—even the ones we like to think of as our allies."

"That's why it can't be an idle threat," Ishan cut in. "We'd have to develop at least two working prototypes. One to demonstrate, as a warning; the other to be held in reserve."

Enaren stepped between Batanides and the Tellarite even as he addressed Ishan. "Sir, the admiral is correct. Reviving the Genesis technology is a recipe for disaster. Might I respectfully suggest a less inflammatory but potentially viable alternative?"

Ishan reclined his chair and folded his hands on his lap. "I'm listening."

"Issue an executive order lifting the ban on the Shedai Meta-Genome data. Make it available to the upper echelons of code-word-clearance personnel. Start a new biomedical research program. This kind of science is what the Federation does best. I'm confident we could take the lead and help the Andorians find the cure before the Typhon Pact does."

The president pro tem narrowed his eyes and studied Enaren with suspicion. "Councillor, the people of Andor rebelled against the Federation less than three years ago. They voted to secede, embarrassing us on the galactic stage and setting in motion a series of near-defections by dozens of other worlds. Now they're letting themselves be courted by the Typhon Pact, our chief rival, a power that has engaged in violent espionage against us . . . and you want me to put my name on an executive order that rewards the Andorians for their betrayal? Are you serious?"

Unfazed by Ishan's tirade, the gray-haired Betazoid replied in a low and level voice. "Sir, this is not a time to serve the whims of wounded pride. We have more to gain through a show of public generosity than we do from—"

"Absolutely not," Ishan said. "If we make a show of trying to win back the Andorians, we'll be telling every Federation member and colony with a grievance that the path to prosperity runs first through secession and then through our treasury. I won't set that precedent. For now, we'll continue with the embargo. As for the next step, I want proposals from each of you, outlining strategies to break the Andorians' will. And since I have to be on a transport to Betazed by the crack of dawn, I'll expect them bright and early. Dismissed."

"I take full responsibility for putting us in league with the Tholians," zh'Thiin confessed as dusk turned to night inside the library. "But how we arrived in this predicament is less important now than how we extricate ourselves from it. And to do that, we need to find the cure."

The Progressive leader shook her head. "That gains us nothing, Professor."

Th'Forris quipped, "It gains us the continuation of our species."

"But the *Treishya* and the Typhon Pact will reap the political benefits," ch'Szaan said.

"Which is why you need to make sure they don't get the credit," zh'Thiin said. "The three of you need to whip your members into line and take the fight to ch'Foruta inside the parliament. Demand hearings, subpoena records and comm logs, do whatever you can to make the people of Andor blame the *Treishya* for the delays in finding the cure."

Her recommendation worried the three politicians. After a fretful moment, ch'Szaan spoke for the group. "If we do that, it could spark civil unrest. Uprisings. Riots."

"Maybe even civil war," th'Forris added.

"Yes, that's a risk," zh'Thiin admitted. "But the alternative is political suicide."

Her remark attracted zh'Tarash's attention. "Why now, Professor? What's the hurry?"

"Because events have been set in motion. Partly against my will, but there's nothing to be done about that now. At any rate, if my colleagues and I are right, not only might we be on the verge of finding a permanent solution to the fertility crisis—we might have an opportunity to discredit the *Treishya* and help guide Andor back toward the future it truly deserves."

"Above all else," Tozrene screeched, *"it is imperative that we be the ones to bring the Andorians the data they need to save*

their species. We must not permit the value of our contributions to be diluted by the tampering of others—either on Andor, or within the Federation."

"On this point," said Thot Naaz, "we are all in agreement. Chairwoman Levat, can the Tal Shiar keep us apprised of political developments in the Parliament Andoria?"

"We will share all reports from our assets in Lor'Vela."

"Good. Then all that remains is to prevent any external interference in the Andorians' work. Our field agents have identified all Starfleet and Federation civilian medical personnel who possess the requisite training and experience to affect the progress of the Andorians' research. As of now, all have been placed under constant surveillance." Electing to end the subspace-channel conference on a positive note, Naaz added, "With perseverance, my friends, it should not be long before we welcome Andor as the newest member of the Typhon Pact."

Six

Bashir vented his impatience by tapping his finger on the desk in his office. The screen in front of him had been paused on the same blue-and-white Federation emblem for nearly ten minutes while he waited for the secure comm channel to make its connection. It had taken him hours to confirm in what sector the *Enterprise* had been deployed. To his relief, it was in the nearby Rolor Sector, en route to Ferenginar; to his consternation, the starship's relative proximity did not seem to have made it any easier to reach via subspace for an impromptu conversation.

Five more minutes, he promised himself, *but after that I—*

The screen snapped from laurels and stars to the face of Doctor Beverly Crusher, the chief medical officer of the *Enterprise.* Her red hair was a tousled mess, and she squinted across the light-years at Bashir. *"Doctor Bashir?"*

He sat up and leaned forward. "Yes, hello." A closer look revealed Crusher's utter exhaustion. "Are you all right?"

Her voice was a weary groan. *"Nothing a long vacation and a time machine won't fix."* She staved off his reply with a tired wave of one hand. *"I have a three-year-old son."*

"I understand. My sympathies."

"Thank you." She pinched the sleep from her eyes. *"Not to be rude, but it's the middle of the night for me, so if we could cut to business?"*

An apologetic nod. "Absolutely. I'm conducting follow-up

research on some work you did about three years ago . . . on Andor."

Hearing him say *Andor* jolted Crusher to attention. *"You need to leave that alone."*

"I'm afraid I can't do that. A friend of mine on Andor thinks the data they need to reverse their dropping fertility rates is somewhere to be found in the genome you identified."

Crusher pressed her fingertips to her lips, a gesture clearly meant to ask Bashir's patience for a moment. *"First of all, I didn't identify it. It was isolated by Professor Marthrossi zh'Thiin and her team at the Science Institute. Second, the moment I sent even a fragment of one of its chromosomes to Starfleet for analysis, it triggered a security alert like nothing I'd ever seen. All I did was ask for a pattern analysis, and I almost got myself court-martialed."* She lowered her voice to a whisper to underscore the gravity of the situation. *"Whatever you're working on, abandon it—and for your own sake, don't let Starfleet even suspect you've seen that genome."*

"I can be discreet and conceal my work from Starfleet, but I need to know more about the genome—what it is, where it came from. And as far as I know, you're the only person I can ask for that information. You're the only one I can trust. Please help me."

His plea weakened Crusher's resolve. *"Starfleet made us redact all data about the genome from the ship's computers. All I can tell you is what I remember."* She waited until Bashir cued her to go on. *"The Meta-Genome is an artificial genetic construct created by an extinct precursor race called the Shedai. They ruled over a large area of local space up until about a million years ago, in the sectors around Pacifica."*

"Where the Tkon Empire used to rule?"

"Same region. Anyway, the Shedai went into a prolonged

*period of hibernation a few hundred thousand years ago, but
before they did, they encoded a vast amount of raw data—on
everything from biology to power generation to you-name-
it—into an impossibly complex set of genetic strings, which
they scattered onto planets all over their former territory. And
then they left behind some kind of key for reassembling all that
information."*

Intrigued, Bashir cut in, "To what end? Did they plan to
resurrect their entire civilization when they woke up?"

She shrugged. *"I guess. I saw twenty-third-century medical files related to the Meta-Genome's discovery. It looks as if
some of our most advanced tissue-regeneration technology was
derived from the Meta-Genome, along with who knows what
other advancements."*

"And that was part of the mission profile for Operation
Vanguard."

A quick nod. *"I think so."*

"And how did the Tholians end up peddling the Meta-
Genome to Andor?"

*"If I remember correctly, there was a suggestion in some
of the Vanguard documentation that the Shedai uplifted the
Tholians to sapience, but enslaved them in the process. After
they emancipated themselves, they took some of their former
masters' knowledge with them."*

Bashir began to appreciate the scope of the Meta-
Genome's history and the potential for widespread chaos its
uncontrolled dissemination might unleash. "If the Federation
has the Meta-Genome data that Andor needs, why aren't we
giving it to them, instead of letting the Tholians play the part
of the benefactor?"

*"Your guess is as good as mine. But I can tell you this:
If you go digging for an answer—or, Heaven help you, a*

cure—the powers that be at Starfleet Command had better not find out it was you, or else think that you're dead. Otherwise, you'll end up wishing you were."

"Point noted."

Crusher's tone sharpened. *"I'm not kidding. Getting caught with the Meta-Genome data would be a career-ending mistake. Do yourself a favor, Doctor, and leave it alone. And if you can't, or won't . . . do me a favor, and forget we ever talked about this."*

"This conversation never happened."

"I should be so lucky. Good night, Doctor."

"Sweet dreams. And thank you."

Her hand blurred into view for a moment, and then the channel was terminated at her end. The screen on Bashir's desk reverted to the blue-and-white Federation emblem, and he was left alone to contemplate just how far he was willing to go in pursuit of a wild hunch. Crusher had said nothing to Bashir about the risks that Shar's holographic missive hadn't already told him, but the genuine fear in her voice gave him pause. He had bucked orders many times in the past, risked reprimand over matters of principle, but somehow this felt different—as if he had been implored to commit a noble crime for a greater good, even though it would cost him everything.

Would I give up my freedom to cure a dying people? Lose my life to save a world?

He was stricken for a moment by unbidden memories of murders he'd committed on Salavat, of strangers who had died by his hand, of black deeds he'd done with the blessing of the government that he was now being implored by a desperate peer to defy in the name of mercy.

His thoughts drifted into a daydream of the Egyptian

afterlife, a remnant from some book of mythology he'd once read. He saw himself standing before Anubis, judge of the dead, facing the *Ma'at*: a scale that would weigh his life's evils against its acts of virtue. If the balance of his soul favored good, he would earn redemption and salvation; but if the measure of his life favored evil, his soul would be handed over to the Devourer of the Dead for damnation and destruction.

If I had to take that test right this moment, Bashir realized, *I honestly don't know which way the scale would tip.* It was a truth he had lived with for far too long.

No longer. He was done with the status quo. It was time for change, and not by degrees. It would be major, and he would make it happen—as soon as possible, and on his own terms.

Sarina Douglas stepped out of the shower and with both hands twisted a torrent of warm water from her blond hair. After long days—of which this had been one—she often reveled in taking an extended retreat beneath a spray of hot water and gentle sonic pulses. It was one of many pleasures she had come to appreciate in the years since Julian had freed her from her prison of medically induced near-catatonia and unleashed the full potential of her genetically engineered body and mind. Of course, a shower didn't hold a candle to wine, or to music, or sex, but coming so late to the joys of the senses had taught her to take nothing for granted.

Every day we draw breath is a victory, she reminded herself.

She wrapped a fresh, light-blue towel around her damp hair and pulled on a knee-length, decadently soft white bathrobe. Its thirsty natural fibers wicked the last drops of water

from her skin as she padded out of the bathroom and across
the carpeted floor of the bedroom she shared with Bashir. To
her surprise, he was sitting on the end of the bed, hunched
forward and hands folded, with a somber expression on his
face. Douglas checked the chrono, then looked back at her
lover. "Aren't you supposed to be on duty in the hospital until
the end of Beta Shift?"

"I need to talk to you."

His monotonal reply alarmed her. She sat beside him,
barely perched on the bed's corner. "Are you all right?" When
he hesitated to speak, she added, "Is this about what you were
saying on Bajor? About what happened on Salavat?"

"No." He stopped and seemed to reconsider his answer.
"Not directly."

Something was haunting his thoughts; she could see it
in the distance of his gaze. "What's going on? How can I
help?"

It took him a moment to begin, but once he did, the
story poured from him. He explained that the summons
from Quark had been a back-channel message from his
old crewmate Shar, on Andor, asking for his help in saving
the Andorian people. Then he told her, in a frantic spill
of information, all about the Shedai Meta-Genome: what
it was, where it came from, why it was needed, and what
would happen to Bashir and anyone else who dared to try
to unlock its secrets. It was a mad torrent of history and
conspiracy theory and science all rolled into a breathless
rant.

Finally, his frustration and righteous anger came to the
fore. "The fact that Starfleet is stifling research into the Meta-
Genome makes no sense! Why have access to something with
so much potential only to lock it away?"

"Sometimes, this kind of knowledge gets buried for a reason."

"I refuse to accept that!" He sprang to his feet and began pacing and combing his graying black hair from his eyes with his hand—mannerisms that reminded Douglas unfavorably of Jack, the eponymous ringleader of "the Jack Pack," Douglas's former comrades in psychiatric exile.

She didn't like playing devil's advocate, but the situation seemed to call for it, if only to calm Bashir down. "Perhaps whoever classified the Meta-Genome data had a good reason."

"Reasons lose their meaning over time. Whatever led someone to suppress this information is long since irrelevant."

"We don't know that."

"Sarina. This has politics written all over it. But how many people are still carrying political grudges from the twenty-third century?"

"You'd be surprised. The Tholians, for one. And as a civilization, the Romulans have been known to stay angry for centuries."

Her pointed logic was unable to pierce his armor of indignation. "It's inhumane. Placing politics or security concerns over the survival of a sentient species is indefensible."

Perhaps conversational judo was in order. "I agree with you completely."

Bashir's rhetorical momentum halted as he looked at Douglas. "You do?"

"In principle? Absolutely. I'm not going to sit here and make an argument to justify doing nothing while innocent people die, never mind an entire species." She stood and gently took hold of Bashir by his shoulders. "But think carefully about the answer to this next question. Precisely what action do you suggest we take to stop it?"

He responded by clutching her shoulders, as well. "I need access to the original Meta-Genome data. All of it. As soon as possible."

"Julian, are you completely deranged? Starfleet would never let you have it. They might even drum you out of the service just for *asking* about it."

His demeanor turned dark and deadly serious. "We won't go through official channels. No one else on the station can know I have the data—not even Captain Ro. And once I have it, I'll have to conduct all my research offline—one query to any Starfleet or Federation database, and I'll be in solitary confinement faster than you can say 'treason.' But it all starts with us getting a copy of the complete Meta-Genome and any supporting documentation we can find from Operation Vanguard. And that's why I need your help."

"To do what? My security clearance isn't anywhere near high enough to pull those files through Starfleet Intelligence. You think you'd get locked up fast? Watch what happens to me if I even mention that program at SI."

Bashir seemed unfazed by her protest. In fact, he looked even more resolute. "I don't want you to get the files from SI." He let Douglas work out the rest on her own.

"No. Dammit, Julian, that's too dangerous. We can't!"

"If we don't, the Andorian race will go extinct."

Douglas fought back against a sick feeling in her gut. "It's a mistake."

"It's the only option we have." He stroked her cheek with the back of his hand and pressed his forehead to hers. "We have to try."

"Okay. But I'm warning you, Julian: If we dance with the devil, we *will* get burned."

He kissed her. "Won't be the first time."

The waiting was the worst part. Douglas had followed the established protocol for setting up a meeting: she had sent a written message containing only a prime number—always the next upcoming prime-numbered day to occur on the Federation standard calendar—to an ostensibly inactive recipient address. As always, her message was immediately bounced back to her with an error message explaining that her intended recipient did not exist, but she knew that her contact monitored all errors bounced from that address, and that her signal would be received.

Once that step had been completed, there was nothing more for Douglas to do but go to the meeting place at the prescribed time—always exactly five hours and nine minutes after she had sent her message—and then wait, for however long it took to get a reply.

On the old Deep Space 9, the rendezvous would have taken place in the main room of her quarters. Now that she lived with Bashir, she found it prudent to take these meetings elsewhere. Someplace more private, safe from eavesdropping or prying eyes: the solitary confinement block of the new station's expansive maximum-security stockade complex.

In keeping with Starfleet's commitment to the ethical treatment of prisoners, the cell in which Douglas sat was comfortable, clean bordering on antiseptic, well-lit, and deathly quiet. She reclined on the bed, which could retract into the bulkhead when not in use, and used her folded hands for a pillow. *If I hadn't turned off the comms down here I could tell the computer to play some music,* she mused with mild regret. *Ah, well. I guess that's the price I pay for privacy.*

"You asked to see me." The husky, feminine voice of L'Haan—Douglas's mysterious Section 31 handler—came from the back of the cell and startled the deputy security chief, who scrambled to her feet as she turned. The Vulcan woman's face was lean and youthful, but a diamond-hard quality in her eyes gave her the air of someone much older. She had changed little if at all since her first meeting with Douglas, years earlier. She still wore 31's signature all-black uniform and her Cleopatra-style coif with chilly pride. "State your business."

"I need a favor."

"Our organization does not exist for the personal benefit of its members."

Douglas reined in her temper. "What I'm asking for can benefit the organization, provided we manage it and its consequences correctly."

L'Haan arched one eyebrow until she became doubt incarnate. "Elaborate."

"The Andorians reached out to Julian a few days ago. They—"

"We know. Bashir's former crewmate ch'Thane contacted him through the Ferengi."

It never failed to unnerve Douglas the way that L'Haan seemed to know all the details of a situation far ahead of everyone else, as if all the people around the Vulcan woman were merely pieces on her astropolitical chessboard. "Do you know what Shar sent to him?"

"Portions of the classified Meta-Genome." She made a subtle, birdlike tilt of her head. "Bashir intends to acquire the full genome for analysis." She had said it as if it were fact, but a nuance of diction made it clear she was asking a question.

"Yes. But neither he nor I have the security clearance to gain access to it without ending up in one of these cells for real. That's why I need you to get it for us. Can it be done?"

"Not without great risk." She paced a few steps, stopped near the entrance of the cell, and turned back. "How would you make such an effort on my part worthwhile?"

"By delivering something else the organization wants very, very much."

The Vulcan seemed irked by Douglas's vague promise. "The release of the full Meta-Genome, even into hands as trusted as yours and Doctor Bashir's, poses grave risks to the security of the Federation—possibly to its very existence. If it were to be stolen or intercepted by hostile powers, there would be dire consequences for the future of our civilization."

She met L'Haan's ire with her own rising temper. "We're well aware of the dangers. He knows not to query any external systems about the genome, and we'll do all we can to maintain total secrecy at every stage in the project."

"And if the good doctor succeeds in his mission to save the Andorians, how will he explain the provenance of his miraculous cure?"

"At that point, he'll invoke his right against self-incrimination. But before we go public with the cure, we'll delete all data about the genome that isn't integrated into the end result, so that only the portions needed for the cure are subjected to peer review."

Her assurances seemed to placate L'Haan. "You still have not told me what would be of such value to the organization that we would incur the risks of obtaining this for you."

It was time to bait the trap. "I think the prize will be what you've had me chasing all along: Doctor Bashir himself."

L'Haan was not easily ensnared. "I doubt he would pledge himself to our cause in the name of reciprocity, no matter how profound his gratitude might be."

"True—especially since he thinks I'll be acquiring this through back channels in Starfleet Intelligence. If he thought we were providing him the Meta-Genome data, he'd refuse it. No, what'll bring him to us is that after years of spurning our invitations, when this little crusade of his is over, no matter the outcome, he'll be ruined in Starfleet. He'll have nowhere else to go."

The Vulcan considered that. "Logical. If his effort fails, he will leave Starfleet in disgrace and become a persona non grata in his profession. If he succeeds, he will become a folk hero to billions, not to mention every living Andorian, but his superiors in Starfleet and the Federation will all but crucify him in the court of public opinion. He will be branded a traitor."

"Bashir hasn't taken our hand because until now, he's never really been drowning." Douglas knew she was telling L'Haan exactly what Section 31 had long hoped to hear. "Get me the Meta-Genome data, any way you can. I guarantee you—once I give it to Julian, it won't be long before he's in over his head. After that . . . the rest'll be up to you."

Seven

Success! After countless failed experiments, a seemingly endless parade of dead-end forays into recombinant retroviral vectors for protein resequencing in active biological matrices, Shar was so enthralled by the tantalizing promise of a real breakthrough that it took him nearly half a minute to realize the Science Institute's general alarm was trumpeting through his laboratory.

What in the name of Uzaveh . . . ? He looked up from the hooded display of his electron microscope and glanced over his shoulder at the flashing red alert panel on the wall. *If this turns out to be another bomb hoax—*

His open-ended vow of vengeance was cut off by the sound of the lab's door sliding open and the arrival of an oddly frazzled Professor zh'Thiin. "Shar! We have to go!" She beckoned him with frantic waves. "Now! Let's go!"

"But I've almost isolated a—"

"Leave it!" He understood now: she wasn't irate, she was terrified. He hit a key on the scanner, saving the latest readings. On his way to the door, he called out toward the ceiling, "Computer! Dump all data to the backup sites, Emergency Protocol *Settesh*. Execute!"

"Burst transmission commencing," the computer replied as Shar followed zh'Thiin out of the lab and into the long, pale-gray corridor outside.

The professor was jogging, and Shar made an effort not to

outrun her but rather to pace her, so that he could remain by her side to protect her, if the situation came to that. "What's happening? Why are we heading to the shuttle platforms?"

Labored breaths slowed zh'Thiin's reply. "The protesters promoted themselves to a mob."

"That didn't take long." It had been only hours since a planet-wide news service sympathetic to the *Treishya*'s political agenda had begun a non-stop series of on-air tirades against the Science Institute and its work on the fertility crisis, with special efforts made to vilify Shar and zh'Thiin. He had written it off as a cheap smear campaign when he came to work that morning; only now did he see it for what it truly was: a call to arms. "I presume we're evacuating the Institute as a precaution?"

The professor's answer was trumped by a thunderous rumble of something exploding a few floors beneath them. Overhead the lights flickered and went dark as power failed throughout the building. Then came the savage roar of blood-thirsty voices. Zh'Thiin pushed herself to an all-out sprint and answered between gasps for air, "Not anymore!"

Without power the turbolifts were useless, so Shar and zh'Thiin detoured down a transverse passage. Rounding the corner, they collided with almost a dozen other researchers at the door to the emergency stairwell, which led to the rooftop. Shar marshaled the panicked scientists into order through force of will and sheer volume. "Single file! Upstairs! Move!" The group surged into the smoke-filled stairwell and ascended by leaps and bounds, driven onward by the clamor of pursuers making their way up from a few flights below.

No one spoke during the retreat to the roof; they were all too busy coughing as they gulped great mouthfuls of choking smoke and winced against the effects of tear gas. The noxious fumes burned the back of Shar's throat as he shepherded his colleagues upstairs toward fresh air, and less than a flight from the top he fell to his knees, blind and suffocating.

Then a rush of cold, clean wind flooded the stairwell, and he could breathe again. *Thank Uzaveh, someone got the door open.* In greedy gulps he filled his lungs and found the strength to get up and keep climbing. Stumbling and weaving like a drunkard he navigated the final switchback. The sight of blue sky pulled him forward, its attraction almost magnetic.

He tripped over the threshold as he passed through the doorway, but Professor zh'Thiin caught him before he faceplanted on the roof. She pulled him to his feet. "Are you okay?"

"Fine." He coughed hard, then pointed at the nearest shuttlecraft. "Let's go."

In too much pain to worry about pride, Shar let the middle-aged *zhen* guide him across the rooftop to the shuttle. As soon as they were inside, a gravel-voiced *thaan* in a lab tech's uniform shut the hatch behind them and shouted to the pilot, "That's everyone! Go!"

Engines whined, and Shar suffered a moment of disequilibrium during liftoff until the inertial dampers kicked in. Their shuttle was airborne in seconds, along with the two others that were kept atop the Science Institute for both official travel and emergencies.

Shar tried to move toward one of the nearby viewports, and zh'Thiin tightened her grip on his arm until he assured her in a steady voice, "I'm fine." She let him go, and he eased over to a viewport to steal a look at the Science Institute, which was shrinking into the distance. Smoke rose from dozens of broken windows on its lower floors, and a ring of bodies surrounded the modern building, blocking all its ground-floor exits. A small mob had arrived on the now-empty rooftop and appeared to have busied itself setting fires.

One of the research fellows, a sweet-tempered young *shen* named Carrinor sh'Feiran, sidled up to Shar to have a gander at the spectacle below. "I never thought I'd see Andorians treat science like this." Her cherubic features turned dark with rage. "It's a disgrace."

"That's putting it mildly." Shar watched the flames on the rooftop climb higher. "From where I'm standing, it looks like someone's trying to start a civil war."

Sh'Feiran looked pained. "I just don't understand those idiots. Don't they know we're trying to help them? To save them? To save our entire species?"

"I guess some people would rather die as they are than risk changing to survive."

"Fine, I'm happy to let them die," sh'Feiran grumbled as she turned away. "But why can't they let the rest of us choose to live?"

Shar added her lament to the long and growing list of questions for which he had no good answers. He forced himself to tear his attention from the mindless destruction on the surface and turn back toward Professor zh'Thiin. "Where are we headed?"

"Our backup site."

"The one in Kathela?"

She shook her head. "No, that one's already under siege. Our 'dark' site."

He searched his memory but drew a blank. "I didn't know we had a dark site."

"No one outside the Institute does. We built it through an intermediary, off the books."

In less violent times, Shar would have found such secrecy regarding public resources suspect, but given their circumstances it seemed prudent. "Can I ask where it is?"

"The Tlanek Ice Cap. Hope you packed a sweater."

Kellessar zh'Tarash had always wondered what the Parliament Andoria looked like from the lofty vantage point of Presider ch'Foruta, who sat alone on the highest tier of the dais at the front of the chamber. From zh'Tarash's assigned place in the fourth hemispherical tier of seats facing the dais, it resembled nothing so much as a frenzied mob teetering on the edge of a riot. Now, reeling from news of the protesters who had overrun the Science Institute, the ever-fragile peace of the planet's ruling political body seemed in greater peril than ever.

The roar of hoarse shouts was tamed for a moment by ch'Szaan's amplified bellowing: "This is an outrage!" the New Restoration Party leader addressed the chamber. "At a time when the people of Andor need to unite, the *Treishya* and their puppets turn us against one another!"

"Lies!" raged the Speaker of the Parliament, a loyal *Treishya* partisan named Marratesh ch'Lhorra. "We had nothing to do with what happened at the Science Institute! That was just the price that Professor zh'Thiin and her kind paid for ignoring the will of the people!"

The speaker's tirade goaded Unity Caucus leader th'Forris into the verbal fray. "How can you say your party isn't responsible? We hear your rants all over that puppet network of yours."

"Andor News Service is no one's puppet."

A bark of derision telegraphed th'Forris's contempt. "We're not blind, you know. We all know ANS is nothing more than your party's propaganda machine, spewing hate and lies around the clock. Do you deny they called for an attack on the Institute?"

"We aren't responsible for what ANS broadcasts."

Before th'Forris could retort, he was accosted from his right by Chayni zh'Moor, the leader of the True Heirs of Andor. "You and the rest of your ilk in the Opposition always spout the same pathetic complaints, blaming ANS for your troubles. You're just angry the people get to hear the truth now, raw and unfiltered by your sycophants in the media."

"Truth?" shouted ch'Szaan. "The only truth here is that your friends are telling people to stand in the way of progress, to sabotage our only hope for survival!"

Thufira sh'Risham, the leader of the Visionist Party, regarded ch'Szaan with fury and disgust. "We counsel the people of Andor to reject abomination in all its forms. We won't let Professor zh'Thiin inflict her mad experiments on us—or mutate us like germs in a dish."

As much as zh'Tarash wanted to remain silent and above the debate, she could not bring herself to let such an ignorant assertion pass without rebuttal. "Genetic therapy is not mutation, it's medicine. The work that Professor zh'Thiin and her team are doing at the Science Institute is a labor for the good of all Andorians, an effort to guarantee the survival of our species."

Speaker ch'Lhorra pounced on zh'Tarash's statement, as if he had been waiting for it. "If genetic engineering is such a medical boon, why did the Federation ban it nearly two centuries ago, with our unanimous support? Could it be, perhaps, that it represents a perversion of nature?"

"Any technology can be abused or misused," zh'Tarash said.

"But you admit the procedure zh'Thiin and her associates propose would mutate us?"

Ch'Szaan interjected, "It would be the correction of an acquired defect in our biology. If anything, it would be the reversal of a previous mutation."

His explanation inflamed the passions of THA leader zh'Moor. "Who are we to question the will and wisdom of Uzaveh? How do we presume to undo the work of His divine will?"

"Uzaveh is a deity of endless possibilities," said th'Forris. "His teachings encourage us to explore and master our own nature."

"But not to tamper with what He made!" sh'Risham erupted.

I can't stand these idiots' affected stupidity, zh'Tarash fumed. "We thwarted Uzaveh's diseases a hundred times through the ages. We purged our bodies of His unwelcome parasites. We hunted half our world's native fauna to extinction. Where were your protests then?"

The speaker cupped the microphone of his headset to add authoritative-sounding bass and resonance to his voice. "Don't try to twist this issue with your semantic tricks and—"

"My logic is straight as an arrow," zh'Tarash cut in. "Only your limited intellect makes it seem twisted, because you're too stupid to follow an argument from A to B."

Following her lead, ch'Szaan added, "We won't stand by and let the *Treishya* hold the people of Andor hostage with scare tactics and obsolete superstitions!"

"You would call faith in Uzaveh the Infinite *superstition*?" sh'Risham screeched. "How *dare* you!" As the Visionist leader prowled through the aisles toward ch'Szaan, zh'Tarash knew her ally had taken his rhetoric a step too far. Before anyone could speak a calming word, fists and feet were flying and blood was being drawn. The huddled mass of the parliament's members devolved into a brawl, a teeming pile of profanities and corporal punishments.

Sharp, explosive reports from the presider's gavel halted the clumsy struggle. Bruised and bloodied eyes turned upward, toward the chamber's highest dais. Presider ch'Foruta slammed his gavel against its block until everyone froze in place. "Stop it! Control yourselves! This is a disgrace! Exhibitions like this make me wonder why Andor even needs a parliament. Perhaps you should all take some time to reflect upon that question. Until such time as I hear persuasive arguments for this body's continued existence, I declare it to be in recess." With a final strike of his gavel he dismissed the shamed parliament.

No one protested. The presider's actions were well within his executive purview, and considering the tenor of the moment, to some his decision might even have seemed prudent. But as the other members of the Parliament Andoria slunk away, and the presider himself made a quick and unceremonious exit from the hall, zh'Tarash was troubled by a twinge of dark suspicion—that Andor was on the brink of a civil war, a social implosion from which it would never recover. The survival of the Andorian species was already in grave peril; a massive and sudden reduction in population would hasten if not guarantee its extinction.

Standing alone in the evacuated hall, zh'Tarash knew she had to steer her government and her people away from certain self-destruction. She was sure that violent revolution was not the answer—but she was just as certain that, no matter how it was done, Ledanyi ch'Foruta and his governing coalition had to be removed from power before it was too late.

Though she was not a religious person, she found herself reflecting upon an oft-quoted line from *The Liturgy of the Temple of Uzaveh*: "The Path of Light can be found only by those who brave the Road of Storms and weather its ceremony of losses."

She was too wedded to reason to believe she would ever find herself upon a Path of Light, but as she watched night settle upon the capital of Andor, she had no doubt that she had begun her own journey into the storm of a lifetime.

"This is getting out of control." Presider ch'Foruta pivoted into his chair while his three senior advisers gathered on the other side of his desk. Outside his office window, a hazy sunset ambered the evening sky along the horizon, pursued by the creeping advance of a starry night. "I wanted pressure on zh'Thiin, not an assault on the Science Institute."

His chief adviser, zh'Rilah, struck an optimistic note. "On the plus side, the riot at the Institute is playing well with our base. As long as we keep sh'Risham and zh'Moor as the face of the religious hard-liners, we can stand back and try to look like peace brokers."

Ch'Foruta was not encouraged. "On the downside, the Science Institute just got burned to the ground on our watch. Forget that our base loves it. How do we spin it for the moderates?"

Sh'Donnos, the senior counselor for justice, set a padd on the presider's desk. "My office can issue a statement deploring the violence. The draft is ready to go. We can order a halt to all violence and threaten swift consequences for anyone who disobeys."

The suggestion earned a nod of approval from zh'Rilah. "That's good. It'll let us keep a lid on anyone thinking about reprisals or escalation and cement the public's perception of us as the law-and-order party." She looked at th'Larro, the senior counselor for intelligence. "Valas?"

"We can use the riot at the Institute as cover the next time we get asked why it's taking so long to develop a cure. That'll help us position the Progressives and their moderate allies against the THA and the Visionists."

"Making all of them look nonviable as governing parties," ch'Foruta said. "It would be nice if we could establish ourselves as something other than 'the least of all evils by default.'"

"We're working on it," zh'Rilah said. "Unfortunately, the riot hurt us with the moderates. We can put out statements and do all the damage control we want, but we're going to take a hit."

It wasn't unexpected news, but it still worried ch'Foruta. "How big a hit?"

"Ten to fifteen points. Maybe more in the eastern provinces."

Th'Larro seemed even more alarmed than the presider felt. "Any way to blunt that?"

The chief adviser rubbed her thumb against her forefinger as she pondered options. "We could distance ourselves from the rants on ANS by pointing the finger at the THA."

The presider waved off that idea. "No, that'll backfire. If we blame the THA, they'll withdraw from the coalition. And the moment that happens—"

"The Progressives call for a no-confidence vote," zh'Rilah said, finishing his thought. "Same thing happens if we blame the Visionists. So what do we do—disavow the protesters?"

A low harrumph from sh'Donnos. "Our base would *love* that."

"So, take the hit," th'Larro said. "What difference does it make? It's not as if sh'Risham or zh'Moor would ever let a no-confidence vote get off the floor. And even if they did, ch'Lhorra would bury it in points of order. Hell, we could drop *thirty* points in the polls and it wouldn't matter. No one's dissolving the government as long as we don't turn our friends against us."

"All true," ch'Foruta said. "But you're not seeing the big picture, Valas. The coalition can stand until the next plebiscite, but we'll still need to win that election—and if our numbers tank because of this mess at the Institute, we'll have to find a way to turn them around and win back the moderates, or else we might as well gift wrap my gavel for the Progressives right now." He reclined his chair and studied his advisers' grave faces. "Any suggestions?"

Th'Larro's antennae twitched with restrained excitement. "What if we start releasing more of the Meta-Genome data to zh'Thiin and her team? Jump-start their research program?"

His idea was met with doubt by zh'Rilah. "We've talked about this, Valas. Any good news out of zh'Thiin's camp plays to the Progressives' advantage. They've been painting them-selves as the party of science for decades now."

"Exactly. So we take it from them—hit them where they're strongest, steal their best issue and make it our own." The *thaan* turned toward ch'Foruta. "They'll never see it com-ing. We give them everything they've been asking for and more. Pump money and data into their operation. Let them do whatever they can to fast-track a solution to the crisis."

The presider knew he was rarely the smartest person in any room, though he was far from stupid—but he had no idea what th'Larro was driving at. "How does that help us, Valas? Our base will go insane if we publicize our support for zh'Thiin's research."

"That's the best part, sir—we *don't* publicize it. We tell zh'Thiin it's not about politics, it's about finding the cure. You know how Progressives think—they won't even question it. Then, as soon as she finds the cure, we let it leak to the press that the Progressives accelerated her research program by promising the Typhon Pact its support for Andor's membership, in exchange for giving zh'Thiin direct access to the Meta-Genome data."

It was diabolical and just what ch'Foruta had wanted. "That's brilliant, Valas. We make zh'Tarash look like a traitor and tarnish the Progressives for at least a generation, maybe two; we secure a majority in the popular vote, so we can stop looking over our shoulder every three years; and, best of all, we get the cure." A satisfied nod. "How long to make it happen?"

"That depends."

"On what?"

"For starters, the Tholians, but I suspect they'll cooperate. The only other obstacle I can foresee would be reestablishing contact with Professor zh'Thiin. She and her people have been off the grid since the riot at the Science Institute's headquarters."

"All right. Get started, and make sure we retain at least some plausible deniability."

Zh'Rilah dismissed the other counselors. "Thank you." She watched her two peers leave, then fixed the presider with a shrewd glare.

Despite being unnerved by the *zhen*'s attention, ch'Foruta met it head-on. "What, Ferra?"

"This is a dangerous game you're playing, sir. If anyone finds out about it—"

"I'll know they got it from one of you three, and I'll have you all shot."

His dark humor only made zh'Rilah more insistent. "Sir, I'm serious. The potential blowback on a disinformation campaign this big could be devastating—not just for us personally, but for the party. It depends on a lot of elements going right, at precisely the right times. If something disrupts the timetable—"

"Relax. Valas knows what he's doing. Besides, it's not as if we're going to live or die by the grace of a million tiny details. The only thing that *really* matters is that we beat zh'Tarash to the punch in the media. Once our version of the truth gets out, the Progressives will be stuck playing defense—or as it's known in politics, *losing.*"

Eight

It was a fact of life for Starfleet personnel that orders of any kind could come with no warning or explanation, only an expectation that they would be obeyed. As much as Douglas had tried to acclimate herself to this arbitrary state of affairs, she still found herself perplexed to receive an early morning summons to the station's hospital complex for a medical exam.

It's been less than seven months since my last physical. Everything checked out fine. Why do they need to see me again so soon?

Sector General, Deep Space 9's expansive and state-of-the-art medical facility, was located in the main body of the station, directly beneath The Plaza, a sprawling level of dining, recreational, and commercial spaces. The hospital occupied more than a quarter of the vast, circular deck. Unlike its bare-bones forebear, the infirmary on the old DS9, Sector General comprised several operating suites; dozens of laboratories; wards for post-operative recovery, intensive care, and quarantine; and dedicated offices for a wide range of medical specialties, including obstetric, pediatric, ophthalmic, and orthopedic medicine, as well as dentistry.

Douglas stepped out of the turbolift into the wide outer passageway that ringed the medical complex. Directly in front of her yawned the broad, brightly lit entrance to the hospital. In the center of the reception area stood a large circular information desk, its façade boldly emblazoned with the words SECTOR GENERAL in Federation Standard, its polished duranium countertop uncluttered and unblemished. Douglas passed by the desk and smiled at the civilian receptionist stationed there. Along the curving wall behind the gatekeeper's post, armed security officers stood at the entrance to a number of corridors that radiated away from the entrance. Navigating by memory, she followed the center corridor to the main suite of exam rooms.

The wide hallway was bright and pristine, and its air was laced with the astringent odor of medical-grade disinfectants. To the ordinary noses of the doctors, nurses, and technicians she passed, the hospital's atmosphere might have come to seem routine, but to Douglas's genetically enhanced perceptions, the place smelled so aggressively clean that it was almost offensive.

Arriving at the intersection that separated the recovery rooms from the exam stations, she stopped at the corner station and caught the attention of the duty nurse, a young male Trill attired in green surgical scrubs. "Pardon me."

"Yes, Commander?"

"I was ordered to report for a physical?"

He pointed down the corridor in front of her. "Exam Eight, fourth door on your right. The doctor's waiting for you."

"Thanks." Still confused but at least relieved to know she wasn't imagining the peculiar orders, she continued walking to the assigned examination room. As she stepped toward it, the door slid open, an implied invitation. *Time to see what this is about.*

She stepped inside; the door closed behind her. The only other person in the room stood off to one side. Her back was to Douglas, but the styling of her raven hair was unmistakable, despite her costume of a long blue physician's jacket over a Starfleet doctor's uniform. L'Haan turned to face Douglas, her hands tucked inside her jacket's pockets. "Late. As always."

There was nothing to be gained from arguing with the Vulcan woman, so Douglas cut to what mattered. "Do you have it?"

"Yes. But I am not sure I should give it to you."

"I don't have time for games, L'Haan."

Steeply arched eyebrows hinted at diminishing patience. "I assure you, Miss Douglas, we do not regard anything about this situation as a game. The events you seek to set in motion pose tremendous dangers to everyone involved."

Douglas resisted the urge to throttle L'Haan. "We've already covered this."

"My superiors are not convinced that you appreciate the gravity of the situation. I've been directed to make sure that you do." She paced in a slow orbit around Douglas, who pivoted to keep the other woman in her sights. "First, as tempting as we find the prospect of using Doctor Bashir's impending disfavor as a means to his recruitment, that's not why we've agreed to help you. The chief purpose of Section Thirty-one is to ensure the safety and continued existence of the Federation. We believe that winning back the friendship of the Andorian people is vital to those objectives, and that the current pro tem administration's embargo against Andor is not just petty, it's self-defeating. It will drive Andor into an alliance with the Typhon Pact, an outcome we cannot permit. For those reasons, we've chosen to support Bashir's efforts."

"I'm sure he'd be deeply touched if he ever found out."

The sarcasm only darkened L'Haan's demeanor. "However, we cannot risk letting the Meta-Genome data be stolen. Consequently, we will monitor Bashir's research. If we see any sign of a threat to his project's secrecy, any hint that a foreign agent has gained access to the data, we will terminate the entire operation with extreme prejudice."

Those final two words were a euphemism Douglas knew well; they had an old pedigree in intelligence work. *Extreme prejudice* was a polite way of saying that Section 31 was prepared to kill Bashir and everyone around him, and to destroy anything and everything necessary, to keep the full Meta-Genome data under exclusive Federation control.

L'Haan stopped in front of Douglas. "Do you understand?"

"Perfectly."

"Good." L'Haan reached into a pocket of her jacket, took out a small translucent envelope containing ten isolinear chips, and handed them to Douglas. "Make certain that Bashir understands *before* he decrypts this data. Once he does, there will be no going back." Then the Vulcan stepped past Douglas and left the exam room, signaling the end of the conversation.

Douglas stood for a moment, staring at the envelope in her hand, then snapped herself back into action. She turned and hurried out the door after L'Haan. "Hey, what about—"

There was no sign of the Section 31 handler in the corridor outside the exam room. The passageway was empty for two sections in either direction, and even when Douglas strained to listen for footfalls that matched L'Haan's stride, she heard nothing but the hum of the life-support systems and the gentle feedback tones of Federation medical equipment.

It was hard not to succumb to envy. *Someday I need to learn how she does that.*

Bashir didn't hear his office's door chime until it warbled for the second time. He sat back from his three-dimensional holo-display and grumbled, "Come in."

The door unlocked at his invitation and slid open with a soft hush to reveal Douglas. She hurried inside and used the manual controls beside the door to close and lock it beside her.

Bashir observed his inamorata with bewilderment. "Is something wrong?" Douglas faced him and began unzipping her uniform jacket. "Sarina, we're on duty. I don't think this is—"

"Be quiet." Affixed to the inside of her jacket with strips of medical adhesive were ten isolinear chips. She extricated them and passed them in two fistfuls to Bashir.

The slender computer chips were cool in his hands despite having been concealed against Douglas's torso. He watched the light play off their variously colored surfaces, then he looked up at his beloved. "Are these . . . ?" She confirmed that what he held in his hands was the Meta-Genome data they had sought through her connections in Section 31. "Who knows?"

"You, me, and the organization." She pressed her palms on his desk and leaned across it to confide in a whisper, "And we have to make sure it stays that way."

It wasn't hard to imagine the caveats with which Section 31 had provided the data. "Let me guess—if anyone finds out, we'll all vanish into the ether."

"Something like that." She placed one hand over the pile of data chips. "Before you start decrypting these, I have to ask: Are you absolutely sure you want to do this?"

"You know I am. I've made that abundantly clear."

"Yes, but at the time the situation was strictly hypothetical. Now we have the data in our hands. This isn't just what-if anymore. This is the moment of truth, Julian." She picked up one chip, stood, and circled around his desk, holding up the small rectangular data-storage device like a holy relic. "For once, think before you act. Once you access the information on these chips, you'll be guilty of espionage against the Federation, and I'll be an accessory."

"If you want to get technical about it, we're already guilty of espionage."

"True. But we could just vaporize these chips right now, and no one would ever be the wiser. Once you retrieve the data and start working on it, we'll have crossed a line. One that could mean the end of our careers and spending the rest of our lives in solitary confinement on rocks with no names, in star systems no one's bothered to put on a map."

"We can't concern ourselves with worst-case scenarios."

"Actually, that's the best-case scenario. Even if everything goes perfectly, and you find a cure, and you get it to the Andorians, once you do you'll be arrested, court-martialed, and in all likelihood disappeared before anyone has a chance to thank you."

He didn't like where this was going. "Dare I ask what constitutes a worst-case outcome?"

"If Section 31 thinks your security has been compromised, or that anything you do poses a risk to the safety of the Federation, they'll kill you, me, and anyone else who might be even tangentially involved. Then they'll erase your research, bury the Meta-Genome data, and probably exterminate the Andorians while framing the Tholians for the genocide."

Bashir reclined and let her sobering assessment sink in. "I see. . . . Well, one has to give them credit for being thorough, I suppose."

"This isn't a joke, Julian. I know we're acting with the best of intentions, but I'm afraid we might be opening Pandora's box here."

It was clear to him that whatever had transpired in her meeting with her Section 31 handler, it had left her shaken. He abandoned his defense mechanism of glib pretense and sat forward. "Do you think we can't keep the data a secret?"

"No operation is ever perfectly secure. No matter what precautions we take, there's a risk our efforts might be observed and analyzed by someone who knows what to look for."

He picked up one of the chips. "Imagine for a moment if it was the human race that was dying. Would we be as quick to throw away a chance like this if our species was on the brink?"

"Maybe not—but that isn't what's really at stake, Julian. If we lose control of the Meta-Genome data, we might be responsible for the deaths of tens of billions of sentient beings, all over the galaxy. Just because we're using it to heal doesn't mean others would be so noble."

"I agree." He gathered up the isolinear chips, plucked the last one from Douglas's fingers, and put them all into the bottom drawer of his desk. "Computer: lock desk drawers."

From an overhead speaker came the synthetic female

voice that seemed ubiquitous to Starfleet computer systems: *"Drawers secured."*

Douglas wore a skeptical expression. "Now what?"

"Well, I can't just plug those chips into my regular work console and start parsing the data. The moment it starts decrypting, we'd likely trigger who knows how many alarms." He stroked his beard pensively, a nervous habit born of his inability to sit still most of the time. "I'll need a dedicated computer core for this project, one that can be partitioned from the station's network. Can we take over one of the auxiliary cores?"

"That won't work. We could isolate one core from the others, but you wouldn't be able to access it without sending signal traffic over the station's network. Even if you encrypt the data in transit, that's no guarantee your work won't send up red flags."

"Then we'll need something completely autonomous." The two of them stood together, concentrating on the challenge ahead of them. Then their eyes widened in unison, and Bashir suspected they had arrived simultaneously at the same solution. He blurted, "A runabout—"

"—is a mobile computer core!" Douglas was almost giddy. "We could swap out all the modular mission systems on the *Tiber* with medical equipment, turn it into a traveling medlab."

"We'll need a cover story. A medical research survey in the Gamma Quadrant, maybe."

The deputy security chief nodded. "That might work. Let me check its mission schedule. If it's clear, I can set you up as soon as tomorrow. Any work you do on the runabout, we can pass off as prep for the survey. The only risk factors will be securing the data chips in transit and making sure no one hacks the runabout's computer core to see what we're working on."

"How do we do that?"

"You worry about finding the cure." She kissed his forehead. "Leave security to me."

Nine

Liberated from the invisible, smothering embrace of the transporter's annular confinement beam, Commander Sam Bowers drew a grateful breath. *I know it's for our safety, but I wonder if we set ours a bit too strong.*

Shaking off the claustrophobic effect, he willed himself into motion and marched down the center aisle of the cargo bay of the civilian freighter *S.S. Ibiza* at a quick step, on a straight line for the person who had summoned him here: the *Aventine*'s chief of security, Lieutenant Lonnoc Kedair. The Takaran woman was tall and cut a trim but imposing figure, with her finely scaled green hide, jet-black mane of hair, and piercing violet eyes, whose hue matched that of the natural, intricate symmetrical markings on her forehead and chin.

She was standing beside the freighter's commanding officer, Captain Satal, a lean, fiftyish Thallonian man whose bleached-white topknot and pencil-thin mustache contrasted sharply with his dark crimson skin and loose-fitting robes of black Tholian silk. He looked to Bowers like someone who aspired to be an Orion merchant prince.

Hoping to avoid being drawn into a pointless argument, Bowers eschewed eye contact with the freighter captain as he addressed Kedair. "Sitrep, Lieutenant."

"We have a small problem, sir. Specifically, jurisdiction."

He'd been expecting news of resistance, not legal minutiae. "Come again?"

Satal interjected, "Your troops have no right to be on my ship—which I told you and your captain before you beamed these jackbooted thugs into my cargo bay."

Now the freighter captain had Bowers's full, irate attention. "We've covered this, Captain Satal. Your ship is registered on Betazed and operates under Federation authority. If you—"

Kedair cleared her throat loudly enough to cut Bowers off. She handed him a civilian version of a padd. "That's what I'm trying to tell you, sir. The *Ibiza*'s license was transferred to Ghidi Prime three days ago. All their paperwork checks out, including the security seal."

The first officer waved his padd at Kedair and Satal. "Then why does this ship still show up in the Federation's merchant marine database?"

"Because it takes your fat-assed bureaucrats six to twelve weeks to update their records and disseminate them to Starfleet."

The security chief's face blushed a darker shade of green, a telltale sign that the freighter commander was firing up her temper. "Unfortunately, Captain Satal is correct. This vessel operates under Typhon Pact authority. It's exempt from Federation law in interstellar space."

Bowers pointed around them at the mountains of shipping containers stacked in orderly rows and columns, all the way up to the ship's lofty overhead. "What about the cargo?"

Satal inched forward, as if trying to provoke a fight. "What about it?"

"Where's it from? I don't care whose flag you fly under, if you're transporting contraband on or off Federation worlds with the intention of delivering it to Andor, we'll beam every last bit of it into deep space on a wide-dispersal setting."

His threat prompted an arrogant smirk from the Thallonian. "Not unless you feel like starting an interstellar incident, Commander. My manifest is on that padd. Have a look." He spread his arms in an all-encompassing gesture toward his cargo. "These are all Typhon Pact goods, aboard a Typhon Pact commercial vessel, bound for a neutral planet."

"We'll see about that." Bowers stepped off to one side and paged through several screens of data on the padd—not enough to read the entire manifest of the *Ibiza*, but enough to get the gist of this elaborate, brazen ploy. He turned back and confronted Satal. "Diverse inventory you have here."

Satal feigned innocence with a shrug. "I just move what the clients pay for."

"So I see. Rare and perishable foodstuffs. Industrial fertilizers and bioengineered seeds. High-end medical equipment, computers, replicators, construction technology, weapons, not to mention two million metric tons of gold-pressed latinum." Bowers feigned surprise. "Who knew the Typhon Pact did such a bustling trade in goods that are specialties of the Federation?"

"Learn something new every day," Satal said.

Bowers handed the padd back to Kedair. "The most interesting thing about this ship's cargo, Lieutenant? It all came from the same corporate client on Ghidi Prime. Captain Satal expects me to believe that one company produces such a wide range of commercial goods."

"I never said they produced any of it. Just that they paid to ship it to Andor. It's not as if Seboz Holdings is the first aggregate retailer in corporate history."

Kedair's anger became a cold fire as she studied the information on the padd. "A Typhon Pact shell company sets up shop on a planet just over the border inside Tzenkethi space.

Using middlemen, they buy up all the Federation goods they know Andor needs most. Then they recruit the *Ibiza* and who knows how many more ships to switch their registries to Ghidi Prime. In a month or two, they have a legally untouchable black-market fleet." She huffed out a snort of derision. "If they set this up correctly, they might even be turning a profit."

"Something I'd like to be doing myself," Satal cut in, "if the two of you would be so kind as to take your goon squad and *get off my ship.*"

Bowers took the padd from Kedair and slapped it against Satal's chest. "With pleasure."

The security chief tapped her combadge. "Kedair to boarding party. Regroup at the transport site, on the double." She and Bowers walked aft to the bay's largest open area, which the *Aventine*'s operations officer, Lieutenant Mirren, had designated as the key site for transport on and off the vessel. Within a minute, the rest of her boarding team met them there.

Satal called out, "Aren't you going to say you're sorry, Commander?"

The taunt compelled Bowers to look back with contempt at the Thallonian. "If you can warp this tub of crap outta range before I give the order to blast it into dust, you can call *that* an apology." He tapped his combadge. "Bowers to *Aventine*. Beam us back. Before I shoot someone."

On the other side of Dax's desk, Bowers prowled back and forth like an animal testing the limits of its cage. "This makes our mission even more pointless. You realize that, right?"

"Sam, please—sit down. Watching you pace is like talking to a tennis match."

He stopped and sighed heavily, then eased himself into one of the guest chairs in front of the captain's desk. "I've got Kedair investigating how many commercial ships have recently resigned their registries from Federation worlds, but ships get decommissioned all the time. We won't know which ones are flying under new flags until we try to impound them and end up with a slap in the face. And I'll bet we're going to start seeing a lot of them, very soon."

"We knew it was only a matter of time before someone exploited that loophole. To be honest, I'm surprised the Ferengi didn't do it first."

"Chalk that up to Grand Nagus Rom courting Starfleet's help to secure his borders against the Tzenkethi." Bowers shook his head. "I'm sorry, Captain. I just don't see any point to this embargo. Now that the Typhon Pact's figured out how to end-run us, we're little more than traffic managers. Hell, I bet the *Ibiza*'s captain crossed our path just so he could thumb his nose at us. After word of this gets out, every fast-buck freighter jockey in the sector's gonna be applying for a Ghidi Prime license and a slot on the Andor run. And there's absolutely nothing we can do about it."

"To be honest, Sam, I'm not sure that's a bad thing." She noted his look of confusion, which turned quickly to one of accusation. "Don't act so shocked. I'm not a monster; I know the embargo's a useless cruelty. Your twice-daily briefings have made sure of that."

Her jape earned an amused glint of faux humility from Bowers. "Just doing my job."

"If only our diplomats were so relentlessly—"

"Charming?"

"Annoying." She swiveled her chair so she could lean one elbow on her desk and stretch her legs. "I'm almost glad the

Typhon Pact aced us on this one. The Andorians need those supplies, and playing politics with people's lives never sat well with me. But you and I still have the same problem we had before: we're under orders to enforce an embargo. Even if most of the ships we challenge are legally immune, we have to at least keep up the pretense. And if, every now and then, we stop a ship that we do have the right to impound, we'll do it. But that doesn't mean we have to like it."

Bowers wore a resigned expression. "I understand why we have to play our part. But I'm concerned that when Starfleet Command"—he corrected himself—"I mean when President Pro Tem Ishan finds out what's happening out here, he won't accept it as the inevitable result of a failed foreign policy. I'm worried he'll see it as a challenge. I'm afraid this mess will escalate."

Anxiety churned the acid in Dax's gut. "So am I, Sam. . . . So am I."

Ten

Parked in the middle of a docking bay designated for its exclusive use, the *Tiber* looked small. Sarina Douglas recalled how bulky the runabouts had seemed inside the narrow hangars of the old Deep Space 9. The maintenance and support areas on this new, Starfleet-built facility were much larger, better equipped, and so new that the odors of industrial chemicals and overheated metal had yet to take up residence.

Her footsteps resounded in the empty space; the echoes returned to her, sharp and clear, from the off-white bulkheads and the pale-gray deck as she crossed from the corridor entrance to the port-side hatch of the *Tiber*. Just as she and Bashir had agreed when setting this plan in motion, the small starship's hatch was closed and locked. She considered letting herself in—after all, she knew the code to unlock the hatch—but decided to hail Bashir instead. A light tap on the comm button next to the hatch's controls opened a channel to the *Tiber*'s interior. "Julian?"

Bashir's voice over the comm was slow and weary. *"Come in."*

That didn't sound promising. She keyed in the door's security code. The magnetic bolts retracted with a low hum and a deep thunk from inside the ship's hull, and the hatch slid open. Douglas stepped inside and turned aft, toward the work area. The runabout's interior was steeped in darkness

and shadow; its few spots of feeble illumination came courtesy of computer displays in the cockpit, a dull standby glow
from the transporter arch, and dim emergency lighting that
marked the center path on the deck. Douglas took her time,
to give her eyes time to adjust. She stepped through the open
internal hatchways, passed through the transporter arch, and
moved through the narrow gap between the medical mission
modules.

Bashir sat hunched, flanked by computer displays, his
face buried in his hands.

Suspecting she knew the answer, Douglas asked, "How's
it going?"

He responded with a muffled, inchoate moan of exhaustion and frustration.

She stood behind his chair and massaged his shoulders,
which tension had turned as hard as oak. "That well, huh?"

He lifted his face from his palms. His hair was mussed
and his throat was rough with stubble below his trimmed
beard. "I had no idea it could be this complex," he murmured,
as if in shock. "I've honestly never seen anything like it. Not
even the Yrythny 'turnkey' genome was this Byzantine." He
pinched the bridge of his nose, then rubbed his eyes. "What
time is it?"

"A little past 2200."

Her answer made him swivel his chair around. His angular features were agape with horror. "You're not serious."

"Julian, please tell me you haven't been sitting here since
yesterday." Bashir looked away for a moment, and then he
seemed to deflate. Douglas leaned down to reestablish eye
contact. "When you didn't come back to our quarters last
night, I figured you'd been called to duty in the hospital. If I'd
realized you were in here, obsessing over this—"

He fended off her concern with raised palms. "It wouldn't have mattered." He gestured from one screen to the next as he continued. "I've tried isolating sections of the Meta-Genome for comparison against the major Andorian genotypes, but there are so many results that I can't begin to tell which ones are promising and which are dead ends."

"What if you break it down by gender?"

A tired head shake. "I tried. Even separated into four subgroups, the amount of raw data involved is staggering." He keyed some commands into the control panel and called up a series of medical reports in side-by-side panels; some were from Starfleet records, others were from the Andorian Science Institute. "Shar and Professor zh'Thiin have documented their protocols to the last detail, so I tried approaching the task from a procedural angle. I compared their recent work to Doctor Crusher's research from three years ago, and then I read through an entire file of top-secret reports written over a hundred years ago, by a Doctor Babitz on the *Starship Sagittarius*." His diminishing patience and growing vexation became increasingly evident. "Few commonalities in their protocols, even fewer repeatable results, and not a clue where to start breaking this down to make it the least bit useful."

Douglas resumed kneading the knots from Bashir's shoulders. "You need sleep."

"No, what I need is help. I've done my fair share of genetic research, but this is far beyond my level of expertise. I have to bring in experts, the best I can find."

She ceased her massage and spun his chair around, then she planted her hands on his forearms and leaned down to confront him, nose to nose. "You know you can't do that, Julian. Never mind the risk to our security—if Thirty-one finds out, you'll have put a death mark on the head of every one of those so-called experts."

"All right. So we warn the experts of the risks before we read them in. Anyone who doesn't think it's worth it can walk away."

"And immediately report us to Starfleet."

"I think you're a bit paranoid."

"And I think you're sleep deprived. Maybe now's not the best time to make plans that affect our lives, the security of the Federation, and the survival of the Andorian species."

He pushed himself up from the chair, and Douglas let go of him and stepped back to give him room. He tamed his tousled hair with a slow push of his hands over his head. "I'm not delusional, Sarina. I know bringing in help increases the risk. But I can't do this alone."

"You've only had the data for one day. Why not wait and see what you can do on your own over the next few months? Give it time to—"

"We can't maintain this charade for that long, and you know it. How long before someone starts asking why I'm never in my office? Or until someone retasks this runabout, and we lose our mobile lab? Time's a factor—one we're quickly running out of."

She knew that look in Bashir's eyes. He was committed to seeing this through, no matter the cost. "How many experts do you need to get this done?"

His eyes roamed over the screens of alien data. "No more than six. The best of the best."

"And how are we supposed to explain why you and half a dozen of Starfleet's top geneticists are huddled inside this runabout for days on end?"

He wrinkled his brow with concentration. Then his mood

brightened. "A medical conference! And we can hold it on Bajor. We'll draw less attention away from the station."

"Not bad. Make it sound boring enough and you can probably quell Starfleet's interest. But your little ruse won't fool Thirty-one."

"No, it won't. That's why I'm counting on you to keep them at bay."

"And how am I supposed to do that?"

A stymied roll of his shoulders. "No idea. But you'll think of something. You always do." He stepped past her on his way forward to the hatch. "If you'll excuse me, I have to go send irresistible invitations to six of the most brilliant genomic-medicine specialists in Starfleet."

Douglas said nothing as she watched Bashir leave, not because she relished letting him have the last word, but because his rash disregard for his own survival—not to mention hers and that of anyone else he was callous enough to embroil in this fiasco—had left her speechless.

Antarctic winds howled like nightmares outside the Science Institute dark site, rattling its ramshackle walls and vibrating the transparent-aluminum windowpanes in their frames. Inside the building, hidden drafts from slipshod construction filled the corridors with frigid air and an omnipresent sepulchral groaning. To Shar, all the lighting inside his project's new base of operations looked sickly green—that is, when it wasn't flickering or failing outright. Had they set up shop at Andor's opposite pole, they could simply have relied on sunlight; unfortunately, the planet's south pole had just entered its annual two-month period of constant darkness.

I would almost rather go back to the building the fanatics burned down.

He tried to turn on the computer terminal in his new office, only to find that it had no power. It took him a few minutes of crawling, first under his desk and then around the room's periphery, to trace the Gordian knot of power cords and data lines to their appointed junctions. The gentle-featured *chan* was squatting with a tangle of wires clenched in his fists, swearing under his breath, when he noted a faint shadow settling over him. Swallowing a mouthful of undignified vulgarities, he turned to see Professor zh'Thiin standing in his doorway. The middle-aged *zhen* offered him friendly sympathy. "Settling in, I see."

"As best I can." He dropped the wires, stood, and clapped his hands clean.

"Doctor th'Noor says he'll have the main server up within the hour. After he runs a few routine diagnostics on the core, we'll be ready to get back to work."

Shar tried to sound excited by the news, but failed. "That's great."

His supervisor edged into the room. "Shar? Is something wrong?"

He threw up his arms at the cracked thermocrete walls, the water-damaged ceilings and floors, the naked wiring. "Look at this place. How are we supposed to perform cutting-edge biomedical research *here*? Was this place even designed as a medical facility?"

"If memory serves, it was built to be a weather station."

He waved toward the window, which was being pelted by wind-driven ice. "Forecast for the future of our project: dark, frozen, and trapped in the middle of nowhere."

"Look on the bright side. We won't get many protesters bothering us."

The light above Shar's head chose that moment to die

with a flash and a fizzle, plunging his desk into shadow. "It won't matter if we do. They won't be able to see us in the dark."

Zh'Thiin stepped one foot back into the corridor outside Shar's office and motioned for him to follow. "Let's grab something warm from the commissary." Shar was in no mood to be cheered up, but he trailed her out of the lab and down the long, drab passage.

He indulged a moment of hope. "Is there any *raktajino* left?"

"Don't count on it." The professor snuck a look at Shar while they walked together. "You're not happy about the new facility."

"What gave it away?"

"I'm serious, Shar. You really think we can't continue our work here?"

Her prodding opened the floodgates of his dudgeon. "How can we? The computers are all decades out of date. We don't have anywhere near the network bandwidth or processing power we need to perform virtual sequencing on something as complicated as the Meta-Genome." He pointed at a dank and foul-smelling room on his left as they passed by it. "Even the lavatories don't work. Not that we'll need them, since all the pantries are empty and the only replicator works only half the time. Frankly, I'm surprised this place hasn't been swallowed by a crack in the ice shelf or blown into the sea by a stiff wind."

"Give it time. Winter's not over yet."

"You think this is a joke? We need to be moving forward, making progress, pushing ahead to find a lasting solution to the fertility crisis. This place is a step backward."

She opened the door to the commissary and ushered him inside. "I'm well aware of this facility's shortcomings, Shar.

But upgrading it is no small challenge, especially if we're to keep its location a secret. That's why our agent in the capital must be patient, careful, and discreet."

He looked around and confirmed that he and zh'Thiin were alone in the commissary. Even so, he lowered his voice. "We have an agent in the capital?"

"Not yet. You leave tonight."

"Me? But—"

"No debates, Shar. Your Starfleet experience makes you the best qualified for this. We need you to go back to Lor'Vela, make contact with our suppliers, and arrange for shipments of equipment and supplies—by routes most circuitous, if you please. And if you find an opportunity to make contact with your friends in the Federation, let them know what's happened to us."

Her instructions caught him off guard. "What about the rest of you?"

"Don't worry about us. Our plans contain contingencies within contingencies."

He accepted her assurances but remained wary of his new mission. "What time do I leave?"

"As soon as you're ready. The transport's waiting. But before you go, remember this: Use great caution in the capital. Be vigilant. Trust no one. We're under siege now, both literally and figuratively. And as of this moment . . . *you* constitute our front line."

Eleven

Officially, the new Deep Space 9 was fully operational, but the tangled logistics of moving thousands of civilian and Starfleet residents into new residential spaces, while also supervising routine daily operations and the opening of new commercial venues on The Plaza, consumed the vast majority of Ro's time from one day to the next. The tragedy several days earlier had led to a cascade of delays, resulting in myriad schedule conflicts regarding the movements of materiel, personnel, and shipping traffic.

In spite of those hiccups in the station's opening, thousands of personnel, both Starfleet and civilian, had already taken up permanent residence aboard the starbase, and a swarm of entrepreneurs had proved eager to sign long-term leases for prime spaces on The Plaza, a retail, dining, and entertainment ring that made the old DS9's Promenade look like a mismanaged Orion tent bazaar. And no matter how many petty glitches seemed to clog the daily operations log, there was never any shortage of starship traffic at the new starbase, which served as a vital port of call for fuel, cargo, R & R, and ferry transfers for persons headed to Bajor.

Most days, Ro counted herself fortunate that she had lived to see so bright a future for her homeworld. Sixteen years earlier, Bajor had been suffering under the brutal Cardassian military occupation, a scourge that had lasted nearly half a century. By the time the Cardassians were finally forced

off the planet, they had pillaged its natural resources, stolen
its treasures, strip-mined its surface, and left behind an im-
poverished and traumatized native population.

Ro had been born into that world of violent oppression
and had watched it destroy her parents. Fleeing Bajor and her
bitter youth to build a new life in Starfleet, she hadn't dared to
dream that she might one day return home to find it flourish-
ing and vibrant, its people free and its beauty restored, all safe
beneath the banner of the United Federation of Planets.

Later, after being twice court-martialed by Starfleet—
once as an ensign, after she was blamed for a fatal error
during an away mission on Jaros II, and the second time in
absentia, after she'd defected to the civilian resistance known
as the Maquis—Ro had expected to be a persona non grata
on all Starfleet vessels, starbases, and facilities for the rest of
her life. But after coming home nine years earlier to accept
an invitation to join the Bajoran militia as an officer, she had
found herself assigned to the old Deep Space 9 as its chief
of security, under Colonel Kira Nerys. Then, after Bajor was
admitted to the Federation and most of the Bajoran Militia's
personnel on the station were absorbed into Starfleet, Ro
had found herself the recipient of an unexpected amnesty.
One of her former commanding officers, Captain Jean-Luc
Picard, had persuaded her to accept the restoration of her
Starfleet commission rather than resign. In the years that had
followed, one thing had led to another. And now she was the
captain of a starbase.

Ro picked up a padd from atop her desk in one hand and
sipped her first *raktajino* of the day, fresh from her office's
replicator nook. The data tablet felt heavy with bureaucratic
minutiae. *I should have resigned when I had the chance.*
She was pondering slipping out the back door of her office,

stealing down the corridor to the turbolift, and making a break for the recreation level . . . until the warbling of the comm intruded on her daydream.

"*Cenn to Captain Ro,*" said Colonel Cenn Desca, Starfleet's liaison to the Bajoran Militia and also the station's executive officer, who was seated a short distance outside Ro's office, presiding over the command operations center, which the crew called simply "the Hub."

"Go ahead."

"*He's here, sir.*"

She straightened her posture and shifted her padd and beverage away from the center of her desk. "Send him in."

The door to the Hub slid open, admitting the steady chatter of comm voices, computer feedback tones, and the low-frequency ambient hum of the wide-open, high-ceilinged circular space. Through the open doorway, Ro spied Cenn in the commander's chair, reviewing reports off a padd, and several junior officers holding a meeting around the situation table in the Well, the sunken area at the center of the level. Officers from the Engineering and Science divisions mingled or manned duty stations around the Hub's upper ring.

Then Bashir sauntered in and blocked her view. "You asked to see me, Captain?"

Ro waved him forward. "Come in."

He continued inside. The door closed, restoring their privacy, as he stopped in front of her desk and stood at ease. "Can we make this quick? I'm supposed to leave in ten minutes."

She leaned forward and folded her hands on her desk. "That's why you're here, Doctor. Why did you file a flight plan before I approved your sabbatical?"

"I just presumed the paperwork would be a formality."

It took all of Ro's willpower not to clench her fists. "A formality? Forgive me, Doctor, but don't you have an entire brand-new hospital to run?"

The question seemed to amuse him. "Have you seen the size of my duty roster? I have six attending physicians, scores of specialists, dozens of residents, more nurses than I can remember, and a small army of medical students and support staff. Sector General practically runs itself."

"If the hospital runs itself, why do I need you?"

"To keep Chief O'Brien from having a midlife crisis?"

She tried to pierce his smokescreen of impertinent quips to gain some small insight into what he really was up to. "Just explain to me what you'll be doing on Bajor."

"Exactly what I said in my leave request."

Ro picked up a padd on which she'd kept open Bashir's application, and she read from its contents. "'A private medical conference to discuss radical new strategies for the use of antigen resequencing in the treatment of Kalla-Nohra Syndrome and Pottrik Syndrome.'"

"Precisely."

"Why can't you host your conference here on the station?"

"Because, Captain, it's been my experience that even when I declare quite clearly that I'm off duty, and I delegate my responsibilities to my subordinates, unless I physically remove myself from the station, somebody will find a way to pull me away from my conference and mire me in one bit of hopeless tedium after another."

"I can't argue with your logic." He sounded sincere, and his candid, almost flippant manner suggested to Ro that he was being forthcoming with his answers . . . but something about his request still felt odd to her. She looked into his eyes, searching for any sign of dissembling or evasion, but all she found was his disarming smile. "When can I expect you to come back to the station and, your hectic schedule permitting, resume doing your job?"

"Not sure, really. Depends how long it takes us to work out the bugs in the protocol." He hooked a thumb toward the door. "If we're done here, Captain?"

"Fine. But keep me informed about your schedule. And you *owe* me, Doctor."

He hurried toward the Hub. "Thank you, Captain! I'll make sure you get regular updates!" He was out the door and on his way like an Academy cadet scrambling to make the most of a seventy-two-hour weekend liberty pass.

Ro sat and watched Bashir slip into a turbolift, and then her office door closed. Though the doctor was far out of earshot, the captain's pride demanded that decorum be observed.

"Dismissed," she grumbled before taking another sip of her morning *raktajino*.

A gauzy fog lingered between the old-growth trees of the Bestri Woods, which resonated with the bright sawing music of insects and birds. The late-morning air was rich with the scents of the nearby seacoast, and except for the conference center—which in a previous incarnation had been a retreat for members of the Vedek Assembly—there was little sign of habitation, even though the southwest region of Rakantha Province was one of Bajor's most densely populated areas.

Bashir emerged from the *Tiber*, which he had landed beside two small shuttlecraft on the large greensward beside the conference center. Known by the locals as the Bement Center, the main building was an X-shaped structure built around an open courtyard. Its architecture was evocative of shapes and patterns found in nature, and its connection to the forest was reinforced by its majestic, mortared-stone foundation, golden timber walls, and intricately thatched rooftops. Even though it boasted a wide array of modern amenities, including replicators, self-contained waste recycling, subspace communications uplinks, and a host of security measures to protect its guests, it looked as if it had been standing unchanged in the forest for centuries.

He crossed the well-manicured lawn of recently transplanted Xenexian dwarf grass, a variety engineered to remain short and simplify its care while reducing its ecological footprint, and bounded up the carved-granite steps to the Bement Center's main entrance. The three-meter-tall transparasteel doors parted silently at his approach, and a gentle cascade of cool air washed over him as he crossed the threshold.

Diffused natural light cast a pacific glow over the center's spare interior. Most of the walls were bare planks, and the floors alternated between polished hardwood and rough stone tiles, giving the place a rustic character that was at odds with the majesty of its lofty, peaked roof, which was lined with dramatic skylights. Amber-shaded sconces lined the walls.

Two wings, those to the northeast and northwest of the courtyard, were lined with luxurious, soundproofed residential suites. The southwest wing comprised several large meeting rooms and a small screening room, while the southeast wing was devoted to operations and management—environmental support, the kitchen and pantry, a laundry facility, and administrative offices. Under normal conditions, the resort would have been staffed by a dozen full-time employees. In the interest of secrecy, Bashir had arranged for the resort's personnel to prepare the suites and the meeting areas, stock the pantry, and lay out a welcome buffet for him and his guests—and then abscond from the premises until and unless called for.

Echoes of a group discussion carried down the corridor from the largest meeting room, and Bashir's enhanced hearing discerned the voices of all his expected guests. Two of his invitees had declined to join him, citing scheduling conflicts. He hoped that the four who had come would be equal to the task ahead of them, and willing to face the risks it would bring.

He stepped through the open doorway of the meeting room, and the conversation stopped as his guests turned to face him.

"If it isn't the man of the hour," said Doctor Katherine Pulaski. The venerated Starfleet surgeon had spent most of the past decade as a senior researcher at the Phlox Institute. Though her early work had focused on such specialties as cardiac surgery and epidemiology, her recent work had pioneered a number of innovative new protocols in the field of genomic therapy.

Bashir greeted Pulaski with a firm handshake. "Thank you for coming on such short notice, Doctor. It's a pleasure to finally make your acquaintance."

"The pleasure's all mine, I assure you."

Moving to the next guest, Bashir refrained from extending his hand and instead lifted it with the fingers separated into an awkward and slightly uncomfortable V. "Doctor Tovak," he said to the white-haired Vulcan civilian with prominent cheekbones. "Welcome to Bajor, sir."

Tovak returned the salute with dry formality. "Thank you, Doctor."

His third guest could not wait to shake Bashir's hand. The portly Benzite almost collided with him as he rushed forward, webbed manus outstretched, warm saline mist overflowing from his ventilator. "Greetings and salutations, Doctor Bashir! I hope you will not think me too familiar, but I have read all your papers, and I even took a special extended leave so I could see your acceptance speech when you received the Carrington Award. A shame you did not win."

Bashir downplayed the lingering sting of defeat. "It was an honor to be nominated."

"Still, after your groundbreaking work finding a treatment for the Teplan blight—"

"You're too kind, Doctor Lemdock, really. Thank you so much for coming." He extricated his hand from Lemdock's and gave the Benzite a conciliatory pat on the shoulder as he stepped around him to greet his fourth and final guest. "Hello, again, Elizabeth."

"Hello, Julian." Doctor Elizabeth Lense, who had been the valedictorian to Bashir's salutatorian during their graduation from Starfleet Medical School nearly seventeen years earlier, still had a youthful cast, though gray strands had found their way into the lithe human woman's curly brown hair and fatigue had etched dark half-moons beneath her eyes.

"You're looking well," Bashir said.

"I look like hell, Julian. That's what happens when you have a kid."

"And how are things at the Forensics Division?"

"A new thrill every minute."

Sensing it was time to change the subject, Bashir turned toward the buffet, to which his guests apparently had already helped themselves. "I trust each of you found something agreeable to your palate in the buffet. If you have any requests for dinner, we—"

"Julian," Pulaski cut in, her voice suddenly as sharp as broken glass. "We're all here, and none of us are getting any younger. I'm sure we've all noticed that we're all experts in genomic medicine. So . . . are you ready to cut the crap and tell us why you *really* brought us here?"

Relieved to be free of the pretense, Bashir grinned. "I thought you'd never ask."

Surrounded by the roar of white-water rapids, Prynn Tenmei fought to keep her kayak upright. Each passing second pulled her into faster water, making her passage of the jutting rock formations more perilous. A sudden drop over a mist-veiled waterfall left her in the vertiginous grip of free fall, her guts pushing up into her throat, until the bottom of the kayak splashed down with bone-jarring force that nearly capsized her. Leaning against the roll and paddling like mad, she fought her way back to equilibrium as the surging current carried her downstream.

These new holosuites are amazing! As much as Tenmei tried to remember that this was only a simulation, its vibrancy and detail made it easy for her to lose herself in the illusion. She loved white-water rafting almost as much as flying; it was one of the fastest ways she knew to sharpen her focus. Riding the rapids, all she saw was what was in front of her; all that mattered was the present moment. Navigating the fury of a river in flood, there was no time to dwell on the past. Alone on an angry churn of white spray, she had no history and no future, only now.

Icy spray stung her face, and then a razor-blade wind added to the verisimilitude of the moment. The program's sensory matrix evoked the Kingman Rapids of Izar down to its tiniest details: the cedar-like fragrance of the forest, the violet and orange flowers that lined the riverbanks, the ruddy rocks that stabbed up from the gray-and-white current and could cleave kayaks molded from some of the most sophisticated polymers known to science. A faint haze of late-spring pollen cast a halo around the red setting sun.

Her kayak sank without warning, and she gulped a breath a fraction of a second before she was plunged in the numbing chill of the river. Her insulated wetsuit protected her from the worst effects of the submersion, but the sting of a saltwater river chilled to barely one degree above its freezing point left her face tingling from the threat of frostbite.

Tenmei gasped, exhilarated. "Whoa! Yes!" Braving the worst that the river could throw at her was a baptism, an immersion into fear that left her reborn into courage. This was what she craved in sport, in action, in life—a sip of death's bitter promise to make life's rewards taste all the more sweet. Her gloved hands tightened on the double-bladed paddle, and she resumed the steady rhythm of her strokes, propelling herself forward, ready to best nature's next challenge.

Another twist in the channel narrowed the river to a creek, accelerating the flow of the water and intensifying the risk. Tenmei could barely see the tips of jutting rocks through the white foam in the high-walled canyon, and as unseen forces threatened to roll her upside down, she shifted her paddle position to a low brace to prevent her kayak from capsizing. Her craft caromed off the stone wall of the canyon, and she barely forced its nose left around the next turn in time to avoid having it sheared off.

Less than three meters around the turn was the edge of another fall. As the kayak shot out into open air, Tenmei leaned back to raise the craft's front end—a technique known in the sport as "boofing," an onomatopoeic term derived from the sound kayaks in such postures made when landing in the churning surf beneath the fall. Her boat did not disappoint her; it made a deep and satisfying splash as it landed, and she executed a fast forward sweep to navigate the next turn, which led to a wider and less steep channel through the canyons.

Despite the shallower grade, her kayak maintained a swift forward momentum thanks to the simulation's faithful depiction of Izar's slightly heavier-than-Earth gravity. She was grateful for the extra speed, because her experiences on the real Kingman Rapids had taught her what to expect in deep, slower water such as this. Drawing a deep breath to slow her staccato pulse and calm her pounding heart, she remembered why the blades on Izar paddles were made of a supple but extremely resilient titanium alloy and sharpened like katanas.

On her left, a serpentine shape lunged from the dark water. Tenmei swung her paddle even as she leaned backward farther than she would have believed possible. One of her paddle blades cut a fearsome gash through the aquatic predator's neck, and her return stroke severed the beast's head with the paddle's other blade.

Two more heads shot up from the water on her right. Her wild slash at the closer monster missed but was enough to make the creature duck back beneath the surface. The other snapped forward like a cobra, its dull yellow fangs bared and open wide enough to engulf Tenmei's head. There was no time to position her paddle for another swing, so she thrust the nearest blade upward, into the mouth of the river snake— a *kajiano*, as the locals called it.

Its jaws clamped around the end of her paddle, and as the

current towed Tenmei and her boat downstream, the *kajiano* did all it could to anchor them in the shallows. Fearing she might be pulled from the kayak, or that more of the creatures might swarm to feast on what they would perceive as trapped prey, she twisted the paddle's handle, turning the sharpened blades inside the beast's mouth like a drill bit.

Fangs snapped and blood sprayed, and the *kajiano*'s mouth stretched open as it brayed a deafening screech of pain that echoed through the canyons. Her paddle free, Tenmei let the river carry her away from the wounded creature, whose copious bleeding would in a matter of moments make it the focus of its companions' hunger.

She guided her boat around another bend, down another wild stretch of hair-thin rapids, and past a formation of rocks that signaled she had reached one of the program's major checkpoints. Her muscles ached in a satisfying way, a pain that had been earned and would soon fade, leaving her that much leaner, that much tougher, that much stronger. Paddling in smooth, slow strokes, she guided her craft ashore and pulled herself out, one leg at a time.

Because she had rented this holosuite for seventy-two consecutive hours, she had come prepared for a full weekend of solo recreation, far away from the day-to-day responsibilities of her post as the *Defiant*'s senior flight controller and second officer. She had nowhere to be and no agenda inside the simulation other than to follow the Kingman River all the way to the open water of the Kadri Sea. The only equipment she had brought into the holosuite was her wetsuit; the rest of the experience, including her kayak, her paddle, and the fish she was catching from the river, were all being either simulated or replicated—and, in the case of her fresh-fish dinner, both. The live fish she would catch would be simulations; at some point between when she caught and cleaned the holographic fish—whose guts felt and smelled more than real enough for her enjoyment—and when she finally took its cooked flesh from her frying pan, the holosuite would replace the illusory fish with a replicated fried-fish dinner.

Time in these new holosuites isn't cheap, but it's worth every credit.

She unpacked her gear from the beached kayak, set up her fishing line, and was about to head into the surrounding forest to gather dry wood for a fire when she realized that she wasn't alone in her holoprogram built for one. Lurking out in the trees was a humanoid form, a shadow that appeared to be watching her every move. Not sure what to expect, she dived toward her kayak, somersaulted over the pebble-covered beach, and rolled to her feet with her lethally sharp-bladed paddle in her hands. Facing the intruder, she shouted, "Who's there?"

Twigs snapped beneath the feet of the approaching interloper. As the shadow drew closer, Tenmei was able to see that it was a woman, one a bit taller than she and in excellent physical condition. Only as the figure emerged from the trees into the dying light of day did Tenmei recognize her. She lowered her paddle and sighed with relief. "Sarina? What the hell are you doing in my holosuite program?"

"Sorry. I need to speak with you—privately." Douglas motioned to some nearby rocks. "We should sit. This is gonna take a while to explain."

Had anyone ever asked Jyri Sarpantha what was the worst part of being a spy—not that anyone had ever asked, nor was anyone ever likely to do so—she would have told them that it was not the long stretches of time away from the comforts and conveniences of home, or the alienation that came with living as an interloper in a foreign culture, or the paranoia produced by the omnipresent fear of exposure; it was the indignity of being surgically altered.

Sarpantha had taken pride in her Silwaan heritage. At least, as much as she could, living behind the anonymizing mask and uniform imposed by the Breen Confederacy upon her people, and on countless others, all in the name of equality. In private, she had reveled in her dark caramel complexion, her amber-colored eyes, her luxurious mane of snow-white hair. Her family, friends, lovers, and even a few strangers who'd had the privilege of seeing her unmasked had told her on numerous occasions that she had been, unequivocally, beautiful.

Then, in the name of duty and country, she had let some butcher with a medical license transform her into the semblance of a Bajoran. Her beautiful ivory locks had been shorn close to her pate and dyed black, and the follicles had been genetically altered to keep her hair that color. Her eyes had been turned a mud brown. And her nose—her elegant, delicate, perfect nose—had been vandalized with grotesque ridges over its bridge, with subtle lines that radiated into her fine snowy eyebrows—which also had been dyed black. The surgeons had even changed her fingerprints, "to match patterns consistent with Bajoran ancestry," and they had altered her voice and retinal patterns. *Even my own mother wouldn't recognize me now,* she lamented.

This was the cost of victory. This was the price she had pledged to pay.

Night fell as she crept through the Bestri Woods, following the prompts on her scanning device. The leads from her handler indicated that a handful of prominent Federation and Starfleet medical experts were convening in an unpublicized conference on Bajor. Though the official invitations had been intercepted and suggested nothing of import, the guest list implied otherwise: five of the quadrant's most accomplished experts in genomic medicine. The Breen Intelligence Directorate had decided that it was of vital importance that Sarpantha learn the true nature of the topic that had brought those minds together.

Sarpantha was half a kilometer from the Bement Center when a silent alert vibrated the scanner in her hand, and she stopped. The device had detected several overlapping, high-energy fields surrounding the secluded conference center where the doctors had gathered. It was encircled by an intruder-detection grid, and just inside that was a scrambling field that prevented her from gathering intelligence about the interior or occupants of the enormous building.

The Breen spy hunkered down behind a fallen tree that rested at an angle, with one end elevated where it met its ragged stump. She shrugged off her backpack and took out the components for a sniper rifle. As she assembled the compact magnetic-coil projectile weapon, the evening song of the forest became deafening. Buzzing and droning insects, whooping birds, howling mammals, croaking amphibians—they all were in competition to be the most distracting noise in the world. *Tune them out,* she told herself. *Focus on the mission. Obey your training.*

In less than a minute she had assembled the rifle and activated its holographic scope. Because it operated strictly on enhanced optics, it would not be affected by the center's scrambling fields. It was Sarpantha's best chance of reconnoitering the doctors' activities from a distance without being detected. Lying prone in a gap beneath the fallen tree and its trunk, she trained her rifle's scope on the Bement Center and methodically surveyed its windows.

All of them were dark and curtained, though there were signs of light and activity on the far side of the X-shaped structure, in the wing opposite the one Sarpantha had approached. It would take time to circle around the center's wide defensive perimeter to scout its other sections, but since there was clearly nothing worth observing from this vantage point, she saw no better alternative. Moving with precision and care, she packed up her rifle, cinched shut her backpack, and stole away into the deepening shadows to find a more favorable angle.

Sooner or later she would get a clear line of sight to whatever was happening inside the rustic forest retreat. Only then would she know whether this mission was as vital as her superiors had insisted, or, as she suspected, a complete waste of time.

"In summary, I'm asking you to join me in risking prosecution, incarceration, and the premature end of our medical careers, for a chance to solve the most dire medical crisis of our time."

Bashir searched the faces of his guests to gauge their reactions, but no one was looking at him. Their attention was unanimously glued to the holographic display of the Meta-Genome that he had projected above the conference table at the beginning of his spiel. Tovak's face was a classic Vulcan cipher, while Lemdock was wide-eyed, like a child admiring a new toy. Pulaski stood in awe of the slowly turning double helix, but Lense's reaction surprised Bashir: her face was pallid with fear, as if the projection might come to life and kill them all.

He stepped in front of the projection, in the hope that he might recapture the group's focus. "Are there any questions? Comments?"

Lense continued to gape at the projection. "Is that what I think it is?"

He had avoided calling the Meta-Genome by name during his presentation, to preserve his guests' plausible deniability. "It might be best if we refer to it as simply, 'the Pattern.'"

His verbal evasion earned him a scathing look from Pulaski. "Oh, come now, Doctor. We all keep up with current events, and we all know what we're looking at. That's the Shedai Meta-Genome. The more pressing question is, how did *you* get your hands on it?"

"*How* I acquired it is irrelevant. Regardless of its source, the mere fact that I possess it means I can be convicted of espionage and treason. Now, that's a chance I'm willing to take to save the Andorian people. But I can't do this alone, not in the limited time I'll have before someone learns the real reason for this conference. So I'm asking all of you for your help."

Tovak steepled his fingers and pressed his hands against his chest as he considered the matter. When he spoke, his voice was as dry as Vulcan's deserts, and his tone conveyed neither condemnation nor approval. "What will you do if one or more of us refuses your request?"

It was a fair question, and Bashir had resolved to answer it honestly when it came up. "If any of you is unable or unwilling to be part of this, for whatever reason, I'll respect that. You'll be free to leave—and for your own protection, I'll advise you to report this meeting as soon as possible to Starfleet and the Federation Security Agency. I'd also advise the rest of you to do the same, and to make any legal arrangements necessary to immunize yourselves from prosecution."

Lense's suspicion turned to concern. "You *want* us to throw you to the wolves?"

"I'd prefer it didn't come to that, but if this benign conspiracy of ours is doomed to die aborning, it seems unfair that any of you should suffer for a crime that so far is mine alone."

Lemdock tore himself away from the Meta-Genome projection and looked at Bashir. "Doctor, in your professional opinion, how likely is it that we could find a solution to a syndrome as complex as the Andorian fertility crisis before this conference disbands?"

"I don't know that I'd use the term *likely*. But I think it's highly possible."

Pulaski's doubt grew more pronounced. "Based on what evidence?"

Bashir entered commands on a padd to replace the Meta-Genome model with a new three-dimensional projection of modified strands of Andorian DNA. "This is the latest work from Professor zh'Thiin and her team on Andor. For the past three years, they've been splicing isolated fragments of the Meta-Genome data into the mutated segments of their DNA that are believed to be interfering with successful fertilizations and embryo transfers." He pointed out a number of chromosomes that had been rebuilt with new, synthetic proteins. "As you can see, they've made tremendous progress . . . but not enough. They believe that someone involved in the relay of the Meta-Genome data—either in their own government, or in the Tholian Assembly—is withholding critical strings of data, most likely for political purposes. Since the only other source of a near-complete copy of the Meta-Genome is the

Starfleet Archives, Professor zh'Thiin and her team sent us a secret request for help."

The Vulcan physician leaned close to the projection and eyed its intricate details. "Fascinating. They have completely redesigned the protein structure of a *thaan*'s gamete. And if I am not mistaken, several key sequences in this *shen*'s alleles have been altered, as have the telomeres in the *chan*'s fertilizing cells." He straightened and faced the group. "One can see why opinion regarding this treatment is divided among the Andorians. Professor zh'Thiin and her peers are proposing significant revisions to the Andorian genome." He lifted one eyebrow. "Andorians who undergo changes so radical might become, in effect, a new species, as different from their forebears as primitive hominids are from their modern descendants."

"True," Pulaski replied, "but at least they won't be extinct."

"Assuming they survive the treatment," Lense said. "Changes on this large a scale give rise to all kinds of cellular replication errors. This 'cure' could be the thing that wipes them out."

"Which is why it's vital that they have as much information at their disposal as possible," Bashir said. "But since we can't just send them the Meta-Genome data, it's up to us to continue their work here—to build on the progress they've already made, and finish what they've started."

Tovak maintained an air of resistance. "You said the primary obstacle to zh'Thiin and her team acquiring this information appears to be political. That would make it an internal issue for the Andorians. Would it not be more prudent to wait and let the matter correct itself?"

"I'm not sure the Andorians can afford to wait," Bashir

said. "And my former crewmate Thirishar ch'Thane, who now works as Professor zh'Thiin's research assistant, believes the delays are part of a plan to enhance the power of the *Treishya*, a faction that's not just hostile to the Federation, but at risk of aligning Andor with the Typhon Pact."

Lense acted as if the whole situation finally made sense. "So this isn't just about the medical needs of the Andorians. It's political. We want to find the cure and be the good guys for Andor so that they don't sign on the dotted line with the Typhon Pact."

Though it offended Bashir to have his altruism tainted by realpolitik, he knew there was no point in ducking the truth. "That's right. It was one of the reasons Shar contacted me. There are a lot of Andorians who are looking for a reason to change their minds about secession, and he thinks this is the issue that can make it happen. But whether we get credit or not, whether this brings Andor back into the Federation or not, this is still the right thing to do." He turned off the holographic projection and stood tall. "It's time to decide. Do we help the Andorians? Or do the four of you walk out of here and call Starfleet to take me into custody?"

Lemdock lifted his chin and mimicked Bashir's stance. "If they arrest you, Doctor, they can arrest me, as well."

Pulaski smiled. "I've always enjoyed a good fight. Count me in, too."

Tovak folded his hands together. "Your proposal is sound, Doctor. If criminal culpability and public shame are the price I pay to save a sapient species from imminent extinction, that is a more than equitable outcome. The good of the many must outweigh the good of the few."

That left only one voice to be heard, one opinion that would decide all their fates. Bashir shot a hopeful look at his former Starfleet Medical School classmate. "Doctor Lense?"

She heaved an exasperated sigh and rolled her eyes. "I think you're all crazy. But then, so am I." With a hint of mischief in her eye, she shook Bashir's hand. "Let's get to work."

Twelve

Nothing made the capital feel so dangerous to Shar as knowing he had no friends left in it. Walking alone down darkened lanes, the soft-spoken *chan* tugged on the cowl of his cloak to hide his face from the city's network of surveillance cameras, many of which fed their signals to facial-recognition programs running on mainframes at the Ministry of Security.

It's insane that I have to hide like a criminal. I've done nothing wrong. I've broken no laws. The more he reminded himself of his innocence, the angrier he became. Now that extremists were in control of his homeworld, he had come to feel like an outcast. Andor was turning into a police state; there was no way to be sure who he could trust anymore. Casual acquaintances might betray him to the *Treishya* simply to curry favor and deflect suspicion from themselves. No one was safe living under the shadow of constant suspicion and scrutiny.

Were those footsteps behind him? He looked back but saw no one there. *That doesn't mean anything. Two weeks ago I didn't see the sentinels until they were almost on top of me.* He ducked through an open gate into a service passage that dipped below street level as it passed between two decrepit residential buildings. A battalion of rodents feeding on mounds of rotting food scattered in a chittering frenzy as he hurried through the narrow space. Some of the braver ones nipped at his feet and ankles until he kicked them away, never breaking stride.

He unlocked the gate at the far end of the passage and scrambled up the steps onto a street busy with pedestrians and street vendors hawking wares from wobble-wheeled carts.

A fat old *shen* tried to tempt Shar with boiled mystery meat on a stick. "Fresh *pilska*! Hot and juicy! Only two credits!" He waved it off, but he knew that in a few hours he might be hungry and desperate enough to eat something very much like it.

From inside a cart packed with junk, a scar-faced *thaan* beckoned. "Tools for every purpose! A gadget for every task!" It was easy for Shar to hear the truth behind the dealer's euphemisms: the *thaan* was a black-market weapons dealer, one smart enough—or maybe just brazen enough—to operate in public. Shar made a point of noting where the *thaan*'s cart was located and what its markings were. *I might need to pay him a visit sometime.*

Leading with his shoulder, Shar bladed through the crowd, certain that if he was being tailed, his shadow would be either exposed or thwarted by the bustling throng. He looked back and still saw no one who looked out of place, nor anyone who appeared intent on following him. *Probably just being paranoid. Have to take a breath.*

He turned left at the next corner and ignored the come-hither leer of an emaciated young *zhen* lurking in an open doorway. At a glance Shar could see she might once have been pretty, perhaps even a beauty, but the planet's constant shortages of food and medicine had taken their toll on the fragile young thing, who now was forced to survive by desperate measures. All he could offer her was a fleeting look of pity as he pushed on into the night.

How long before I get so lonely that I take comfort with someone like her?

Each turn took Shar down a road more deserted than the last, until he found himself treading lightly through a back alley, then down a steep flight of spiral stairs hewn from blue-and-white marbled stone, and around a corner to a basement door marked with alien symbols. He knocked twice with his knuckles—three taps, a brief pause, and then a single tap.

Seconds later, a metal panel on the door slid open, and a glowing mechanical eye on a stalk jutted out and bathed him in chartreuse light. A voice, guttural and synthetic, snapped from an unseen speaker, *"A deal is a deal."*

"Until a better one comes along."

The mechanical eye retracted, the panel shut, and the door's bolts unlocked with a *clunk*. The portal slid open, and Shar slipped through it into the unlicensed speakeasy club that served as both a sideline and a front for the Science Institute's secret equipment suppliers.

At the end of a short, dim corridor, a rust-maned, snaggle-fanged Chalnoth bouncer scanned Shar for weapons before waving him through the open doorway to the club beyond. The steady, bass-heavy thump of electronic music was so loud that Shar wondered if it was being used to drive away vermin—a hypothesis he ruled out when he got a good look at the club's diverse alien clientele. Nausicaans, Balduks, Talarians—it was as if someone had rounded up prime specimens of the quadrant's most undesirable off-world neighbors and locked them all in this seedy, strobe-lit, smoke-filled abscess festering beneath the planet's capital. As the *chan* crossed the room to meet his contact, a hulking Orion man collided with his shoulder as if trying to provoke a fight. In no mood for a bar brawl, Shar ignored him and made his way to a curtained, circular booth in the club's farthest corner.

His host, Torv, was already there, puffing on something

sickly sweet and narcotic from an Orion-style hookah. The water pipe burbled and vented pale violet vapors as the fat Ferengi diplomat inhaled through the pipe's long curled hose. Then he grinned and exhaled through his maw of fearsome, pointed yellow teeth. "Nice to see you again, Shar."

"Can we make this quick?"

"What's your hurry? Have a drink." Torv waved over a scantily clad Trill waitress. "Bring my friend here a Solarian Sunrise." The woman nodded and went back to the bar.

"Did you get the list I sent?"

The Ferengi took another long toke on the hookah. He seemed to enjoy nothing more than wasting other people's time, a passive-aggressive trait that Shar wished he could correct with some swift negative reinforcement of the corporal variety.

"I got your list. We're working on it. But the price has gone up."

"Why?" As soon as he'd asked, Shar was able to fill in the answer. "The embargo."

Torv blew a cloud of smoke that enveloped them both. "Precisely. Much of what you want is made in the Federation. And moving it past their blockade gets harder every day."

Shar waved away the smoke, which stung his eyes and left him light-headed. "How much more to get what we need?"

"A ten-percent surcharge."

"Five."

"I didn't call you here to negotiate. The price is the price."

"There's always room to haggle, Torv. Seven percent."

The fat ambassador shrugged. "I'm not the one who needs the shipment. Ten."

Someday I'll make him pay for this in blood. "Fine. Ten. How soon?"

"As soon as we can get it here."

"You promised to deliver it by tomorrow."

"The embargo—"

"Every day you're late, we knock ten thousand off your fee. As per the contract."

"Nice to see you people still know how to read the fine print. We'll let you know when it arrives. We can settle up then."

"Good." Satisfied they were finished, Shar started to get up.

"Before you go, I have a message for you. My contact in External Audits says to tell you, 'Work has begun.' I trust you know what that means?"

It was the best news Shar had heard in weeks, and it took all his willpower not to let slip just how great a relief the message was. "I understand. Thank you."

He walked away, careful not to betray his heightened emotional state. *If Bashir's working on it, we might have a chance. Maybe we can find the answer while there's still time.*

Venturing alone into the streets of Andor's capital, shrouded in night's protective cloak, Shar permitted himself a luxury so long denied that he'd nearly forgotten what it felt like.

He smiled.

"From our vantage point, *Cha* Presider, it appears your *Treishya*-run government is doing more to obstruct your scientists' search for a cure than to promote it."

"I assure you, we have made every effort to advance the search for a solution to the fertility crisis." Ch'Foruta found Tholians a most disconcerting species. Even wrapped in the billowing, iridescent silk of their environment suits, their multi-limbed crystalline bodies, faceted heads, and eyes burning with volcanic fires were the stuff of his nightmares. Political decorum demanded that he mask his unease at all costs, but being confronted here in his own office, face-to-face, by Dezskene, the new official envoy from the Tholian Assembly, had left him on edge. The fact that Dezskene's presence also meant there was a Tholian battleship in orbit only exacerbated the presider's already considerable anxiety.

The deep, dark scratching sound of Dezskene's vocoder-translated voice reminded ch'Foruta of a diamond blade cutting through obsidian. "Reliable sources inform us that your scientists have sought aid from off-world specialists. Why would they resort to such measures if you had delivered to them all that we have given you, as we have pledged?"

"I suspect your sources have been the victims of a miscommunication." Ch'Foruta recalled the talking points on which zh'Rilah had briefed him before this meeting. "Professor zh'Thiin and her peers are only seeking independent confirmation of their findings. It's a standard practice in scientific research. And, as I've already said, we've made available to her team all the Meta-Genome data you've so generously provided."

The fire in Dezskene's eyes burned a bit brighter. "But you do nothing to shield their work from the extremists who constitute the bulk of your own political faction."

Obeying his political instincts, ch'Foruta pivoted toward denial. "I don't know what—"

"A mob of your *Treishya* partisans set fire to your Science Institute's headquarters."

The presider held up both hands. "Those were fringe elements and not representative of the *Treishya* party or its platform, as we can—"

"Do not lie to me, *Cha* Presider. We monitor your

broadcast and textual media. Those zealots are no more outliers from your party's orthodoxy than you or your fellow parliamentarians."

It was time to deflect and obfuscate. "Obviously, these are anxious times for my people. The sorts of dramatic changes we face were always bound to lead to social unrest."

"Especially when your apologists in the media go to such lengths to incite it."

The envoy's criticism left ch'Foruta dumbstruck. *Am I really being lectured on social justice by a Tholian?* He took a deep breath and focused his thoughts on remaining polite. "Did you come to express a specific concern regarding our research?"

Dezskene spread his forelimbs in an expansive gesture. "The entirety of your program is of great concern to us. Andorian science is most advanced. One would expect your medical researchers to have found what they needed after this much time. The fact that your efforts seem to have been stalled for so long on the verge of success leads us to . . . unflattering conclusions."

"Such as?"

"That your researchers are taking advantage of our generosity by prolonging their investigations in order to weaponize the information contained in the Meta-Genome."

All of ch'Foruta's advisers had warned him that sequestering the Meta-Genome data to buy time for the *Treishya* to entrench themselves politically might backfire. None of them, however, had warned him of this scenario. "I assure you, we are doing nothing of the sort. We understand the charitable nature of your people's gift, and we will not abuse it."

"We want to believe you. And it is important to us that our efforts not be in vain. We are prepared to send to your planet's surface a team of our best scientists, experts who possess unparalleled experience with the Shedai Meta-Genome. They would bring with them all of our extant files regarding the genome, and they would help your Professor zh'Thiin and her colleagues accelerate their research."

The Tholians' act of charity was a potential disaster in the making, but ch'Foruta did his best to dismiss the offer as if it were a silly luxury no one would take seriously. "That won't be necessary. Our people have the matter under control, and a cure is at hand."

"We are most relieved to hear that." The envoy leaned forward a few centimeters, just enough to make ch'Foruta tense with fear. "We would be most grateful if, when your scientists announce their cure, we could have representatives present to remind your people of the role played by the Assembly and its partners in the Typhon Pact."

"Of course. In light of the great kindness you've shown us, it would be only fitting." *Except for the fact that it makes me look like a puppet with a Tholian's orthorhombic appendage rammed up my backside, with its pincers working my mouth.*

Dezskene raised himself up from the platform that had been set up in advance of his visit, a cumbersome block of obsidian that the presider's staff had needed an antigrav pallet to move. The envoy's environmental garment shimmered as he moved. "We will look forward to news of your people's renaissance—and to discussing our future of mutual interests."

The presider stood and bade Dezskene farewell with a half-bow. "As do I." He watched his imperial guards escort the Tholian out of his office. As the door hushed closed behind them, ch'Foruta keyed the desk comm channel reserved for his chief adviser. "Ferra?"

As always, zh'Rilah was at the ready. *"Yes, sir?"*

"Tell Valas we've got to find zh'Thiin and light a fire under her—and then we have to make sure we have the Parliament under control once and for all."

Few events better exemplified what Commander Dalit Sarai considered wrong with Starfleet Command than the tedium of its morning senior staff briefing.

Ever since she had been transferred from hands-on work as a field agent for Starfleet Intelligence to administrative duties as a liaison officer inside the San Francisco headquarters complex on Earth, she had felt marginalized and ignored. All her years of experience gathering vital information for the Federation and preventing its enemies from wreaking havoc on its citizens and infrastructure had been reduced to collating reports, conducting threat-assessment analyses that she suspected no one ever read, and being condescended to by superior officers.

This place is a waste of my talents, the young Efrosian woman fumed. *I could be out there making a difference instead of in here, making presentations.* How long was her past going to haunt her? For how long would she be made to pay for the same mistake? Was one friendly-fire civilian casualty really worth derailing an entire career?

She knew there were those who would say she got off lightly, that she escaped any real consequences for her actions. That she was negligent. That she should have held her fire. The critics, pundits, and politicos all loved to second-guess events that had erupted in seconds. It was easy to posit alternatives when one had days to think of them.

She mourned that child. The little Bolian boy's face would follow her forever. In her dreams he would stalk her like a revenant, an accusing shade whose persecution of her failure would never relent. Her empathic senses had felt his pain, his anguish, his final moments of fear and loneliness. Sarai was certain she knew that boy better in his final moments than his parents ever had, and his death had cut her deeper than she had ever admitted, to anyone. His dying light would live in her heart, a constant reminder of the price of her own shortcomings.

Her mandatory presence at the Starfleet Command daily senior staff meeting was the salt rubbed into that lingering psychic injury.

"Next item," intoned Fleet Admiral Leonard James Akaar. His rich voice suited him; he was a giant of a man, barrel-chested, square-jawed, and muscular. Despite being old enough that his face had become a map of his life's long road of pain, and his hair had long since gone white of its own accord, he still looked robust enough to manually dismember large men half his age.

Admiral Marta Batanides, the flag officer in charge of Starfleet Intelligence, slid a padd down the table to the fleet admiral. "Reports of Breen signal traffic in the Murami Sector."

Akaar lifted the padd and snuck a look at its screen. "Cloaked-ship activity?"

Batanides's angular features hardened. "Not sure. We're setting up a tachyon network, just in case. But this could be long-range SLF comms to assets on the ground."

The fleet admiral's piercing blue eyes looked up from beneath thick white eyebrows. "On the ground where? In our space or the Tzenkethi's?"

"We won't know until we triangulate it."

The burly chief flag officer slid the padd back down the table to Batanides. "Good luck with that. I predict the signals will be gone by the time your network is active." He looked down the table and scanned the faces gazing back at him. "Next?"

Rear Admiral Soth Romar, an Argelian who commanded the Ninth Fleet, which was based out of Gamma Hydra, leaned forward to catch the fleet admiral's eye. "Romulan fleet activity suggests they've resumed coreward exploration in the Beta Quadrant. This could put them in direct contact with our *Luna*-class explorers. I'd like to recommend a Level Three advisory be sent to all starship commanders operating in the sectors beyond the Vela Cluster."

"Make it happen." Akaar slapped his palms on the conference room table, his customary prelude to adjourning the meeting. "If there's nothing else?"

Defying her better judgment, Sarai lifted her hand.

Starfleet's senior officer squinted at her. "Commander . . . ?"

"Sarai, sir. I'm the SI adjutant." As soon as she had started speaking, she felt Batanides glaring at her, willing her silently to shut up, but she pressed onward. "I have reason to think there's been a breach of security regarding the Meta-Genome data."

Akaar shifted toward Batanides. "Admiral? Why wasn't this in your report?"

SI's commanding officer shot a steely look at Sarai, then softened her countenance before answering her superior. "I reviewed Commander Sarai's report. It's inconclusive, at best."

The fleet admiral was wary but curious. "Commander? What do you have?"

Sarai relayed the data on her padd to the conference room's main wall display. "Doctor Julian Bashir, the chief medical officer of Deep Space Nine, has convened a medical conference on extremely short notice. Its stated subject is 'strategies for the use of antigen resequencing in the treatment of Kalla-Nohra Syndrome and Pottrik Syndrome,' but in attendance are four of the Federation's leading experts in genomic medicine." She added to the display a number of internal log files from the new starbase. "Just days before this conference, Bashir was called back from personal leave on Bajor by an urgent message from the Ferengi Ambassador to Bajor—his old friend, Quark. And, as you can see, we have reason to believe the Ferengi are acting as a diplomatic back channel on Andor, sneaking messages in and out."

Akaar scrunched his brow at the screen full of circumstantial evidence. "I fail to see how any of this suggests to you a breach of security with regard to the Meta-Genome."

Could they be this obtuse? Or was their blindness a willing charade? "Sir, if Bashir has been in contact with one or more persons on Andor via the Ferengi, my review of his dossier suggests his contact is very likely Thirishar ch'Thane, who currently is working as a senior research fellow for Professor Marthrossi zh'Thiin. She and her team have access to a large volume of Shedai Meta-Genome data provided by the Tholians. And since it's not likely that Doctor Bashir would gather his four most eminent peers in genomic medicine to discuss Kalla-Nohra Syndrome, I think it's reasonable to conclude that he and his colleagues are conducting unauthorized research into the potential of the Meta-Genome."

The fleet admiral delegated his reply to Admiral Alynna Nechayev with a single glance. The aquiline-featured woman, who had earned the respect and fear of most everyone in Starfleet, turned her withering glower toward Sarai. "Commander, that was a lot of words to express the thought, 'I have no concrete evidence to support my theory.' Perhaps you should withdraw your report and concentrate on the assignments given to you, rather than inventing your own."

Headstrong but not career-suicidal, Sarai backed down. "Understood, Admiral."

Akaar took a last gander around the room. "Anything else?" No one spoke. "I'll see department heads at nineteen hundred. We're adjourned." He pushed back from the table and made a fast exit, with Batanides and Nechayev close behind him.

Sarai turned off her padd and vowed this was the last time she would be ignored and humiliated. *If Admiral Akaar won't listen to me, I'll find someone who will.*

Thirteen

It had been years since Bashir had stayed awake so long without pharmaceutical assistance that he'd started to suffer double vision. The most recent instance that he recalled had occurred in the Dominion War, during the siege of AR-558, when, in the face of an imminent Jem'Hadar attack, the luxury of sleep had come to seem tantamount to suicide. Before that, the last time he could remember had been during his final year of training at Starfleet Medical School, balancing the demands of full-time classes with his residency and the rigors of basic training for officers.

Which explains why I just knocked espresso all over the countertop. He set down his mug on the nearby table and chastised himself in softly spoken curses as he found a spare cloth with which to wipe up his spill. *I'd forgotten how easy it is to lose track of time, working on something as immersive as this.* He sopped up the last traces of the java puddle, wrung out the cloth in the commissary's sink, and then draped the rag over the faucet to dry.

He poured enough cream into his drink to turn it a pale shade of beige, then added a shot of simple syrup to make it go down just that much easier. His first long sip restored only the slightest fraction of his clarity; he hoped the rest of the beverage would prove more restorative. Mug in hand, he plodded out of the commissary and down the wing's main corridor to meet with his colleagues, each of

whom had spent most of the last twenty-four hours sequestered in separate rooms, tasked with investigating specific
aspects of the Meta-Genome and how its encoded information could be applied to reversing the decline in Andorian
fertility.

The others were waiting for him in the main conference
room. He saluted them with his mug. "Hello, again. I've made
a few discoveries since last we spoke; I hope all of you have
progress to report, as well. Would one of you like to start? Or
shall I?"

Pulaski and Lense both tried to deflect Bashir's invitation with glances at each other, only to both wind up gazing
blankly into space, wide-eyed with fatigue. A shrug from
Lemdock led Tovak to cross his arms and suggest to Bashir,
"Perhaps you should start us off, Doctor."

"Very well." Bashir used the interface beside the wall-
mounted display screen to access the work he'd saved to
the computer core aboard the *Tiber*, which was serving as
the group's shared computer. A slideshow of images—some
static, some moving—played across the screen. "As you can
see from these animated simulations, I've isolated the segments of the Andorian ova that Professor zh'Thiin and her
team have identified as having suffered harmful mutations
over the past five hundred generations. The Andorians' research identified a few sequences in the Meta-Genome that
appeared promising in reversing the damage to the ova, but
all of the combinations they've tried so far have rendered the
ova either sterile or incompatible with other Andorian cells."
He halted the presentation playback on a split screen that
showed two different flow charts. "This suggests there are two
ways to address this issue. The first is to seek out a sequence
that enables us to restore the ova to a stable form while

preserving its compatibility with existing Andorian genotypes. The second is to focus on developing the most stable
and robust form of ova possible with sequences spliced from
the Meta-Genome, and to then re-engineer the fertilizing
cells of the *thaan* and *chan* genotypes, as well as the placental
chemistry of the Andorian *zhen*, to render them compatible
with this new genetic morphology." He turned to face the
others. "Thoughts? Anyone?"

Pulaski eyed the screen with guarded optimism. "I have
to admit, it sounds extremely promising. I suspect the Andorians would prefer your first approach to the material—
fitting the Meta-Genome to them, rather than reshaping
them to fit it."

"I think you're right about that, though it might not be
the most successful approach."

Lense adopted a more dubious stance. "Politics aside, I
think that the more we tamper with the Andorian genome,
the greater the risk that we'll end up destroying it in order
to save it. If the goal is to come up with a solution the Andorian people will actually accept, I'd suggest approaching it
with an eye toward minimizing the alterations to their core
biology."

Bashir affirmed her suggestion with a nod. "Yes, that's
reasonable. However, that's the method zh'Thiin and her
team have been pursuing for years, with no success. I don't
want to rule out any avenue of discovery on the basis of
politics, ideology, or emotion. We need to focus on what will
work, regardless of how popular, or infamous, it might ulti-
mately prove to be."

"A noble sentiment," Tovak replied. "If logic were the
only criterion on which our work would be judged, I would
agree without reservation. However, your colleagues raise

valid points. If we propose a solution that would alter the Andorian people so profoundly at the genetic level that they might no longer be able to claim true kinship with their immediate ancestors, then it would be difficult to imagine them embracing such a cure, even in the face of extinction."

"I admit it's a radical idea, but right now we can't afford to rule anything out. But your points are all well-taken. We'll postpone exploring that option until we've exhausted all the less-invasive approaches to retroviral resequencing." Shifting the group's focus by turning himself squarely toward Pulaski, he changed the topic. "What findings can you report, Doctor?"

The elderly human woman stood. "I'm glad you asked. Though I've not yet isolated any sequences specific to the Andorian reproductive problem, I saw that the Meta-Genome contains several sequences that could point to new anti-aging therapies. One sequence in particular seems designed to rebuild other genes' telomeres, thereby prolonging vitality and postponing cellular senescence. I also have reason to believe there is a variant of this sequence that serves to restore the telomeres on the first sequence, which means the two would be mutually restorative. If I can isolate that second sequence, it might be possible to develop a vaccine against aging—in effect, a recipe for permanent biological youth without decay. Immortality."

Bashir's jaw slackened. He forced himself back into a semblance of composure. "That's a most impressive discovery, Doctor. But how does it help us deal with the Andorian crisis?"

"Well, it doesn't—not directly. But as I'm sure you know, research sometimes takes us in unexpected directions, and those can—"

"Doctor," Bashir cut in. "I'm not belittling your discovery. But we've gathered for a specific purpose. As promising as this new lead might be, I must ask you to postpone its exploration for another time. Do I make myself clear?" He noted Pulaski's embarrassed nod and took it as his cue to continue. "Very well. I would be most grateful if you could begin analyzing the J chromosomes in the fertilizing cells of the *thaan* genotype and see if any sequences in the Meta-Genome can restabilize them without compromising their compatibility with the repaired *shen* ova." He turned to Doctor Tovak, who met his inquiry with cool reserve. "Doctor? Did your investigation yield any actionable data?"

The Vulcan activated his own presentation on the conference room's viewscreen. "Indeed. As you will no doubt see here, the Meta-Genome sequence labeled Aleph-Tau-Beta-Nine-Nine-Three-Eight-Sigma is an extremely versatile and opportunistic bit of genetic material. It bonds well with a number of receptors, and in most cases it enhances and strengthens those cells with which it fuses. It is most compatible with synaptic tissue, but it also has proved capable of mimicking and replacing memory engrams, a variety of ganglionic fibers, and several types of working tissues in the deep brain. Of note is its restorative quality with regard to damaged—"

Bashir lifted his hand to interrupt. "How does brain tissue regeneration relate to our work on the Andorian—"

"Not at all," Tovak said, anticipating the end of Bashir's question. "However, as my primary area of medical specialty is in the treatment of cognitive, mnemonic, and sensory issues related to neurobiology and neurochemistry, the sections of the Meta-Genome that I recognized first were those relevant to my expertise." He switched to another, mostly blank slide in his presentation. "I made an effort to apply my findings to the fertilization cells contributed by the *chan* genotype, but as of yet I have made no progress in that area."

Bashir grew annoyed, but not enough to engage a Vulcan in debate. He buried his bad mood and turned to face Doctor Lense. "Please tell me you have something relevant to report."

"Sort of."

"Sort of?"

"There's an amazing chimeric sequence in the Meta-Genome that I think could be the key to a truly universal pan-immunity vaccine. And by universal, I mean a single vaccine that could render any individual of any species, carbon-based or otherwise, immune to any external organic pathogen, without risk of a self-destructive autoimmune response. If I could have a few more weeks to analyze the full Meta-Genome, I could—"

"—completely derail this entire project and condemn the Andorian species to extinction." An angry sound, a cross between a sigh and a grumble, rolled deep inside Bashir's throat. "Did any of you pay even the least bit of attention to my request?"

Doctor Lemdock raised one webbed manus. "I did, Doctor."

Bashir was not ready to get his hopes up. Not without evidence. "Prove it."

Exhaling a vaporous plume, the Benzite reached over to the table and activated his own report on the room's viewscreen. "I focused my studies on the placental chemistry of the Andorian *zhen*. Because the *zhen* is the only

Andorian gender that contributes no genetic material to the reproductive process, I speculated that Andorian biology evolved to make the genome of the *zhen* as universal as possible. Existing data supports this hypothesis." He switched to a screen showing side-by-side comparisons of Andorian cells. "Of the four genders, the *zhen* is the least likely to suffer from autoimmune disorders or allergies. They also are the most likely to successfully receive transplanted tissues and organs, and transfused blood. The reason for this is their blood chemistry is the same species-wide, regardless of parentage. It is antigen-free, and their immune systems are programmed to accept all Andorian genetic material as friendly." The Benzite updated the image on the screen to show damaged cells. "I concur with Professor zh'Thiin's hypothesis that one of the root causes of her people's fertility crisis is overactive immune-system responses that have inflicted genetic damage *in utero*. Based on these findings, I would suggest one tactic we might wish to explore would be to re-engineer the immune systems of the other three Andorian genotypes to match that of the *zhen*."

Lense shook her head. "No, that'd be a disaster. The *zhen* have a better record for transplants and transfusions, but their infection rates are also much higher. Take away the other genders' strong immune systems, and you could be looking at a species-wide die-off caused by viruses and bacteria instead of declining fertility."

All at once, Bashir saw his peers' research detours in a new light. "Hang on—could you tailor your hypothetical pan-immunity vaccine to be part of an antigen-resequencing therapy?"

The idea took root behind Lense's wide-open eyes.

"Yes. . . . Yes! We could put all four Andorian genders on equal footing while removing one of the root causes of their long-term genetic damage, which would prevent the syndrome from recurring in the future."

"Something else to consider," Pulaski interjected. "The telomere-repairing genes I've isolated could be repurposed to make the Andorian genome self-repairing."

"Excellent. Now we're getting somewhere. Why don't we all take six hours to get some rest, and then we'll reconvene to discuss our next steps."

Tovak nodded his approval. "A sensible idea."

Lemdock waved one webbed hand at Bashir. "I have a question, Doctor. I do hope you'll forgive me, as I probably should have asked before we began our research, but . . . whose name will appear first on the paper when we publish our findings?"

As if they were all marionettes controlled by the same master, Bashir, Lense, Pulaski, and Tovak each raised one eyebrow as they regarded Lemdock with skeptical derision.

"You know we can't publish our results," Bashir said. "Our best-case scenario is that we find the cure, deliver it to the Andorians before anyone knows we've been working on it, let them claim they developed it on their own, and hope no one finds out it came from us."

The Benzite shrank with disappointment. "So no one will ever know it was us."

"Not unless we get caught," Lense grumped.

Her moment of snark gave Lemdock back his optimism. "Then there is hope!" He hurried toward the door and paused at its threshold to look back at the others. "See you all in six hours!" Then he was out the door, on his way back to his guest room in the northwest wing.

Lense stood beside Bashir and stared daggers at the departing Benzite. Her voice was low and bitter. "He's gonna get us all thrown in the stockade, isn't he?"

"If we're lucky."

That drew a worried glance from Pulaski. "And if we're not?"

Bashir pondered the true worst-case scenario—the nightmare that would descend upon them if Section 31 decided their work had become a danger to the Federation. He sighed.

"Trust me. You don't even want to know."

Day and night had come and gone, marching in their endless cycle while Jyri Sarpantha cowered under camouflage in the Bestri Woods. Several hours had passed since she had succeeded in making a long-range visual observation of a meeting between Bashir and his fellow physicians. She had made sure to document all she could about their work; there had been images of molecules, cells, and complicated chemical formulas. None of it had meant much to Sarpantha, but she knew her superiors would want as much raw intelligence as possible for analysis.

Nothing to do now but lurk in the dark, she brooded.

Sleep had proved elusive. It was impossible to get comfortable on the rocky ground, but even if she found the softest spot on the forest floor, it would make little difference. Her training had taught her to remain alert while on deployment; losing focus could be fatal during a forward recon assignment. Not only did she need to remain aware of all activity by her targets, she had to be watchful for any sign that she had been detected by counterintelligence agents.

There was also the very real danger posed by natural

predators. Bajor was home to massive feline and canine species, either one of which was more than capable of rending an unwary humanoid into tartare within seconds. In a forest shrouded in moonless darkness, every snapping twig or rustled leaf jolted Sarpantha back to full alertness.

All the doctors still appeared to be in their guest suites, sleeping after a marathon session of work. *Maybe I should eat something, before the sun comes up and they all start moving again.* She didn't need to open her pack to know what she had left. There were a few compact meals, dried and vacuum-packed; some dehydrated fruit; a few single-serving tubes of water that she could consume and discard, in order to avoid having her stealth profile compromised by half-full canteens or a too-full bladder; and a can of *raktajino*.

Sarpantha was still debating which field ration to tear open when her comm vibrated against her hip. She checked the device. The message on its screen was terse and unambiguous: TERMINATE CONFERENCE AND ALL PARTICIPANTS IMMEDIATELY, WITH EXTREME PREJUDICE.

So much for dinner.

The slender Silwaan-in-disguise tucked away the comm and opened her pack's munitions pouch. She pulled out a brick of high-yield soft explosive with a molecular fuse. A quick check confirmed the detonator was functional; she set it to standby mode. Then she poked her head up from cover and surveyed the ground between her position and the conference center.

It was heavily wooded, mostly level terrain. There were a few gulches and dry creek beds that would be hard to see in the dark, but she had learned their locations on her numerous trips around the building, so she wasn't concerned about falling into them; they would pose more danger to her pursuers than to her. *Luckily, I don't need to reach the center—just the runabout.*

The small Starfleet ship sat beside other, smaller spacecraft in the wide clearing that flanked the conference center. As the vessel with the largest warp drive and antideuterium fuel payload, it offered the potential for the most devastating explosion. The dangerous part of planting the bomb for maximum effect was that she would need to place it directly adjacent to the antideuterium tanks, which were located on the top of the spacecraft, near its aft bulkhead.

Her only other concern would be triggering the conference center's intruder alert once she entered its sensor perimeter. She had a biometric scrambler that could mask her life signs and fool the security system into thinking she was a large forest animal, but that ruse would work only so long as she wasn't seen. *I'll have to reach the runabout, plant the bomb, and get back to cover before any of the doctors thinks to look out a window and check on their ships.*

It was approximately four hundred twenty-five meters from her sniper's blind to the runabout. Over open ground, Sarpantha could sprint that distance in just over a minute, but in thick forest such as this, even with the benefit of her naturally superior night vision, it would take her closer to ninety seconds to reach her target. If the conference center's sensors were fooled by her biometric spoof-circuit, the alarm might not sound at all; otherwise, it would probably alert the doctors to her approach within ten seconds. Still, they were all asleep, and their first instinct might be to check the center's security system before seeking a visual confirmation in the dark. By the time any of them got as far as opening a curtain, she could be back beyond the tree line.

Worth a shot, she decided, shrugging off her backpack.

Wind kissed her face as she sprinted toward the clearing, the explosive charge gripped in one white-knuckled fist. Trees blurred past, silver lines in the haze of night, and her footfalls crunched and thudded over the hard ground. Sarpantha dashed out onto the broad greensward that encircled the conference center. Around her the night was cool and still. There was no whoop of alarms from the center; its windows all stood dark.

Moving with grace and silence, she scaled the side of the runabout, using its warp nacelle as a step to its curved pylon. Crouched atop the small vessel, she tucked the explosive into a narrow gap between the two antideuterium pods attached to its dorsal hull. Its magnetic clamp locked it into place with a soft thump. Then she armed its detonator and set its timer for two hours—more than enough time for her to fall back to the exfiltration site and call in to request a prioritized extraction. A final check verified that the timer had started its countdown.

Her steps were soft as she stole away, down the side of the runabout—and then she froze at the sight of a blond human woman in a Starfleet uniform aiming a phaser at her.

"Open your hands and raise them over your head. You're under arrest."

Where had she come from? Had she been there all along? Sarpantha had no time to seek answers to those questions, only a moment in which to act. Looking the human in the eye, the Breen field agent made a desperate reach for the detonator's override switch.

Then she was blinded by a flash of orange light—from the phaser.

Few things stripped the shine off a new day for Ro Laren like having to referee a jurisdictional dispute between Starfleet and the Bajoran Militia.

A golden shimmer and a semi-musical wash of sound lingered as the transporter effect faded, revealing the Bement Center, its encircling clearing, and the towering dark majesty of the Bestri Woods that surrounded the site. Shafts of late-morning sunlight angled through the trees, and the warm air was heavy with the fragrance of flowers and the scent of wet earth. The once-secluded redoubt of vedeks seeking inner peace now was swarmed by armed people in uniforms. Members of the Bajoran Militia outnumbered the Starfleet personnel nearly two to one, but the Starfleet teams had come bearing combat weapons and high-tech forensic gear that both were at least a decade more advanced than anything available to the Bajoran troops.

Starfleet security officers surrounded the *Tiber,* while inside their protective cordon a forensic investigation unit worked on top of and around the runabout. The militia troops remained at a discreet distance, but they watched the Starfleet teams as if they were invaders.

Everywhere that Ro looked, the two forces acted like oil and water, moving around each other but never really mixing. Outside the center's entrance was a tense but hushed confrontation between Lieutenant Commander Douglas and a male Bajoran Militia officer wearing a major's rank. Their eyes were ablaze with anger, and fingers were being pointed for emphasis.

I'd better step in before Douglas sparks another secession from the Federation.

There was no subtle way to separate the arguing duo. Ro shouldered her way between them, favoring neither and forcing them to step apart to let her in. "What's the problem?"

"Your *deputy* chief of security is interfering in my investigation."

Douglas looked ready to rip out the man's jugular. "This site is under *Starfleet* authority."

"Your authority ends where Bajor's atmosphere begins."

Ro spread her arms to force the pair even farther apart. "Enough! First of all, who am I speaking to, Major . . . ?"

"Honn," the officer said. "Major Honn Kero, adjutant commander, Rakantha Province."

"All right, Major Honn. I signed the orders authorizing this conference, and I have orders from your superiors, including the First Minister, loaning us the center and its grounds."

"I'm aware of that, Captain."

"Then you should also be aware that the agreement cedes authority for securing the site to Starfleet. Did you miss that part of the briefing?"

"No, sir. But we have reports that a Breen spy was apprehended on Bajoran soil. That makes this a matter for the Bajoran Militia."

Douglas had the taut quality of a coiled spring. "The hell it does. Captain, that spy didn't come here looking to steal Bajor's recipe for perfect *hasperat*. She was sent here to kill five of the Federation's most accomplished medical scientists. This was a military operation, and it deserves a military response." Stepping forward to challenge Honn, she added, "And since I was the one who caught her, I plan on being the first one to interrogate her."

The situation was not cooling as quickly as Ro had hoped. "Where's the spy now?"

"On a shuttle," Douglas said. "Being taken to Deep Space Nine under armed guard."

"Understood, Commander. I'll see you inside." She staved off Douglas's protest with a sharp look, and the human woman withdrew to the conference center while Ro faced off with Honn. "We're both soldiers, so let's cut the crap. You're not getting the Breen spy. You could ask Bajor's delegate to the Federation Council to file an extradition request, but I think you'd have better luck gambling your life's savings in Quark's Bar. Do yourself a favor and go home."

Honn stewed in his resentment but kept his mouth shut as Ro followed Douglas inside the conference center. As she entered the building, a wash of cool air greeted her. The deputy chief of security stood in the foyer, awaiting her next order. Ro gave it to her. "Take me to Bashir."

"This way, Captain." Douglas led her down one long corridor of the X-shaped conference center, past meeting rooms littered with dirty plates, half-filled glasses, and stacks of padds. The chaotic clutter reminded Ro of the cadet lounges at Starfleet Academy during exams weeks.

Slumped in a chair in a long meeting room at the end of the corridor, Bashir looked as if he hadn't slept in days, and his general aura of musky funk suggested it had been at least a couple of days since he had showered. The subtle strands of gray in his tousled black hair were made more obvious by its greasy sheen, and his uniform echoed his disheveled state. He welcomed Ro with a weary lifting of his head. "Good morning, Captain."

Ro looked over her shoulder at Douglas. "Give us the

room." The security officer slipped out, and the door closed. Staring at Bashir made Ro so furious that her voice became at once hard but quiet, a knife-edged whisper. "What are you *really* working on down here, Doctor?"

"As my sabbatical request said, a new therapeutic regimen—"

"Stop lying to me. I'm not stupid. The Typhon Pact might've sent a spy to see what you and your friends were up to, but if it had no strategic importance, they wouldn't have tried to vaporize half of Rakantha Province to put a stop to it." She leaned forward and planted her hands on the arms of Bashir's chair, trapping him. "You're up to something. Something huge. And if it's this important, I need to know about it."

A pained grimace. "I don't think that would benefit either of us."

Her nose was barely a hair away from his. "Let me be the judge of that. I'm giving you a direct order: Tell me what you and your conference guests are working on."

"We're trying to rescue the people of Andor from extinction."

"And why can't you do that on the station?"

He sighed. "Because it involves applying classified information that Starfleet and the Federation government have, in their infinite wisdom, declared forbidden. Information, I might add, that our rivals the Tholians have been all too eager to share with the Andorians."

Memories of classified reports and security briefings came back to Ro, and she stepped back as the magnitude of Bashir's latest misadventure became clear to her. "Tell me you haven't been working with the . . . I'm sorry, what was it called?"

"The Meta-Genome."

"Right. Tell me you—"

"We have. And we're making incredible progress."

She covered her eyes to mask her frustration and fury. "Are you out of your mind?"

"Quite the contrary. If we can isolate a few more critical sequences, we—"

"Stop talking." Ro turned in a tight circle, suddenly feeling trapped by her circumstances. "You know me, Julian. You know I'm not above bending rules to get things done. But this isn't the kind of regulation you can bend. This kind of thing only ends one way, and you know it: with a court-martial and a fast-track to solitary confinement."

"I'd assumed as much from the start. I'd hoped to keep my efforts a secret so that no one but me would have to take the fall for this . . . but I seem to attract accomplices."

Ro eyed the viewscreen on the wall beside the door and found herself impressed by the simultaneous elegance and complexity of the virtual gene sequences Bashir and his team had designed. She was no medical expert, but even she could see that something amazing was taking shape inside the conference center. Something too big for one person to judge.

She looked at Bashir. "How much more time do you need?"

"It's hard to say. It might be days, or it could be weeks. The key—"

"I'll buy you as much time as I can." Her declaration shocked Bashir into silence. "If anyone asks, you and I never had this conversation. I don't know what you're working on."

"Understood."

"But know this, Doctor: If the Typhon Pact was smart

enough to know your little meeting was worth checking out, it's a good bet somebody at Starfleet Command is doing the same. Which means it's only a matter of time before your mercy mission gets shut down for good." She opened the door and tossed her parting words over her shoulder as she left. "Work quickly."

Fourteen

It's too quiet, Tenmei thought as she stepped onto the *Defiant's* bridge. Having served on the ship's overnight watch as a junior officer, she had been prepared to find the bridge's ambience subdued during Gamma Shift, but this was a different degree of quiet. It was creepy, like an empty library or a crypt. *It's because we're docked at Deep Space 9*, she reminded herself. That was why all the duty stations were dark and unoccupied except for the center seat.

Thanks to the bridge's padded and carpeted deck, the ensign in the command chair didn't hear Tenmei until she was all but on top of her. Catching sight of the lieutenant out of the corner of her eye, the magenta-haired young woman blurted "Ack!" as she leaped to her feet.

Tenmei extended one hand in apology. "Sorry. Didn't mean to startle you."

"No worries, sir," the ensign said with a soft southern accent. "What can I do for you?"

"Actually, I'm here to do something for you. What's your name?"

"Crosswhite, sir. Ensign Rhylie Crosswhite."

She took Crosswhite by one shoulder and led her aft, away from the command chair. "Ensign, I'm here to relieve you for the rest of the shift."

"I don't understand."

"I'll stand the overnight watch for you."

"But I have orders—"

"—from Colonel Cenn to man the conn until you're properly relieved. That's what I'm doing, Ensign. Relieving you and assuming responsibility for the conn."

Crosswhite's face scrunched with confusion at Tenmei's charitable offer. "Sir? Isn't Gamma port watch when junior officers pay dues and malcontents draw punishment detail?"

"What's your point, Ensign? Are you suggesting I'm here for breaking regs?"

"No, sir, I wouldn't—"

"You think I haven't paid my dues? I've been on this boat for *nine* years."

"Of course, sir! It's just— I mean, I only transferred over last month, so why—"

"Ensign, one of the most important things you need to learn is to not ask 'why' when senior officers give you orders that do you favors. The correct response is to say, 'Thank you, sir,' and then get gone before they change their minds. Do I make myself clear, *Ensign*?"

"Yes, sir! Thank you, sir!" Still perplexed but also smiling, Crosswhite hurried out the aft port hatchway and made haste aft toward the nearest turbolift.

Oh, to be so young again, Tenmei mused as she sealed the bridge hatches and locked them with her command code. Then she turned and walked forward to the wraparound console that served as the ship's combined helm and operations post. A few gingerly taps on its glossy black surface brought the interface panel to colorful life and filled the bridge with the gentle thrumming of power and the soft music of feedback tones.

She circled around the console and kneeled in front of it, then fished an all-purpose sonic tool from a pocket inside her uniform jacket. The device made quick work of removing the access panel on the forward side of the helm-operations console, revealing its inner maze of isolinear chips, ODN cables, plasma relay capacitors, and command circuits.

Sonic tool in hand, she turned her torso sideways and snaked her arm through a narrow gap in the tightly packed machinery, to reach a junction tucked deep inside the console. Probing by touch memory using only her little finger, she found the node she was looking for. In slow, precise motions she positioned the tool. It activated with a pleasant, steady buzzing.

And away we go. . . .

Pulaski looked at the window and half imagined she could see the forest outside the Bement Center, but night had long since fallen and all she saw was her soft-edged reflection. She wasn't tired—no, that wasn't true; she was alert but exhausted. The anasomazine she'd injected into her carotid artery a few hours earlier had left her senses sharp and canceled out the neurochemical effects of her sleep deprivation, which had just entered its one-hundred-seventh hour. From a medical point of view, she did not need to sleep. But from a practical point of view, she needed to do anything else but work. She and the others had been staring at the Meta-Genome for nearly a week, and it was all beginning to look the same. The noise was occluding the pattern.

Doctor Lense trudged through an open doorway into the commissary. Pulaski watched the younger woman's reflection as she plodded to the replicator and thumped her head against the wall above it. "Club soda with a slice of orange, cold." The carbonated beverage appeared in a flurry of light, with a sound like a miniature calliope being switched quickly on and off. Lense picked up the glass, whose faceted surface glistened with condensation, and carried it to the seat next to Pulaski's. She groaned as she sank into the thick-cushioned armchair. "If I spend one more second thinking about the goddamn Meta-Genome, I'll go insane." She tilted her head back and fixed her blank stare on the ceiling for several seconds. "There. I'm insane now."

"Is that all it takes? If so, I'm pretty sure I had a psychotic break sometime on Tuesday."

"Today is Tuesday."

Days bled together when one spent this long awake, so Pulaski took her word for it. She shifted to face Lense. "How are you holding up?"

"At least I know what day it is." She was quick to soften the verbal jab. "Just kidding. Truth is, I'm not sure I can see straight. My thinking feels clear, but my eyes feel shot."

"I sympathize." Quiet desperation turned her head toward the replicator. "Maybe I should punch up a drink with electrolytes and antioxidants. Try to jump-start my body. . . . Again."

Lense sipped her soda. "Might as well. There'll be plenty of time to sleep once we're all in custody." She blinked slowly at their imperfect reflection. "Are we doing something dumb? It all sounded so heroic when we started, but I can't remember anymore."

The older woman shook her head. "No idea. I'd like to think we're taking a stand for . . . something important. Ethics? The Andorians? Science? Whatever it is, I hope it's worth it."

"I just worry that once politics gets involved, no one'll be listening to us and our big ideas and our fancy words. It'll all come down to talking heads shouting, 'Treason!' Once that happens, people tend to tune out, which means the last thing they'll hear is the accusation."

"That's how the universe works. I know I came here with the best of intentions, and I'm sure all the rest of us did, too. What scares me is the possibility that no one will care. If Bashir's right and we make this work, Starfleet Command and the Federation Council might want to pin medals on us—right up until the moment they find out how we did it. That's when they'll turn on us. That's when it'll get ugly."

Anxious silence yawned between them. Lense was pensive. "What if it all goes as planned? I mean, say we find the cure, and Bashir sneaks it to his friends on Andor. It'll be one of the biggest news stories of the century. Do we really think no one's ever going to figure out we were part of it? What happens if it comes out years from now and looks like a cover-up?"

"I hadn't thought of that." All-new worst-case scenarios spun themselves whole from the gray wool of Pulaski's beleaguered imagination. "The conspiracy-minded would accuse us of running a covert Starfleet operation for no better reason than to influence Andorian politics."

"Far too optimistic." Lense shook her head. "The hardcore kooks will say we were running a clandestine genetic-engineering program to turn the Andorians into the Federation's version of the Jem'Hadar, warrior-slaves we secretly control with rationed drugs in their water."

"Are you sure the replicator didn't spike your soda?"

"I'm serious," Lense insisted. "I'm not talking about reputable news sources like FNS or INS. I'm talking about the fringe channels. The loons with vid-visors and public uplinks."

She dismissed Lense's fear of the paranoid. "Their kind

will always be with us, Elizabeth. We can't shy away from bold work on the off chance that some deluded fool will try to tar us with ridiculous lies."

Her protest got a dour chuckle from Lense. "They aren't the ones who concern me. I worry about the ones who might tar us with the truth—even if only by accident."

"You knew this job was dangerous when you took it."

"That I did. Unfortunately, I forgot to explain that to my seven-year-old daughter." Lense downed the rest of her soda in three quick gulps, then stifled a belch by pressing the side of her fist to her lips. She stood up and stretched. "You've been lovely company, but I have to go and find a dense pillow so I can spend a few minutes screaming my way to inner peace."

Pulaski pointed toward the administrative wing. "Try the manager's office. I think I heard Julian mention it was soundproofed."

"Good to know."

Lense moved in stiff, heavy steps toward the doorway— then stopped as Lemdock barged through it and collided with the doorframe hard enough to knock his vaporator off-kilter. Gasping for air, he croaked, "Come quickly!" Staggering backward, he beckoned Pulaski and Lense with broad waves of his webbed hand. "Hurry!" Then the flustered Benzite jogged off, back the way he had come.

Intrigued and full of guarded hope, Pulaski got up and followed him, and Lense hurried along beside her. Neither of them said anything. *Maybe because we don't want to get each other's hopes up,* Pulaski reasoned.

Lemdock led them to the spacious meeting room that had been set aside for Bashir's exclusive use. Waiting just outside its open doorway was Tovak. The Vulcan stood with his arms crossed. His face was a portrait of hard, unyielding focus. Pulaski, Lense, and Lemdock gathered at his back and peered over his shoulder at the virtual genome model Bashir was assembling.

Brimming with optimism and impatience, Lense whispered, "What's he found?"

Tovak was either unwilling or unable to tear his eyes off Bashir's work as he replied in a tone of hushed respect, "The answer."

Lense and Pulaski traded wide-eyed looks of joyous disbelief. Pulaski scrutinized the genome model projected in front of Bashir, then she glanced up at Tovak. "You mean—?"

"Unless I am gravely mistaken . . . I think Doctor Bashir has designed a stable new genetic model for the Andorian species."

Fifteen

I've never seen so many personnel evaluations. Deep Space 9's department heads had taken until the last possible moment to complete their scheduled crew reviews, a consequence of the backlogs inflicted by Bacco's assassination and the delays it had caused in the rest of the station's unusually crunched schedule. It was almost enough to make Ro Laren turn to religion and worship the Prophets as deities, just so she could beg them to strike her dead, to spare her the agony of signing off on more than two thousand paraphrasings of "performs to expectations."

Where to start? The Engineering division? Its reports were the driest and most mind-numbing. Ro was sure half the words engineers used didn't actually exist but had been cooked up just to pad their files with empty jargon and acronyms. The Medical division? Doctors were the only ones whose professional patois made engineers sound intelligible. Command division? Reading three hundred eighty-four junior officers' variations on why they felt they'd demonstrated exceptional leadership skills meriting promotion sounded to Ro like a probable contributing factor to suicide. *The Security division it is, then.* At least its reports tended to include funny stories about all the other departments' personnel and their myriad screwups.

She had just called up the Security division's evaluations on her padd when her office's overhead speaker beeped softly, granting her what she hoped would be an interesting reprieve. Colonel Cenn's voice filtered down, loud and clear. *"Captain, you have a Priority One subspace signal from Federation President Pro Tem Ishan Anjar."*

Ro tried to stay calm, but her jaw clenched, her muscles tensed, and her left hand closed into a fist. She had never met Ishan Anjar, even though they both had been active during the final decade of the Bajoran insurgency against the Cardassian Occupation. All she really knew of the man was his reputation, which was sketchy, at best. As far as Ro knew, Ishan had never been accused of any wrongdoing, but whispered intimations of back-room deals always seemed to follow his name everywhere Ro had traveled on Bajor since its liberation.

His ascent through the ranks of power in the Bajoran government had been so swift that he had escaped all but a cursory vetting from the people. Some Bajorans had dismissed his election to the Federation Council as a dead-end career move. Instead, his panache for striking bargains had elevated him temporarily to the summit of Federation political power—a move he was looking to make permanent in just a couple of months. Now most Bajorans hailed him as a hero, a triumphant native son. Ro was not one of those people. To her, he was just another politician looking to complicate her already lousy day.

She stood, moved to the middle of the room, and faced the viewscreen mounted on the bulkhead, above the sofa opposite her desk. "Put him through, Colonel."

The diagram of Deep Space 9 that normally occupied the large screen was replaced by a subspace feed from President Pro Tem Ishan. A string of icons in the lower left corner confirmed that the channel was encrypted and secure, while side-by-side chronometers in the lower right corner informed Ro that while it was morning on the station, it was late at night at Ishan's location on nearby Betazed, where he was busy campaigning for the upcoming special election.

Ishan's chiseled features were crowned by dark hair accented with distinguished streaks of steel gray. His nasal ridges were subtle and upswept, and he met Ro's normally implacable gaze with a stare that she was sure could unnerve almost anyone.

"*Captain Ro. I hope you'll forgive me if I cut straight to business.*"

"By all means, sir."

"*What, exactly, is the purpose of Doctor Julian Bashir's medical conference on Bajor?*"

The question raised the hackles on Ro's neck. *Please tell me he doesn't know.* She opted to stall for time. "His sabbatical request said he'd be working on new therapies for Kalla-Nohra Syndrome and Pottrik Syndrome."

Ishan held up a padd. "*I know what it says. I have a copy of it right here.*" He cast the tablet aside. "*I also have a report from Starfleet Security that says your people captured a Breen spy who was trying to blow up the conference center four days ago.*"

"Our interrogation of the Breen agent is ongoing, sir."

A Tellarite leaned into the frame and whispered something into Ishan's right ear. The president pro tem's hazel-green eyes narrowed. "*Captain, it's been brought to my attention that Doctor Bashir has been in contact with an Andorian citizen, most likely his former crewmate Thirishar ch'Thane, via secret diplomatic channels provided by the Ferengi. As you might be aware, ch'Thane works with Professor zh'Thiin on research involving the Shedai Meta-Genome. That, and the fact that Bashir has gathered four of our preeminent genomic-medicine specialists for a conference with no published agenda, has led me and key members of my staff to suspect that Bashir and his compatriots are working on the Andorian medical crisis—something they would be unable to do without access to classified information about the Meta-Genome."*

Ro knew she had to tread with great caution. A fine line separated artful omission from outright lying to the appointed head of the civilian government. No matter what her personal opinion of the man might be, she was bound by oath to respect his office. "Sir, do you have any solid evidence of wrongdoing on the part of Doctor Bashir or his colleagues?"

"This isn't a court of law, Captain. I'm responding to what I consider to be a credible threat to the security of the Federation. If Bashir and the others are working with the Meta-Genome, and the Typhon Pact knows enough about it that they tried to sabotage it, there's a significant chance they could escalate to acts of mass destruction to achieve their goal. Even more alarming is the possibility that some other player on the interstellar stage will steal the data and use it to invent something too horrible to imagine. We can't let that happen."

It galled her to admit he was right. "What are your orders, sir?"

"Take a Starfleet security team to Bajor and find out what they're working on. If it's the Meta-Genome—for that matter, if it's anything to do with the Andorian crisis—shut them down and take them all into maximum-security custody immediately, and until further notice."

"Understood, sir."

"Notify my office when it's done. Thank you, Captain." He closed the channel, switching the screen momentarily to the Federation emblem before it reverted to its usual station diagrams.

Ro walked out of her office and snapped orders at Cenn on her way to the turbolift. "Have Blackmer and Douglas meet me with an armed security detail at the *Rio Grande* in five minutes. We're heading back to Bajor."

An electric mood infused the room. Bashir hunched forward, manipulating the three-dimensional holographic magnification of the modified Andorian genomes he had designed, while his four peers huddled close behind his shoulders, admiring his work with rapt attention.

He triggered a new round of recombination simulations. "As you can see, regardless of which regional, ethnic variant genes we introduce into the simulation, the fertilization and integration paradigms remain stable. Even double pregnancies should be stable and healthy."

Wonderment lit up Pulaski's careworn features. "Don't sell your work short, Doctor. You've done more than stabilize their fertility problem. You've eliminated more than three dozen known congenital defects from their genome by replacing their weakest chromosome."

"Most remarkable," Tovak said. "I see you incorporated my suggestion regarding the error-correction gene. That should permanently suppress the recessive gene that gave rise to the original problem over a millennium ago."

Bashir nodded. "It was an inspired notion, Doctor." He looked back at his colleagues. "You all made amazing contributions. Thanks to your work, not only can we fix the Andorians' fertility issues, we can extend their life spans, increase their average intelligence, and render them immune to a wide variety of diseases and syndromes that have plagued them for centuries." He felt as light in his head as he was dead on his feet. "This may be the finest work of my career."

Lense rested a hand on Bashir's shoulder. "Mine, too." Lemdock and Pulaski patted him on the back, and Tovak honored him with a subtle lowering of his chin.

Their moment of celebration was dispelled by the heavy rhythm of marching feet, drawing closer in the corridor outside. Bashir turned off the holographic projector, shut down the runabout's computer, and met his friends' looks of concern with cool resignation. "We knew this was coming." He stood, stepped between the others and the conference room's door, and smoothed the front of his uniform. Seconds later the door slid open, and their guests arrived.

A squad of ten Starfleet security personnel filed into the room and fanned out to circle behind the five doctors and surround them. None of the security officers drew their phasers, but they all rested their hands on their weapons' grips and stood ready to react.

The last three people to enter were Sarina Douglas, Captain Ro, and Deep Space 9's chief of security, Lieutenant Commander Jefferson Blackmer. Ro's countenance was red with anger. Douglas looked both embarrassed and apologetic. The security chief's expression was absolutely neutral, a perfect poker face. The captain focused her fury on Bashir. "You've got a real knack for finding trouble, Doctor."

"I consider it a gift."

"Well, I don't. Would you care to guess who sent us here?" It was obvious to Bashir that her query was rhetorical, and that the only correct response was to stay quiet until she continued. "The president pro tem *himself* ordered me to arrest you and impound your work."

It was Elizabeth Lense who shot back, "Did you tell him what we're working on?"

"He seems to have a fairly good idea." Ro fixed Bashir with a look that could slice through a starship's hull. "And that's exactly what I warned you about, four days ago." For a moment she shut her eyes and pressed her palm to her forehead, as if to push past a brutal headache. She turned toward Blackmer. "Jeff? Impound their computers—*all* of them: their padds, the conference center mainframe, every isolinear chip, and all the cores on their shuttles and the *Tiber*. Put it all under guard with transport scramblers, and tell Cenn to launch the *Defiant* to come take it all back to the station. Once it's secured, I'll brief Starfleet Command."

"Aye, sir." Blackmer waved the other security officers into motion. The mustard-collared personnel started gathering up all of the doctors' equipment and storage media.

Ro edged into Bashir's personal space. "Do you have any idea what you've done here, Doctor?"

"Yes, I do. If anyone's failing to see the big picture, Captain, it's you."

"Spell it out for me."

"We *have* the cure, Captain. We *found* it." Petty as it was, Bashir took a small measure of satisfaction in watching Ro recoil from his news. "That's right. By using the last three years of Professor zh'Thiin's work on the

Meta-Genome as a springboard and filling in all the gaps in their data with sequences from the complete Meta-Genome . . . we've cured the Andorian fertility crisis. You just ordered Blackmer to box up the Andorians' only hope for survival."

The angular beauty of her face went pale as the truth sank in. Then her lips vanished into a hard frown, and the creases in her forehead deepened with her resolve. "It doesn't matter anymore. We have executive orders to place you all under arrest."

"Do you think this is what President Bacco would have done?"

"She's dead, Doctor. What she would've done doesn't matter anymore."

Bashir felt his pulse quicken and throb in his temples as he watched security officers cart away all his work and shut down the conference center's computer network. "This is insane! At least let me talk to Ishan."

The captain's reaction was incredulous at best. "What do you think that'll accomplish?"

"Maybe once he sees that we're not just talking about a hypothetical, he'll see the value in what we've done! With the cure in hand, we could win back the goodwill of the Andorians and keep the Typhon Pact off our doorstep."

Ro tilted her head. "That actually doesn't sound crazy."

"Is that a 'yes,' Captain? You'll let me talk to Ishan before you shut us down?"

"No, we're still shutting you down. But I'll let you talk to him before I hand you over for a one-way trip to solitary confinement."

"Too kind."

"You know me: I'm just a big softy." Ro headed for the

door and stopped beside Blackmer on her way out. "Keep him here while I open a channel to Ishan."

Blackmer looked at Bashir, then at Ro. "You sure that's a good idea?"

"Why not? How much worse can this get?" The captain pointed a threatening finger at Bashir. "Do *not* make me sorry I just said that."

Sixteen

"*B*y what right do you presume to question my orders, Doctor?"

Confronted by a larger-than-life viewscreen image of Ishan, Bashir noted that the president pro tem looked older and more weary than his public image on the newsfeeds. Fatigue had underscored his eyes with puffy, dark crescents, and his dark hair had streaks the dull gray of lunar regolith. But for all his apparent frailty, he projected a steely will and a fierce temper.

"With all respect, Mister President Pro Tem, as a physician I am in some cases bound more by my Hippocratic oath and my own conscience than by the law."

His heartfelt assertion deepened Ishan's ire. "*Is it your contention that because you're a medical doctor, you should be exempt from Federation law? Or from executive orders?*"

"Not at all, sir." He looked down for half a second to gather his thoughts. As he took a breath, he felt the nervous anticipation of Ro, Blackmer, and Douglas, who stood off to one side of the conference room, auditing his conversation with the temporary head of the Federation government. "I'm just trying to explain that my actions aren't the result of any wish to harm the Federation. They're the product of my vow to defend life before all other considerations."

Ishan's hard, hazel-green eyes narrowed. "*Correct me if*

I'm wrong, Doctor, but didn't you also take an oath of service to Starfleet and the Federation?"

"Yes, sir."

"So how do you justify betraying that oath to serve an-other?"

"In my opinion, sir, I am doing no such thing. If you would hear me out, I think I can show that my actions in fact serve the best interests of both Starfleet and the Federation."

The skeptical Bajoran crossed his arms. *"I'm listening."*

"First and foremost, sir—it's the right thing to do."

"I disagree."

"This is no mere abstraction, sir! The lives of real, sentient beings are at stake here! Even now the Andorian species is nearing a biological tipping point, one from which it will be almost impossible to revive a genetically robust population. It's time to put aside our resentment over their secession and give them the cure."

Ishan shook his head. *"My staff and I have already discussed this. Andor betrayed the Federation once when it seceded, and a second time when it entered into treaty negotiations with the Typhon Pact. We can't be seen to reward that kind of behavior with concessions. It would be an invitation to every member world in the Federation to secede in order to extort us."*

"The only reason the Meta-Genome became a political issue on Andor was because we'd hidden the data, and then the Tholians called us on it. Since then, the Tholians have capitalized on their monopoly over the Meta-Genome data, and they've been using it to pull Andor farther from our political influence and deeper into their own. But if we share the cure with them, freely and without condition—"

"We'd be handing the Typhon Pact a blueprint of the full Meta-Genome, something we're not sure the Tholians actually have."

"No, sir, we wouldn't. The cure contains only the tiniest fraction of the complete Meta-Genome. And now that my team and I have isolated the segments needed for the cure, we've already deleted the remainder of the Meta-Genome data from our drives." Bashir paused for a few seconds as Ishan looked to someone off-screen for confirmation of that fact. "The cure would not reveal any of the other countless secrets of the Meta-Genome. Nor can I or my team."

"I and many other people genuinely appreciate the efforts you've made to contain the damage from your little misadventure, Doctor. But that doesn't change the fact that you put the safety of the Federation itself at risk for the benefit of a planet that's no longer a member."

Bashir deliberately mimicked Ishan's earlier choice of words. "Well, *correct me if I'm wrong,* sir, but it's my understanding that there are still nearly forty-one million Andorians who hold Federation citizenship on worlds other than Andor, and nearly a hundred thousand Andorians still serving loyally in Starfleet. Don't *they* deserve this cure?"

The president pro tem's face reddened as his brow knitted with anger. *"This isn't some semantic game, Doctor. If we let this cure out into the galaxy at large, it's only a matter of time before it makes its way back to Andor."*

"Then why not send it there ourselves and take credit for it? Beat the Typhon Pact at its own game! If we let the Tholians guide the Andorians to this cure, I guarantee we'll lose Andor and its people to the Typhon Pact—for at least a generation, if not forever. Is that an outcome you're ready to risk? A wager you're willing to make when the lives of the Andorian people are the stakes?"

"*I won't be seen as weak, Doctor. Not by the people of the Federation, not by our allies, and certainly not by the Typhon Pact.*"

His intransigence baffled Bashir. "Weak? What about coldhearted? Or vindictive?"

"*Those can be seen as virtues during an election.*"

"That's what this is? Posturing for the special election? You're shining up your foreign-policy credentials with the blood of the Andorians?" The ruthlessness of Ishan's political calculation made Bashir sick. "If this is an example of how you plan to use power, I think it's an excellent argument for why you should never be allowed to wield it."

"*I've been lectured by nobler men than you, Doctor. But they're dead, and I'm still here. History is written by the winners. Remember that.*" He raised his voice. "*Captain Ro?*"

Ro stepped in from the room's periphery to stand beside Bashir. "Sir?"

"*Take the good doctor into custody, as I'd originally ordered.*"

"Yes, sir."

"*And make sure no one interrogates him or his associates. They're all to be transferred to a secure facility as soon as we can make arrangements for their transport.*"

"We could use the *Defiant*—"

"*No, thank you, Captain. For reasons of operational security, I'm afraid the ultimate location of the doctors' incarceration will have to be kept on a need-to-know basis.*"

A chastised nod. "Understood, sir."

Ishan terminated the transmission without the courtesy

of a simple farewell. The screen changed to the Federation emblem for a moment before fading to black.

No one said a word, but Blackmer wasted no time drawing his phaser and aiming it at Bashir. "Sorry, sir. It's protocol."

"I understand. No hard feelings."

Blackmer looked at Ro. "Orders?"

"Hold him and the others in the empty conference room down the hall. After I beam up to the *Defiant* with the away team and the computers, have Douglas take Bashir back to the station in the *Rio Grande,* and you take the others back in the *Tiber.*"

He seemed uncomfortable with her decision. "Are you sure that's a good idea, sir?"

She threw a look at Bashir. For a moment, he thought he caught a glimmer of amusement on her face. "Something tells me they'll have a lot to talk about on the way home."

It never failed to impress Bashir how quickly a place one thought of as a refuge could become a prison. Ensign Liizsk and Petty Officer Damrose from Deep Space 9's security division ushered him down the conference center corridor. They stayed a few paces behind him, a respectable distance, phasers drawn and aimed squarely at the center of his back.

Liizsk hissed, "Stop." The broad-shouldered, long-limbed Saurian stepped past Bashir and unlocked the door to the lounge. As the portal slid open with a hushed sigh, Bashir saw his confederates gathered inside the room. Then, from behind him, came Damrose's gruff voice: "In." The square-jawed Iotian seemed impervious to Bashir's reproachfully arched eyebrow, so the doctor did as he was told and stepped inside the lounge without complaint. The Saurian entered commands on the door's keypad, closing and locking the room's only exit.

Bashir met his peers with good humor. "And how are all of you holding up?"

Lense gestured toward the transparasteel windows. "We're great. It's a beautiful day, and we have a lovely view of your friends from the station carting off all our work."

Pulaski took a less confrontational tack. "How was your talk with Ishan?"

"It could have been better." His façade slipped, betraying some of his frustration. "I can't tell if he's driven more by spite or by ambition. With one breath he talks about punishing the Andorians for betraying the Federation, with the next he talks about denying them the cure just so he won't look weak before the election. He's playing dice with the fate of an entire species!"

A fleeting hint of cold contempt slipped past Tovak's stoic façade. "The president pro tem appears to be a most disagreeable individual. To prioritize politics over the preservation of sentient life is illogical and amoral."

Lemdock honored Tovak by bowing his head. "Well-said, Doctor." He gesticulated with his webbed hands at the parade of security officers and technicians visible through the window. "But it does nothing to address the fact that our work is being confiscated. What happens now?"

A low, mirthless chortle from Lense. "Now we get lawyers."

Bashir saw the truth in her black humor. "She's right. My advice to all of you would be to refuse to answer any questions without your JAG counsels present, and to collectively point the finger at me. Deny any knowledge of the true nature or origin of the Meta-Genome."

His suggestion was met by Lense with anger and confusion.

"How the hell are we supposed to do that? And who'd believe us if we did?"

"It's all about plausible deniability," Bashir said. "As long as you all tell the same story, you'll be fine. Tell your counsels that I lied to you, that I told you we were working with a synthetic genome I'd found in the Gamma Quadrant."

Now it was Pulaski's turn to voice her doubts. "Why would they believe us?"

"Because that's the story I'm going to tell them: that none of you knew you were breaking the law—only I knew."

Tovak shook his head. "They will not believe it."

"But they won't be able to prove otherwise." He lifted his hands to forestall their protests. "Trust me. You've all risked more, and done more, than I ever could have hoped. There's no reason your careers should have to end with mine. Please, trust me on this."

Lemdock slumped into a chair, despondent. "While we're busy saving ourselves, who's going to save the Andorians? What happens to our work?"

Pulaski rested a consoling hand on the Benzite's shoulder. "There's still a chance the Andorians could find the cure on their own. If we did, maybe they can, too."

"Unlikely, I fear," Tovak said, further dashing Lemdock's feeble hopes for a happy conclusion to their medical odyssey. "Based on the research notes that came with the classified data, the sequences that helped Doctor Bashir craft a stable Andorian matrix are exclusive to Starfleet's record of the Meta-Genome. It is possible even the Tholians do not have all the sequences we used. If they lack even one of them, they will not be able to create this cure."

All the bad news drove Lense to bury her face in her hands. "So that's it? It's over?"

"Not quite," Bashir said. That snared the others' full attention. "Starfleet impounded our computers and storage media, but they haven't secured all copies of the Andorian cure. Yet."

His suggestion put a gleam of mischief in Pulaski's eyes. "Explain, Doctor."

"The Andorian cure is a tailored retrovirus, one that remains stable but inert until introduced into an Andorian's bloodstream. As such it poses no risk to other species." A sly tilt of his head. "Such as humans, for instance."

Eyes wide, Lense leaped to her feet and grabbed Bashir's shoulders. "You injected *yourself* with the retrovirus? It's dormant in your bloodstream *right now*?" Her look of shock brightened into glee. She grasped the sides of his head and planted a firm, fast kiss on his lips, an act not of passion but of gratitude and congratulations. "You magnificent bastard!"

"All part of the service."

The others gathered around him, slapped his back, shook his hand, and patted his shoulders in commendation. Pulaski was the first to gather her wits and get back to business. "So, now what? You've got the cure, but you're still a prisoner. How do we get it to Andor?"

"Let's just say I expected something like this would happen." Bashir stepped clear of the group's adoration and moved toward the door. "Consequently, preparations have been made."

Lemdock looked fearful. "Such as?"

"In the interest of preserving your plausible deniability, let's just say, *I have a plan*."

The door opened behind Bashir. He turned to see Sarina Douglas standing in the doorway with her hand resting on her sidearm phaser. "Julian? I have orders to take you to the stockade complex on Deep Space Nine and place you in solitary confinement, effective immediately." She beckoned him with a tilt of her head. "Shall we?"

Bashir bade his fellow physicians farewell with a small nod. "If you'll pardon me . . . I believe my chariot awaits."

Seventeen

Outside the climate-controlled conference center, the midday air was sultry and rich with scents of the forest and the sea. It was a short walk from the main entrance to the waiting *Rio Grande,* but Bashir felt beads of perspiration forming on his forehead by the time he and Douglas had descended the steps and crossed the walkway to traverse the lawn. The grass and soil were pleasantly elastic under his feet, a welcome change from walking on hard surfaces.

Douglas kept a firm grip on Bashir's left elbow as she led him toward the runabout. Her lips barely moved as she spoke, and her voice was almost a whisper. "Last chance to back out."

"We didn't come this far to give up," he mumbled back, casting surreptitious glances around the area to see if they were being observed with more than casual attention.

"Defying executive orders isn't run-of-the-mill insubordination, Julian. The plan was for you to go AWOL, not become public enemy number one."

"The facts on the ground have changed. We have to roll with it."

"You could have injected me. I—"

"There wasn't time." He paused as a pair of security officers passed them, walking in the opposite direction. As soon as they moved out of earshot, he continued. "I dosed myself as soon as I was sure the genome was stable. If I'd waited for you, I'd have missed my chance."

They walked in troubled silence for a few moments, and the runabout loomed larger in Bashir's field of view. Douglas's voice trembled with anxiety. "Are you sure you want to do this? Once it's done, there's nothing more I can do to help you."

"I don't see that I have a choice, do you? If I surrender, either the Andorians die as a species for no good reason, or, worse, Ishan steals the cure and uses it to blackmail them."

"Let's not start embracing insane conspiracy theories," Douglas warned.

"Why not? Ishan's willing to risk letting them die so he can win an election. If he'll do that, what's to stop him from leveraging the cure after he's elected? From using it to force concessions from them? Or bully them back into the Federation? What then?"

"Don't obsess over what-ifs. There's no point getting worked up over crimes nobody's committed yet. Stick to what we know: the Andorians are dying."

As usual, Douglas's advice was sound. Bashir focused himself on the here and now. "Fine. That's still more than enough reason, as far as I'm concerned."

"Me, too." A worried look. "You know they'll crucify you for this. They'll take your rank, your medical license. And they'll smear your name. They'll have to, to save face."

He weighed those sacrifices against his sins on Salavat. "A small price to pay."

They were only a dozen meters from the *Rio Grande*. Its side hatch stood open, and its engines hummed in preflight mode. Douglas took a deep breath. "I wish I was going with you."

"So do I. But I need your cover intact so you can bring me inside Thirty-one."

She chuckled softly. "Another harebrained plan—but I guess we should see if you survive this lunatic scheme before I start breaking your balls about the next one."

"Too kind." He stopped and faced her, and she mirrored him as he leaned closer. Part of him feared this might be the last time he saw her. "Don't forget to deliver my messages."

She pressed her forehead to his. Her blond hair tickled his face. "I won't."

He kissed her, and he looked into her blue eyes. "I apologize for this, by the way."

"It's okay. My career depends on it, so make it look good."

They stepped apart to regard each other—and then he coldcocked her with a punishing right cross to her jaw. The punch snapped her head sharply to the side, a perfect knockout blow. She collapsed onto the grass, and Bashir made no effort to catch her because he was already sprinting flat out for the runabout, hoping he reached cover inside it before someone opened fire.

Panicked shouts filled the noonday air, and as he ducked through the port-side hatch of the *Rio Grande,* a stun-level phaser beam caromed off the small starship's hull, leaving a dull gray scorch. He slapped the CLOSE EMERGENCY HATCH panel on his way in and pivoted left into the cockpit. As promised, the ship was warmed up and ready for flight.

First things first. He pried open the main control panel, reached inside its optronic viscera, and extracted the ship's transponder circuit with surgical precision. *Can't have them seizing remote control of my ship.* As the yelling from outside grew louder and more bellicose, the *Rio Grande* shuddered under a barrage of small-arms fire.

Bashir dropped into the pilot's seat and activated the antigrav coils to lift the ship off the ground. As it made a smooth and level vertical ascent, he armed the ship's forward phaser cannons. Working the helm with his right hand and the weapons controls with his left, he pivoted the runabout in a slow 120-degree turn and crippled the engines of his colleagues' shuttlecraft with three pinpoint shots. Then he pointed the ship's nose upward and punched in the impulse drive. Blue sky faded within seconds to the black vault of space and its treasure of stars.

Voices crackled from the overhead comm—commands from the Bajor Planetary Operations Center, or BPOC, to correct his flight path overlapped with orders from the *Defiant* in orbit and the *Tiber* below him to stand down and surrender his vessel. He ignored them all, raised the *Rio Grande*'s shields, and set his course for Andor at maximum warp.

His hand hovered over the warp drive controls. *I hope Sarina's okay.*

An explosion buffeted the runabout—it was a warning shot from the *Defiant*. Over the comm, Captain Ro was saying something, but her message was garbled by crosstalk from BPOC.

As the *Rio Grande* jumped to warp, the last thing Bashir heard was Ro swearing.

It happened so quickly that Jefferson Blackmer almost missed it.

Only a few moments earlier, the security chief had been sitting in the cockpit of the *Tiber,* conducting a routine pre-flight check. He had looked up through the forward viewport and made a mental note of Lieutenant Commander Douglas walking Bashir toward the *Rio Grande.* He had turned away for only a few seconds, just long enough to bring the impulse core online, when angry shrieks of phaser fire turned his head. Outside, Douglas was down, Bashir was running toward the *Rio Grande,* and someone was shooting at him from a distance.

What the hell just happened?

Bashir scrambled inside the *Rio Grande* and closed its hatch. Security officers sprinted toward the small starship and peppered it with stun-level phaser blasts.

Blackmer opened a ship-to-ship channel to the other runabout. "*Tiber* to *Rio Grande*! Don't do anything stupid, Doctor! There's nowhere to run!" He saw the telltale glow of charging warp coils inside the *Rio Grande*'s nacelles. He tapped a panel to close the *Tiber*'s open hatch. "Doctor! Can you hear me? Stand down and surrender the *Rio Grande* immediately!"

The *Rio Grande* rose from the ground as its antigrav system engaged, and it pivoted while firing phasers on the other grounded shuttlecraft's engines. Blackmer reached for the *Tiber*'s helm console to power up the engines. "This is your last warning, Doctor! Don't make me chase you down." There was no reply as the *Rio Grande* pointed its nose skyward. Cursing under his breath, Blackmer charged the *Tiber*'s antigrav circuits to prepare the ship for takeoff. His runabout lifted off the ground like an air bubble floating to the surface of a pool—and then Blackmer was surprised by a split-second sensation of free fall, followed by a jarring impact.

The *Tiber* was back on the ground. Its controls stuttered and went dark, and then the tiny ship fell as silent as the grave. Blackmer sensed this was no ordinary malfunction: it was sabotage. *Bashir must have booby-trapped his runabout as a precaution.* Through the cockpit viewport he watched as the *Rio Grande* streaked away like a missile into the cloudless blue sky. Blackmer tapped the combadge on his uniform. "Blackmer to *Defiant*."

Captain Ro answered. *"This is* Defiant. *Go ahead."*

"Doctor Bashir has escaped custody and stolen the *Rio Grande*. He's heading for orbit."

As Blackmer's report of Bashir's flight from Bajor filtered down from the bridge's overhead comm, Prynn Tenmei glanced over her shoulder from the *Defiant*'s forward console to gauge Captain Ro's reaction. The Bajoran commanding officer's stern face gave nothing away, and her voice was level and calm as she responded to Blackmer. "Can you join the pursuit?"

"Negative. He sabotaged the Tiber. *It's down for the count."*

"Understood. *Defiant* out." Ro looked toward Ensign Crosswhite at the tactical console and made a quick slashing gesture. Crosswhite closed the comm channel as Ro stood from the command chair. "Tactical, get a lock on the *Rio Grande*. Helm, set an intercept course."

Crosswhite and Tenmei both replied "Aye, sir" as they executed Ro's commands. The magenta-haired tactical officer was the first to add, "I have a lock on the runabout."

Ro folded her hands behind her back and projected quiet confidence. "Raise shields, charge tractor beam, and arm phasers, one-quarter power. Target the *Rio Grande*'s engines."

"All systems ready," Crosswhite said. "The *Rio Grande* will enter weapons range in nine seconds." Sensor data appeared on the main viewscreen, superimposed over the runabout.

All eyes were on the viewscreen or on Ro, so no one noticed as, with a subtle tap of one little finger, Tenmei triggered the sabotage she'd prepared four days earlier.

Thunder resounded through the hull as the ship lurched and heaved, knocking the captain off her feet and pinning the rest of the bridge officers against their consoles. On the viewscreen, the heavens pitched and rolled, turning bright stars into chaotic streaks. The overhead lights stuttered into darkness, and Tenmei winced and braced herself for her pièce de résistance.

The bottom half of her duty station erupted into sparks and shrapnel, and she barely jumped clear of a fireball that belched from her fractured wraparound console, blackening the overhead. She hit the deck with her hands singed and bleeding and her uniform smoldering from dozens of tiny bits of red-hot debris.

Captain Ro kneeled and swatted glowing embers off Tenmei's torso and arms. "Lieutenant! Are you hurt?"

Tenmei's voice was hoarse from the toxic smoke she'd inhaled. "I'll live."

Reassured, the captain turned to get answers from Crosswhite. "Report!"

"Primary systems offline." The ensign struggled in vain to coax information from her console. "We have comms, but sensors are down. Not sure what hit us, or where it started."

Ro slapped her combadge. "Bridge to engineering! Damage report!"

Chief O'Brien sounded calm over the comm despite the cacophony of shouting and warning sirens in the engineering compartment. *"No damage to the engines, but command-and-control systems are shot—even the auxiliaries. I hate to say it, sir . . . but we're adrift."*

The captain simmered for a moment. Then she turned her eyes upward, as if she saw something far off, through the ship's bulkheads. She tapped her combadge. "Ro to *Rio*

Grande. Well-played, Doctor. I salute you. But if I ever catch you, I am going to *kick your ass.*"

Crosswhite silenced a soft chirping on the communications panel. "BPOC reports the *Rio Grande* has gone to warp, Captain."

"Noted, Ensign. Hail the station and tell Commander Stinson to send the *Glyrhond* to tow us home for repairs." Ro extended a hand to Tenmei, clasped her forearm, and helped her to her feet. "Go get yourself patched up."

Tenmei shook her head. "I'll be fine, Captain."

"I didn't ask you for a status report. I gave you an order." A jog of her head. "Go."

"Aye, sir." Tenmei left the bridge holding her burned and shrapnel-torn palms in front of her chest like a surgeon with ungloved clean hands heading into an operating room.

As she made her way aft to the turbolift and down one deck to the medical bay, she reflected on the fact that there was little chance any hard evidence would ever be found to link her to the sabotage of the *Defiant.* Inevitably, someone would note the anomaly of her unscheduled relief of Crosswhite from the overnight watch a few days earlier, but that alone would not be enough to merit a court-martial.

But even if Tenmei hadn't been certain of that—even if her role in Bashir's escape would have cost her everything—she knew she would still have done her part, and done it gladly.

For Julian, her friend.

For the people of Andor.

And not least of all . . . for Shar.

Once, long ago, she and Shar had been in love. Or at least, they had thought they were. Circumstances had pulled them apart by subjecting them to forces greater than they could resist: family, duty, old vows, and, more than anything, an ever-widening gulf of time and space. But even though she was no longer *in love* with him, she still loved him, and there was nothing she wouldn't do to help him and his beautiful, tragic, passionate people.

The medical bay door opened ahead of her, and she held up her scorched hands to show Doctor Pascal Boudreaux the reason for her visit. The stout, dark-haired Louisiana native motioned for Tenmei to take a seat on the nearer of the compartment's two biobeds.

As she settled in, Boudreaux grabbed a medical tricorder, a hypospray, and a dermal regenerator, then he joined her and turned on his bedside manner. "Lay back." She admired his rich Creole accent and did as he said. He eased the hypospray to her throat. She felt a negligible tingle as he injected her and explained, "For the pain." Like a promise fulfilled, the analgesic dulled the persistent hot stinging in her hands and left her woozy.

His hands moved with slow, methodical precision, guiding the dermal regenerator's beam over her seared flesh, restoring it to unblemished perfection while she watched. He noticed her attention and paused after treating her left arm. "How do you feel, Lieutenant? You are okay?"

She answered with a calm heart. "Yeah, Doc. . . . I think I am."

Eighteen

Leonard James Akaar was a powerful man, in many senses of the word. A scion of Capellan royalty, the son of a *teer,* he had inherited a fearsome physique. Taller than most other humanoids, his broad shoulders, barrel chest, and pronounced musculature would impress even the most jaded Klingon warrior, and despite having just celebrated his one hundred eighteenth birthday (by Earth reckoning), he was still healthy and robust, and his mind was as sharp as the blades of a *kligat.* Only his bone-white hair betrayed his age, though his subordinates assured him frequently that it made him look not elderly but "distinguished."

He knew that all his physical attributes and prowess, however striking, were nothing compared to the true power he wielded as Starfleet's highest-ranking general officer. When he gave the word, great fleets moved, armies took action, and the fates of billions were decided. Countless beings lived or perished each day by the force of his commands. In his right hand he held the power of life, and clutched in his left was the dark might of death.

So why did he constantly feel as if he were at the mercy of events beyond his control?

He trained his focus on the Efrosian woman from Starfleet Intelligence who had barged into his office moments earlier. "Repeat that, please?"

"Doctor Julian Bashir has escaped custody on Bajor."

Commander Sarai's report remained as much a non se-
quitur now as it had the first time Akaar had heard it. "I was
not aware that Doctor Bashir was *in* custody."

"He was, sir. President Pro Tem Ishan ordered his arrest
three hours ago, from Betazed."

Akaar suspected there was more to Sarai's narrative. "On
what grounds?"

"Conspiracy to commit espionage, and illegal access to
the Shedai Meta-Genome."

Her report jogged Akaar's memory. "You mentioned
something about that in a staff meeting last week, didn't you?"

"Five days ago, sir. At the Monday morning senior staff
briefing."

"And I seem to recall you were ordered not to pursue
this."

"I didn't."

"So, it's a *coincidence* that the president pro tem issued
an arrest order based on a report that was never supposed to
leave this headquarters?" Her pause was damning. "We'll re-
visit that in a moment. Were Bashir and his colleagues working on the Andorian cure, as you suspected?"

"Aye, sir. Their computers and storage systems were impounded, but it seems as if all the Meta-Genome data had
been securely deleted before we arrived."

"What about the cure? Did they find it?"

"If they did, they left no trace of it, sir."

Her news perplexed Akaar. "Why would they go to
so much effort, only to erase all their work?" A troubling
thought occurred to him. "Do we know where Bashir's
headed?"

"His departure trajectory from the Bajor system suggests
he's en route to Andor."

More notions and theories spun in the admiral's imagination. "Why go to Andor, unless . . . unless he *already has the cure*. He must have hidden it, smuggled it out somehow."

"Sir, if we can make that deduction, the Typhon Pact likely can as well. It's against their interests to let Bashir deliver that cure to Andor. If they capture him, they could present the cure to Andor as their own work—and that would be a political disaster for the Federation."

She was right, and that vexed him. He paced behind his desk. "We need to handle this with care. One mistake and we could end up in a shooting war with the Typhon Pact." He tapped the internal comm switch on his desk. "Yeoman, get in here."

Seconds later his office door slid open, admitting the low bustling of comm chatter, muted conversations, and computer feedback tones from the command center on the lower level outside Akaar's office. His yeoman, an absurdly young-looking Vulcan man whose name Akaar had yet to learn, hurried in clutching a padd and a stylus. "Yes, Admiral?"

"Get admirals Nechayev, Batanides, and Bennett in here, on the double."

The Vulcan furrowed his steep brows. "Admiral James Bennett from the JAG office?"

"Do you know of *another* admiral in Starfleet named Bennett?"

The yeoman about-faced as he answered. "No, sir. Right away, sir."

"Get back here." Akaar waited while the Vulcan pivoted around to stand at attention.

"Sir?"

"Track down the *Aventine* and get me Captain Dax on a

real-time subspace channel." He shooed the Vulcan out of his office with urgent waves. "That's all. Proceed. Move."

The yeoman made a hasty exit. As the door closed, Akaar returned to his desk and sat down. He folded his hands on the desktop and trained the full force of his stone-faced condemnation on the Efrosian subordinate in front of him. "Now, then, Commander—let's take a moment to discuss what I'm going to do about *you*."

Nineteen

It was an inescapable fact of life in Starfleet, Ezri Dax had decided, that on the *Aventine* crises only ever happened when she was trying to sleep. After tossing and sprawling for nearly two hours after she had turned in for the night, she had drifted off sometime just after 0315—which made the shrilling of the overhead comm so damned unwelcome at 0439.

"Bridge to Captain Dax." It was the ship's senior science officer and third-in-command, Lieutenant Commander Gruhn Helkara. The young Zakdorn's voice trembled with urgency.

Dax stifled a groan and a softly muttered curse, then pinched the sleep from the corners of her eyes as she sat up. "Gruhn, unless we're under attack—"

"Fleet Admiral Akaar is waiting to talk with you on a secure channel from Earth."

That explained Gruhn's tone of alarm. "Patch it down to my quarters."

She pushed off the covers and forced her weary limbs out of bed. A yawn contorted her face as she scooped up her dark-blue bathrobe from the bench at the foot of her bed and wrapped it around herself on the short walk to her quarters' main room where a secure comm terminal sat on a desk, its incoming-signal light blinking in the darkness.

With both hands, Dax pushed her sleep-mussed black hair from her forehead, then sat down in front of the terminal. She opened the channel and squinted slightly as the screen burst to brilliant life with a sunlit image of Starfleet's white-haired, stern-faced commander. "Admiral. Sorry to keep you waiting."

Akaar skipped the preambles and pleasantries. *"I have new orders for you. Because of their sensitive and personal nature, I want to discuss them with you directly."*

"Personal for *who*, sir?"

"For you, Captain." There was regret in his eyes as he continued. *"I'm to understand you once had an intimate relationship with Doctor Julian Bashir, did you not?"*

The inquiry summoned old habits of defensiveness Dax had thought long expunged. "I did, sir. But that was years ago. It's long behind us."

The admiral's demeanor turned cagey. *"But you remain close, correct?"*

Where was he going with this? "We're still friends, yes. Has something happened?"

"Doctor Bashir is facing charges of espionage and high treason. He was arrested on Bajor a few hours ago, but he broke custody and fled in the Rio Grande. *Attempts to pursue him were foiled by acts of sabotage on the* Tiber *and the* Defiant."

Uncharitable as it was, Dax imagined such a fiasco must somehow be connected to Bashir's romance with former Starfleet Intelligence field agent Sarina Douglas—but she pushed away that notion for lack of proof. "Admiral, there must be some mistake—"

"I wish there were, Captain. But there is more than ample evidence that Doctor Bashir and his accomplices acquired classified Starfleet Intelligence archive files through—"

"Pardon me, sir—accomplices?"

Akaar's expression darkened. *"Four of the Federation's preeminent medical experts appear to have been helping him analyze and repurpose the stolen intel."*

"To what end?"

Her question seemed to put Akaar on the spot. His mandibular muscles clenched and relaxed, as if he were grinding his teeth. *"That's not important, Captain. What matters is that we believe he escaped with a copy of some or all of this classified information, and it's imperative that we capture him and recover the data before it falls into the wrong hands."*

"And you feel the *Aventine* is best suited to this mission because . . . ?"

"You know him, Captain. How he works, how he thinks, what he's capable of. Who he might turn to for help. And because we suspect his current destination is Andor, you and your ship are perfectly positioned to intercept him."

Dax had to concede the admiral's reasoning was sound, but questions lingered. "Why do you think he's heading to Andor?"

Another pause by Akaar signaled another attempt to deflect Dax's question. *"Again, Captain, for now we think it's best to compartmentalize such intel on a need-to-know—"*

"Sir, if you want me to get inside Julian's"—she cleared her throat—"inside Doctor Bashir's head, I need to know as much as possible about what he's doing, and even more important, what *he* thinks he's doing. If you need me to withhold certain details from my crew, so be it. But I can't even begin to predict his behavior unless I know his objective."

Her argument left Akaar mute for a moment. When the admiral looked up, he wore a resigned expression. *"Very well, Captain. The following information is for you only—it is not to be shared with your crew, not even with your XO."*

"Understood, sir."

"Through channels of which we are currently unaware, Doctor Bashir acquired a copy of Starfleet's archive file about the Shedai Meta-Genome. He and his colleagues claim that they used the Meta-Genome to design a cure to the Andorian fertility crisis. That's what we think he's trying to deliver to someone on Andor, most likely Professor Marthrossi zh'Thiin, or your mutual former crewmate Thirishar ch'Thane. Our orders are to prevent that delivery, recover all copies of the cure, and take Doctor Bashir into custody, as quickly as possible."

Confusion and indignation made Dax recoil slightly in her chair. "Admiral, are you telling me that we've been ordered to stop him from completing a *mercy* mission?"

"Ours is not to reason why, Captain. Ours is but to obey the whims of the chief executive."

"Sir, enacting a politically motivated embargo is one thing, but—"

"Let me clarify the situation, Captain." Akaar leaned in, filling the screen with his weathered visage. *"I am under direct orders from the president pro tem to apprehend Bashir with all due haste. To that end, he has directed me to redeploy all ships currently tasked to the Andor embargo to the capture of Doctor Bashir. If someone other than you finds him first, I would dread to think how they might interpret Ishan's subsequent orders. I, for one, would sleep better tonight if I knew that Bashir was safely in custody aboard the* Aventine.*"*

Dax knew better than to ask the admiral to elaborate on what "subsequent orders" Starfleet might receive from the president pro tem following Bashir's arrest. Realizing that she was being tasked not with a manhunt but with a clandestine search and rescue, she accepted the orders in the spirit they had been given. "Understood, sir."

"Good. And Captain? Work quickly. Your 'reinforcements' are closer than you think."

Stars flashed past the *Rio Grande,* slipping away like all the years and days and hours of Bashir's life that had led him to this moment. He couldn't deny that it was exhilarating to be a fugitive, to be on the run. His heart was beating faster, his breathing had grown deeper. He felt more alive than he had in months. For the first time in years, he felt as if his actions *meant something.*

Not much time left, he realized with a look at the long-range sensors. He accessed the ship's log system and initiated a new recording. "Personal log, supplemental. Doctor Julian Bashir recording. By the time this log is recovered and reviewed, my efforts to bring a cure to the Andorian people will be over—either because I'll have succeeded or because I was captured in the attempt. Some will call me a traitor for defying the orders of the lawful civilian government of the Federation. I don't imagine my chosen defense—that those orders are immoral—will carry much weight in a court-martial. And though I've taken steps to shift the venue in which my case might be heard, I hold little hope that I will succeed. I know that, from a legal standpoint, I am grasping at straws. Unfortunately, even if I should enjoy the best of circumstances, I fear my life will be irrevocably altered. Long ago, Thomas Wolfe wrote, 'You can't go home again.' He meant it figuratively, but in my case it will also be literally true. I can never go back to Deep Space Nine . . . or to Earth . . . or, for that matter, to the Federation. And even if some future government were to pardon me, I doubt Starfleet would be so forgiving.

"So know that I have not undertaken this course of action lightly. My actions were done with full awareness of their consequences, and I will accept them all. But place no blame on those I duped into helping me. My fellow physicians, my peers—none of them knew the true origin of what they were working on. Only I possessed that knowledge, just as I alone now carry the last chance of survival for the Andorian people in my blood.

"Call me a traitor if you wish. Call me a hero. Or forget my name completely. It makes no difference. As long as I complete my mission, the continued existence of the Andorian people will be my legacy. Everything else . . . is mere sound and fury."

He switched off the log recorder and saved his message.

On the other side of the runabout's cockpit, an alert warbled. Bashir got up and moved to the tactical station. One of the scenarios he had programmed the sensors to watch for had just transpired: long-range scans had detected multiple Starfleet vessels adjusting their headings and velocities to move into the sector from which the *Rio Grande* was approaching Andor.

Fortunately, with the transponder disabled, they won't recognize me right away. He checked the registry codes of the vessels that appeared to be tasked with intercepting him. One was a short-range patrol cruiser, the *Sarrakesh*; it was too slow and too far away to pose any real danger to the *Rio Grande,* so Bashir put it out of his thoughts. Two larger vessels, the *Falchion* and the *Warspite,* were of greater concern. While the *Falchion* was only a *Sabre*-class light cruiser, she was extremely fast—much faster than the runabout. And the *Warspite* was a formidable threat indeed: a huge *Sovereign*-class starship under the command of a noteworthy young captain. That was not a confrontation Bashir had any desire to hasten.

But more worrisome than any of those was the fourth Starfleet vessel, which was cutting a swift path through subspace and heading directly for the *Rio Grande*.

A good thing, then, that I did not think stealing a runabout would be the answer to all my problems. He adjusted his course slightly and then started disabling several of the safety systems in the runabout's warp core. Outrunning the *Falchion* and the *Warspite* would pose no great challenge, as long as they didn't isolate his ship as their target in the next two hours. A few radical changes to the ship's warp-field geometry, combined with pushing it nearly a full warp factor past its rated maximum speed, would mask the *Rio Grande's* identity well enough.

A whine of protest from the warp coils resonated through the little ship's hull. Bashir began shutting down systems and diverting their power to the inertial dampers. He started with the tactical grid, figuring he had no real chance of prevailing in an armed conflict with even the least of his pursuers; next he sealed the aft compartments and shut down their life support. Then he routed all the reserve battery power to the ship's structural integrity field. By slow degrees, the whining from the warp coils faded away, restoring the runabout's normal ambience—a deep, steady thrumming of the engines punctuated by soft computer noise.

He checked his speed and position. *So far, so good. I just might make it to Andor alive.*

But still his eyes kept returning to that fourth, troubling sensor reading. His fastest pursuer. The one that his gut told him would ruin everything. He reminded himself that he had the advantage of a genetically engineered intellect, but it was little solace; he was up against a captain with nine lives of experience who knew all his quirks, all his tricks, and all his fears.

With each passing second, Captain Dax and the *U.S.S. Aventine* drew closer, and Bashir knew there would be no outrunning it, no outfighting it, and no stopping it—or her.

He turned his eyes toward the stars and resigned himself to whatever came next.

Let the games begin.

Twenty

If there was one thing above all else that Ro Laren missed about the life she'd led before taking command of Deep Space 9 nearly six years earlier, it was the priceless gift of relative public anonymity. She stepped through the parting airlock doors onto the main concourse of the new station's horizontal *x*-ring and was met by a clamor of shouting voices and a crushing wave of bodies all thrusting recording devices into her face.

The reporters' frantic queries bled together. "Captain Ro! Is it true that Doctor Bashir hijacked one of the station's runabouts?" "Captain! How was the *Defiant* disabled?" "Was the Typhon Pact involved?" "Has Doctor Bashir been charged with a crime?" "Does Starfleet know where Bashir is going?" "What were Bashir and his colleagues working on at the conference center?" "Is Bashir a Typhon Pact spy?" "Do you think Doctor Bashir is guilty?"

Ro shouldered through the throng and tuned out their barrage of questions. The knot of journalists followed her for several meters down the concourse until their paths were blocked by a security detail that let Ro pass before forming a shoulder-to-shoulder line across the passage. Anchoring the line at its center was Ensign Nyyl Saygur, a Brikar who Ro had been assured was small for his species, even though he looked like a walking hillside compared to every other member of the station's crew. Saygur halted the procession of reporters by holding out one massive, three-fingered bronze hand and intoning in his thunderous baritone, "No."

The flurry of inquiries that had peppered Ro came to an abrupt halt. Satisfied that none of the correspondents were foolhardy enough to challenge the high-density humanoid, who was surprisingly light on his feet thanks to the gravity compensator he wore as part of his uniform, Ro continued on her way and slipped inside a waiting turbolift. "The Hub," she said.

Her lift car sped away toward one of the spokes that linked the ring to the station's core. Though there was no sensation of motion, the car's position indicator tracked its progress through the station, changing perspective and scale as appropriate. Once the turbolift reached an intersection with a vertical ring, it made a swift ascent to the command level that crowned the new Frontier-class starbase.

Ro stepped out of the turbolift. As she walked to her office, Colonel Cenn rose from his seat overlooking the Hub and fell into step beside her. He kept his voice low for the sake of discretion. "I just reviewed the latest updates on the hunt for the *Rio Grande*. Still no contact."

"Have we computed its maximum possible flight distance?"

Cenn held up a padd with a small star chart on it. "We have two scenarios. One for the *Rio Grande* as rated, and one that assumes Bashir will overdrive the warp coils."

"Go with the second one. And get sensor logs from every listening post, sensor buoy, and independent array between here and Andor. Flag any ship we can't identify."

"Already on it, sir. We're analyzing a small mountain of data right now." They reached the door to her office, and Cenn stepped in front of it, blocking Ro's path. "One more thing, Captain. You have a message waiting for you . . . from Doctor Bashir."

"How do you know what messages I have?"

His voice dropped to a whisper. "Because he copied all senior staff on the message, as well as the station's JAG office and the chief attending physician at Sector General."

"I'm not gonna like what it says, am I?"

"I wouldn't presume to speculate, sir."

She inhaled angrily and reminded herself to breathe, slowly and evenly. "Continue the search, and let me know if we get any leads on the *Rio Grande*."

"Aye, sir." Cenn stepped clear of the office's doorway. He watched Ro enter her office, and then he returned to his seat and resumed monitoring reports on his command panel.

Ro strode to her desk. "Computer, lock door." The order was acknowledged by a quick double-tone. Confident of her privacy, she settled in at her desk and called up the message from Bashir. It was a simple written missive, sent from his account on the station. Its subject line was terse and unambiguous: LETTER OF RESIGNATION.

The body of the message was nearly as sparse:

14 September 2385
Stardate 62703.9

Captain Ro Laren, Commanding Officer
Starbase Deep Space 9, Bajor Sector

Captain Ro,

I hereby resign my Starfleet commission and my billet as chief medical officer of Deep Space 9, with immediate effect.

The immoral nature of the orders given to me by President
Pro Tem Ishan Anjar have left me no choice but to end my
Starfleet career and follow the dictates of my conscience
as a medical doctor and a citizen of the United Federation
of Planets.

With profound regret,
Commander Julian S. Bashir, M.D.

Ro read and reread the words on her display and felt a
cold sensation brew in her gut. As many times as Bashir had
disobeyed orders or defied regulations in the name of principle, he had never before taken the step of formally severing
his relationship with Starfleet. Only now, as Ro sat and read
Bashir's pointedly accusatory resignation, did she realize
that the headstrong physician had no intention of seeking a
compromise or accepting some half-measure in order to save
himself. He had declared his career and commission forfeit in
the name of his cause.

*He's more committed than anyone suspected. Which means
he's also far more dangerous.* She wondered: If he was willing
to do this, how much further would he go? Would he set aside
his Hippocratic oath long enough to use force to accomplish
his mission? Would he decide the preservation of a species
outweighed the value of individual lives?

She had no way to answer those questions, but this
change in Bashir's status quo was clearly a warning sign that
this crisis was not one to be treated lightly. She opened an
internal comm channel to Cenn's post outside in the Hub.
"Colonel, has Doctor Bashir's message been transmitted yet
to Starfleet Command?"

*"No, sir. It seems he expects either you or the senior JAG
officer to do that."*

"As per protocol. Naturally."

Cenn struck a cautious note. *"Sir? Should I direct the JAG office to hold the letter?"*

For a moment, Ro considered doing Bashir a favor—deleting all copies of his message from the station's archives and instructing the JAG office to disregard it. Then she realized that it was not her call to make—and that doing so might inflict more harm than good on Bashir. *He made this decision for a reason. Let him live with it.* "No. Tell Commander Desjardins to forward the letter to Starfleet Command, ASAP. And alert the ships hunting the *Rio Grande* that Doctor Bashir is no longer a Starfleet officer . . . and should be treated as a civilian criminal."

Music mingled with the ringing of gambling machines and the bright noise of celebratory voices, filling Quark's with a joyous roar.

Sarina Douglas huddled over a pint of Bajoran ale and kept to herself at one end of the bar. She seemed to be the only customer drinking alone that evening.

The mixed-species crew of a civilian freighter had taken over a block of tables in the center of the main room on the first floor, and their raucous drinking songs and gales of throaty laughter had forced all of the bar's other patrons to be that much louder just to be heard over the merchant crew's revels. Legions of empty glasses littered their tables, the tops slick with spilled exotic libations whose origins read like a travelogue of known space.

A cluster of half-in-the-bag Starfleet enlisted personnel and noncommissioned officers had commandeered the just-installed dartboard for an impromptu championship. Chief Petty Officer Wilik held a comfortable lead over his nearest

challenger—a feat that Douglas chalked up to the absence
of chief engineer Miles O'Brien, who had secluded himself
in his quarters since Bashir's hijacking of the *Rio Grande*.
Douglas couldn't blame O'Brien for seeking solitude. Bashir
had been so intent on his top-secret project that he hadn't
even said good-bye to his best friend before leaving the station to work on Bajor—and his only farewell had been a letter
of resignation.

Using the reflective surface of the bartop, she snuck a
look at the two faces peeking down through the railing of
the bar's second level, from directly above her: a pair of
undercover Starfleet Intelligence agents posing as civilians.
An untrained observer would not have distinguished the
pair from the other patrons that flanked them, but Douglas
had noted the way the Denobulan man and Trill woman
surveyed the bar at regular intervals and how discreet they
tried to be when concluding each sweep with a downward
glance in her direction. She also recognized the SI-standard
comm on the woman's belt; its presence had been betrayed
when the woman's shirt had ridden up slightly as she sat
down.

Someone's keeping tabs on me, Douglas mused. It
wasn't unexpected. Her relationship with Bashir was common knowledge among her crewmates, and in the wake
of his flight from custody, everything associated with him
was under heavy scrutiny—including and especially her
actions, both on Bajor and back here on the station. She
had first spotted the two SI agents on The Plaza, when
she'd spied their reflections following hers in storefront
windows.

Just as predictable as being placed under surveillance,

she had been placed on inactive status pending the conclusion of the investigation into Bashir's crimes against
Starfleet and the Federation. Though she had been careful
to cover her tracks and distance herself from any incrimi-
nating evidence, she expected it would be weeks, at least,
before she was permitted to return to duty. Whether anyone
would still trust her at that point, or ever again, remained
to be seen. *A damn shame. Just when it felt like I was one of
the gang.*

Quark walked quickly behind his line of bartenders,
double-checking their work and offering unsubtle correc-
tions when he found flaws, which was often. Each tense
exchange left the middle-aged Ferengi's lobes flushed a
half-shade brighter pink. He was a few meters away and
about to step in Douglas's direction. She checked the
reflection in the bartop and waited until her SI minders
swept their stares past her. As soon as she was free of their
direct scrutiny, she used her best sleight of hand to sneak
a nearly flat isolinear chip underneath her napkin. Then
she summoned Quark with a tiny lift of her chin. "I could
use a refill."

He picked up her empty glass. "Jalanda Midnight Ale?"

"That's the one."

He dropped the empty glass down a matter-reclamator
slot, grabbed a clean pint from a shelf under the bar, and
lifted it to an old-fashioned tap spout. A tug on the handle,
and he was filling the glass with amber liquid topped by a
thick, foamy head. "You know your brews. The Bajorans
are so proud of this one, they won't let me replicate it. Gas-
powered kegs or nothing."

"I know. That's why I like it." Another stolen glance

confirmed her minders were focused elsewhere for a few seconds. She lowered her voice. "I need a favor."

"Favors cost extra."

"As always. I need you to pass a message through your diplomatic channels."

"To whom?"

"Shar. On Andor."

The Ferengi cast a furtive look at the SI agents' reflected faces on the bartop between them. "I don't think your new pals would like that."

"What they don't know won't hurt us, Quark."

"And what I don't get involved in won't hurt me at all. I like my way better."

"It's just eight simple words, coded on a chip under my napkin."

He drained off a bit of excess foam from the top of her beer. "Bringing a message in was one thing. Everyone's on their guard now. And between you and me, I don't like getting in the middle of messes like this one—especially when it means lying to Ro."

"I have fifty thousand Federation credits standing by for a transfer to your account."

With balletic grace, he swept away her napkin and the isolinear chip it concealed while dropping a coaster in their place, and then he set down her new pint of ale and grinned. "Always a pleasure to serve you, Commander. Let me know if you need anything else."

"I will, Quark. Thanks."

She noted the preternatural skill with which Quark tucked the palmed isolinear chip into his pocket while distracting casual onlookers by making a show of crumpling and discarding the napkin, all while walking away from Douglas to berate another one of his employees.

Douglas chanced a direct look at the two agents on the level above her. They were still there, and neither seemed aware of the transaction that had just occurred under their noses. Her poker face as steady as her hands, she picked up her ale and took a long, slow sip.

My part's done, she told herself. *The rest is up to Julian.*

Twenty-one

Status lights along the bridge bulkheads flashed amber at long intervals, a steady reminder that the *Aventine* was at Yellow Alert as it closed in on the *Rio Grande*. All around Dax her crew worked with keen efficiency, sharing data and coordinating their efforts, while she sat in her command chair, her focus keen on the image of the runabout on the main viewer.

A flurry of ionized particles jetted from the runabout's starboard warp nacelle as it veered to port at high warp speed. At the helm, Lieutenant Tharp adjusted the *Aventine*'s heading to match. "Another course change, Captain. Compensating." The Bolian flight control officer checked his instruments. "Speed constant at warp seven-point-eight."

Seated at the console to Tharp's left was Lieutenant Oliana Mirren, the senior operations officer. She monitored the sensor readings that were being routed to her console. "The *Rio Grande*'s shields are still up, Captain." The lithe, dark-haired human woman looked back at Dax. "Should I send another hail to Doctor Bashir, sir?"

"Repeat our last."

Mirren acknowledged the order and pressed a key to transmit a recording of the message they had sent to the *Rio Grande* four times already: a direct order to Bashir to stand down, drop to impulse, surrender his vessel, and prepare to be boarded. She waited several seconds, then shook her head. "No reply, Captain."

Dax leaned forward and watched the runabout begin another series of sloppy evasive maneuvers. Intercepting the little ship had been easy for the *Aventine*. With its slipstream drive and pinpoint-precise navigation, the *Vesta*-class explorer had catapulted nearly two dozen light-years in a matter of minutes once the *Rio Grande* had been identified. And now that the runabout was in the *Aventine*'s sights, it was only a matter of time until the smaller ship was captured. So why was Bashir prolonging the inevitable? Dax was baffled. *He must know he has no chance of outrunning us or outgunning us. So what the hell is he doing?*

She resigned herself to the need for the use of force and turned toward her first officer, who as usual stood to the right of her command chair, even though he had a chair of his own. "Sam? Do we have a weapons lock on the runabout's shield emitters and warp core?"

Bowers threw a questioning look at the security chief. Kedair nodded once and poised her hand over the phaser controls on her console. The XO glanced at the *Rio Grande*, and he seemed as unhappy about the situation as Dax did. "Weapons locked, sir."

"Set phasers to one-quarter power and fire to disable."

The XO nodded to Kedair, who fired the ship's phasers. On the main viewscreen, brilliant orange pulses hammered the *Rio Grande*, and in just three hits the ship's shields collapsed and it tumbled out of warp speed. Bowers reacted with calm precision. "Tharp, come about, bring us out of warp, and put us at station twenty thousand kilometers from the *Rio Grande*. Mirren, stand by to put a tractor beam on the runabout."

In less than a minute the *Aventine* was hovering above and behind the *Rio Grande*, which appeared to be drifting without impulse power. A pale golden shaft of energy lanced through the void and snared the runabout. "Tractor beam engaged." Mirren looked troubled by new sensor data on her panel. "Sirs? I'm reading no life-forms aboard the runabout."

Dax sprang to her feet and doled out orders on the move. "I'm going over there. Sam, Lonnoc, with me. Gruhn, you have the conn."

Helkara handed off his post to a junior officer and moved to the center seat. "Aye, sir."

Kedair sidestepped from her station to block Dax's path to the turbolift. "Captain, I respectfully suggest you let me secure the runabout before you beam over."

"Suggestion noted and overruled." She stepped around the Takaran security chief and led her and Bowers into the turbolift. "Let's move."

Bowers and Kedair said nothing on the turbolift ride, nor on the short walk to the transporter room. A male human chief petty officer stood behind the transporter console and nodded at Dax and the others as they entered and stepped onto the platform, found their way to separate pads, and faced forward. The chief powered up the system with a pass of his hand and looked to the captain for clearance to proceed. Dax took a breath. "Energize."

The chief swept his hand across the controls, and the energizer coils overhead and underfoot filled the compartment with a swiftly rising hum. Then came a shimmering veil and a moment of paralysis, followed by a pulse of white light—

—that faded to reveal the cockpit of the *Rio Grande*. Kedair moved aft, toward the crew-support module. Dax studied the commander's console.

Bowers pivoted toward the helm. "Autopilot's engaged. Not sure for how long. Looks like Bashir disabled the flight data recorder along with the transponder." He poked at the controls. "So much for figuring out how long since he ditched."

Dax studied the cramped cockpit with trained eyes. "There are ways of finding out. I'll have a forensic team sweep the ship for anything Julian left behind. Even skin cells might be revealing, if we find them soon enough."

Kedair returned from the aft section of the runabout. "Empty. Bashir's definitely not on board, and the transport and sensor logs have been wiped. He must have abandoned ship."

Bowers motioned past Dax toward the commander's console. "What's that?"

"A personal log." Dax tapped the screen to play it back.

Bashir's recorded voice emanated from the overhead speakers.

"Personal log, supplemental. Doctor Julian Bashir recording. By the time this log is recovered and reviewed, my efforts to bring a cure to the Andorian people will be over—either because I'll have succeeded or because I was captured in the attempt. Some will call me a traitor for defying the orders of the lawful civilian government of the Federation. I don't imagine my chosen defense—that those orders are immoral—will carry much weight in a court-martial. And though I've taken steps—"

Dax halted the playback. "I've heard enough. Lonnoc, copy it and send it back to the ship for analysis. Sam, send a copy to Starfleet Command. I'm sure they'll want it as evidence." She tapped her combadge. "Dax to *Aventine.*"

Helkara answered. *"Go ahead, Captain."*

"Tow the *Rio Grande* into Shuttlebay Two and beam us back, on the double."

"Aye, sir. Stand by for transport."

As they waited to be transported, Dax secretly fumed at being outmaneuvered by Bashir. "Julian wouldn't have beamed off this ship unless he had somewhere else to go. And since he hasn't reached Andor yet, he must be on another ship. Whatever it is, wherever it is—*find it.*"

Shadows roamed the streets of the Andorian capital. Everywhere Shar went, he felt spied upon. As night settled on Lor'Vela, its ancient, narrow cobblestone boulevards took on a darkling cast that put the young *chan* on his guard. He was keenly aware of his isolation; all his friends and allies were far away, and they felt more distant with each passing day. Should he find himself imprisoned again, this time there would be no one to secure his freedom. He would fade away, forlorn and forsaken, in the catacombs carved deep within the bedrock.

Ruddy light bled through careworn curtains, a meager glow all but swallowed by the night. Shar kept the hood of his cowl draped low to hide his face as he walked, but even so, a cruel wind snaked inside and chilled his antennae. A cold, dark season had dawned.

In the ten days since he had returned to the city, he hadn't stayed anywhere more than two consecutive nights. He had stashed clothes and weapons in small bags in hidden spaces all over the capital, and thanks to his Ferengi contacts, he had untraceable credit chips that he could use for small purchases such as meals or for short-distance trips in hired transports so that he could avoid being detected by the surveillance systems that monitored all public transit nodes. Living in a state of near-constant motion had worn him down quickly and left him wandering at times as if in a daze, plagued by dull headaches and a steady sensation of unsatisfied hunger.

A far cry from the life I used to lead.

He turned a corner and began the riskiest part of his evening walk. Each night, regardless of what roundabout route he had taken to get here, he strolled down this particular block, looking for any evidence that his contact was trying to signal him. By itself, walking here night after night was no crime, but Shar was wary of doing anything that might be detected as forming a pattern of behavior, so he made an effort to vary the timing of his visits. Sometimes he swung past at dusk; sometimes he passed this way before midnight; a few nights he had delayed his visit until an hour before sunrise. Each time, the signal had been dark.

Tonight it was lit: a single red candle burned in the alley-facing window of a decrepit, three-level dwelling. Whoever lived there likely had no idea of the significance of the signal or for whom it was intended. Based on Shar's admittedly limited understanding of espionage tradecraft, the resident of that dwelling was probably someone who was paid to light the candle when told and to not ask any questions, about anything, ever.

It was important not to draw attention to himself. He continued walking, his stride even and regular. His next objective was to retrieve the message. He tucked his hands inside his pockets, both to keep them warm and to confirm he still had his personal comm.

He left behind the residential sector the moment he crossed one of the capital's main thoroughfares, the aptly named Division Boulevard. A sparse traffic of hovercars cruised above the broad, four-lane roadway—automated vehicles serving the needs of the city's nighthawks. Shar kept his head down as he crossed the street into Sakina Commons, a commercial sector known for hosting a variety of around-the-clock businesses, most of them bars and restaurants. The area was a favorite of young professionals, particularly those who worked for the members of the Parliament Andoria.

Navigating by memory, he made his way to one of the quarter's less popular eateries. Its name was hand-painted in alien symbols above its tall arched gateway, which led to a long and narrow roofed path that reeked of stale urine. This evening the odor was so rank that Shar was relieved to get through the restaurant's front double doors and have his nose offended instead by some of the most nauseating victuals he had ever encountered.

SopveQpu' Gishka served a fusion menu: Klingon-Ferengi cuisine. Someone had made the dubious observation that both species had a penchant for eating live food and had hit upon the disgusting notion of melding such stomach-turning Klingon classics as *rokeg* blood pie or *gagh* with the Ferengi's emetic masterpieces, live tube grubs and Kytherian soft-shelled crabs. The only thing Shar liked about visiting this culinary house of horrors to pick up his messages was that, no matter how hungry he was before he came in, his appetite vanished the moment he stepped inside, and it often didn't return for several hours after he left.

If I could reduce this place to a hypospray, I'd have the ultimate diet aid.

He made his way to the back booth, which was always obstructed by a conical sign on the floor. Its warning was written in Klingon script, but Shar deduced it probably translated as CAUTION—WET FLOOR. He ignored it and slid into the booth. Then he waited.

A few minutes later, a fat middle-aged Klingon chef with prodigious jowls lumbered over to Shar's table. The exertion of propelling his own bulk the length of his restaurant left him struggling to catch his breath as he spoke. "What . . . do you . . . want?"

"I'll have the vegetarian plate."

There was nothing like a Klingon giving one the stink eye. "Sold out."

"My friend called ahead. He said you'd hold it for me."

"What . . . is your friend's . . . name?"

"Opportunity."

Disgusted, the Klingon chef plodded away in slow, rocking steps and vanished into his kitchen. Shar suspected the man didn't like him. *I can't imagine why; I'm quite likable.*

A few minutes later, the chef returned holding a large tin plate in one hand and a rolled napkin in the other. He dropped the platter on the table with such flair that its freight of wriggling *gree* worms scattered across the tabletop. Then he tossed the napkin into Shar's lap like an insult. "Grass-fed worms. *Qapla' novpu'.*"

There was something almost hypnotic about watching the worms spread out on the table, but Shar had seen and smelled enough of SopveQpu' Gishka. He unfurled the napkin and retrieved the isolinear chip hidden inside it. After a quick look around to make sure he wasn't being watched, he inserted the chip into a reader slot on his comm device and detached an in-ear transceiver that would let him listen to the chip's message without fear of eavesdroppers.

Through the earpiece, he heard a woman's voice read eight simple words.

"He has the answer. He's coming. Be ready."

He put away his earpiece, removed the isolinear chip from his comm, dropped the fragile strip of polymer onto the floor, and crushed it under his boot heel. Then he got up and made a quick exit to the street.

The message was better news than Shar had dared to hope for, and it had come much sooner than he had thought possible. Part of him knew he should be overjoyed. But he knew that not everyone on Andor would welcome Bashir and his cure. The *Treishya,* their political allies, and their Typhon Pact patrons would almost certainly do everything in their power to seize the cure for themselves if they found out about it.

As of that moment, Shar knew his mission had changed.

He also knew he was going to need help—and that he had only one place left to turn.

A quick about-face combined with a moment of inattention collided Bashir's head with a low overhead beam and left him seeing a red haze of pain for a few seconds. The crew spaces aboard the *S.S. Parham* were even more confined than those aboard the *Rio Grande,* despite the ship's greater size. Most of the interior volume of the *Caretta*-class freighter was devoted to cargo storage without life support, leaving only a few cramped berthing spaces, a narrow mess with a single combination replicator-reclamator, and a common head and sonic shower.

After changing into civilian clothes and stowing his single small duffel under the rack in the ship's guest quarters—which amounted to an empty storage closet with a bunk built into the bulkhead—he ducked through the low doorway into the main passage that ran down the center of the ship's only deck. The corridor was barely large enough for him to walk through without his shoulders touching the sides. He made his way forward, past the ship's sole escape pod, and ducked through another low, round-cornered hatchway into the cockpit.

Slouched in the port-side chair was the ship's owner, pilot, captain, and chief mechanic. Emerson Harris was a human man in his early thirties. There didn't seem to be a lot of muscle on his lean and wiry frame, but his hands bore the calluses of hard work. His long, square face was framed by short dark hair and distinguished by a low brow, a rudder-straight nose, and a pointed chin. Grime and food stains marred his red plaid shirt, whose sleeves he had torn off either for comfort or to avoid getting them snagged while he was making repairs on some hard-to-reach part of his rattletrap of a ship. Underneath the stained plaid pseudo-vest he wore an equally soiled white T-shirt, and both hung loosely over the top of his frayed and weathered work pants.

Harris greeted him with a broad grin and a soft Tennessee drawl. "Y'all settled in?"

Bashir dropped into the other cockpit seat. "Yes, thank you."

"Hope you don't mind the tight fit. Don't get many passengers."

"Well, then, thank you for making an exception."

He dismissed the courtesy with a wave. "Ain't nothin'. Least I could do after you fixed that problem for me last week."

"It seemed like the right thing to do."

Seven days earlier, the *Parham* had been docked at Deep Space 9 for a refueling stop when it was flagged for a random health and safety inspection by the dockmaster.

After Harris's ship had been cited for numerous violations, Douglas had brought the case to Bashir's attention and recommended that he grant the freighter pilot a blanket exemption—in return for a small favor: postponing his next run for up to one month, in order to wait and maintain comm silence at an arbitrary set of coordinates in interstellar space, until and unless hailed with a specific code phrase. At first Harris had balked at the suggestion, but a generous donation to his operating costs had persuaded him to take the deal rather than face the revocation of his flight license.

Bashir suspected that Douglas had arranged the *Parham*'s failed inspection, but judging from the slovenly conditions inside the vessel, she likely hadn't needed to make much of an effort to push the *Parham* over the line into full-blown code violations.

"So, uh, Doc . . . I don't mean to pry or nothin'—"

"Then don't."

Harris grew uneasy. "Sorry, but I gotta. I mean, look at this from where I'm sittin', Doc. You hail me from a Starfleet runabout—a damn fine ship, by the way. Faster than mine, with a cozier bunk, and armed to boot. And you ping me lookin' for a ride? What gives?"

It would do no good to spook the man, but he was already suspicious. Lying to him might make matters worse, depending upon how much he already knew about the situation. Bashir watched the man's face for revealing microexpressions as he asked, "What have you heard?"

The query made Harris look away, as if he were hiding something, too. He chewed on his answer for a second. "Comm blasts from Starfleet are callin' you a criminal. . . . Are you?"

"I guess that depends on one's point of view. What do you think?"

"I try not to judge, Doc."

"If you knew there was a warrant for my arrest, why did you meet me?"

Harris looked offended. "I gave my word, Doc. Said I'd be there for you, and I am."

"I appreciate that. Really, I do. I'd have been lost without you."

That seemed to quell some of Harris's doubt and anxiety. "So, what's on Andor?"

"People who need my help. Speaking of which, can't we go any faster?"

"Not much, no. But even if we could, I'd advise against it."

Bashir tried not to let his impatience show. "Why not?"

"Commercial traffic on the Andor Run averages warp five. We start haulin' ass, you might get there a few hours sooner, but we'd kick up a shitload of red flags doin' it. And seein' as there's a price on your head, I'd reckon that's the last thing you'd want."

Mollified, Bashir sat back and relaxed. "You make a fair point."

"Damn straight I do." He fiddled with the ship's flight controls for a few seconds, then turned back toward Bashir. "So, who're these people you're out to help? Friends of yours? Maybe got yourself a sweet blue honey down there?"

"No, nothing of the kind."

The skipper looked confused. "What's the rush, then? Someone owe you money?"

"I'm not in this for profit. Or for glory, in case that was your next question."

"Then level with me, Doc. What the hell am I mixed up in? Why does Starfleet want your butt in a sling?"

Bashir's first instinct was to deflect, lie, or somehow put an end to the conversation. Then his conscience stung him, and he realized that whether he had meant to do so or not, he had just put Harris's life in very real danger. *If I expect him to risk getting killed, I owe him the truth.*

"How much do you know about why Andor seceded from the Federation?"

The disheveled pilot shrugged. "Just what I hear on the news. Somethin' about they're dying off, and they blame us for hiding some top-secret files they think might've helped 'em find a cure. Then the Tholians said they have it and they'd share, so Andor told us to get lost."

"As it happens, every word of that is true. Now, even with the Tholians' help, the Andorians still haven't found their cure—but I have. And with your help, I plan to bring it to them."

"And what's in it for you?"

"Absolutely nothing. In fact, I fully expect more than a few interested parties will reward my efforts by trying to kill me before I complete my mission. . . . And you with me, I'm afraid."

To his surprise, Harris looked pleased. "All right, then. Sounds like a plan, Doc."

"You're taking this far better than I might have expected."

"Don't get much call to do good deeds. Figure it'll be a nice change of pace."

"Even though you'll be in terrible danger?"

Harris grinned. "I'm a ship captain, Doc. Risk is my business."

"You're the captain of an unarmed one-man freighter."

The younger man's mirth faltered. "Okay, so my business is delivering cargo." His jovial demeanor returned. "But I've been meaning to diversify."

It wasn't dawn itself to which Kellessar zh'Tarash objected; it was the fact that she was obliged to rouse herself from bed each day at sunrise—and sometimes earlier—when she would have much preferred to slumber until the crack of noon.

The buzzing of her alarm pulled apart her fragile curtain of dreams, and she forced herself out of bed with a weary groan. *Every year it gets harder,* she lamented, but just as quickly she felt self-conscious about her self-pity. She wasn't as young as she used to be—not that anyone else was, either—but she was far from old. She was in good health, and for an Andorian, she had barely begun to creep up on the lower threshold of middle age.

Gray predawn light bled around the edges of her bedroom curtains, enabling zh'Tarash to discern the elegant features of her sleeping lover, Rane. She was a lovely *shen,* but never more so than when she slept. Awake, her beauty was marred by the lingering shade of sorrow, just as zh'Tarash's was. Others rarely recognized that darkness in them, that void where love once had dwelled, but she and Rane knew each other so well that they no longer needed to speak of it. They had been bondmates, pledged to each other since their youth, consecrated in their union with the gentle grace of Isal, their group's *chan,* and the fierce pride of its *thaan,* Hosh.

More than four years had passed since the Borg invasion. Since the day that a sickly green bolt of fire cast down from orbit had leveled the planet's former capital and consumed

Hosh and Isal. Since the day that she and Rane had seen their lives cut in half.

She closed her eyes and pushed away the memories.

We will not speak of it. Not today. Not ever.

A deep breath, and zh'Tarash got out of bed. She collected her dressing gown from the chair in the corner, put it on, and tied it closed over her pajamas. On her way out of the bedroom, she let her fingertips whisper across Rane's cheek, and she felt a moment of mild envy that, as an artist, Rane enjoyed the privilege of sleeping in pretty much every day.

In another time, before the decimation of the homeworld by the Borg, before the scourge of the fertility crisis, zh'Tarash might have feared that her political rivals, or even society at large, might have tried to publicly shame her and Rane for their relationship. They had made no secret of their *tezha*—their exclusive sexual union outside the reproductive ritual of *shelthreth*—but then neither had many other fractured bondgroups that had suffered the ravages of the recent past. Faced with perils of a more existential quality, the Andorian people had begun to shift their mores. Lifestyles and behaviors that had once been condemned were becoming mainstream, or at the least tolerated as an inevitability.

Of course it helped that she and Rane had an additional rationale for remaining together and refusing new bondmates: their *thei*, Sennifaal th'Tarash. Crossing the hallway with gingerly steps, she cracked open his bedroom door. The six-year-old was still fast asleep; his antennae twitched ever so slightly, signaling that he was deep within a dream cycle.

May the winds of Uzaveh bring you gentle dreams, my thei.

Later, when he awoke, he would rouse Rane, who would make him breakfast and see him off to school. Then Rane would return home and paint in her studio until it was time to go back and bring Senn home for lunch and homework. It was a routine like any other, but zh'Tarash was grateful for it every day. She knew that she and her bondmates were among the few lucky ones, those who had succeeded in siring a healthy offspring when so many millions of others had endured the heartbreak of repeated miscarriages. On some level, she wondered if the tragic deaths of Isal and Hosh had been Uzaveh the Infinite's price for their child. If so, it was a price she would pay again—with her own life, if necessary.

She eased Senn's door shut and continued in feather steps down the hall and around the corner toward the kitchen, to conjure herself a mug of hot *katheka* from the replicator and jolt her brain into full consciousness before showering and making her way to the Parliament Andoria to endure another day of pointless prattle by ch'Foruta and his *Treishya* demagogues.

As she started to cross the living room, she stopped.

A stranger was sitting on the sofa, facing her.

Should I scream? Should I run? Terrified, she looked back toward the bedrooms. *What about Senn? Rane?* Seeing no option for retreat, she steeled herself and invoked her steadiest and most defiant tone of voice. "Who are you? And what are you doing in my home?"

The *chan* held up empty hands. "I beg your forgiveness, *Zha*. My name is Thirishar ch'Thane. I work with Professor zh'Thiin at the Science Institute."

She knew his name, and as her eyes adjusted to the dim light in the room, she recognized his face from briefings and news footage. "How did you get past my guards? And the alarms?"

A coy twitch of his antennae. "Sorry. Trade secret."

"And you've broken into my home because—?"

"I need to speak with you, but I can't risk coming to your office at Parliament."

"Why not?"

"Because your enemies are my enemies. The *Treishya* was behind the mob that burned down the Institute's headquarters. If they knew I was in the capital, they'd come after me."

She recalled ch'Thane's arrest a couple of weeks earlier. "You do seem to be at the top of their most-wanted list. But just because we share an enemy, that doesn't make us friends."

"Not yet, it doesn't. But it's a good place to start."

He remained seated as she edged into the room and stood in front of him. "All right. You want my trust? Tell me where to find Professor zh'Thiin and the rest of the Institute staff."

"All I can tell you is that they're someplace safe—for now."

"That's not the answer I was hoping for."

"Best I can give you."

She studied his face, seeking any telltale signs of a lie taking shape. "Why don't they come back? Things have been quieting down in the capital."

He shook his head. "Not for much longer. Something major is about to break, something that'll put the *Treishya* on the defensive. That's why I need your help."

The more he spoke, the more worried zh'Tarash became. "What kind of help?"

"I need you to facilitate safe passage and amnesty for Julian Bashir."

The human's name and an account of his crimes had topped the previous night's Parliamentary security briefing. "He's a fugitive from Starfleet justice. After all the work I've done to try to mend fences with the Federation, why would I antagonize them by helping *him*?"

"Because he's in trouble for trying to help *us*. I sent him the Shedai Meta-Genome data we got from the Tholians, along with all the work the professor and I had done over the last three years. And I just got a message back from him: He has the cure, and he's on his way here."

His news robbed her of her equilibrium, forcing her to sit down across from him. "You're telling me he has *the* cure? *The* solution to our fertility crisis?"

"That's what his message said, yes."

As a politician, suspicion came easily to zh'Tarash. "How can you be sure he's telling you the truth?"

His conviction was steady. "I served with him. I trust him. I *believe* in him."

"We've been led down the garden path before—by you and your Yrythny cure, as I recall. What if Bashir's wrong, too? What if he only *thinks* he has the cure?"

"He's risked *everything* to bring this to us: his commission, his career, his reputation. And if he's intercepted by the Tholians or the *Treishya*, perhaps his life. He wouldn't make such a dangerous wager unless he was certain it was worth it. And if he's sure, *I'm* sure."

"Your faith in him is touching. But it doesn't change the political reality that I alone do not control the government. I have no legal authority to direct the military or grant amnesties."

The young scientist was undeterred. "True. But the rules of parliamentary politics contain several mechanisms that protect the interests of the minority and empower the loyal opposition."

"I don't need *you* to teach me the nuances of politics."

"Then stop acting like a helpless *grayth* in the parliament chamber. It's time to take a stand, *Zha,* and you're the only one in a position to do so."

How brash of him! "It's not as simple as that. Manipulating the process for advantage takes time. I'll need to rally my allies and try to seduce vulnerable votes from the other side."

"Do what you have to, but do it quickly. We don't have much time before Bashir arrives. If he gets here and we're not ready, ch'Foruta will end up holding all the cards."

His sense of urgency was contagious. "I'll try. But the gears of state grind slowly, and they never move without a cost. Making this happen will mean expending political capital."

"Well, if you've been saving it up, this would be a moment worth spending it on."

She couldn't tell if his enthusiasm was the product of idealism, naïveté, or both. "So you say. But if I burn up all my favors and influence on this, and it ends up going wrong, the result would be political suicide. The Progressive Caucus would be ruined—and it might drag its allies down with it. Is that really a price you're willing to pay?"

The *chan* stood. "If your party and its allies fall, my colleagues and I fall with you." He walked to the back door that led to her walled garden, turned its handle, and paused to look back. "On the other hand, if you back Bashir and it turns out he's right, you'll be known as the ones who saved all of Andor. Whatever you decide to do . . . I'll be watching."

He opened the door, stepped out, and closed it gently behind him.

After a second's hesitation, zh'Tarash sprang from her chair and dashed to the back door. When she looked out into the lush confines of her garden, there was no sign of ch'Thane.

She looked back toward the bedrooms and thought of Senn, and of Rane.

Then she thought of all the Andorians who had been denied the joy of raising families.

There would be *katheka* at the office, and no one would care if she didn't shower today. She hurried back to her bedroom to get dressed.

Zh'Tarash had a long day ahead. She planned to make it one to be proud of.

Twenty-two

Stepping inside a holodeck when it was in Stellar Cartography Mode felt to Ezri Dax like space walking without the encumbrance of an environmental suit. As soon as she was through the door, she felt gravity release its hold on her, and she drifted up from the deck into the enveloping simulation of interstellar space. Somewhere behind and below her, she heard the doors close, and the illusion was complete. She was alone, adrift in the endless vault of night, surrounded in all directions by all the stars known to Federation science.

"Computer, bring me to the others."

The heavens pinwheeled and sped past as the simulation adjusted Dax's vantage point relative to the simulation. As was typical in holodeck programs that were often shared by several personnel in a department, the *Aventine*'s computer had initially segregated Dax into her own partition of the program, in case her research objectives were different from those already in progress by other users. After a few seconds of vertiginous galactic adjustment, the starfield settled once more, and from the darkness emerged Helkara, Kedair, and Bowers. The trio was surrounded by several highlighted icons that represented ships and faint lines—most straight, some arced—that indicated the different vessels' flight paths and anticipated headings.

Dax took stock of the amassed evidence. "Where are we so far?"

By virtue of rank and his colleagues' silence, the burden of response fell on Bowers. "We've compiled this from every flight plan, tracking station report, starship sensor log, and long-range surveillance array we could scrape together." The first officer gestured between two brilliant points of light. "We've identified all uncloaked starships traveling in the sectors between Bajor and Andor that are within range of a rendezvous with the *Rio Grande* in the past day."

Dax eyed the scant number of targets. "There had to have been more than this."

At a look from Bowers, Kedair said, "Computer: Overlay eliminated subjects." All at once the simulation was choked with hundreds of icons and course trajectories. "We're ignoring any ship that's not traveling to Andor or that's been stopped and searched during the window of time since we think Bashir abandoned the runabout."

An approving nod. "Good work. Let's talk about what's left."

The security chief glanced upward. "Computer: Remove overlay." The simulation returned to the state it had been in moments before. Kedair highlighted three of the ships' icons with quick taps. "Although we currently count ten ships as possible rides for Bashir, that's based on the broadest available definition of 'possible.' These three would have to have risked warp core overloads in order to make the necessary deviations from their original course to meet the *Rio Grande* and then return to their original headings without losing ground. Since none of the sensor arrays monitoring this sector detected any unusual energy signatures consistent with overdriven warp cores, I'd like your permission to rule these three out."

"Done," Dax said, and Kedair dismissed the highlighted icons with a wave of her hand.

Helkara highlighted three more vessels. "Although these could have made the rendezvous with the *Rio Grande*, I would suggest it is extremely unlikely that any of them did."

His certainty intrigued Dax. "Because?"

"The first is a Sheliak commercial freighter. Given their extreme xenophobia, I would think it highly doubtful that they would offer Doctor Bashir, or any non-Sheliak, transportation to Andor, or to anywhere else. The second of these vessels is an automated cargo transport. While it's not impossible that Bashir might have remotely accessed its navigational systems to arrange a transfer, he would find it a most uncomfortable conveyance, as it has no life-support systems, and no inertial damping outside its sealed cargo containers. It also is policed by robotic sentries that would be most inhospitable to an organic stowaway. As for the third vessel, it's a Klingon battle cruiser, the *I.K.S. ghung'HoH* out of Mempa."

"Point taken."

With a sweep of his hand, Helkara made his three subjects and their data vanish.

Dax looked at Bowers. "And then there were four."

"Three, in my opinion." He tapped the icon for the ship closest to the *Aventine*'s position. "This is a Tholian battleship. If they'd intercepted Bashir, it's a good bet they'd have destroyed the runabout. So I think we can rule them out." He flicked the data point into oblivion.

"What do we know about the last three?"

"Unarmed commercial freighters," Kedair said, "all with recent registry transfers to Ghidi Prime. Computer: Show registry and technical specs on remaining subjects." Beside and beneath each of the three remaining icons appeared long scrolls of information: license and registration paperwork, recent flight histories, biographical data on their owners, commanders, and crews, as well as full ship schematics. "The *Fortune's Fool* is a Ferengi-owned container ship, crew complement of forty-seven, and the fastest one of the bunch—but also currently the farthest from Andor." She switched her attention to the second ship. "The *Parham* is a one-man boat. The owner's strictly small-time, specializing in artisanal goods, custom cargo, and light courier work. It's presently on course for Andor, ETA twelve minutes." Her focus turned keen and cold as she noted the third vessel's details. "I've saved my favorite for last: the *Mogonus,* an Orion merchantman with a long history of sentient trafficking, smuggling, and black-market ties. Its captain and crew have been implicated"—a note of resentment tainted her voice as she continued—"but *never charged* in more than four dozen unsolved acts of deep-space piracy."

Bowers lifted his chin at the data sheet for the *Mogonus.* "Where is it now?"

"En route to Andor, ETA three hours and nine minutes," Kedair said.

The three officers looked at Dax, and Bowers struck an upbeat note. "Orders, Captain?"

Dax reviewed the facts in front of her and made a decision. "Set an intercept course for the *Parham.*"

Confused looks passed among the other three officers. Kedair pointed at the icon for the Orion ship. "But Captain, the *Mogonus*—"

"Would have cost more credits to hire than Julian's ever had in his life. But more important is the *Parham's* maintenance-and-inspection record: It failed a health-and-safety inspection on Deep Space Nine just over a week ago—right before it got a clean certificate from Julian. I'm willing to bet that was no coincidence."

"Computer," Bowers said, "end program." The illusory cosmos dissipated like vapor as the holodeck gradually lowered the four officers to the deck and reactivated its artificial gravity. Just as they touched down, Bowers noted, "To catch the *Parham* before it lands on Andor will mean using the slipstream drive—and even that'll be cutting it close."

"Do whatever it takes, Sam." The four of them set foot on the deck and moved together toward the exit, which opened ahead of them. "Julian's on that ship. Catch it. That's an order."

"Grab your socks, Doc, we're droppin' outta warp in three . . . two . . . *now*."

Bashir's pulse quickened as warp-stretched starlight shrank back into discrete points—and then his breath caught for half a second in his chest as Captain Harris swung the *Parham* through a tight turn that brought the northern hemisphere of Andor into majestic view. They were close to the planet, definitely within standard orbital distance, and the blue-and-white orb dominated their field of view. The *Parham*'s cockpit windows polarized to reduce the blinding effect of the planet's reflected light, causing the stars behind the planet to vanish into darkness.

For a world that had been placed under unilateral economic sanctions by the Federation, Andor had no shortage of starship traffic. With just his naked eye, Bashir counted several dozen vessels of various origins and sizes coming and going. Some were in standard orbits from which they could transfer personnel and cargo via transporters, while others shuttled to and from the planet's surface. Cresting the curve of the planet's northern hemisphere was a Tholian battleship. All that activity transpired at the bidding of Andor Control and under the watchful auspices of two Andorian military starships, which patrolled from antipodal high orbits.

Harris keyed a short string of digits into his ship's comm and pressed TRANSMIT. "Hang tight, Doc. Soon as Control gives me landing coordinates, we'll set down and get you on your—"

A flash of bluish-white light from outside the ship forced Bashir to shield his eyes with one arm. When the painful radiance began to fade, he lowered his arm to see one of his worst fears realized. The *Aventine* had just arrived in orbit between the *Parham* and Andor, by means of what he could only surmise had been a terrifyingly precise quantum-slipstream jump.

Angry voices clamored over the Andor Control comm channel, and the two Andorian warships began accelerating away from their patrol positions to intercept and flank the *Aventine*, which was pivoting its bow with preternatural grace toward the *Parham*.

The small freighter's owner-pilot gaped at the huge, *Vesta*-class starship looming over his ship. "They're chargin' weapons and a tractor beam. I'm guessin' that ain't good."

"Correct." As if on cue, the comm over Bashir's head chirped twice to announce an incoming audio signal from the *Aventine*.

Harris reached up and thumbed open the channel. "Yo."

"Attention, commander, S.S. Parham. This is Captain Ezri Dax, commanding the Federation Starship Aventine. Stand down and prepare to be boarded."

Bashir pressed a finger against his lips and looked at Harris: *Say nothing about me.* Harris raised his hands away from the helm controls, as if someone on the *Aventine* were watching him through a viewport. "Sorry, Cap'n, but I reckon y'all have made some kinda mistake."

Another voice—masculine and gruff—joined the conversation. *"Attention, commander, Aventine. This is Captain Kainon th'Liro, commanding the Andorian Imperial warship* Ilmarriven. *You have no legal authority here. You and your vessel are ordered to withdraw."*

"Negative," Dax replied. *"We are in pursuit of a fugitive from Starfleet justice, one whom we have reason to suspect is being harbored aboard the civilian vessel* Parham."

Harris and Bashir watched the two Andorian battleships take up positions on the *Aventine's* aft flanks, one above the Federation ship, the other beneath it. The Andorian commander's voice remained unyielding. *"Aventine, can you identify the suspect?"*

"Affirmative. Starfleet officer Doctor Julian Bashir. Rank, commander."

"Parham commander," th'Liro said. *"Identify yourself."*

"Captain Emerson Harris. I'm on file with Andor Control."

"Captain Harris, is the Starfleet fugitive aboard your vessel?"

Harris started to reach for the mute switch, no doubt to concoct some lie to protect Bashir, but the fiasco had gone far enough. Bashir caught Harris's hand and answered for him. "Captain th'Liro, this is Doctor Julian Bashir."

"Captain Dax," th'Liro continued, *"with what crimes is Doctor Bashir charged?"*

"Treason, espionage, assault on an officer, theft of Starfleet property, and desertion."

"That's absurd! You can't charge me with desertion. I resigned my commission before I left the Bajor system."

"Really, Julian? That's the charge you want to contest?"

"I'm just saying, if you're going to sully my name, at least get your facts straight."

"I think you ought to be a bit more concerned about the—"

"*Doctor Bashir,*" th'Liro cut in. "*Do you confess to being a fugitive from Starfleet?*"

"Yes—and at this time, I formally request asylum on Andor."

Dax's voice pitched upward with anger. "*What? On what grounds? If you think I'm—*"

"*Captain Dax, I remind you that you have no authority here. Doctor Bashir's petition is by no means assured of approval, but until we receive a ruling from our government, your ship will stand down. If the* Parham *makes any attempt to flee, we will deal with it. And if Doctor Bashir is to be taken into custody pending extradition, that will also be under our jurisdiction.*"

After a tension-filled pause, Dax replied, "*Acknowledged, Ilmarriven.*"

The Andorian commander continued. "*Doctor Bashir: What is your reason for requesting asylum on Andor?*"

"To bring you the cure for your people's fertility crisis—which also happens to be the reason that Starfleet and the Federation want to see me behind bars."

His statement was met by a long silence, followed by a soft-spoken reply. "*Acknowledged.*" After another pause, th'Liro added, "*Stand by.*"

Changing status indicators on the *Parham*'s master control console made it possible for the freighter captain to let go of the breath he'd been holding. "They're powering down."

"For now. The real question is, what happens next?"

"Beats the hell outta me. I'd usually kick back with a beer while waiting on a bureaucrat, but with all that firepower pointed our way, I'm a bit too wound up to swallow right now."

"I understand, believe me."

Bashir's thoughts turned toward the planet's surface. Had his message reached Shar? Had his old friend known what to do with news of his imminent arrival? He had been counting on Shar and his colleagues to have a network in place for manufacturing and distributing the cure once they'd extracted it from his bloodstream. But knowing who was in control of the Andorian government, he couldn't risk surrendering himself to just anyone. If what Shar had told him was correct, Andor's current presider had every reason to want Bashir to fail.

If someone's on my side down there, maybe I have a chance, Bashir told himself in a halfhearted bid to prop up his faltering courage. *But if not . . . then this is about to become the biggest blunder of my entire life.*

Presider ch'Foruta jogged through the stately, high-ceilinged main passage of the Parliament Andoria, his chief of staff at his side, and silently cursed whomever had decided to shield the interior of the new government's capital building with transporter scramblers. He struggled to expel words between labored breaths. "How in the name of Uzaveh did it get called for a vote?"

Already hard-pressed to keep pace with the presider, zh'Rilah lost a few more steps using valuable air to answer him. "Leader zh'Tarash forced a quorum call."

I should have known. Damn the lawyers and their dirty tricks! It didn't bother ch'Foruta that the forced quorum tactic was one that his own party had employed several times in the past few years to push through its own preferred legislation and ratify controversial executive orders. All it took was a lot of patience on one side and a lack of attention on the other.

One party waited until Parliament was in session but effectively in recess for routine state business off the floor. Then its members would return to the main chamber, one or a few at a time, and try to remain inconspicuous until enough members of the Parliament were present—by decree, one half of all its elected members, plus one—and a vote could be called. Then, if the party orchestrating the trick held a majority among those present in the hall, one of its members would call a point of order, introduce a binding resolution, and motion for an immediate referendum on the resolution. If the process was executed quickly enough, before opposing votes could be marshaled into the chamber, the minority could defy the majority—for a moment.

Such a moment was taking shape right then in the Parliament Andoria.

The Progressives' leader is becoming a bigger problem than I'd expected, ch'Foruta brooded. Since no one had been able to locate Professor zh'Thiin to extend to her the diabolical offer that ch'Foruta's intelligence counselor th'Farro had concocted, the presider had tried to arrange a meeting with the elusive scientist through Leader zh'Tarash. The result had been nothing, not even the professional courtesy of a brusque refusal—merely cold silence.

Who does this upstart zhen *think she is?*

A pair of uniformed guards pulled open a pair of tall, ornately adorned outward-swinging doors that led to the presider's private entrance behind the main chamber's elevated dais. The imperial soldiers pushed the doors closed behind zh'Rilah. Her footsteps and ch'Foruta's were loud and met by crisp echoes as they hurried down the passageway. The presider threw a look at his chief of staff. "How are we doing on the quorum call?"

The *zhen* touched her ear to better listen to reports from the chamber floor. "It's going to be close. Sounds like zh'Tarash is trying to close the vote, and we're running out of delays."

"We'll see about that."

He left zh'Rilah behind and lurched ahead, to a door through which she was not allowed to follow him. It opened ahead of him, and the roar of voices hit him like an ocean swell—the Parliament Andoria had devolved into pandemonium.

The presider bounded up a short flight of stairs to his ceremonial seat overlooking the chamber from its highest point. Fewer than two-thirds of the members were present, but zh'Tarash had expertly rallied all her Progressives and a few of their allies in other minority parties. A shouting match in the hemispherical seating tiers escalated swiftly to pointed fingers and threatened to degenerate into a brawl at any moment.

Projecting calm authority, ch'Foruta sat down, picked up his gavel, and pounded it against the block until the deafening reports subdued the chaos below him. He leaned forward and looked down to his ally, Marratesh ch'Lhorra. "*Cha* Speaker, a point of order."

"We recognize the Presider."

"I formally request a review of the resolution's specific terms."

The Speaker of the Parliament picked up a padd and read from it while more members of the *Treishya* hurried into the chamber through its multiple entrances behind the uppermost tier of seats. "Parliament Resolution Four-seventeen, introduced by Leader zh'Tarash and co-sponsored by Leader th'Forris: 'Be it resolved, and ratified by a majority vote, that the Parliament Andoria grants, with immediate effect, the asylum request received this day from United Federation of Planets citizen Julian Subatoi Bashir.' The resolution currently stands at one hundred sixty-six votes in favor, one hundred fifty-eight opposed, with no abstentions."

Another dozen *Treishya* had arrived while ch'Lhorra was talking. Quashing zh'Tarash's bill would now be a simple matter. The presider stood to address the chamber. "*Cha* Speaker, at this time I move we extend the voting on this resolution, to gauge its support among those of our number now joining us."

"Seconded," added sh'Risham, the Visionist Leader.

"The presider's motion carries," ch'Lhorra declared. "Voting will continue."

In less than a minute, the nay votes surpassed the yeas by a margin that confirmed the motion's irreversible defeat. *One disaster contained*, ch'Foruta gloated. *Now to preempt another*. "*Cha* Speaker, at this time, be informed on behalf of the Parliament that I am issuing an executive order to our imperial forces in orbit, directing them to stand down and permit the Starfleet vessel to take the Federation fugitive into custody without an extradition hearing."

He was answered by an enraged outburst from New Restoration Party Leader ch'Szaan. "This is a travesty of justice! What kind of message does it send if we allow our sovereignty to be usurped in our own orbit? We have every right to demand proof of this human's crimes before we permit a foreign power to arrest him inside *our* jurisdiction!"

"This is a matter requiring the utmost diplomacy." Ch'Foruta struck his most condescending tone. "The Federation might no longer be our trusted friend, but neither is it our enemy, and we would be wise not to make a foe of them through acts of intransigence."

The next verbal jab came from an unexpected direction—his ally, Leader zh'Moor. "Leader ch'Szaan speaks the truth, Presider! Setting aside the law, with its guarantees of due process and impartial judgment based on evidence, in favor of executive decree, sets a very dangerous precedent—one the True Heirs of Andor will *not* support."

Some backbencher *shen* from the maddeningly neutral Alliance Party shouted out, "Bashir says he's trying to bring us the cure to the fertility crisis! We can't just turn him away!"

A surge of voices assailed ch'Foruta, who stood dumbfounded. He couldn't argue his case based on the truth of the matter—that he wanted Bashir out of the equation because he couldn't permit the human to deliver the cure and shift the credit for Andor's salvation away from the *Treishya* and its allies. Instead, he was forced to stand his ground on the thin ice of a hastily concocted lie. "We have no reason to believe that Bashir is telling the truth about having the cure—"

"All the more reason for a fair hearing," zh'Tarash shot back, wading into the fray. "If he's lying, I'll be the first to vote for his extradition. But the law demands he be given the chance to present his evidence and be heard!"

The mood in the chamber was turning ugly, and votes that ch'Foruta would have taken for granted only minutes earlier suddenly seemed in danger of turning against him. There was no time to adhere to the quaint details of protocol. It was a moment for blunt-force politics.

"The executive order has been issued." He transmitted the directive to the ships in orbit from his personal padd. "*Cha* Speaker, I move we recess until tomorrow."

Rage flooded up toward ch'Foruta from all sides. Cries

of condemnation, calls for his gavel, demands for justice—
but no one to second his motion. He shot a baleful glare at
ch'Lhorra, who understood what the presider wanted.

The speaker cupped his hand over his headset to make
his amplified voice audible over the commotion: "Motion is
seconded and carried." Even though it was a clear violation of
protocol for him to second the presider's motion, he swung
his own gavel three times against its block and declared, "This
body stands in recess until midday tomorrow."

Dozens of parliament members pelted ch'Lhorra and
ch'Foruta with a storm of small thrown objects as the two
Treishya fled their elevated stations and retreated through
their respective private exits. Harried by styluses and data
chips, ch'Foruta ducked back into his private corridor where
zh'Rilah stood waiting for him. She fell into step with him as
they ran for the large doors that led out to the main passage.
"What just happened in there?"

"Unless we play our next move perfectly," ch'Foruta
snapped, "the start of a coup."

"Doc? I ain't tryin' to be a nervous Nellie, but I think the
Tholians are headin' our way."

Bashir tried to reassure Harris with a calm hand on the
man's shoulder. "Relax. It's all posturing. They just want to
show the Andorians that they're backing them up. Since they
know this likely won't turn violent, it costs them nothing to
look supportive."

The captain heaved a worried sigh. "Hope you're right,
Doc. That thing's *real* big."

Watching the Tholian battleship loom large ahead of
them, Bashir found himself sharing a small degree of Harris's
apprehension. "It certainly is."

The comm crackled slightly as th'Liro hailed them. *"Attention, civilian vessel* Parham *and Starfleet vessel* Aventine. *We have received an executive order directing us to stand down. Captain Dax, you're free to take Doctor Bashir and his accomplice into custody and depart."*

Dax replied, *"Acknowledged,* Ilmarriven. *We'll make this quick and painless."*

Enraged, Harris muted the comm. "Those blue bastards! They sold us out!"

"Captain, stay calm. I'll need your help if I'm—" Bashir's plea was interrupted by a jolt that rocked the tramp freighter. A blinding golden radiance filled the cockpit. He lifted a hand to shield his eyes. "Tractor beam. You'd best power down, Captain."

Harris trembled with fury. "I ain't gettin' reeled in like a prize marlin." He jabbed at switches on his master control console, and the next thing Bashir saw was a holographic targeting sight superimposed over the viewport in front of Harris.

"You said this vessel was unarmed!"

"Officially? It is." Harris locked the *Parham*'s concealed phaser cannon onto the unshielded *Aventine.* "Unofficially? I got sick of being hassled by pirates. Never thought I'd have to use this on a Starfleet ship, but there's a first time for everything, I guess."

"Stop!" Bashir lunged to pry Harris's hands from the controls, but by the time he seized the captain's wrists, it was too late—Harris had fired. A cloud of orange flames and blackened debris erupted from the *Aventine*'s main deflector dish. The tractor beam faltered and ceased, and for a moment the *Parham* floated free as its would-be captor listed sharply to port.

Then everything went straight to hell, just as Bashir had always feared it would.

That does it, Dax fumed. *No more kid gloves.* She white-knuckled her command chair's armrest as operations officer Mirren struggled to bring *Aventine's* inertial dampers back online and flight controller Tharp fought to restore the ship to its previous attitude.

Bowers's deep voice cut through the whooping alarms and frantic chatter. "Damage reports! Now!" He pivoted toward Kedair. "Target the *Parham* and fire to disable!"

"Locking phasers. Firing. One hit." The security chief reacted to an alert on her console. "Holding fire—one of the Andorian ships is blocking our shot."

"Magnify." Dax watched as Kedair adjusted the image on the forward viewscreen to show the second Andorian battle cruiser, the *Tuonetar,* maneuvering into a defensive posture that prevented the *Aventine* from targeting the escaping tramp freighter. "Mirren, hail that ship, and get me the captain of the *Ilmarriven.* Tharp, come about, Pursuit Pattern Indigo. Get us a shot at the *Parham* before she enters the atmosphere."

While the others carried out her orders, Bowers stepped to his customary post at the right of Dax's chair. "We took a direct hit to the main deflector dish. Damage to all primary sensors, including the ones we need for slipstream. Be warned, our targeting's also going to be impaired."

"Wonderful." Despite the *Aventine's* maneuvering, the image on the viewscreen continued to show the *Tuonetar* dead ahead. Dax leaned forward. "Tharp, report."

"The *Tuonetar's* moving with us, Captain. I can't get around her."

Mirren swiveled her chair to look back at Dax. "I have Captain th'Liro on audio."

Dax stood up to better project her voice, though her rising swell of anger likely would have done the job just fine all on its own. "Captain th'Liro, why is your sister ship impeding our effort to capture the *Parham*?"

"Unknown. We've ordered Captain sh'Naar to stand down, but she refuses to respond to our hails."

Kedair silenced a shrill alert on the tactical console. "Captain, the *Tuonetar* is raising shields and charging its weapons, and the Tholian battleship is moving to attack position."

"Shields up," Dax said, almost as if by reflex.

Bowers leaned close to confide, "Without the main deflector, we have no forward shields. So I recommend we avoid taking any punches on the nose, Captain."

She whispered back, "Noted." Then she raised her voice for the comm discussion. "Captain sh'Naar, this is Captain Dax aboard the Starfleet vessel *Aventine*. We have no quarrel with you or the Andorian people. Please stand down and let us—"

A flash of light on the viewscreen was matched by a thunderous boom that resonated through the deck and bulkheads and sent Dax and Bowers tumbling across the pitching deck of the bridge. They slammed against each other as they collided with the access panels beneath the starboard consoles. The roar of the blast faded but left Dax's ears ringing.

Kedair reported with cool detachment, "The *Tuonetar* fired on us, Captain."

All eyes on the bridge turned toward Dax, who realized that her next orders would mean the difference between peace and war for billions, as well as the life or death of her crew.

"All power to shields, Lieutenant. And get me a shot on the *Parham* before it's too late."

Captain Lemarliten sh'Naar was desperate. "Hit them again! Target their impulse drive! Helm, keep us ahead of them! Someone hail the *Parham,* tell them to use us for cover!"

Fearful glances skipped from one junior officer to another, and another, as if everyone on the bridge of the *Tuonetar* was waiting for someone else to second-guess their commander. By default, the task fell to her first officer, Commander th'Desh.

Her second-in-command was reed-thin and taller than a hermit's tale. He towered over her as he interposed himself between her and the rest of the crew, no doubt to stop her from giving them more orders. His voice was trip-wire taut. "Captain, we had no order to fire."

"It's my order, Commander. Carry it out."

I don't have time for this, sh'Naar raged as th'Desh stalked away from her command chair. *None of us do.* In her heart, she knew time was running out, not only for her and her bondmates—who after three attempts had yet to accomplish even a single successful fertilization—but for the Andorian people as a culture and as a species.

The communications officer turned from his panel to face sh'Naar. "Captain, no response from the *Parham*—but Presider ch'Foruta has ordered me to put him on the shipwide comm." He tapped a blinking icon on his panel, and then the presider's voice resounded through the ship.

"*Attention, officers and crew of the* Tuonetar. *Your attack on the Starfleet vessel is in direct defiance of my executive order. This is a direct order: Stand down, before this conflict escalates into—*" Sh'Naar cut off the presider's message in mid-sentence with a tap on her command console, then she opened her own channel to address the crew.

"Attention, all decks, this is the captain speaking. I know I don't need to tell any of you that our people stand on the brink of extinction. So, with all due respect to President ch'Foruta, I will not let that Starfleet vessel leave our space with a man who says he has brought us the cure. I can't guarantee that Bashir is truthful. Or that he's right. But for the sake of our families—for the sake of *our people*—I intend to give him a chance to prove that he is both. Remain at your posts, and carry out your orders. That is all." She closed the channel and turned her chair toward her tactical officer. "You have your orders. Don't make me repeat them."

"Yes, Captain." The young *chan* avoided eye contact with sh'Naar and focused on his panel as he fired the *Tuonetar's* phasers at the *Aventine*. Then he looked up, terrified. "Sir, the *Ilmarriven* is raising shields and charging weapons—and ordering us to stand down."

She watched the *Ilmarriven* maneuver into prime firing position against the *Tuonetar*. Every second was priceless now; unless sh'Naar could bring the *Parham* aboard the *Tuonetar* to let her crew evaluate Bashir's alleged cure, the opportunity would be lost. Regardless, even if her gamble proved justified, she knew this would mean the end of her military career—but all she cared about in that moment was the family she had been so long denied.

Sh'Naar resigned herself to the will of Uzaveh and cast aside caution.

"Helm, catch up to the *Parham* right now . . . no matter what it takes."

It was impossible to see the *Parham*'s command console through the toxic smoke filling the cockpit, but Bashir guessed from the sickly whining and groaning of the ship's damaged impulse engines that Captain Harris's ill-advised escape attempt wasn't setting any speed records. "Evasive, starboard! Get us out of the crossfire!"

"Jus' sit back, Doc! I know what I'm—"

A nearby barrage of phaser fire turned everything retina-searing white for a split second. Then a stray shot volleyed between the two Andorian starships on either side of the *Parham* clipped the tramp freighter with a glancing blow that showered Bashir and Harris in sparks. The lights dimmed, and the consoles hiccuped on and off for a moment before half of them went dark and stayed that way. Harris thumped one screen with the side of his fist and coaxed it back to life for a few seconds, long enough to parse an automated damage report. "Cannon's fried, warp drive's toast. Starboard might've been a good call, after all."

Bashir made a quick survey of which systems were still functional. "Shut down main power and use the manual thrusters to push us toward the atmosphere."

Harris gawked as if Bashir were a gibbering *mugato*. "Are you outta your mind, Doc? Dive into atmo without main power? We'd go up like a cricket in a campfire."

How had Harris survived this long flying a ship by himself? "I'm not suggesting we leave main power off all the way down. Just long enough to drop off everyone's primary sensors for a few seconds so we can make a run for the surface."

"The surface? Maybe you missed the memo, Doc, but

they're not exactly rolling out the red carpet for you. It's my ship, and I say we boogie."

"With no warp drive? How far do you think you'll get before—"

A metallic-sounding vocoder voice screeched over the comm. *"Attention, commander,* Parham. *This is Commander Rezthene of the* Tanj'k Tholis. *Prepare to be taken in tow for your own safety. Failure to comply will be interpreted as a hostile act."*

The two men frantically waved away the cloud of smoke in front of them to see the Tholian battleship cruising directly toward them. The sight of the triple-wedge-shaped vessel bearing down on them impelled Bashir to push himself as far back into his chair as he could go. "Captain, if I was you, right about now I would be—"

"Leaving! What a wonderful idea!" Harris patched every last bit of power he could dredge from his ship's batteries and wounded impulse core and set a course for full retreat from the *Tanj'k Tholis*—even though that meant risking another run through the gauntlet of phaser fire dancing between the *Tuonetar* and the *Ilmarriven*.

The *Parham* lurched to a halt, and its hull creaked like a rusty hinge being twisted apart. Harris checked his instruments. "Tractor beam. But it ain't the bugs, it's—"

"Captain Harris," said a woman's voice, *"this is the* Tuonetar. *We have you in a tractor beam. Shut down your engines and let us bring you aboard."*

Reacting to Bashir's affirming nod, Harris replied, "Whatever you say, ma'am." He reached up, closed the channel, and looked at Bashir. "So, is that it? Mission accomplished?"

Outside, salvos of phaser fire leaped in all directions

between the *Tuonetar* and the *Ilmarriven*—and the *Parham* quaked as the tractor beam enfolding it stuttered.

"Not yet," Bashir said. "Not even close."

It was all spiraling out of control. A new enemy rose at every turn, and sh'Naar knew at once that her ship was outmatched. The *Parham* was being towed into the *Tuonetar*'s main hangar, but the *Aventine* was proving more resilient than she had expected, and now the *Ilmarriven* had turned against sh'Naar, firing multiple shots that had left the *Tuonetar* hobbled.

"Aft shields failing," called out the engineering officer. "We're losing main power!"

Damage reports raced up the command display beside sh'Naar's chair. "Patch in the reserves, and divert power from life support to the tractor beam." A tap on the console switched it from damage control to tactical. As belligerent as the Tholians were, they were courting Andor, so sh'Naar was sure the *Tanj'k Tholis* wouldn't fire. As for Captain th'Liro and the *Ilmarriven*, she had a hunch they would pull their punches long enough for her to finish this. "Tactical, keep an eye on the *Aventine*, but target all weapons on the *Ilmarriven*, and angle our aft quarter toward the Tholians. Fire on my mark!"

"Belay that order," th'Desh said, loud enough for everyone on the bridge to hear. "Cease fire, drop shields, and open a channel to the *Aventine* and the *Ilmarriven*." All at once, battle activity on the bridge halted, and everyone looked up with both hope and fear.

Sh'Naar turned to see her first officer holding her at phaser-point. "Mutiny?"

The gaunt-faced *thaan* glanced at the communications officer, who confirmed with a nod that the channel was open. "Captain sh'Naar: By authority of a lawful executive order from Presider ch'Foruta of the Parliament Andoria, and in accordance with Andorian Imperial Fleet regulations, I relieve you of your command, on the grounds that you have acted against the orders of a superior, and are, in the professional estimation of myself and Doctor zh'Phair, psychologically unfit for command." Neither his hand nor his voice wavered as he added, "Lieutenant ch'Mas, take Captain sh'Naar into custody and escort her to the brig."

There was nothing to say, so sh'Naar waited until the tactical officer drew his phaser and ushered her toward the turbolift. As they walked to the waiting lift car, she heard th'Desh issue his first order as the new acting captain of the *Tuonetar*.

"Release the tractor beam on the *Parham,* and tell Captain Dax it's all hers."

Standing at the center of a smoke-filled bridge, surrounded by fragged consoles and plasma conduits raining erratic sparks from the overhead, Dax was torn between feeling grateful that the Tholians had stayed out of the altercation and that no one on either side seemed to have been seriously hurt, and feeling borderline homicidal that Harris, Bashir, and a rogue Andorian starship commander had put her and her crew in this position in the first place.

Bowers finished his circuit of the bridge and joined Dax in front of their side-by-side command chairs. "Heavy damage to the main deflector, sensors, and shields. Minor damage to the port warp nacelle and its slipstream coils. A few injuries, no fatalities."

"Bottom line it for me."

"We're looking at two to three days of repairs before we can leave orbit."

It was all Dax could do to keep her temper in check. "Dammit. I was ready to go easy on that civilian until he did this. Now I plan to make sure he never breathes free air again."

"You and me both, Captain." Bowers motioned toward the flashing alert panels on the bulkheads. "Should we stand down from Yellow Alert?"

"No. Captain sh'Naar's reaction makes it clear this whole mess is a lot more incendiary than we thought. There's no telling where the next blowup might come from, so stay sharp, and keep the shields up, just in case."

"Understood."

Mirren got up from the operations console and walked back to join Dax and Bowers. "Sirs? The main shuttlebay reports the *Parham* is aboard. On my recommendation, we're waiting until a security detail arrives before we pressurize the bay."

Finally, some good news. "Smartly done, Lieutenant." Dax turned toward the security chief. "Lonnoc. Take a team to the shuttlebay and arrest Captain Harris and Doctor Bashir."

Twenty-three

Framed within the desktop monitor, Fleet Admiral Akaar was the very portrait of stoicism. He seemed less pleased by Dax's news than she had hoped he would be, accepting her report of Bashir's capture with a slow, dour nod. *"Have you debriefed him yet?"*

"No, sir. My security chief arrested him and his accomplice a few minutes ago. They've been searched and confined to separate sections of the brig."

"Well done, Captain. Now bring Bashir back to Earth, as soon as possible."

It was time for the bad news. "I'm afraid our return has been delayed, sir."

Concern creased the white-haired admiral's brow. *"Explain."*

"During our initial attempt to tow the *Parham* aboard, it fired on us, using a concealed weapons system. We returned fire and disabled the freighter's weapons and warp drive, but before we could reestablish our tractor beam, the Andorian cruiser *Tuonetar* fired on us." She picked up a padd from her ready room's desk. "Long story short, we've sustained some—"

"Stop—the Andorians fired on you?"

"I was hoping I might gloss over that part."

"Keep hoping." His concern intensified. *"Please tell me you did* not *return fire."*

She shook her head. "No, sir, we didn't. Within less than a minute of the *Tuonetar*'s first shots, it was intercepted by its sister ship the *Ilmarriven,* and the *Tuonetar*'s first officer relieved its captain by order of the Andorian presider."

"So this can remain a strictly internal matter for the Andorians?"

"Yes, sir, that's my understanding. We've just received formal apologies from both the Parliament Andoria and the Andorian Imperial Command."

Akaar's fierce mask of anxiety relaxed a bit. *"Good. I know it can't have been easy to hold your fire in such circumstances, Captain. I commend you and your crew for your restraint."*

"Thank you, Admiral."

"Now, if you can, please explain to me why the Andorians fired on you."

She dreaded his reaction to her next revelation. "He told the Andorians that he came bearing the cure to their fertility crisis. And he asked their government for political asylum."

He closed his eyes and massaged his temples with his thumbs. *"Did they believe him?"*

"Hard to say. They denied his request, if that means anything."

"Did your crew find any trace of such a cure aboard the captured ship, or on Bashir?"

"Not yet, but we're still looking. What should I do if he really has it?"

"Leave that for the politicians to worry about. Our orders are to contain the situation to the maximum possible degree. However, no matter what we do, sooner or later news of Bashir's claim will make it to the media. We need to have him off the political stage before that happens, and every moment he remains in orbit of Andor, even if he's in custody,

is another moment we risk this debacle turning into a diplo-matic crisis."

"I agree, sir. Which is why I have my crew working double shifts to bring the warp drive back online as soon as possible."

Akaar shook his head. *"I fear that won't suffice, Captain. As I said when I tasked your ship with this mission, the* Falchion *and* Warspite *were assigned to act as your backup, should the need arise. I'm directing them now to rendezvous with you at Andor. They should arrive within six hours. At that time, you will transfer Bashir and his accomplice to the custody of Captain Unverzagt on the* Warspite."

Dax didn't like the sound of that. "Admiral, I don't really think that's—"

"The decision's made, Captain. Those are *your orders."*

It was clear there was no room for discussion, so Dax acquiesced with a nod. "Yes, sir." She took a moment to collect herself. "Can I ask what'll happen to Doctor Bashir?"

"First, a closed-proceedings court-martial. Then, barring some heretofore unknown manner of thermodynamic miracle, a swift conviction followed by a sentencing hearing."

"I see."

Perhaps detecting the note of sympathy in her voice, Akaar put an edge on his. *"Captain, feel no pity for Doctor Bashir. Put aside your personal history with the man and see his actions for what they are: espionage and treason. No matter how noble his motives might be, he risked the security of the Federation—and that decision was not his to make. So resist the temptation to see him as some kind of hero. For now, treat him as a prisoner, and nothing more."*

There was truth in what Akaar was saying, but it stung all the same. "Yes, sir."

"Let me know if his briefing yields any actionable intelligence."

"I will."

"Starfleet Command out." Akaar ended the transmission, and the image on Dax's ready room monitor switched for a moment to the Starfleet emblem before fading to black.

Torn between the demands of duty and the bonds of affection, Dax stood from her desk and resigned herself to that which needed to be done. It was time for her to talk to Bashir.

It wasn't the isolation of the brig that bothered Bashir, or the indignity of being locked up and kept under remote supervision, like some kind of animal. It was the tedium; the boredom of being cooped up with nothing to do and no one to talk to. In a full-time Federation correctional facility, there would be reading materials, ranging from bland to boring, and access to music. But this was a starship's brig, designed for short-term detention pending transfer to a larger venue, such as a starbase or a planetside penal colony.

Thanks to his genetically enhanced memory, he had the option of replaying a vast range of music in his imagination, and he could recall word-for-word most if not all of the books and papers he had ever read. Such measures were taxing and tended to be unsatisfying; he yearned for novelty, for discovery, for the allure of new experiences.

I can always look forward to long-term incarceration, he consoled himself ironically. *That should present me with a boundless frontier of new experiences.*

From beyond the force field that demarcated the edge of his cell he heard a door sigh open, followed by the approach of footsteps as the door hushed closed. He knew the weight and cadence of those footfalls.

Dax stepped around the corner into Bashir's limited field of view. She stood in front of his cell and crossed her arms, then regarded him with disappointment. "Julian."

Bashir stood and showed her the courtesy of facing her. "Ezri."

"Are you all right?"

"You mean physically? I'm fine, thank you for asking." She eyed the cell, though Bashir couldn't tell if she was assessing its comforts or its weaknesses. *Knowing her, probably both at the same time.* He interrupted her survey by leaning into her line of sight. "Something I can do for you? Or did you just pop in to say good-bye before Starfleet drops me down a black hole?"

He had hoped to lighten the moment, but Dax was in no mood for his brand of humor. "Starfleet Command wants you back on Earth in a big hurry. Since we're stuck here making repairs for a few days, they're sending two more ships to take you off our hands."

"How thoughtful of them."

"You joke, but this'll end badly for you, Julian."

He swallowed the urge to laugh. "I always figured it would."

Earnest and desperate, she asked, "Then why did you do it?"

Bashir looked at Dax, and for a moment he was sure he saw in her a spark of the young, idealistic counselor he'd once loved, and the spirit of the proud scientist-soldier she had been in her life before this one. "You know why."

She dropped her arms and started pacing, as if she were the one who had been caged. "For the *Andorians*? They turned their backs on us!"

"Not all of them. Just a slim majority—some of whom acted out of passion."

Dax took his point in stride. "They are *passionate*. Have to give them that." She turned to confront him. "But this? Stealing top-secret data from your own government? Throwing away your career? Your reputation? What did the Andorians ever do to deserve this kind of sacrifice?"

"Nothing. They didn't have to. Innocent people shouldn't be made to beg for their lives. The weak and the suffering shouldn't have to kowtow to receive help, from us or anyone else."

He could see from her shocked expression that he'd struck a chord in her conscience. She turned away, embracing denial over truth. "Principle is all well and good, Julian, but you also swore an oath as a Starfleet officer. To defend the Federation. To obey lawful orders."

"I also seem to recall more than one ethics instructor at Starfleet Academy teaching us that more was expected of us than blind obedience. That we had a higher duty, to the truth, and an obligation to resist orders that are immoral."

Dax tensed, as if he had offended her. "What part of 'don't steal top-secret data from your own government and give it to a foreign power' struck you as immoral, Julian?"

"The part that expects me to ignore my oath as a medical doctor and be a passive bystander to the slow death of a sentient species."

Back on the defensive, Dax once again crossed her arms. "So now your Hippocratic oath trumps your oath of service? Or your obligations as a Federation citizen?"

"Yes, I think it does."

"The law disagrees."

"Laws are written by fallible beings. Sometimes the law is wrong." Bashir felt a trembling in his limbs and realized the argument with Dax was flooding his bloodstream with adrenaline. He started to pace just to expend some of the pent-up energy coursing inside him. "Ezri, if you could've heard my conversation with Ishan, if you'd heard how callous he was when I told him we had the chance to cure the Andorians, you'd understand why I'm so angry."

"If the president pro tem ordered you to stand down, he must have his reasons."

Her apology for authority bolstered his indignation. "His political ambitions aren't worth condemning the Andorian species to slow extinction by chronic miscarriage."

"Is it possible you're exaggerating just a bit?"

"I don't think so. Ishan's suppressing the cure for the same reason he ordered a pointless embargo. He's using the Andorians as scapegoats, as an easy way for him to score cheap political points during the run-up to the special election. At best, he's a crass opportunist; at worst, he's a genocidal thug in the making."

Another pregnant pause made Bashir wonder if his criticisms had finally found their mark. Then Dax shook her head. "Even if you're right, he's still the one in charge, and I have my orders. I'm not saying I don't sympathize with your reasons, Julian. It's just that as a starship captain, I don't have the luxury of indulging my conscience. . . . I'm sorry."

Bashir was crestfallen; he had hoped for better from her. All he could do now was try to salvage some small measure of victory from his moment of defeat. "I understand. And it was always my intention to turn myself in when this was over. All I'm asking is that you not make my sacrifices be in vain. Before you hand me over, let me deliver the cure to the Andorians."

"I can't do that, Julian, and you know it."

"All I'm asking for is an hour on the planet's surface, just to meet with Shar and—"

"I can't. As long as you're in here, you're under my authority. The moment I let you set foot on Andor, you'd be under their jurisdiction, and there's no telling how that would play out. That's not a risk any sane commander in my position would take."

Desperation welled up from within him. "All right, I see your point, and that's reasonable. But I don't need to leave the ship. The cure is in my bloodstream, as a dormant retrovirus that will repair the Andorian genome. Just let Simon come in and take a sample of my blood, and then he can beam it down to Shar and—"

"That's not happening, either, Julian. Your cure contains segments of classified intel that I've been ordered to contain at all costs. Humanitarian concerns aside, I have orders not to let you deliver that cure, on the grounds that it would compromise Federation security."

It was such an absurd statement that Bashir exploded with rage. "And you *believe* that? Does that rationale make *any* sense to you? Or does it sound like some politician's ginned-up excuse to play God with the lives of people who can never hold him accountable?"

Her eyes burned with cold resentment. "Everything with you has to be an extreme, doesn't it, Julian? Heroes and villains. Good and evil. Right and wrong. Never any room in your worldview for subtlety or nuance, is there? If someone doesn't agree with you, they must be stupid, or selfish, or part of a grand conspiracy. Well, I hate to break it to you, Julian: Sometimes people are just struggling to make the best of bad situations. Like this one."

She walked away without a look back. Bashir listened as the unseen door slid open, and then the echoes of Dax's footsteps receded until the door hushed closed, restoring the brig's ambience of deathly quiet.

Too wired to relax, Bashir paced until his adrenaline levels dropped, and then he flopped back onto the bunk and stared at the overhead. Alone with his thoughts, he recalled every argument he and Ezri had ever had as a couple; though this latest contretemps bore little resemblance in substance to their long-ago lovers' tiffs, the style had been eerily familiar.

He had always assumed that as he and those around him grew older, they all would change, some no doubt in unexpected ways. Now he saw the opposite was true; neither he nor Ezri was any different than they had been a decade earlier. If anything, they had become more like themselves over the years, as if time had distilled them to their essences.

We didn't grow apart, he realized. *We were* always *apart. We just didn't know it.*

Twenty-four

Shar walked at a brisk pace, one gloved hand pressed to his ear to muffle the sounds of the busy capital street so he could hear Torv's mealymouthed whining over his in-ear transceiver.

"*Yes, Shar, we're sure. The Starfleet ship has Bashir in custody, but they're not going anywhere. Sounds like you've got a few hours before their friends come to get the doctor.*"

He kept his voice down to minimize the risk of his side of the conversation being overheard by the daytime throng of pedestrians surrounding him. "How many hours?"

"*Who knows? It's not like Starfleet publicizes the movements of its starships.*"

"Fine, it doesn't matter at this point. Have you uploaded the comm recordings?"

"*They're on the transfer node. I've deducted my fee from your account.*"

Shar suppressed his rising urge to indulge in sarcasm. "Thank you, Torv."

The Ferengi remained snide in the face of courtesy. "*Anything else?*"

"Not at the moment, but stay by the comm. Shar out." He reached down to his belt and tapped the master switch on his personal comm, ending the private call.

Not wanting to attract attention, he stepped out of the flow of foot traffic and put his back to the wall of one of the avenue's stately old skyscrapers, a marvel of carved stone and mirrored glass. Though some people felt the new capital's past as one of Andor's commercial centers made it seem less dignified than the old capital, Shar admired the modernity and sleek style of Lor'Vela. Most of the buildings in this part of the city were pressed up against one another with nary a sliver of air between them. Most blocks hid enclosures shared by multiple buildings, large open squares converted to fountains and green spaces. Deprived of the convenience of back alleys, the lofty towers of commerce bunched their service entrances on the side streets.

Another knot of well-dressed civilians drifted past Shar, who merged into their ranks with ease. He had prepared for this outing by adjusting his attire to match the environment: a well tailored midnight blue suit with a light-gray shirt, black shoes polished to an almost obscene mirror-perfect finish, and a bespoke charcoal overcoat of the softest, warmest natural fibers he had ever touched. His ultra-fashionable sunglasses hid his paranoid eyes as he broke from the pack, picking up his pace as he turned the corner.

He reached under his jacket to the small of his back as he neared one of the service doors and pulled out a Starfleet-issue tricorder. A quick tweak of its settings, and he was ready.

No one was approaching in either direction on his side of the street, and no one on the other side seemed to be paying him any mind. Shar checked the markings on the service door, just to make sure he'd targeted the right one. A small stenciled warning at eye level read ANS EMPLOYEES ONLY—NO TRESPASSING.

I'm not trespassing. Just visiting unannounced.

A single pulse from the tricorder released the door's computer-controlled magnetic locks. He pulled it open, slipped inside, and pulled it shut behind him. The cinderblock corridor on the other side was narrow and lit with sickly green lights. He jogged around a couple of tight corners and up a few short flights of stairs. Tucked into one of the building's dusty back corners was a freight elevator. It had been designed to move cargo and equipment delivered by shuttles to the rooftop platform, and as such its lone car was spacious and high-ceilinged. Shar pressed the elevator call button and waited. A status screen beside the call button informed him of the elevator's downward progress to his sublevel. As it drew near, he stepped to one side and took cover behind some stacked boxes, in case the lift proved to be occupied.

A chime heralded its arrival. The double-layered doors opened, one retracting upward, the other descending to fill the gap between the car and the floor, to better facilitate the transfer of cargo on old-fashioned wheeled load lifters. There was no sound from inside the lift, so Shar emerged from hiding and stepped inside it.

Its control panel was keycard secured. That was a wrinkle Shar hadn't anticipated. He was searching the tricorder's settings to see if it could bypass this obstacle, when a weathered, brawny young *thaan* in a grimy red maintenance coverall interrupted his labors.

"Who are you? And what are you doing with that?"

Shar greeted his would-be interrogator. "Hi! I'm an engineer in the IS department—just started, actually—and this is one of our newest inventions. Here, check it out." He handed his tricorder to the *thaan* with cheerful enthusiasm. The *thaan* wrinkled his brow but took the device from Shar. When the maintenance worker turned his eyes toward the device's screen, Shar punched him in the throat, boxed his antennae with a fierce clap of his hands, and landed a swift kick to his groin. As the *thaan* dropped to his knees, Shar plucked his tricorder out of the *thaan*'s hand, then he kneed the worker in the jaw to finish the fight.

"Sorry about that." He dragged the unconscious *thaan* inside the freight elevator and snagged the access keycard from the front chest pocket of the *thaan*'s coveralls. "But you'll thank me someday."

He swiped the card in and out of the reader beside the controls, then pressed the pad for the rooftop. It lit up, the doors closed, and the lift car began its swift ascent. *Ten seconds to the roof,* Shar noted. *Might as well put the time to use.* He powered up his tricorder, logged on to his private data-transfer node, and downloaded the file Torv had uploaded using Shar's public encryption key. It was one of the oldest methods of anonymous, secure communications and data transfer, but it remained one of the most effective, even after several centuries of use.

The lift doors opened, and a frozen edge of wind slashed at him. Winter's gusts were stronger and colder atop the building than at street level. Up here there was no shelter, nothing to stand in the path of the gale and bear the brunt of its frigid wrath. Shar traded his tricorder for a Type-1 phaser and fired a single shot into the elevator's controls. Then he clutched the lapels of his overcoat shut with one hand and held on to his phaser in the other as he made his way across the rooftop. He paused at the door to the emergency stairs and fragged its lock controls, then moved on to the structure that housed the building's orbital communications uplink. He opened its door with another precision phaser blast and ducked inside, out of the lacerating cold.

Banks of circuitry and walls of hardware blinked and hummed with power—this was a system Shar understood well. He had seen many like it during his service in Starfleet, on his way to earning a top rating in communications systems while serving aboard the *Tamberlaine*. The uplink was the Andor News Service's portal to the galaxy at large, its means of sending and receiving subspace signals from distant worlds and ships in orbit. But to a skilled technician such as Shar, it was even more than that: it was a backdoor into ANS's hard-wired planetary network. From here, he could take advantage of the entire network's formidable broadcast capabilities.

It wouldn't take long for the network's engineers to deduce what Shar had done, or from where, so he knew he would have to make the most of this infiltration of their system. Using a suite of Starfleet cyberwarfare applications on his tricorder, he broke into the ANS system as an administrative user and locked out anyone else with top-level authority.

As he'd expected, his efforts triggered alerts almost immediately. *They're very good,* he observed. *But not good enough.* He uploaded the audio recordings snagged by his Ferengi contact into the ANS system and marked them as public access files, a designation that meant they were to be shared over unencrypted networks with all of the planet's news services and made freely available to the public at large. The data transferred in less than a second, and he uploaded a Trojan horse application that would hide backup copies of the recordings under various names throughout the network and restore any deleted primary copy within seconds. *Don't even bother trying to kill this bit of truth; it won't stay dead, no matter what you do.*

All that remained now was to add his own, personal touch.

He activated the RECORD function on his tricorder.

"People of Andor: My name is Thirishar ch'Thane. Many of you know who I am. For those of you who don't, I work at the Science Institute with Professor Marthrossi zh'Thiin. She and I, and many others, have been working these past three years to devise a cure to our centuries-long fertility crisis using the Shedai Meta-Genome data provided by the Tholians.

"Many of you are demanding to know why we seem no closer to a cure today than we did three years ago. I had my suspicions, as did many others, but it was not until today that my worst fears were confirmed. Presider Ledanyi ch'Foruta and his *Treishya* allies have blocked our access to portions of the data provided by the Tholians, in the hope that slowing our research will harm the political fortunes of the Progressive Caucus and give the *Treishya* an unbreakable hold on power in the capital. Our lives have become the stakes in their cruel political game.

"I have uploaded to the public news nets a recording made less than an hour ago, of communications between our government and four starships currently in orbit: the Imperial warships *Ilmarriven* and *Tuonetar,* the Starfleet vessel *Aventine,* and a private freighter, the *Parham*. Traveling on the *Parham* was my friend and former crewmate Doctor Julian Bashir. He requested asylum on Andor so that he could bring us the cure to our fertility crisis, a cure that he devised based on data and research that I shared with him a few weeks ago. The *Treishya* and their political allies denied Bashir's request for asylum, and Presider ch'Foruta, in defiance of the Parliament Andoria, handed Bashir over to Starfleet without any kind of due process.

"Starfleet and the Federation will tell you lies about Doctor Bashir. They will call him a criminal, a spy, a deserter, a thief, a traitor, a liar with delusions of grandeur. But I assure you that he is none of those things. He is a man of genius, vision, and principle who has risked everything he had, and all that he ever will have, to bring us help in our hour of greatest need. Julian Bashir is no traitor, he's a hero—*our* hero.

"So why is our government turning him away? Why not grant him the courtesy of reviewing his case? If he's mistaken, or if he's lying and I've been deceived, then by all means extradite him. But if, as I believe, he speaks the truth and has the cure, we must welcome him. We must not let the Federation, or Presider ch'Foruta, deny us this glimmer of hope.

"I tried, many years ago, to suss a cure from the turnkey gene of the Yrythny genome, which I'd found in the Gamma Quadrant; I failed. I know many of you blame me for tragedies that were caused by that research; some of you resent me for filling your hearts with false hope. I understand your anger. I deserve it. But now I must ask you to trust me, one last time.

"March on the capital. Today! Now! This minute! Contact your members in Parliament. Tell them it's time for the presider to step aside and let wiser heads guide our fate. Because, my fellow Andorians, this time . . . the future of our civilization truly hangs in the balance.

"Decide. And act."

He stopped the recording and uploaded his message into the ANS network—then triggered an all-channels signal interruption to make sure every active monitor on the planet would hear what he had to say. No doubt the recording would be picked up by other news services and repeated, ad nauseam. Whether it would prove sufficient to goad a once-proud but now tired and despairing people into decisive action, only time would tell.

Running footsteps and shouting voices echoed behind the emergency stairwell door. In a few moments, Shar knew, the roof would be swarming with armed private security.

He clutched the tricorder to his chest and walked to the roof's edge.

A metallic bang cut through the wind noise as someone kicked open the stairwell door. Shar triggered his tricorder's built-in emergency beacon.

An angry *thaan* with beady eyes and a sharp chin charged forward, his sidearm aimed at Shar's face. "Whatever you're holding, drop it! Hands up! On your knees!" More armed guards poured out of the staircase behind him. They fanned out to either side of the leader, all of them brandishing potentially lethal weapons with the trembling hands of underpaid amateurs.

Shar stepped up and back, atop the low barrier wall that ringed the roof's perimeter. An indicator light on his tricorder's screen switched from red to green.

Then he stepped backward, off the roof.

He imagined their horrified faces, their silent slack-jawed shock. After a few seconds, one of them would muster the will to look over the edge, only to see . . . no sign of him.

The annular confinement beam negated his momentum as it took hold of him, and his blurred view of the cityscape washed to white before fading to reveal the familiar accoutrements of a Starfleet transporter room. Behind the transporter control console, a wide-eyed young human woman whose uniform was marked by crimson trim and an ensign's pips regarded him with curious suspicion. Standing in front of the console and aiming a phaser at him was a green-scaled, black-haired Takaran woman. Next to her was a familiar face.

"Sam!" Shar stepped forward, arms outstretched to embrace his old friend Bowers.

The brown-skinned, shaved-headed human man held Shar at arm's length. "Sorry, Shar. I'm afraid the reunion has to wait." He turned to the Takaran. "Place him under arrest."

In all her life, zh'Tarash had never seen a scandal erupt so quickly into riots—but then, until now, she had never seen a scandal in which the very survival of her species had been at stake.

Shar's message had spread like fire through paper, igniting the fuses on fears old and new around the world in the span of a few hours. His vid and the communication recording he'd uploaded seemed to be the only things that anyone on Andor was watching, or talking about, or writing about. He'd struck his rhetorical blow at midday in the capital. Now, as the sun dipped below the horizon, millions of enraged Andorians had descended upon Lor'Vela. They had come in private transports, or on the maglev trains, or through the planetary transporter network. It was terrifying to zh'Tarash how rapidly their numbers had swelled to fill the streets and plazas.

Now the mob had surrounded the capital building. Even within the protected space of the parliament's meeting chamber, there was no escaping the low and ominous chanting of the people outside. All their rallying cries bled into a wall of noise, a sonic tide that felt as if it might crest the barricades and swamp them all at any moment.

Tonight the Andorian people were white-hot with fury, a blade burning bright, fresh from the forge—and Kellessar zh'Tarash was determined to be the hammer that would give them a new edge and a stronger temper. It was time to strike, before their passions cooled.

The presider and his lackey speaker had forced the Parliament Andoria into recess, but this time they had overstepped their bounds. Tall with pride, zh'Tarash strode down the main passageway to the meeting chamber's upper-tier entrances. Walking just behind and to either side of her were her allies, Ulloresh th'Forris, leader of the Unity Caucus, and Narwanit ch'Szaan, leader of the New Restoration Party. Marching behind them was every member of their respective parties, the entirety of the Loyal Opposition, as well as a majority of the unaligned Alliance party—and, hounding the procession from its flanks, a gaggle of journalists and correspondents from every news service on Andor.

A male Trill reporter, whom zh'Tarash thought looked too young to be out on a school night, thrust a pen recorder toward the Progressive leader while speed walking backward beside her. "Leader zh'Tarash, what do you hope to accomplish while the Parliament is in recess?"

"You need to brush up on the bylaws of the Parliament Andoria, young man. If a majority of the elected ministers are present and wish to do so, they can compel the speaker or the presider to gavel parliament back into session. And if they refuse, or if neither can be reached in a time frame deemed reasonable, a pro tem speaker can be appointed to open the proceedings."

The reporter perked up, sensing the story was bigger than he expected. "Why would the speaker or presider refuse to gavel Parliament back into session?"

"Ask them. Here they come now."

She lifted her chin, and the reporter nearly tripped over his own feet as he turned to see Presider ch'Foruta and Speaker ch'Lhorra leading the members of their governing coalition—the *Treishya*, True Heirs of Andor, and

Visionists—down the main passageway from the opposite direction. For a moment, the two groups resembled armies converging, and zh'Tarash reflected on an old Andorian saying: Politics is merely war by other means. Then the great portals of the meeting chamber swung open to admit its elected members, and like rivers diverted, they flowed down the tiers and segregated themselves into their ideological tidal pools.

The media crowded into the public galleries that looked down on the chamber. Surveying the room from her desk, zh'Tarash drew a deep breath; the air was heavy with fear and charged with rancor. Everyone knew why they were gathered, and zh'Tarash felt a grudging respect for ch'Foruta and his partisans that they had chosen to face this moment head-on rather than seek to delay the inevitable.

Speaker ch'Lhorra picked up his gavel, cracked it thrice against its block, and declared to the chamber, "The Parliament Andoria stands in session."

Before the speaker had finished his sentence, zh'Tarash was on her feet. "*Cha* Speaker, I move for a vote of no confidence against this government."

"Seconded," interjected Unity Leader th'Forris.

The speaker said what was required of him in a glum and tired croak of a voice. "Voting shall commence at once and will last until all members present have voted or abstained."

On an ordinary vote, the various whips might spend an hour or more cajoling votes from the more reluctant members of their respective parties, trading favors or wielding threats as circumstance dictated. But this was no ordinary vote; this was a radical moment, a mirror image of the debacle that had set Andor on a lonely and self-destructive path three years earlier. This, zh'Tarash hoped and prayed, would be remembered as the day that Andor reclaimed its heritage.

The tolling of a sonorous bell signaled that voting was completed. A glance at the chrono confirmed what zh'Tarash had expected: less than twelve minutes had elapsed since her motion. All eyes turned to the speaker, who reviewed the vote count, which was visible for all to see on a display above the presider's dais.

The outcome was already known, but protocol had to be observed.

"The motion carries. This government stands dissolved." He struck his gavel once.

It was ch'Szaan's turn to stand. The head of the New Restoration Party rose and lifted his voice to fill the chamber. "I move for the formation of a new governing coalition, uniting the New Restoration Party with the Unity Caucus, the Progressive Caucus, and the Alliance Party."

Zh'Tarash called out, "Seconded!"

"Motion carries," th'Forris declared. "Members of the named parties: Confirm or reject this new coalition. Voting will continue until all members present have voted or abstained."

As quickly as one government had fallen, another rose to take its place. Within minutes the votes had been cast and counted, and the new coalition was confirmed.

The speaker set down his gavel and left it behind as he exited his dais. Above him, the presider also withdrew without fanfare. No doubt they would retire to their offices and collect their personal effects, escorted by capital security as a matter of protocol.

Watching from the fourth tier, zh'Tarash wanted to feel overjoyed. A few days earlier, a political upheaval such as this would have seemed impossible—as impossible as a cure for the fertility crisis. Now she stood at the summit of Andorian politics, and hope for her people seemed almost within reach. On its face, it was a moment that should have felt like victory.

Unfortunately, now she and her peers had to contend with a bloodthirsty mob on their doorstep, a Tholian envoy who would pressure them to bend to the Typhon Pact's whims, and a shortsighted hawkish Bajoran ideologue who saw bullying Andor and its people as his ticket to the Federation presidency. There were few moments when it was ever good to be in charge of a government, but this seemed to zh'Tarash like the worst possible moment to assume responsibility for running Andor.

So be it. If change is all they want, change is what we'll give them.

She sat back and savored the moment. Perhaps it would be a good day, after all.

Twenty-five

"**W**hat the hell is happening on Andor? Is this more of Starfleet's excellence on display?"

Not many people enjoyed the privilege of shouting at Admiral Akaar. His wife was one; the other two were the sitting President of the United Federation of Planets and, when necessary, the president's chief of staff. As the head of Starfleet endured the verbal abuse of Ishan Anjar and his Tellarite lackey Galif jav Velk, he kept his temper in check by telling himself that these two were only temporary occupants of the Federation's executive office.

Unless Ishan wins the special election, his inner pessimist reminded him.

"To the best of my knowledge, Mister President, neither Captain Dax nor any member of her crew had anything to do with the political shift in the Parliament Andoria."

"A political shift? Is that a new euphemism for 'radical upheaval' you just invented?"

Akaar let his exhaustion mask his fading patience with stony indifference. "Given that the membership of the Parliament Andoria remains unchanged despite the realignment of its internal factions and the fact that the transfer of power occurred legally within the parameters of Andor's parliamentary procedure, 'shift' seemed the most apt description of the situation."

Ishan stewed in his anger on the other end of the subspace

channel. Velk, at least, was keeping a cooler head on his side of the split-screen communication. *"Admiral, we sent Captain Dax to Andor to prevent Bashir and his outlandish claims from becoming a political issue."*

"We understand that, sir. However, there was only so much that could be done to restrict the flow of information in that scenario. And I think it should be noted that Captain Dax and her crew demonstrated exceptional restraint in not retaliating when they were fired upon by rogue Andorian forces. Had they shot back, this crisis could have escalated far more dramatically."

Velk took it upon himself to answer for Ishan. *"The president pro tem and I appreciate all their sacrifices and courage, Admiral. What's important now is containing the situation and keeping control of the narrative for the press and public."*

"If you say so."

Ishan cocked one eyebrow. *"How long until* Aventine *reaches Earth with Bashir?"*

"The *Aventine* is too badly damaged to leave orbit. I've sent the *Falchion* and the *Warspite* to rendezvous with her within the hour and to take custody of Bashir."

"That's all well and good, but how long until Aventine *departs?"*

"The current estimate is just under two days, sir."

The stern-faced Bajoran shook his head. *"That won't do, Admiral. The political climate on Andor is far too volatile to risk any further contact. I want the* Aventine *homeward bound with Bashir, even if your other two ships have to tow her home at warp one."*

"Captain Dax might object to that, sir."

"Then make it an order. This won't be a subject for debate.

I want both Doctor Bashir and the Aventine *back at McKinley Station by the time I return on* Starfleet One."

A grudging nod. "As you wish, sir. Regarding the political situation on Andor, I think we might consider taking this opportunity to lift the embargo as a gesture of goodwill."

Ishan turned defensive. *"Excuse me?"*

"This change in the governing alliance shifts the tenor of the Andorian government in a way that might be favorable to us, sir. With the Progressive Caucus leading the new governing coalition, there might be a chance to normalize political relations with Andor and maybe even broach the possibility of bringing them back into the Federation. If you were to rescind the trade sanctions you imposed and give me permission to end the embargo—"

"Absolutely not. The change in the Parliament Andoria only proves my policies are working even better than expected."

"With all respect, sir, the political situation on Andor is complex and driven more by internal factors than by external pressures. To ascribe credit for the parliament's realignment to a unilateral policy that has barely had time to—"

"Admiral, why are we talking about this?" interjected Velk. *"I don't recall your portfolio including oversight of interstellar trade policy or external diplomatic missions. Did I miss a meeting? Were those cabinet responsibilities recently reassigned to your office?"*

Akaar forced himself not to tense his muscles, hunch his shoulders, or clench his jaw. To the president pro tem and chief of staff, he knew he would appear calm and unemotional. But deep inside, in the dark pit of his warrior soul that he hid from all who knew him, he imagined what it would feel like to seize Ishan and Velk and break them like dry twigs.

He answered Velk in as level and unaffected a timbre as he could muster. "No."

"Then I suggest you stick to running Starfleet and leave the politics to us."

"Whatever you think best, sir."

Ishan frowned. *"Contact us the minute the* Falchion *and* Warspite *are under way with the* Aventine. *And reassign whatever resources you need to maintain the embargo. That's all."* He reached forward, and the screen switched to the Starfleet emblem before fading to darkness.

Akaar fumed at the blank screen on his office desktop. His pulse pounded out a devil's beat in his temples, and he clenched his left fist until his fingernails bit into his palm. Ishan was legally his commander in chief, and Akaar was bound by oath to obey his orders to the letter. But the *letter* was not the *spirit,* so that was where Akaar resolved to begin his rebellion—by fixing his moral compass on what he knew was right and letting his conscience be his guide.

Hearing the brig's door open, Bashir found himself hoping, for reasons he couldn't articulate, that Dax had come back. He hid his mild disappointment when Doctor Simon Tarses turned the corner and stood facing him through his cell's invisible force field.

The younger man was a few inches shorter than Bashir and slight of build. A medical satchel was slung at his left hip and a medical tricorder occupied the pocket on the side of his right thigh. The years since he and Bashir had served together on the old Deep Space 9 had been kind to the quarter-Romulan physician; his dark hair was now distinguished by a few gray hairs at his temples and subtle creases lived at the edges of his smile, but otherwise he remained gallingly youthful.

He greeted Bashir with a genial nod. "Hello, Julian."

Bashir rolled off his bunk and stood. "Simon. What can I do for you?"

Tarses patted his satchel. "Just need to give you a quick exam. For the record."

"Ah, yes. The standard evaluation for new prisoners. Proceed."

The young chief medical officer powered up his tricorder and took out its small, cylinder-shaped metallic scanning device, which he aimed at Bashir. "How are you feeling?"

"About as well as can be expected."

"That badly, eh? I've heard a lot of gossip about you in the last day."

"Such as?"

Tarses shrugged. "Some people are calling you a traitor."

Bashir searched his old friend's eyes for some hint of his true feelings. "And what are *you* calling me?"

"At the moment? My patient." He trained the sensor on Bashir's midsection. "Any discomfort or lingering physical pains? Any reason to suspect you suffered blunt-force trauma when your ship got caught in the crossfire?"

A weary sigh signaled Bashir's waning patience. "I feel fine, Simon."

"Just doing my job, Julian. Bear with me." He glanced up from his tricorder and cast a sly look at Bashir. "Mind if I ask you a non-medical question?"

"If you like."

"Why'd you do it?"

Bashir hesitated to answer. Was this some sort of trap?

Some ruse to elicit a confession that would soon be used against him? He didn't think that Simon Tarses was the sort of person who would collude in such a betrayal, but then he hadn't served with him in nearly five years. People could change a great deal in far less time than that, as Bashir had learned with Ezri Dax. For the moment, he chose to err on the side of self-preservation. "Why did I do what?"

"What do you think? Steal classified data. Hijack a runabout. Throw away your career."

"I didn't steal the classified data." Technically, that was true; one or more agents of Section 31 had stolen the data. It was merely a convenient omission on his part that he failed to reveal he had solicited the crime. He continued, "I only *used* it."

Tarses switched off the small scanner and put it away. "You know what? I'm not a lawyer. I don't care about the semantics of what you did or didn't do. If it makes you more comfortable, we can speak hypothetically. If you stole classified data and used it to cook up a cure for the Andorian fertility problem, what would be your rationale for throwing away your career and risking life in prison?"

"Simply this: It's the right thing to do."

An understanding nod. "Somehow, I knew that's what you'd say." He adjusted the settings on his tricorder and looked down at its display as he continued. "Did you hear we have Shar in custody?"

Bashir's cool façade vanished, and he barely stopped himself from lunging forward into the force field. "When? How?"

"He used a Starfleet emergency beacon on a tricorder to get himself beamed out of a jam on the planet's surface. Apparently, he seized control of the planet's broadcast networks to plead your case to the people. And I think it worked. They stormed the capital, and something happened to shift the balance of power in the parliament. Just like that"—he snapped his fingers—"Andor has a new government. How do you like that?"

"Not a bad day's work. . . . So, Shar's on the *Aventine* right now?"

Tarses tilted his head. "Yup. Just a few cells over. Next to your pal Captain Harris." He paused to study something on the tricorder, then he switched it off and slung it back by his hip. "So, you developed the cure as a benign retrovirus and injected it into your bloodstream, eh?"

"It seemed like a good idea at the time."

"So the cure isn't something you can just dump onto an isolinear chip. You're the cure. You're the package that has to be delivered to Andor."

An embarrassed shrug. "That was the plan. Alas, it seems to have hit a snag."

"Prepare to be un-snagged." He tapped his combadge. "Tarses to sh'Pash. Ready."

As the brig's outer door opened, Tarses tapped the control pad beside Bashir's cell and lowered the force field. Moments later, an attractive young Andorian *shen* wearing a gold-trimmed Starfleet uniform and carrying a Type-II phaser rounded the corner, followed by Shar and Captain Harris. The *chan* nodded at Bashir, who nodded back.

Sh'Pash handed Bashir a combadge as he stepped out of his cell and regarded Tarses with new admiration. "Simon, you know they'll crucify you for this."

Tarses grasped Bashir's shoulder. "If you succeed, it'll be worth it."

The *shen* gestured toward the exit. "Doctors? Are you ready to go?"

Tarses started walking. "Let's go."

Bashir followed with pleasure. "I thought you'd never ask."

"You wanted to see me, Captain?"

Dax sat at her dining table and looked up at Bowers, who stood outside her quarters, leaning his head through the open doorway. She beckoned him. "Come in."

He crossed the room to stand in front of her. She pushed an empty glass across the table to him, then nodded at the bottle of Aldebaran whiskey between them. "Fill up and sit down."

Bowers poured himself a generous double shot of the amber liquor and lifted the glass to his nose for an appreciative sniff. "The good stuff." A small sip led to a deeper taste, and he settled into the chair opposite Dax's. "What's the occasion?"

"My annual crisis of conscience." She downed another swig of the floral, caramel-scented alcohol and savored its oaky aftertaste and soothing warmth. "Did you ever find yourself taking a stand for something you didn't really believe? Just because you had to?"

The XO shrugged. "I've certainly had to defend decisions other people made that I didn't agree with. But that's part of wearing a uniform."

"So I keep telling myself." She drummed her fingers on the tabletop a few times. "Like when you were telling me what a stupid idea the embargo was. Or how ineffectual and pointless the blockade would be. I knew you were right, but I had no choice but to argue against you."

He cast his eyes down again, into his drink. "We all have our orders."

"Yes, we do. But when did I start following mine so

blindly? I used to have a mind of my own. At least, I thought I did. Was I only imagining that?"

Bowers shook his head. "No. During the Borg invasion, you were downright roguish."

"I *was,* right?" She quaffed another half-mouthful; this time her lips puckered at the whiskey's sour notes. "At some point I started living by the book instead of my conscience."

"Can we drop the ranks for a second?"

"Absolutely. Don't take this the wrong way, but I need a friend right now way more than I need a first officer."

He put down his drink. "Speaking as your friend, Ezri, I'm wondering what has you all spun up like this. Was it your talk with Bashir?"

Dax nodded. "I heard everything he said, and inside my head, I agreed with him. Everything he's doing, and his reasons for doing it—they all made perfect sense to me. But every word out of my mouth was an argument. It was like I couldn't bring myself to agree with him. Like I'd spent so long arguing with him over the past few years that even now, with all that behind us, I fell back into the same old pattern of opposing any idea he supports."

"If you don't mind my asking, can you be more specific?"

She took another sip of whiskey to calm her ragged nerves. "We have orders to recover and suppress all the Meta-Genome Data, including whatever part of it might be included in the cure Julian says he created. But what if Julian's right? What if the value of that information lies in our ability to share it instead of our ability to hide it?" She put her drink down, then pushed it aside. "I mean, isn't ensuring the survival of the Andorian people more important than trying to shove a hundred-year-old secret back inside a box?"

"I certainly think so. Apparently, so does Julian."

"So why do I sit here telling myself lies?" She got up and paced toward sloped ports that lined one side of her quarters and looked out on the northern hemisphere of Andor. "Why do I defend the inexcusable policies of a politician whose beliefs I despise?"

Bowers peered ruefully into his drink. "Because you swore an oath, just as I did—and so did every other officer of Starfleet."

"But Ishan is so clearly in the wrong, Sam. He's smug, and conniving, and something about him just rubs me the wrong way. I wish I could explain it better than that."

"No, I think that sums up the little weasel perfectly."

Dax looked back at Bowers. "Thanks." She returned to the table. "Here's the thing, Sam. Julian told me that he's hiding the cure for the Andorians in his own bloodstream. He doesn't even need to go to Andor to deliver it. We could have Simon draw some blood from him, and then we could beam it down to Shar's associates with instructions from Julian on how to extract it and mass-produce it."

"Except that we're under orders not to let the Andorians acquire the cure."

"Precisely. And that's the order that sticks in my craw. The Andorians are teetering on the edge of extinction. Their future as a species is at stake. And we're sitting on the cure because . . . why? Some ill-defined fear about 'national security'? We hold their fate in our hands, Sam. Don't we have a higher duty, not just as Starfleet officers but as sentient beings, to act out of compassion rather than blind obedience? If we deny them the cure, and they pass the tipping point, won't that make us guilty of genocide? That's not something I want to live with."

Bowers put down his glass. "You could obey your conscience instead of Starfleet and the president pro tem, but that path comes with consequences."

"I know. And so did Julian, but it didn't stop him from doing the right thing." She moved to stand at Bowers's side and looked him in the eye. "What do you think I should do?"

He looked at the table. "Whatever your conscience tells you."

"Don't duck the question, Sam. I'm looking for an honest opinion, here. And I'm asking you as a friend, not as my XO, and not as an officer. We're just two people talking here."

He lifted his eyes to meet hers. "No, we're not. I'm your first officer, and you're my captain. Where you lead, I follow. You tell me what you want to accomplish, and I'll make it happen, come hell or high water. So, you tell me, Captain: What's the mission?"

His profession of loyalty caught her so by surprise that for a moment she was speechless. After a deep breath, she gathered her courage and settled her mind upon a course of action.

Then the whooping cry of a Red Alert echoed through the ship, and Lieutenant Kedair's voice resounded over the intraship PA system.

"Attention, all decks! Three prisoners have escaped the brig: civilian Emerson Harris and former Starfleet officers Thirishar ch'Thane and Julian Bashir. Report to General Quarters and secure all decks. If you spot the prisoners, alert your deck officer. Bridge out."

Dax sighed and shot a glum look at Bowers as they walked together toward the door to the corridor. "Looks like someone just made my decision for me."

Sprinting for their lives, Bashir followed Shar, Harris, and Tarses inside the transporter room. Lieutenant sh'Pash stood beside the open doorway; with one hand she waved them through like an Academy drill instructor herding cadets through an obstacle course, while with her other hand she swiveled a phaser back and forth, covering both sides of the corridor.

Just before she darted inside, she fired a few shots in either direction, then she locked the door and melted its control pad with a single blast of her weapon. "We have company," sh'Pash said as Tarses crossed to the transporter console.

"Shar, Doctor, Captain, get on the pad," Tarses snapped. "You, too, Thyla."

Before Bashir could ask what would happen to Tarses, the other surgeon's Andorian partner in crime herded Shar and the two human men onto the transporter platform. "Quickly." As soon as the four of them stepped onto the elevated platform, its energizer coils hummed to life, and Bashir felt a galvanic tingling travel over his body from crown to toe.

Tarses looked up from the controls at sh'Pash. "You preset the coordinates?"

"It's good to go," the *shen* replied. "Energize!"

The young doctor passed his hands over the console's touchscreen interface, and a white embrace of light and sound washed away the details of the room just as the whine of phaser fire began to howl at its door—

—and the glow faded to reveal the interior of the *Aventine*'s main shuttlebay, where the battered hulk of the *Parham* stood with its starboard hatch open and gangplank extended.

Two security officers leveled phasers in the trio's direction, but sh'Pash fired first and stunned her two shipmates with unnervingly precise marksmanship. She waved Shar, Bashir, and Harris toward the *Parham*. "Into the ship!"

Harris and Shar ran for the freighter's gangplank, but Bashir grabbed sh'Pash by her sleeve and spun her around to face him. "Why didn't we beam to the planet?"

The Andorian yanked her arm free. "We're running with shields up! Intraship beaming was the best I could do. Now go! I'll get to the control room and open the bay doors."

She didn't wait for him to agree or thank her, she just sprinted away, focused on the next step of her mission to set Bashir and his cohorts free.

Bashir took off at a full run and chased Harris and Shar up the gangplank into the *Parham*. As he crossed the threshold a step behind Shar, Harris shouted over his shoulder, "Retract the plank and seal the hatch!" Shar turned back and helped Bashir carry out Harris's orders, and then the two former Starfleet officers hurried forward into the *Parham*'s cockpit.

Outside the forward viewport a narrow strip of stars appeared and then rapidly widened as the *Aventine*'s shuttlebay doors glided apart. Harris punched in commands on the master console, fired up the freighter's damaged impulse engine, and nudged his ship into motion.

As soon as they cleared the shuttlebay's force field, phaser blasts lanced through the darkness on all sides of the little ship, rocking it like a dinghy trapped in a tempest. As Harris steered a wild path through the fiery mayhem, he flashed a devil-may-care grin over his shoulder at his passengers. "Grab somethin' heavy, gents. I get the feelin' we're in for a rough ride."

A manic atmosphere reigned on the bridge of the *Aventine* as Dax rushed from the turbolift with Bowers close at her back. On the main viewscreen was an image of the *Parham* diving toward Andor. Dax hurried into her command chair as she called out to Kedair, "Tactical, report!"

"The *Parham* has left the shuttlebay and is making a run for the surface."

Bowers kept his eyes on the screen as he ordered, "Tractor beam! Now!"

The security chief keyed in the command, only to be met by an unhappy feedback tone. "Malfunction, Captain. Tractor beam emitter levels are at less than four percent power."

"Helm, maintain pursuit course, keep us in range. Mirren, how long to restore tractor beam power?"

The operations manager swiveled around from her panel, her expression urgent. "Sir, someone sabotaged the tractor beam's main plasma relay."

Dax nodded. "Probably the same someone who broke our prisoners out of the brig and helped the *Parham* leave the shuttlebay."

Bowers reviewed the latest update on his console. "Captain, a security team just arrested Lieutenant sh'Pash and Doctor Tarses for aiding and abetting the prisoners' escape."

Just when I thought this day couldn't get much worse.

From the tactical station, Kedair asked, "Should I arm phasers, Captain?"

"Negative. That ship's too badly damaged. One shot could vaporize her."

Kedair moved her hand away from the phaser controls. "Aye, sir."

A blinding beam of orange energy slashed across the main viewscreen, and as Dax's eyes recovered from the flash, she saw a starship's phaser blast rip into the *Parham*'s impulse engine, which erupted in a white-hot burst of ignited plasma.

Dax watched the small freighter spiral erratically into

the atmosphere. Enraged, she sprang to her feet. "What was *that*?"

Everyone raced to update their consoles. Kedair answered first. "Not us, sir! That shot came from the *Warspite*!" The image on the main screen switched to show the *Sovereign*-class starship cruising into orbit from behind the *Aventine*.

An alert chimed on Mirren's panel. "They're charging up for another shot!"

"Helm! Put us between them and the *Parham*! Mirren, hail the *Warspite*!"

The *Aventine*'s engines whined and its hull groaned in protest as Tharp forced the ship through a sudden deceleration and turn into its sister ship's line of fire. At the operations console, Mirren worked with speed born of terror before she looked back at Dax. "I have commander, *Warspite*, on channel one."

"On-screen." Dax strode forward to present the most formidable image possible.

Looking back at her from the main viewscreen was Captain Steven Unverzagt. The human commanding officer of the *Warspite* was an imposing figure: tall, broad-shouldered, and densely muscled. His face was defined by a strong, proud chin, a dark and well-kept beard, and a head of thick black hair worn slightly longer than was considered customary for Starfleet officers. His gray eyes and heavy brow combined to give him an intense stare that seemed engineered to shred lies and break down pretenses. He leaned forward on one elbow and eyed Dax with unfiltered irritation. *"Captain, what do you think you're doing?"*

"Hold your fire, Captain."

"I'll do no such thing. Move your ship out of my firing solution."

Dax glanced back at Kedair. "Lieutenant, shields to full, and lock phasers and torpedoes on the *Warspite*. If they fire on the freighter again, return fire."

"Aye, Captain."

Unverzagt simmered behind narrowed eyes. *"You're letting Bashir get away."*

"No, I'm stopping you from causing an interstellar incident. The *Parham* was inside Andor's atmosphere when you fired on it. That means you attacked a civilian ship with deadly force while it was under *Andorian* jurisdiction. That's a *crime,* Captain." She threw another look back at Kedair. "Lieutenant?"

"Weapons locked on the *Warspite,* sir."

Faced off against her burly, bearish peer, Dax exorcised any trace of anxiety from her face or her voice. "Final warning, Captain. Stand down or I *will* fire on your ship."

Unverzagt's resentment was plain to see. *"You'll regret this, Captain."*

The transmission ended without notice, but a moment later Mirren noted a change on her console. "The *Warspite* has powered down its weapons and lowered its shields."

Bowers faced the viewscreen. "Looks like the damage is done, though."

Dax's heart sank as she watched the *Parham* plunge toward Andor's surface in a flat spin, trailing smoke and shedding debris from its unshielded and overheated hull. If Bashir and the others were trapped inside the crippled freighter, they were as good as dead.

All that Bashir could see or smell was smoke. It tasted of burnt plastics and overheated metal, and it was blacker than night. Its heavy particulate dust was a sticky, insidious poison that adhered to his skin and infiltrated his nostrils, his ears, his pores.

It was all but impossible to imagine anything being loud enough to rise above the death wail of the *Parham*'s crippled engines and power core, but somehow Captain Harris's violent cursing cut through the high-pitched shriek of rushing wind and shredding metal. The scrappy pilot remained strapped into his command chair at the helm, fighting and failing to make his hobbled ship obey even the simplest commands. Bashir and Shar alternated between being pinned to one bulkhead or another and being hurled about like rag dolls in a broken centrifuge.

A crack cut across the ship's forward viewport, and half a second later hundreds of fissures branched off that first break and one another, spiderwebbing the transparasteel panel.

Harris craned his head back, over the top of his seat, and shouted something at Shar and Bashir. The words got lost in the banshee howl of the *Parham*'s uncontrolled descent. Bashir looked at Shar to see if he'd understood, only to see his own confused expression mirrored on the young Andorian's soot-stained face. They both shook their heads at Harris, who rolled his eyes, drew a chestful of air, and bellowed, "Get in the goddamn escape pod! Now!"

Shar was next to the pod's open hatchway, and he pulled himself through it just before another wild roll of the ship would have hurled him aft. He powered up the controls for the pod as Bashir fought his way across the narrow passageway. At the hatchway's edge, Shar stopped him from entering and pointed at the hatch and ejection-system control panel. It showed nothing but a jumble of symbols and half-formed interface graphics, none of which were functional. Bashir pointed inside the pod at the guidance controls, which flickered to life. Shar leaned back, checked the panel, then turned back toward Bashir to flash a thumbs-up confirmation.

Bashir pulled himself forward, toward the cockpit. As he edged inside the cramped space, one of the secondary starboard consoles exploded, filling the cockpit with smoky bits of polymer shrapnel. Harris ducked behind his raised arm for cover, then saw Bashir as he lowered his hand. "What the hell are you doin', Doc? Get in the pod!"

"The ejection controls are fried!"

"I know. Been meanin' to get 'em fixed. Serves me right, I guess."

A hard jolt rocked the ship to port, and then its nose plunged, and Bashir was pinned to the back of Harris's chair. "What do you mean?"

Harris's hands flew across his console, struggling to route every last bit of power to just two systems: the structural integrity field and the escape pod. His voice began to crack from the strain of besting the noise. "I can launch the pod from here. Get in and I'll do the rest."

Yelling over the roar of the blazing wreck left Bashir hoarse. "What about you?"

"I'm done for, Doc. I fired on a Starfleet ship. They'll never let me fly again, and I ain't goin' to jail. This is it for me, so go! I'll hold her steady."

He grabbed Harris's shoulder and made the man look at him. "You're sure?"

There was no fear in Harris's eyes. "Doc, this is the best thing I've ever done. . . . Go."

Bashir left Harris and clawed his way over sparking consoles and imploding bulkhead panels to the escape pod. He motioned Shar deeper inside, then clambered in after him.

As soon as Bashir was fully inside the pod, the hatch rolled shut behind him. Deep thumps and vibrations in the hull signaled the release of the magnetic clamps, and half a second later he and Shar were pinned to the aft hatch as the pod rocketed away from the *Parham*, streaking through Andor's mesosphere like a bullet shrouded in fire.

The inertial dampers kicked in a few seconds later, and the two old friends tumbled in free fall. Shar tapped a command into the guidance system, and the pod ceased its rolling. Once the view through the aft hatch's viewport stabilized, they both looked back.

In the distance, trapped in the hazy realm between the vacuum of space and the cushion of atmosphere, the *Parham* was a dark projectile, tumbling and rolling, spewing smoke and casting off pieces of its hull. Then a great flash consumed the vessel from within, and its shattered remains spread across the sky like a flower of smoke.

Bashir pushed back against his sorrow; there was no time for it—not yet. All he could do was promise himself he would make sure the name of Emerson Harris was remembered with his own when people spoke of who helped save the Andorians from a premature oblivion.

Shar placed a consoling hand on Bashir's shoulder. "My condolences, Julian. We were lucky you had such a brave friend."

It shamed Bashir to admit the truth. "Actually, I barely knew him."

"Then we should count ourselves doubly fortunate. Most people don't inspire such courage in strangers." The *chan* pulled himself back toward the guidance controls and started programming landing coordinates.

Bashir watched over Shar's shoulder. "We're heading for the plains of Kathela?"

"No, but this pod is. I can't take a chance on anyone tracking us to the Science Institute's dark site. Even with the change in the government, secrecy is the only protection they have." He finished his computations and locked in the pod's descent profile. Then he turned to the communications panel, set up an encrypted channel, and sent out a simple message consisting only of what looked to Bashir like random numerals.

A moment later came the reply—another string of numerals, followed by symbols. Shar copied the new information and added it to his comm's cipher code. Then he opened an audio channel. "Shar to Professor zh'Thiin. Do you read me, Professor?"

A crackle of static was followed by a woman's voice. *"Yes, Shar. Go ahead."*

"I'm with Doctor Bashir, and he has the cure. We're in an escape pod on approach, and we need you to beam us down as soon as possible."

"Acknowledged. Locking onto your signal now. Stand by to transport."

Bashir shot a quizzical look at his friend. "Where, exactly, *are* we going?"

"Let me put it this way: If you like ice fishing, you're in for a treat."

Twenty-six

"*I am forced to conclude, Admiral, that you have lost all control over the mission to Andor.*"

On the face of it, the president pro tem's assertion was hard for Akaar to refute. "This situation is complex and potentially explosive, Mister President. Given the delicate state of our political relationship with Andor, I would argue that Captain Dax's actions were in the best—"

"*They were insubordinate,*" Ishan cut in, his anger verging on incandescent, "*not to mention harmful to the interests of Federation security.*"

Akaar smothered his temper as he faced his commander in chief via the secure subspace channel being transmitted from the high-warp transport designated as *Starfleet One*. "So far, sir, I see no actual harm. Handled correctly, we could turn these events to our advantage."

The Bajoran waved off Akaar's suggestion. "*I don't want to hear any more about your agenda for peace, Admiral. I want to hear how you plan to deal with Captain Dax.*"

"At the moment, I see no reason to take a hand in the matter."

"*She threatened to fire on another Starfleet vessel!*"

The accusation hung between them, unanswered, while Akaar wondered how the president pro tem had already acquired such detailed intelligence regarding the confrontation between the *Aventine* and the *Warspite*. Akaar had already transferred Commander Sarai out of Starfleet Command to a less sensitive posting on Luna, so if Ishan or one of his senior advisers had a source inside Starfleet's headquarters, he had no idea who it might be. Then he considered the possibility that Ishan, who had already demonstrated a keen disregard for the protocols of the chain of command, might have bypassed him and made direct contact with Captain Unverzagt on the *Warspite*. Either way, his up-to-the-minute knowledge of events in the field boded ill.

"Under the circumstances, sir, I think Captain Dax acted within the law. If anyone is deserving of a closer review, I would suggest it's Captain Unverzagt."

Ishan's seemingly omnipresent Tellarite adviser, Velk, leaned into the frame and whispered in his ear. The Bajoran gave his counselor a quick nod, then motioned him away. *"Let's move on for now, shall we? What are we doing to get Bashir off Andor?"*

The question, to Akaar's chagrin, was just what he'd expected. "Legally, we have no right to do so. If the Andorians capture him, we can ask them to extradite him."

"The Andorians? Why would they arrest him? As far as they're concerned, his only crime so far might be trespassing." Ishan grumbled under his breath and shook his head in frustration. *"No, Admiral. We can't just sit back and wait for them to hand Bashir back to us. We need to go in there and get him before he turns over classified data that could do us real harm."*

Akaar feared the conversation's next turn. "What are you suggesting, sir?"

"Don't pretend we aren't speaking the same language, Admiral. I want you to arrange a covert operation on the surface of Andor, to find Bashir and return him alive to the Warspite.*"*

"Such an operation would be a violation of Andorian sovereignty, sir."

"Which is why it has to be covert. The Falchion will arrive at Andor in a few minutes. I want you to task them with keeping the Aventine neutralized while the Warspite completes its mission. Is that understood?"

The more Akaar heard, the more discomfited he became. "Sir, please clarify what you mean when you say you want the *Falchion* to 'neutralize' the *Aventine.*"

"Captain Dax has demonstrated a propensity for ignoring, subverting, and outright disobeying my orders. I have no doubt that if she is informed of our intention to recapture Bashir, she'll take action to prevent it. So I'll make this as clear as I can, Admiral: Captain Dax is not to be informed of this operation in any way, either generally or specifically. To that end, the Falchion's mission will be to isolate the Aventine from the chain of command and prevent it from communicating with other ships or entities on the planet's surface. If the Aventine tries to take action against this operation, or if it does anything that seems contrary to our interest in containing the Meta-Genome data, the Falchion is authorized to do anything necessary to stop her. Confirm for me that you understand my order and that you will carry it out."

"I understand your orders, sir, but I also have a responsibility to warn you of their potential consequences. If a covert operation on Andor goes wrong, or inflicts any degree of collateral damage, it could serve to alienate the Andorians even further from the Federation—perhaps far enough to drive them into an alliance with the Typhon Pact."

His warning seemed to amuse Ishan. *"Then so be it. If Andor allies itself with our rivals, I'll have no choice but to show them what a grievous mistake that is—and let them serve* as an example to the rest of our member-worlds that they're better off with us than against us."

Akaar gave up any hope of reasoning with the man. It was clear that Ishan had made up his mind—or that someone had made it up for him—on everything from foreign policy to the minutiae of Starfleet's command-and-control process, and contrary opinions were unwelcome. "Very well, sir. I'll relay your orders to Captain Unverzagt. Unless, of course, someone in your office has already taken the liberty of relieving me of that necessity."

A brief but venomous silence conveyed Ishan's displeasure at Akaar's dry jibe. "*I'll look forward to hearing from you as soon as you have Bashir back in custody. Good luck, Admiral.*" Without waiting for acknowledgment or valediction, Ishan ended the transmission.

There was no question in Akaar's mind of what he had to do. He had his orders, and he would see them carried out in good faith, just as he had sworn to do many decades ago. But whether the mission at hand ended in success or tragedy, he knew that it would set a terrible precedent. It was not merely that Ishan was overly belligerent and too quick to resort to force that troubled Akaar. It was that Ishan was reckless, vindictive, and petty. These were not admirable qualities in any leader; in the person of a Federation president, they could be disastrous.

One crisis at a time, Akaar reminded himself as he left his office to set in motion the president pro tem's ill-considered plan. *For now, I must deal with this and do all I can to prevent a calamity. And tomorrow, when this is done . . . then I will begin to deal with Ishan.*

The drawing of blood for analysis was a simple procedure, one that required only two persons: a patient from whom blood was being taken, and a phlebotomist to perform the procedure. In fact, there was no reason why, given the conveniences of modern medical science, a trained medical professional could not draw a sample of his or her own blood, completely unassisted.

Consequently, it struck Bashir as a touch of overkill that nearly every member of Professor zh'Thiin's staff at the Science Institute's dark site was pressed in upon the two of them in a tight huddle, in the middle of the main laboratory. A host of Andorian faces representing all of the species's ethnic variations—antennae in front or in back, skin tones in more than a dozen hues of blue, and countless subtleties of physiognomy and antenna shape—watched with wide eyes and bated breath as zh'Thiin used a hypospray to draw a primary sample of Bashir's blood. No one spoke as she switched out the removable ampoule on the hypospray and drew a second backup sample. Then she passed the two clear cylinders filled with red human blood to one of the mesmerized witnesses. "Get these into the sequencer and isolate the retrovirus."

The lanky researcher hurried across the lab, and the gathered knot of his peers parted ahead of him, their deference to his passage almost reverent. Half the group followed him to the molecular sequencer at the far end of the vast room, while the rest lingered around Bashir, Shar, and Professor zh'Thiin, who put away her hypo syringe.

Bashir massaged the tender spot on his forearm from which the serum samples had been extracted. "How long will it take you to isolate the retrovirus?"

"If it's as unique as you said, we should be able to separate it from your blood and map its gene sequence in under an hour."

Shar's mood was less optimistic. "The real problem is what to do with it after that."

"What do you mean?" Bashir rolled down his sleeve. He looked back and forth between Shar and zh'Thiin. "Are you saying you don't have mass-production capabilities?"

"We do," zh'Thiin said. "Several of them, all over the planet. What we don't have right now is a secure way of getting the quantum pattern to them for industrial replication."

Noting the confusion on Bashir's face, Shar added, "It's the riots, Julian. Comm networks are failing all over the planet. Some are going down because of traffic spikes, and some are being crippled by physical sabotage of the signal routers."

Bashir pondered the problem and all its complexities. "What about the transporter system you used to beam us off the escape pod?"

The professor shook her head. "Most industrial facilities are shielded against transporter beams. Routine counter-espionage tactics since the Dominion War."

Bashir was perplexed. "Can't you hail them? Ask them to lower their defenses?"

That got a rueful chuckle out of Shar. "In the middle of a global uprising?"

"Ah. I see. Never mind."

Professor zh'Thiin sighed. "The other problem is that the *Treishya* probably still want to stall the cure, to improve their chances of regaining control of the Parliament. The moment one of their people hears we're sending out the cure's pattern, they'll cut the power to the pharmaceutical factories. The only way this works is if we can rapidly distribute the cure and get it into mass production before the *Treishya* have time to stop it."

A worrying thought occurred to Bashir. "But if they know I'm already on the surface, won't they already be looking to block you from delivering the pattern to the manufacturers?"

"That's what we're afraid of," Shar said. "It's also part of why I sent the escape pod toward Kathela. I'm hoping the *Treishya* are wasting time and manpower searching for us near the pod and looking for this lab on the wrong side of the planet."

The professor turned a concerned glance toward the scientists working on the far side of the lab. "There's another risk we have to consider. Even if we can restore data-line connections to the manufacturing facilities, sending out a signal this huge to multiple recipients will make it easy for the *Treishya*—and anyone else—to trace it back to this site. Assuming that ch'Foruta and his followers are itching for payback, we could be looking at a very unfriendly visit within an hour of sending out the cure. Getting murdered at night in the snow might end up being our reward for saving the world."

"Reminds me of an old Earth saying," Bashir said. "'No good deed goes unpunished.'"

Shar replied, "That proverb has a long history on Andor, as well."

Bashir chortled at the morbid absurdity of their predicament. "I guess some concepts really *are* universal."

Sequestered in her ready room, Dax passed each interminable minute hoping for good news from the planet's surface. There had been reports on several Andorian military channels that the escape pod from the *Parham* had been recovered intact, but with no sign of any survivors. It seemed unlikely that anyone could have evaded detection fleeing on foot from the crash-landed pod, so Dax was left wondering whether its passengers had been plucked off the pod before it made planetfall—or if, perhaps, no one had survived to board the pod in the first place.

Can't think like that, she chastised herself. *I have to hold on to hope.*

Her door signal cut through the maudlin silence. She took a breath, sat down at her desk, and cleared her thoughts. "Come in."

The door slid open, and Bowers entered. He stood at ease in front of her desk as the door closed. "Captain, I thought you'd want to know that the *Falchion* has arrived in orbit."

"I know. I saw them through my viewport."

Bowers looked out the viewport behind Dax. "Aha. Starship spotting the old-fashioned way."

"I go with what works. Something else on your mind, Sam?"

He looked only mildly abashed at being so easily read. "Any fallout from your showdown with Captain Unverzagt?"

Dax recalled her subspace conversation with Admiral Akaar, whose tolerance for crisis and controversy seemed to be nearing an end. "Not yet. But the day is young."

The first officer processed that news. "Can I ask why you let the *Parham* go?"

"She was too far away for a tractor beam—not that we had one—and I didn't think the situation merited the use of deadly force." Memories of the *Parham*'s fiery end haunted her thoughts. "Unfortunately, the *Warspite*'s captain disagreed."

"I suspect the president pro tem had a hand in that outcome."

"Gee? You think?" She stood and turned to face out the viewport and admire the stark beauty of Andor. "Let Ishan make all the noise he wants. I stand by my decision."

Two soft tones from the overhead comm were followed by Lieutenant Kedair's voice. *"Captain, Commander, you're both needed on the bridge."*

"On our way." Dax gestured at Bowers to lead the way. She followed him out the door to the bridge and felt the ambient tension ratchet sharply upward.

As soon as the two of them had reached their side-by-side command chairs, Kedair looked up from the tactical console to report. "Captain, we've detected encrypted subspace signal traffic coming and going from both the *Warspite* and the *Falchion*. I've confirmed the source of the signal is Starfleet Command."

Alarm and suspicion traveled in swift whispers from one bridge officer to another. Dax turned to Bowers and leaned close to confer with him in a tense hush. "Why is Starfleet Command talking to our escort ships but not to us?"

"Best guess?" Bowers glanced at the images of the *Falchion* and the *Warspite* on the main viewscreen. "Someone's telling them to do something we won't like, and since the powers that be no longer trust us to do as we're told, we're being cut out of the loop."

His explanation fit the facts, but Dax remained baffled. "But what are they gearing up to do? What *can* they do? Even if Bashir's alive, he's on Andorian soil."

"Maybe the people giving the orders don't give a rat's ass about that."

Mirren swiveled around from the ops panel. "Captain? We're being hailed by the *Falchion*. Its captain says we're to be towed out of orbit and into warp for the trip home."

"Like hell we are." Dax strode forward, looking for a confrontation. "Put the *Falchion*'s captain on-screen, right now."

After a few seconds of futile tapping and confused

reactions, Mirren looked back at Dax. "I can't, sir. I'm getting nothing but static on all frequencies."

"That's because the *Falchion*'s jamming our comms," Kedair said. "Looks like someone wants us gagged for the ride home."

The *Sabre*-class starship grew larger on the viewscreen as Mirren reported, "They're maneuvering into position for warp-capable towing."

Dax went back to her command chair, determined not to lay down without a fight. "Helm, evasive. Tactical, auxiliary power to shields. Mirren, get me eyes on the *Warspite*."

Bowers took his seat and advised Dax sotto voce, "We weren't really in any shape for a fight with one ship, Captain. Maybe antagonizing two at once isn't such a great idea."

"Who's *antagonizing*? I'm just *resisting*. . . . For now."

Mirren split the image on the viewscreen to show the *Falchion* on one side and the *Warspite* on the other. "Captain, the *Warspite* is powering up her subspace antennas and main deflector dish. The *Falchion* has initiated a pursuit course and is accelerating to overtake us."

"Helm, keep us out of the *Falchion*'s reach." She swiveled toward her Zakdorn science officer. "Gruhn, program a feedback pulse that'll use the *Falchion*'s jamming signal to fry its own comms." Looking at the evidence in front of her, Dax was forced to arrive at the logical conclusion. "Sam, they're going after Julian, and their first move is to get us out of the way."

"Orders, Captain?"

"Get the *Falchion* off our tail, and get us back in the game. And make it fast—if I'm right, Julian doesn't have much time. Which means neither do we."

Captain Steven Unverzagt—known as "Zot" to his close friends, none of whom he allowed to serve on his ship—epitomized the concept of economy of effort. Seated in his command chair, hearing and seeing all that transpired around him, he was the still point at the center of the action that filled the bridge of the *Warspite*. He kept his eyes on the main viewscreen, watching the movements of the *Falchion* and the *Aventine*, even as he imagined a seemingly endless variety of possible outcomes to his ever-changing circumstances.

His executive officer, Commander Sarjat Ramapoor, finished a whispered conference with Lieutenant Zimm, the Nalori chief of security, and cut across the bridge to Unverzagt's side. "Captain, the *Aventine* is evading the *Falchion*'s attempts to take them in tow."

Unverzagt kept his eyes on the screen. "I can see that. Tell me something new."

"The *Aventine* has reinforced her shields and charged her phasers, and now she's scanning *us*."

"Is she? If for nothing else, let's give Captain Dax a small measure of credit for tenacity."

Ramapoor turned a worried eye toward the viewscreen. "Should we postpone the operation until after we've removed the *Aventine* from the equation?"

"Absolutely not. She was never going anywhere. And to be perfectly blunt, we need her. I'm counting on Captain Dax to be my ace in the hole." He checked the tactical update on the display to the left of his command chair. "Let's see how much steel Dax really has in her spine. Order the *Falchion* to ramp up its jamming of the *Aventine*. Comms, sensors, the works."

"Aye, sir." Ramapoor walked forward to relay orders to the operations officer, a fresh-faced Denobulan ensign named Korl.

Unverzagt turned his chair just enough to shoot a

sidelong look at the tactical officer. "Lieutenant Zimm. Is the cyberwarfare team ready to proceed?"

"Yes, sir." The Nalori, whose jet-black skin, teeth, and eyes contrasted so majestically with his pale aqua crew cut and drooping mustache, looked up with pride. "All teams report ready to engage Operation Bright Storm, on your mark."

"Begin. Tell me when we've finished Phase One."

Zimm transmitted the order to the ship's cyberwarfare unit, which was safely ensconced on one of the *Warspite*'s lower decks, near the main deflector dish and sensor modules. Their mission profile was the model of simplicity: infiltrate, corrupt, and disrupt all of Andor's extant medical information networks and their known or potential backups.

The entire operation was anticipated to last only two to five minutes from initiation to completion. Once it was over, most of Andor's civil and military information networks would be hopelessly crashed. The best estimates Unverzagt had seen for the Andorians' projected recovery time was no less than two days.

More than enough time to carry out Phase Two, Unverzagt mused. The next step in the operation involved locating Bashir's precise coordinates on the planet's surface, beaming down an armed covert operations team, taking him into custody, and beaming him back aboard the *Warspite* for his immediate journey back to Earth, where a military tribunal stood waiting.

Ramapoor returned to stand beside his captain. "Andorian data networks are collapsing, sir. We should have information superiority in less than two minutes."

"Very good, Number One. Keep the strike team and transporter chief on hot standby."

"Of course, sir. But, if I might ask an operational

question?" With a curt nod, Unverzagt cued the man to continue. "How do we plan to find Bashir before the Andorian military forces us out of orbit?"

Unverzagt kept his eyes on the main viewscreen, on which the *Aventine* loomed larger with each passing moment. "As soon as all data networks on the surface are disrupted, order the *Falchion* to create a gap in their jamming signal, and to make certain it looks like an accident."

The first officer still did not seem to grasp the overarching strategy. "And then?"

"And then, Number One . . . we sit back, and we wait."

Twenty-seven

"What do you mean you can't transmit the pattern?"
Bashir hoped he had heard Shar wrong, because all his risks and sacrifices would be rendered meaningless unless the Science Institute could disseminate the quantum replication pattern for the Andorian retrovirus. "Is something jamming the channel?"

The young *chan* grew more distraught the longer he tried and failed to make the comm terminal do his bidding. "It's not jammed. I think it's dead."

Nervous whispers susurrated among the scientists gathered behind Shar and Bashir. Professor zh'Thiin cut through the murmuring with a sharp-edged command. "Carri! Run a diagnostic on the network. Are we getting valid pingbacks from the other nodes?"

Doctor sh'Feiran pushed her way free of the clustered researchers, found a free terminal, and started running simple tests. Bashir watched the *shen*'s face shift from hope to dejection in a matter of seconds. She halted the last test and looked up at zh'Thiin. "Nothing. No signal at all."

Shar leaned back from the terminal and slumped low in his chair. "That's it, then."

Bashir looked back and forth between Shar and zh'Thiin. "What does this mean?"

"It means someone shut down the planet's entire data

network," zh'Thiin said. "Without it, there's no way to transmit quantum replication patterns."

"Can't we send the data over a standard subspace comm channel?"

"Normally, yes," Shar said. "Unfortunately, someone's jamming all of Andor's civilian channels, and our comm equipment isn't capable of operating on military frequencies."

The precision and efficiency of the disruption left Bashir with no doubt who had caused it. "These are Starfleet information-warfare tactics."

Shar shook his head. "Just like they taught at the Academy—by the book."

"We'll just wait them out," zh'Thiin said. "It won't take long for someone else to realize what's happening. When they do, the Andorian military will force the Starfleet ships to leave."

Bashir and Shar exchanged grim looks of mutual recognition. The *chan* broke the news to his colleague. "We don't have that much time, Professor. If we wait until the Starfleet vessels leave, the *Treishya* will use that delay to seize control of all the production facilities. If we lower our screens to try and call for help, the *Warspite* will lock on to our signal and come in force to capture Bashir—and the cure."

His bad news only added urgency to zh'Thiin's resolve. "Then we'll make multiple copies of the quantum pattern, one for each of us, and we'll all leave here and split up. We'll become couriers and bring the cure directly to the manufacturing sites."

Shar was more than dubious. "A sudden large-scale departure? They'd detect that for sure. And even if they didn't, you know the *Treishya* won't stop looking for us just because they're out of the majority. They won't let us deliver the pattern if they can stop us."

"He's right," Bashir said. "The only safe way to deliver the pattern is by transmission."

"Whatever we do," Shar added, "we'd best do it soon. If Starfleet storms this lab before we get the cure disseminated, that'll be game over."

A desperate plan formed in Bashir's imagination. He leaned in beside Shar and pointed at the comm terminals. "Show me all the comm frequencies that are being blocked."

The *chan* called up the data on the screen. "What are you thinking, Julian?"

Bashir made a swift perusal of the information, which confirmed his suspicions. "They're blocking only Andorian frequencies." He reached into one of his jacket pockets and pulled out the combadge sh'Pash had given him during his escape from the brig a few hours earlier. "Which means I should be able to contact the *Aventine* using this."

Shar raised his hands. "Hold on. Why hail the people who're hunting you?"

"Because I don't think Ezri is the one jamming the comms or disrupting the data network." Replaying the tragic confrontation in his memory, Bashir pictured which ships had fired at which time. "After we slipped the *Aventine*'s tractor beam and entered the atmosphere, they didn't chase us. But the *Warspite* did—they fired on us, and they were shooting to kill. And they'd have finished us off if the *Aventine* hadn't stepped in to block their shot." The more he thought about it, the more sense it made. "I think Ezri was trying to help us, and not just to preserve Starfleet's rules of engagement. I think she's the one person in orbit we can trust right now." He met Shar's doubt with his own unflagging certainty. "I *have* to talk to her."

"Julian, to do that, we'd have to drop the lab's energy

screen. The moment we do, we'll show up on *everybody's* sensors, Andorian and Starfleet alike. At that point, we might as well go outside and put a neon bull's-eye on the roof."

Professor zh'Thiin shook her head and turned away. "It's too dangerous."

"I know it's not an ideal solution," Bashir admitted, "but I think it's our only chance."

Fearful looks traveled from one set of eyes to another. No one seemed content to sit and await the bitter end, but neither were any of them in a hurry to hasten its arrival. Petrified, zh'Thiin looked at Shar for counsel. "You know this woman, don't you? Can we trust her?"

"I don't know. We served together for a while, but I haven't seen her in years." He shifted the burden of account-ability to Bashir with a single glance. "But she and Julian used to be in love. If anyone knows her, he does."

The gathered scientists turned their collective gaze toward Bashir. He had no idea what to tell them except the plain truth. "I can't promise that Ezri will help us. I know that if she betrays us, this is all over. We can't even contact her without giving away our position. That seems to be by design; I think someone, probably the captain of the *Warspite*, wants me to reach out to Dax. So in that respect, yes, I'll be playing straight into his trap. I wish there was a better way, and that I could give you more reason for hope, but all I can tell you is this: Dax is one of the bravest souls I have ever known. Irrational as it might be . . . I believe in her."

Shar looked at zh'Thiin for a decision.

The professor sighed and addressed the room. "What will be, will be. Shar, patch Doctor Bashir's combadge into the comms and try to encrypt his signal to the *Aventine*, for whatever good it does. The rest of you, find weapons. I suspect we're about to need them."

Dax turned as her security chief announced, "Captain? We're being hailed by Doctor Bashir."

"In my ready room." The Trill captain moved at a quick step toward her sanctum just off the *Aventine*'s bridge. "Sam, you have the conn. Keep the *Falchion* busy."

Bowers pivoted into the command chair. "Aye, Captain."

Behind Dax, the bridge crew continued to work in well-rehearsed concert, marshaling their varied forms of expertise toward the singular goal of rendering the *Falchion* deaf, dumb, blind, and toothless. Knowing the counter-offensive was well in hand, she pushed it from her thoughts as she hurried into the chair behind her desk and opened the comm channel on her holographic display. Bashir's face snapped into crisp focus; he looked haggard and worn.

"Julian! Are you all right?"

"I'm fine, Ezri, but we don't have much time. We're being jammed—"

"By the *Warspite*, I know. But you shouldn't be hailing us, they'll—"

"Trace the signal back to us. It was a risk we had to take. We need your help."

He was desperate. She couldn't remember ever hearing such genuine trepidation from Bashir, who had always prided himself on putting up a cool front. "What do you need?"

"The planet's data networks have crashed, and the civilian comm channels are jammed. Without them, we can't get the cure to the pharmaceutical factories. I need you to help deliver the retrovirus's quantum pattern to those sites, as soon as possible."

She froze. It was an open call to insubordination. Letting him escape through strict adherence to the rules of engagement had been one thing; actively defying explicit orders from Starfleet Command and the Federation government was another. "Julian . . . I . . ."

"It's ready to go, on a portable data card. We just need to get the pattern to the plants."

"You're talking about a court-martial offense."

He calmed himself, and the fear left his voice. *"I know I've asked the impossible, Ezri. And I know I have no right to put you in this position. For that, I apologize. But whatever you choose to do . . . and no matter what happens to me . . . I will always be your friend. I hope I can still call you mine."* A blue finger tapped on Bashir's shoulder, and he looked away for a moment. *"If you'll pardon me, I'm told we need to go prepare for the inevitable."*

As he turned away, Dax's eyes misted with tears and her heart swelled with admiration and affection for this quixotic man she'd once loved. "Julian!" Her exclamation turned him back toward the conversation. "Are you *positive* you have the cure?"

His answer was calm and devoid of ego. *"I'm absolutely certain."*

She was going to regret this. "Stay right there, and *don't move.*"

Six pillars of light shimmered into being at the far end of the lab, and Bashir felt his throat tighten as he realized the figures that materialized inside the transporter beams were clearly holding phaser rifles. Had the *Warspite's* forces found them first? Or was this Dax coming to arrest them all herself? Beside him, Shar tensed as he watched the humanoid forms solidify inside the swirling columns of fading particles, and Professor zh'Thiin clasped one slender hand onto Shar's shoulder.

Standing at the front of the away team was Dax. She held a phaser rifle in her hands, just like the personnel behind her. As soon as the last remnants of the transporter effect released them, she strode toward Bashir, followed by her team of security personnel, who were being led by the *Aventine*'s Takaran chief of security, Lieutenant Kedair.

Dax pointed toward the exits and snapped orders over her shoulder. "Lonnoc, we need to secure this wing of the complex. I want transport scramblers placed and active in thirty seconds. Rendezvous at the center junction in ninety seconds. Set all weapons for heavy stun, fire for effect. Move!" Kedair and the security team left the laboratory at a full run, and as they passed Bashir he saw that each of them wore a transporter inhibitor with retractable tripod base strapped across his or her back. Meanwhile, Dax joined Bashir and Shar at the comm terminal. "You two okay?" They nodded affirmations, so Dax turned her attention to the scientists. "Those of you who have weapons, set them for stun and help set up barricades at the main intersection. Those of you without weapons, find some place to hide and stay there till we come for you. I'll be here with Shar and the professor. Go!"

The other researchers hurried out, leaving zh'Thiin, Shar, Bashir, and Dax to speak in private. The Trill looked at Shar. "Julian said you have the pattern on a data card?" Shar nodded, and Dax extended one hand. "Give it to me. Quickly."

Shar looked at zh'Thiin, who nodded her permission. He reached under the comm terminal and retrieved the card from its hiding place, then handed it to Dax. She plucked a spare combadge from a pocket on her belt and affixed it to the card. Then she set it on the floor, tapped the combadge, and stepped back from it. "Dax to *Aventine*. Lock onto this signal and beam it directly to the bridge. Energize."

It took only about a second for a new transporter effect to fill the lab with white noise and prismatic light, and then the data card was gone. Dax tapped her own combadge. "Dax to *Aventine*. Report, Sam."

Bowers replied, *"Ready, Captain."*

"Sam, copy the data on that card and relay it to every pharmaceutical factory on the planet. This is an Alpha One command, and until it's completed, you are to consider all other mission priorities rescinded. Is that clear?"

"Understood, Captain. All other priorities rescinded."

"Good. Now wish us luck. Things are about to get pretty hairy down here."

"Be careful, Captain."

"Same to you. Dax out."

Poised at the edge of calamity, Bashir felt suddenly, strangely light of spirit. Then Dax turned and accosted him with mock reproach. "What are you smiling at?"

"Keep this up and I might fall in love with you again."

She drew a pistol-grip phaser from her belt holster and handed it to him with a rakish smirk. "Julian, I'm here to save your ass—this is no time to start *threatening* me."

Twenty-eight

The rifle was cool in Dax's hands, which she held steady despite the bone-deep chill that pervaded the snow-bound science facility. Hunkered behind some improvised cover—a large lab table pushed over onto one side—she peeked over the top edge, on the lookout for company.

Bashir crouched on her right and peeked around the side of the barrier with one eye behind the phaser she'd loaned to him. "What are they waiting for?"

"Probably trying to figure out how much firepower they'll need to blow through this choke point." She looked back at the other two branches of the crossroads-shaped intersection they were defending, with help from Kedair, a handful of security personnel, and half a dozen lightly armed Andorian scientists who looked as if they had never fired a shot in anger in their lives. "The scramblers we set will keep them from beaming into the south wing, and I have two of my people guarding its only exit, so they won't have much luck attacking from outside."

"Which means they'll have to—"

Phaser shots screeched overhead, loud and bright enough to make Dax and everyone around her squint in pain. More shots slammed against the barricades, and behind the furious shriek of energy weapons was the thunder of running feet. Overcoming her natural instinct to duck and hide, Dax forced herself to lift her rifle up and over the barrier to face her attackers.

"Weapons free!"

Her order snapped the rest of her compatriots out of their fetal curls and into action. As soon as they began to return fire, the oncoming wave of aggressors ducked into doorways and nooks, forced to slow their advance by resorting to two-by-two, leapfrogging cover-and-move tactics. Within seconds the metal lab table glowed a dull orange and grew too hot to touch.

Easy to forget how much punch a phaser on heavy stun really packs, Dax noted as she edged back to protect herself from getting burned through carelessness.

Dax popped her head up to check the corridor—then ducked to avoid another barrage of incoming fire. More shots flew over her head from behind, reminding her that the enemy had the advantage of attacking a single point from multiple directions.

A lucky shot sent one of the defending Andorians sprawling backward, unconscious. Then a full-power blast ripped through part of the ceiling over Dax's head. Smoldering debris rained down, along with blazing-hot motes of charged plasma. She lifted the muzzle of her rifle above her barrier's edge and fired blind, filling the west passageway with a random surge of suppressing fire as she shouted to Kedair, "Time for Plan B!"

The security chief ducked low as she pulled a small cylinder from her belt and armed it with a single press on its top button. Then she yelled over the clamor of phaser fire to a Kaferian member of her security team, "Zisk! Grenade!" The bipedal insectoid followed Kedair's lead, ducked low, armed a grenade from his belt, and signaled Kedair with the best approximation of a thumbs-up he could manage with his three-digit manus. Then Dax drew her own grenade while Bashir peppered the south passage with random phaser blasts.

Kedair, Dax, and Zisk sprang to their feet and hurled the explosives overhand with speed and precision. Kedair's flew down the north passageway, Zisk's arced away to the east, Dax's to the west. Then they dove for the floor, and Dax shouted for one and all, "Down!"

The nearly simultaneous pulses of searing white light were followed by peals of thunder so close they felt as if they could break bones by sonic force alone. Hot gusts full of dust and smoke billowed down the corridors and rolled over the intersection blockade. Fine silicate dust stuck to hair, skin, and uniforms, turning everyone identical shades of faintly metallic gray.

Risking a peek over the barricade, Dax saw the west passage blocked by heaps of smoking wreckage, broken thermo-crete, and twisted metal. Glowing spurts of superheated plasma jetted from ruptured conduits, and a firefall of sparks from severed live wires overhead danced and scattered across the debris. *That ought to buy us a few minutes,* Dax figured.

Her combadge chirped to announce an incoming signal. She hoped for good news, but was greeted instead by the enraged bellowing of Captain Unverzagt. His voice was loud enough in the dusty confinement of the intersection for everyone present to hear him with perfect clarity. "*Warspite to Captain Dax! Are you reading me, Captain?*"

Dax coughed to clear the dust from her mouth. "This is Dax. I read you."

He sounded apoplectic with fury. "*What the holy hell do you think you're doing?*"

She spied Bashir's approving smile in the hazy half-light and felt an odd sense of calm as she told Unverzagt the unvarnished truth.

"What's right, Captain. . . . I'm doing what's *right*."

In theory, Bowers knew it was possible for him to monitor all of the synchronous tactical challenges facing the *Aventine* from the central position of the command chair, but he was too wound up to remain seated. He moved from station to station as reports flooded in, hoping that he could keep this perilous juggling act in motion for just a few minutes more.

He arrived at the tactical console. "Kandel, where's the *Falchion*?"

The bald Deltan woman answered without looking up. "Still trying to maneuver back into jamming range, but her main antenna is still offline. We can hold her off."

"What about the *Warspite*?"

Kandel shifted the focus of her panel to Andor's southern pole. "Moving into a close-support profile for its strike team on the surface." She silenced a new alert. "They're beaming down additional troops. It looks like they have the lab complex surrounded."

"Keep me posted if anything changes." Bowers moved on, crossing the bridge toward science officer Helkara's station.

The first officer was halfway to Helkara when Mirren turned from the ops console and caught his eye. "Sir, we're receiving an emergency signal from *Starfleet One*." As if Bowers wouldn't know what that meant, she added, "Sir, it's President Pro Tem Ishan."

"I know who it is, Lieutenant. Do *not* open that channel."

"But it's—"

"Oliana, we're carrying out an Alpha One command from the captain. All other priorities have been rescinded. That means no new incoming orders or communications. Understood?"

Discomfited, Mirren returned to work at her insistently chirruping console.

Bowers crowded in on Helkara and perused his progress. "How much longer, Gruhn?"

The svelte Zakdorn's overlapping facial ridges mirrored his brow, which was creased with fierce concentration. "Almost there, Commander. The *Warspite*'s still trying to block the major channels, but I'm working around that by splitting the data into asynchronous packets on parallel subharmonic—"

"That's nice, keep working, tell me when you're done." Bowers gave the second officer a complimentary slap on the shoulder, then moved on.

He was a few steps shy of the command chair when Mirren hissed at him, "Ishan is *ordering* us to acknowledge his transmission, sir."

Bowers settled into the command chair. "Tell Ishan . . . it's good to want things."

A ruddy glow in the north passageway, backed by a rising cry of steady phaser fire, made it clear to Dax where the *Warspite*'s forces intended to break through her improvised defenses. "Lonnoc, we'll hold the line here. Julian, take the scientists and fall back to the end of the south passage."

Kedair began waving the Andorian defenders back, away from the flashpoint of the conflict to come. Bashir, however, remained at Dax's side. "I'm not going anywhere."

"This is about to get ugly, Julian. You don't want to be here."

A half shrug. "I've done my part for Andor. Now my place is here. With you."

A burst of light and a roar of noise filled the north passage.

Kedair cried out, "They're breaking through! Get down!"

Dax and Bashir took cover behind the north side's cobbled-together barrier of desks and filing cabinets. Kedair and Zisk flanked them, and the rest of the *Aventine* security team that had come with Dax huddled up close behind them, a second line against impossible odds.

Dozens of orange phaser beams lashed through the dusty darkness over their heads. High-power shots scarred the walls with carbonized burns, and smoke quickly filled the intersection.

Beneath the steady whine of phaser fire came a bright metallic clinking—

Thunder and blinding light, a concussive wave, then darkness—

. . . and Dax was alone in the blue twilight, stunned, immobile, her vision blurred, her hearing muffled. All around her, bodies lay strewn on the floor, some writhing in agony, some deathly still and half-buried in rubble. Her symbiont felt more present than usual, its mind more active. It was pushing her into action, taking command of her muddled senses in the name of self-preservation. Her body felt like lead mired in mud. It was so hard to move. . . .

A slow blink and her vision sharpened. Phaser shots were flying. Voices shouted.

A Starfleet Special Ops strike team, clad in solid black

field combat uniforms, charged through their freshly blasted gap in the north passageway's wall of debris.

Standing against them, alone in the corridor, was Kedair. She stood in the open, relying on her expert marksmanship and her Takaran distributed physiology to protect her in the face of overwhelming force. Undaunted, she stood as phaser beams lanced through her, leaving her dotted with holes. But thanks to a biology that had no vital organs, she remained on her feet, defiant and firing with unerring precision, picking off anyone who dared to brave the breach. Turning sideways to reduce her profile as a target, she held her ground, and between stunning the attackers, she brought down more chunks of the building on top of their heads.

Dax looked to her right and saw Bashir fighting his way back to consciousness. She crawled to him and dragged him behind cover. As they collapsed into a corner, he coughed out a mouthful of red spittle and grinned at her with bloodied teeth. "Are we dead yet?"

"Not for lack of trying. Good to go again?"

"Ready when you are . . . Captain."

She helped him up, and together they staggered back out into the fray to stand beside Kedair and tempt fate by holding the line for just a few moments more.

"That's the last one!" Helkara exclaimed. The Zakdorn spun from his station to face Bowers. "All sites have confirmed receipt and verified the pattern data!"

A cleansing sigh left Bowers ready for what he knew had to come next. "Mirren, put Ishan on-screen, please." He stood from his chair and held up his chin with pride.

The president pro tem appeared on the main viewscreen,

his ashen face tinted with rage. *"Identify yourself! To whom am I speaking?"*

"Commander Samaritan Bowers, first officer of the *Aventine*."

"Captain Unverzagt informs me your captain is assisting the fugitive Bashir on the planet's surface. Is that true, Commander?"

Bowers feigned ignorance. "Captain Dax didn't specify a reason for her away mission."

"Commander Bowers, effective immediately, you are to relieve Captain Dax of her command and place her under arrest for conspiracy to commit espionage and high treason."

"I understand, sir. Please stand by while I relay your order to our chief of security." Bowers pulled his thumb across his throat, a slashing gesture that signaled Mirren to mute the channel and terminate the outgoing visual feed. She confirmed the switch with a nod, and he added, "Get me Captain Dax, on the double."

Mirren worked quickly, then answered, "Channel open, sir."

"Captain, this is *Aventine*. Do you copy?"

Dax's reply was hoarse and half drowned under the whine of phaser fire. *"Go ahead."*

"Mission accomplished, and I have President Ishan on the comm."

"Is it what we expected?"

"To the letter, Captain."

A brief pause. *"Then you know what to do, Sam."*

"Aye, sir. Good luck." Bowers stepped forward to stand over Mirren's shoulder. "Hail the *Warspite* and tell Captain Unverzagt that Captain Dax and Doctor Bashir surrender."

Bashir looked on, dumbstruck as Dax dropped her phaser rifle and kicked it away. Then the young Trill starship commander caught Kedair's eye. "It's time, Lonnoc. Do it."

Peppered with phaser wounds that slowly fused shut, Kedair turned and aimed her phaser at Dax and Bashir. "Captain Dax, Doctor Bashir—you're both under arrest." For the benefit of the *Warspite* personnel who were gathered on the far side of the collapse blocking the passageway, she called out, "Cease fire! Captain Dax has been relieved of her command and taken into custody. I repeat— *cease fire!*"

The shooting stopped, and cautious eyes peered out through the smoky gloom. As the team from the *Warspite* advanced in slow steps through the breach, Kedair shouted back to the other *Aventine* personnel and the Andorians, "Stand down! Lower your weapons, and hold your fire! That's a direct order."

Bashir looked at Dax, pleading with his eyes for reassurance. Under her breath she confided, "It's okay, Julian. It's done."

No one spoke as the teams from the two starships met, wary of each other, both sides anticipating betrayal. Then reason prevailed, and Kedair stepped aside to confer in private with the leader of the Special Ops team from the *Warspite*. After a moment of hushed negotiation, they shook hands, and Kedair stood aside as the hulking black-furred Caitian lieutenant pointed at Dax and Bashir and snapped at his troops, "Arrest those two and prepare to beam up."

Commandos in black surrounded Bashir and Dax and pulled their arms behind their backs. Then each of them was restrained with a pair of cold, tight-fitting magnetic manacles.

Dax seemed tickled by their predicament. "How sweet! Matching jewelry."

Bashir couldn't help but chuckle. "There's the Dax I know and love."

As the commandos led the two of them away, she flashed Bashir a bittersweet smile that felt to him like friendship incarnate. "What can I say? You always did bring out the best in me."

Twenty-nine

Standing outside Ishan's circle of senior advisers, Admiral Akaar felt like an uninvited guest at a party. Lurking behind the president pro tem's shoulder was his Tellarite chief of staff, Velk, who acted as the traffic manager and gate-keeper, shushing some and inviting others to speak. Despite his best efforts, the tenor of the office on the fifteenth floor of the Palais de la Concorde was one of chaos straining at the leash of order and threatening to slips its bonds. All that Akaar could do was wince and try to shut out the din of over-lapping voices.

"Sir, if you could just look at next year's estimates for grain yields on Acamar—"

"We need an answer for the Sheliak Ambassador on the Tagoras problem before—"

"Polls show you ahead on Betazed, but only by one and a half points, and only against a single unspecified challenger, but if we run the numbers with multiple candidates—"

Ishan raised his hands and his voice. "All of you, stop! One at a time, damn you." He pointed at Safranski, a Rigel-lian who had served as the late President Bacco's secretary of the exterior and who continued in that capacity, pending the special election of a new president. "You were about to give me your read on the Andor situation."

"Yes, sir." Safranski cleared his throat, and Akaar noted that the Rigellian made a point of avoiding eye contact with

Velk. "In the seventy-two hours since the governing coalition of the *Treishya*, True Heirs of Andor, and the Visionists was dissolved by a no-confidence vote and replaced by the Progressive–New Restoration–Unity–Alliance coalition, several changes have taken place. Shadow cabinet members from the new coalition have been appointed to the front bench offices, and as of this morning, the Parliament Andoria has named a new presider."

The news put Ishan in a glum mood. "Let me guess: the Progressive leader, zh'Tarash."

There was genuine surprise in Safranski's reply. "No, sir. They elected Solloven zh'Felleth of the Unity Caucus."

Velk's porcine features took on a sinister cast. "Clever. Instead of elevating one of their own, the Progressives bought themselves some goodwill by backing their coalition partners. Would I be correct in assuming the cabinet posts have been equitably divided between the new coalition's member parties?"

Safranski continued to address his remarks to Ishan. "That would be correct. And just this morning, the Parliament Andoria passed its first binding resolution: a repeal of its Secession Act. It passed along party lines, and Presider zh'Felleth contacted the Federation Council in person to submit Andor's application for readmission to the Federation."

That revelation put Ishan visibly ill at ease, as if he had no idea how to react to it in mixed company. "I see. Most interesting." He forced a thin and patently insincere smile. "That should give the Council something to debate about for a while."

"Not likely." Joy brightened Safranski's face. "Several dozen senior members of the Council have already pledged to support Andor's readmission, and Councillor Enaren of Betazed has promised to fast-track the application out of committee over the weekend and move it to a floor vote. Andor's membership could be reinstated as soon as Monday afternoon."

Ishan's smile tightened almost to the point of vanishing. "Excellent. Anything else?"

"Just one more item." At last, Safranski turned his focus toward Velk, almost as if he expected to savor the moment to come. "As soon as Andor's membership is formally restored, its Progressive Caucus leader, Kellessar zh'Tarash, will announce her candidacy for the Federation presidency." The Rigellian looked pleased with himself as Velk winced at the news. Then Safranski added, to Ishan, "Looks like your campaign's about to get even *more* interesting, sir."

"I can hardly wait." Ishan turned away from Safranski to invite someone, anyone, to change the topic. "What's next?"

A cascade of voices filled the room, and Akaar remained outside the verbal scrum, in no mood to compete with bureaucrats for the pleasure of chewing on a rhetorical bone. He watched Safranski make a dignified departure from the office, and part of Akaar wished that he was leaving, as well.

Over the course of half an hour, one manufactured crisis at a time, the knot of supplicants surrounding Ishan's desk thinned. The last one to leave was the Bajoran's annoyingly cocksure campaign strategist, Rellim Eryjem, a pollster for hire whose last turn on the political stage had saddled the Federation with the belligerent ineptitude of Min Zife's second term. Only after the half-human, half-Orion political operative had left the office did Ishan and Velk even deign to note that Akaar remained at attention, mere meters from the president pro tem's desk.

Velk offered Akaar one open hand. "Admiral, our apologies for keeping—"

"Give us the room." Akaar's demeanor brooked no argument. "I need to have a word with Mister Ishan. In private."

Ishan motioned for Velk to leave. Then he noted Akaar's glance toward the agent assigned to Ishan by the Protection Detail, and the president pro tem waved his Vulcan bodyguard out of the room with casual indifference. The agent, to his credit, was reluctant to leave his post, but he seemed reassured when Akaar promised, "We'll be only a minute."

The agent followed Velk out the door, which closed after them.

Akaar stood in front of Ishan's desk and towered over the seated chief executive, whose countenance soured without the benefit of an audience. "So, Admiral. What's this about?"

"The chain of command, sir."

Ishan's eyes dulled with boredom. "What about it?"

"You need to learn to use it, sir."

Faced with a direct challenge, Ishan bristled and sat forward. "Excuse me?"

"Sir, during the past week, you have, on no fewer than three occasions, bypassed Starfleet Command and issued orders directly to active-duty Starfleet personnel in the field. On stardate 62703.9, you ordered Captain Ro Laren of Starbase Deep Space Nine to proceed to Bajor and arrest Doctor Julian Bashir. On stardate 62708.1, you requested a sitrep directly from Captain Steven Unverzagt of the *Starship Warspite*. Finally, on stardate 62708.7, you ordered Commander Samaritan Bowers of the *Starship Aventine* to relieve his commanding officer and take her into custody. I also have reason to believe that you or a member of your staff encouraged insubordinate activity by a Starfleet Intelligence liaison assigned to my office."

The middle-aged Bajoran arched one gray eyebrow with

disdain. "Are you challenging my authority as the civilian commander in chief?"

"No, sir. But the manner in which you exercised your authority was not only improper, it was in violation of Federation law and the Starfleet Code of Military Justice. If you wish to micromanage the actions of Starfleet, that is your prerogative. However, Starfleet's protocols of command and control require that you issue all military directives through Starfleet Command. When you bypass my office and issue orders directly to starship commanders, you undermine my authority and make it impossible for me to perform my duties as a general officer." Akaar planted his fists on the desktop and leaned in to emphasize his final point. "Especially when you plan to launch covert military operations that could lead us into war . . . *sir.*"

Ishan's glare was sullen. "Your point is noted. Thank you, Admiral."

He did not have to tell Akaar that he was dismissed. It was implied and understood.

"Thank you, sir." Akaar turned away and departed, his craggy mien a deliberate cipher. There would be idle chatter about their closed-door meeting, and no doubt there were already some in the Palais and in Starfleet Command who were spreading anxious whispers of Ishan's usurpation of Akaar's military authority. As much as Akaar regretted fanning the flames of rumor and innuendo by confronting Ishan this way, the president pro tem had forced his hand.

Crossing through the outer office, he spied Velk huddled in a corner, plotting under his breath with Eryjem while staring daggers in Akaar's direction.

I'm beset by serpents on all sides, Akaar brooded as he stepped inside a transporter alcove for the return to Starfleet

Command. *Even in my own headquarters, officers under my command betray my trust. I need someone untouched by this pro tem administration. Someone above reproach. Someone I can trust to help me get to the root of Ishan's hidden agenda.*

As the first hum of the transporter filled Akaar's ears, hope rekindled in his heart.

He knew just the man for the job.

Thirty

There were worse prison cells in the galaxy; Julian Bashir knew as much from bitter experience. He had been a prisoner of the Breen during the Dominion War, and he'd seen the insides of his share of starship brigs and alien jails. The key difference between those incidents and his present situation was that this was the first time he knew he actually deserved to be there.

He paced back and forth across his four-square-meter solitary confinement cell. Incarceration vexed him as much as it did most people, though he took comfort in the fact that it was, at least, a Federation-run facility. That meant it was sanitary, temperate, and well lit. His bunk was only slightly uncomfortable, but not so much as to constitute a hardship. At regular intervals nutritious meals appeared in his replicator nook, which had no user interface—a standard security precaution, to prevent sabotage or tampering. When he wanted something to read, as long as it wasn't classified or sensitive material, it was uploaded to his padd. He even was allowed a modicum of control over his cell's primary overhead light.

And I certainly can't complain about a lack of privacy.

No one had questioned him. Following his arrest on Andor, he and Dax had both been beamed up to the *Warspite*. After they had left the transporter room, they were ushered in different directions. He and Dax had shared a valedictory glance as they parted ways.

That was the last he had seen or heard of her.

One week of high-warp travel later, he had been delivered to this ostensibly nameless rock in a star system so insignificant it likely was known by a catalog number rather than a name. There had been no interrogations, no abuse, no attempt to elicit a confession of his crimes. Just four walls, a featureless door, a smooth floor, and a blank ceiling, all cast from the same haze-gray thermocrete. The overhead light fixture cast a steady if sickly chartreuse glow.

The worst part of his detention, in his opinion, was the silence.

Some sadist had decided to deny him the privilege of listening to music in his cell. Bashir saw no obvious reason for the deprivation other than that it annoyed him; someone was playing games, showing him who was in charge. After all, it wasn't as if they had withheld a vital need; there was no provision in the Federation Charter of Rights and Freedoms that stipulated prisoners had to be permitted to enjoy musical entertainment. Even so, it irritated him—not just because it was arbitrary, but because it was so damnably *petty*.

Let them take what they will. They can't touch what matters.

The only person who had spoken to him since his arrest had been a JAG officer aboard the *Warspite*. The young female lieutenant had read the charges against Bashir in a voice so cold and unfeeling that he had wondered for a moment if she were actually a poorly programmed hologram. It was an impressive criminal complaint: high treason, espionage, insubordination, disobeying a superior officer, multiple counts of assaulting a fellow officer, three counts of criminal destruction of private property, two counts of sabotage—one for the *Defiant,* the other for the *Tiber*—stealing a Federation starship, and, of course, the all-purpose charge that linked the others: conspiracy.

Good work if you can get it.

He circled like a wild thing fresh to a cage, as if by walking his cell's perimeter he would somehow suss out its weaknesses and begin charting a course to freedom. But there was no chance of that. This penal facility, wherever in the galaxy it happened to lie, was buried deep inside an asteroid, an airless chunk of rock drifting unknown through the darkness, one speck of silicon and carbon lost in a spray of planetary debris between distant planets. Even if he escaped his cell, there was nowhere to go from there, and no surface on which to hide.

That was all right with him. He had no desire to escape, no reason to flee.

I chose this, and I accept it. No turning back now.

He stopped pacing and sat on his bunk. Leaden silence settled upon him. In theory, he would eventually be brought before a court-martial, despite having resigned his commission. It might take a day or two for the prosecutor to present all the evidence according to proper JAG procedure, but when it was done, Bashir had no doubt he would be convicted and sentenced to live out his days in this forsaken place. He was facing the end of his Starfleet career, the revocation of his medical license, and the loss of everything he had worked for in his life.

It was the best he had felt in years.

No punishment they could impose could make him forget what he had done for the people of Andor or erase from his memory the image of Sarina gazing upon him with love and respect as she watched him embark upon the greatest fool's errand of his life. If this was the price he had to pay for doing what he knew was right, he could live with it.

He looked at his drab, utilitarian prison cell and his matching gray coveralls. Then he caught his reflection in the mirror over his retractable sink and refresher. For the first time in years, he wasn't ashamed of the man looking back at him.

Locked away inside a rock with no name, Julian Bashir felt . . . *free*.

One Year Later

Epilogue

"Look at them, Tala. They're so *beautiful*."

Selleshtala zh'Lothas marveled at the tiny life cradled in her arms, wrapped in swaddling clothes and gazing up at her with the most beautiful eyes she had ever seen. *My lovely shei. You have no idea how long we've waited to welcome you to the world.*

Her entire bondgroup huddled together in the recovery room off the maternity ward of Kathela General Hospital, all admiring their healthy new offspring with tearful wonder. Shayl, the *thaan,* squatted beside Tala's bed and draped his arm over her shoulders, while the group's *chan,* Thar, hovered over and doted on Mara, their *shen*, who held their other newborn, their *thei,* against her breast and surrendered to bliss, mesmerized with love for their precious child.

"I'd almost given up hope," Thar confessed. "After all we'd been through—"

"Love sustained us." Shayl stroked a sweaty lock of Tala's hair from her forehead, then he cupped his palm with gentle grace over the tiny *shei*'s delicate bald head. "Thank Uzaveh for Bashir's miracle and for the courage of all who defended him."

Mara wiped away a tear and kissed the head of their infant *thaan*. "They need names."

The bondmates nodded in agreement. According to custom, the right of naming belonged to a child's *zhavey*. Shayl clasped Tala's hand. "What shall we call them, *zh'yi*?"

She lifted her *shei* in both hands over her head. "I declare before Uzaveh that your name shall be Ezrishar sh'Lothas." She lowered the *shei* and handed her to Shayl. Then Mara shifted their *thei* into Tala's hands, and she lifted him up toward Mother Stars and the Maker of All Things. "I declare before Uzaveh that your name shall be . . . Bashir th'Lothas."

Shayl beamed with paternal approval. "Excellent names, *zh'yi*."

The bondgroup gathered around Tala, enfolding her in their loving embrace, shutting out the world so they could be alone with their joy, safe from the envy of strangers' eyes.

United around their children, they spoke of the past and of the future. At last they could share their links to their forebears dating back to ancient times, and they could dare to look ahead and imagine the shape of their scions' tomorrows. That moment and its exultation would be but one among countless others stretching backward and forward in time, connecting all who were with all who would be, uniting them in the dream incarnate of Uzaveh the Infinite.

One family at a time . . . the Andorian people were healing.

Acknowledgments

Thanks go first to my loving and amazing wife, Kara, without whom I could do none of the things that I all too often take for granted in my life.

Second, my gratitude goes out to my editors at Simon & Schuster for their guidance; my agent, Lucienne Diver, for keeping the business side of my life from spiraling into chaos; and my fellow authors on this ambitious miniseries for all their patience and assistance.

At this juncture, let me also offer belated thanks to who-ever invented bourbon.

Lastly, I thank you, the readers, whose interest makes all this effort worth the trouble.

About the Author

David Mack has left the building.

Find him at his website:
www.davidmack.pro